Sky Dog turned, his face locked in a grim mask

"Running Bird and three others rode all night to get here. They were hunting when they came across a large party of *wasicun* about sixty miles north-westward."

"Roamers?" Kane inquired.

Sky Dog shook his head, black tresses flying. "Not unless Roamers have traded in horses for Sandcats and their rags for black armor."

A cold fist seemed to punch deep into Kane's belly, from the inside out. He was barely aware of saying, "Mags."

Sky Dog nodded gravely, fear glinting in his jet-black eyes. "If they're on their way to the Darks—"

"I think that's a safe bet," broke in Grant.

"—they'll pass right by our settlement. And if they started rolling at sunrise…" Sky Dog's words trailed off as he tilted his head back to consult the position of the sun.

Kane finished the shaman's sentence. "They could be here any minute."

Other titles in this series:

JAMES AXLER

OUTLANDERS™

OUTER DARKNESS

THE
LOST
EARTH
SAGA

BOOK 3

A GOLD EAGLE BOOK FROM

WORLDWIDE®

TORONTO • NEW YORK • LONDON
AMSTERDAM • PARIS • SYDNEY • HAMBURG
STOCKHOLM • ATHENS • TOKYO • MILAN
MADRID • WARSAW • BUDAPEST • AUCKLAND

To Melissa—who is equal parts Brigid, Fand and completely herself.

First edition September 1999
ISBN 0-373-63823-X

OUTER DARKNESS

Special thanks to Mark Ellis for his contribution to the Outlanders concept, developed for Gold Eagle Books.

From Brig o' Dread when thou may'st pass,
On Purgatory Road thou travel at last.
—Old English dirge

The Road to Outlands—
From Secret Government Files to the Future

Almost two hundred years after the global holocaust, Kane, a former Magistrate of Cobaltville, often thought the world had been lucky to survive at all after a nuclear device detonated in the Russian embassy in Washington, D.C. The aftermath—forever known as skydark—reshaped continents and turned civilization into ashes.

Nearly depopulated, America became the Deathlands—poisoned by radiation, home to chaos and mutated life forms. Feudal rule reappeared in the form of baronies, while remote outposts clung to a brutish existence.

What eventually helped shape this wasteland were the redoubts, the secret preholocaust military installations with stores of weapons, and the home of gateways, the locational matter-transfer facilities. Some of the redoubts hid clues that had once fed wild theories of government cover-ups and alien visitations.

Rearmed from redoubt stockpiles, the barons consolidated their power and reclaimed technology for the villes. Their power, supported by some invisible authority, extended beyond their fortified walls to what was now called the Outlands. It was here that the rootstock of humanity survived, living with hellzones and chemical storms, hounded by Magistrates.

In the villes, rigid laws were enforced—to atone for the sins of the past and prepare the way for a better future. That was the barons' public credo and their right-to-rule.

Kane, along with friend and fellow Magistrate Grant, had upheld that claim until a fateful Outlands expedition. A displaced piece of technology...a question to a keeper of the archives...a vague clue about alien masters—and their world shifted radically. Suddenly, Brigid Baptiste, the archivist, faced summary execution, and

Grant a quick termination. For Kane there was forgiveness if he pledged his unquestioning allegiance to Baron Cobalt and his unknown masters and abandoned his friends.

But that allegiance would make him support a mysterious and alien power and deny loyalty and friends. Then what else was there?

Kane had been brought up solely to serve the ville. Brigid's only link with her family was her mother's red-gold hair, green eyes and supple form. Grant's clues to his lineage were his ebony skin and powerful physique. But Domi, she of the white hair, was an Outlander pressed into sexual servitude in Cobaltville. She at least knew her roots and was a reminder to the exiles that the outcasts belonged in the human family.

Parents, friends, community—the very rootedness of humanity was denied. With no continuity, there was no forward momentum to the future. And that was the crux—when Kane began to wonder if there *was* a future.

For Kane, it wouldn't do. So the only way was out—way, way out.

After their escape, they found shelter at the forgotten Cerberus redoubt headed by Lakesh, a scientist, Cobaltville's head archivist, and secret opponent of the barons.

With their past turned into a lie, their future threatened, only one thing was left to give meaning to the outcasts. The hunger for freedom, the will to resist the hostile influences. And perhaps, by opposing, end them.

Chapter 1

Abrams looked at the distant jagged peaks looming against the backdrop of stars. The Bitterroot Range reminded him of fangs, and the glittering constellations above them were like the multitudinous eyes of an enormous predator, waiting hungrily for prey to come within reach.

Abrams repressed a shiver as a chill wind gusted across the flatlands. As the flames of the campfire leaped and flickered, black shadows writhed across the ground. On the far side of the camp, colossal aspen trees rose amid tangled, thorny thickets. He didn't like the woods, either, his imagination populating them with all variety of menaces, from mutie wolves to mutie people.

Nearly thirty years had passed since Abrams had worn the combat armor of a Cobaltville magistrate. During those years he'd become the administrator of the Magistrate Division. He'd liked his position and he'd been good at it. Now all of that was on the line—along with his life.

He was tall with a neatly clipped gray beard that was presently stained white from the road dust he'd been exposed to all day. Judging from the dryness hitting the back of his throat with every breath, and the heaviness in his lungs, he'd been inhaling that dust as well. Sitting on the outside of the camp where the Mag force had bedded down for the night after a day's hard travel, he watched over the other eleven men who sat around the two Sandcats they'd brought with them from Cobaltville.

Abrams hurt all over, especially the leg that Kane, the renegade former Magistrate, had lamed. He'd forgotten how much the Mag armor could chafe when a man had to wear it all day. And he stank. He'd also forgotten about that part. He'd have given anything for a bath and a bed, but he didn't know when he'd see either one of those again.

He was still resentful of Baron Cobalt for ordering him to take a Mag team over the road himself instead of simply assigning a team to the mission. But the baron had told Abrams more than he should have, had revealed more of the baron's weaknesses than a man trained to follow command should ever know.

Baron Cobalt had told him that Salvo had been telling the truth; Lakesh *was* working with Kane. In addition, the baron had told him he hadn't been in touch with the Archons. Both of those declarations had shaken Abrams's belief systems.

Abrams sighed and sipped his lukewarm coffee sub. He accepted his lot with a warrior's stoicism, but with an experienced man's resentment of an unexpected reversal of fortune. Looking up at the starlit sky, he realized that if all went according to plan, the squad would arrive at the foothills by sometime tomorrow afternoon.

Somewhere in that mass of mountains was a buried redoubt. Abrams knew that for certain. Once, it had been called Redoubt Bravo, but Lakesh had pronounced it unsalvageable. At that time, Baron Cobalt had trusted the old chief archivist of the Historical

Division. That was no longer true. In fact, if the baron's information was correct, Lakesh was an even bigger traitor than Kane.

Baron Cobalt had declared that the redoubt was actually the hidden base that Kane and Lakesh were operating out of with other fugitives. Abrams sipped his coffee sub again, watching the other members of his own team. Sometime over the next two days, he'd find out if the redoubt actually was abandoned and unsalvageable or if Kane was holed up in it.

If the redoubt was abandoned, Abrams was convinced Baron Cobalt was going to be angry enough to have his head from his shoulders for proving him wrong. And if Kane really was there, even with a full force of twelve Mags, Abrams knew they were going to be in a fight for their lives. There would be no stopping a full squad of hard-contact Mags, but Kane and Grant would undoubtedly kill some of them.

Abrams tried to smother his rising apprehension. The Darks had long been shrouded by superstition, the deeply shadowed ravines exuding an almost palpable atmosphere of death and fear. He thought he could detect the odor of malevolence on the breeze blowing from the peaks.

Some of the other Magistrates smelled it, too, judging by the way they paced restlessly around the perimeter, eyeing the silhouetted mountain range over their shoulders. Most of them sat around the fire, sharing the last of the night's ration of food from the self-heat packages. Weary after a dawn-to-dusk ride in the bellies of the Sandcats, they stared at the flames, then at the Darks as they smothered yawns.

Leaning against the heavy metal hull of one of the vehicles, Abrams dashed the rest of the coffee sub out of his cup and did his best to fight off the fit of melancholy gloom. Every member of his squad was supremely well trained, they were well armed and, in tandem with the Sandcats, they were an essentially invincible force.

Built as a fast-attack-vehicle, the Sandcat had flat, retractable tracks supporting the low-slung, blunt-lined chassis. Armored topside gun turrets concealed a pair of USMG-73 heavy machine guns. The wag's armor was composed of a ceramic-armaglass bond, shielded against both intense heat and ambient radiation.

The interiors comfortably held eight people. At the front of the compartment, right beneath the canopy, were the pilot's and copilot's chairs. In the rear, a double row of three jump seats faced each other.

As Abrams thought of the man who had shattered his knee, his gloved hand tightened on his cane. The prospect of finding Kane somewhere in the mountains did not make him feel differently about the mission. Abrams was not on a vengeance trail, but Baron Cobalt, despite his reasoned justification for dispatching the squad, secretly harbored revenge as the ultimate goal.

The official reason for the mission was that it was part of a cooperative initiative of the nine villes that ruled the former United States of America. Nearly a year before, Kane and Grant—two veteran Cobaltville Magistrates—turned renegade, escaping the ville and taking a condemned prisoner with them. In the process, they had chilled several fellow Mags, shot down two Deathbirds, assaulted the baron himself and—Abrams grimaced as his poorly reconstructed knee twinged—crippled him.

After that, the insurrectionists had vanished into thin air, falling so completely from sight it was as if they had never existed at all. Abrams knew they had uncovered, either by accident or by design, one of the most ruthlessly guarded secrets of the pre- and postdark generations—the mat-trans units, known sometimes as gateways.

As Abrams understood it, the matter-transfer gateways were major aspects of the predark scientific project known as the Totality Concept. Most of the units were buried in subterranean military complexes, known as redoubts, in the United States. Only a handful of people knew they even existed, and only half a handful knew all their locations. The knowledge had been lost after the nukecaust, rediscovered a century later, then jealously guarded. There were, however, units in other countries, so it was possible that Kane, Baptiste, Grant, Lakesh and even Salvo himself could be anywhere on Earth.

"Sir? Am I disturbing you?" whispered a husky voice.

Abrams started, snatching up his cane before he recognized Pollard looming in the wedge of shadow between the two Sandcats. Like all the other men, Pollard was a veteran hard-contact Mag, and his burly body was encased in the black polycarbonate armor. The close-fitting exoskeleton was molded to conform to the biceps, triceps, pectorals and abdomen. Even with its Kevlar undersheathing, the armor was lightweight and provided no loose folds that could snag on projections. The only spot of color anywhere on the armor was the small, crimson, disk-shaped badge of office emblazoned on the left pectoral. The stylized, balanced scales of justice were superimposed over a nine-spoked wheel. The badge symbolized the Magistrate's oath, of keeping the wheels of justice turning in the nine villes.

Pollard carried his helmet under his left arm, keeping his right hand, his gun hand, free. Like the body armor, the helmet was made of black polycarbonate, and fitted over the upper half and back of his head, leaving only a portion of the mouth and chin exposed. The slightly concave, red-tinted visor served several functions: it protected the eyes from foreign particles, and the electrochemical polymer was connected to a passive nightsight that intensified ambient light to permit one-color night vision. The tiny image-enhancer sensor mounted on the forehead of the helmet did not emit detectable rays. However, its range was only twenty-five feet, even on a fairly clear night with strong moonlight.

The Magistrate-issue side arm, the Sin Eater, was holstered to Pollard's right forearm. A big-bored automatic handblaster, the Sin Eater was less than fourteen inches in length at full extension, the magazine carrying twenty 9 mm rounds. When not in use, the stock folded over the top of the blaster, lying along the frame, reducing its holstered length to ten inches.

When the Sin Eater was needed, all a Mag needed to do was tense his wrist tendons. Sensitive actuators activated a flexible cable in the holster and snapped the weapon smoothly into his waiting hand, the stock unfolding in the same motion. Since the Sin Eater had no trigger guard or safety, the blaster fired immediately upon touching the Mag's crooked index finger.

Pollard had not been selected for this field duty, but enthusiastically volunteered. Stocky and blunt jawed, he was the perfect Mag. But Abrams knew he was not driven by duty. Like Baron Cobalt, Pollard's motivation bubbled from a wellspring of vengeance.

He was the sole surviving member of Salvo's ill-fated Grudge Task Force, an elite squad tasked specifically to apprehend Kane, Grant and the fugitive archivist, Brigid Baptiste. Pollard had suffered two indignities at the hands of the insurgents. First Kane had shot down his Deathbird, and months later Grant had tricked, then very nearly beaten him to death.

Under ordinary circumstances, Pollard would have faced a termination warrant for witnessing a mat-trans unit in operation as it whisked the fugitives out of the reach of ville justice. However, Salvo had named Pollard as his lieutenant in the task force. When Salvo vanished, apparently spirited out of Co-baltville by Kane and Grant, Pollard had been allowed to live, since he could provide information, and his commander was suspected of being in ca-hoots with the criminals. Later, when Baron Cobalt announced that his initial assessment of Salvo's treachery had been hasty, Pollard pounced on the chance to redeem himself.

The other Mags in the squad did not share Pollard's passion. Although Grant and Kane might not have been loved by their fellow Magistrates, they were respected and admired. Their abrupt disappearance and conviction in absentia of sedition and murder had seriously damaged Mag Division morale.

"What is it?" Abrams asked, his tone stiffly formal.

Pollard's bulldog features twitched a trifle, as if he resented the thinly veiled disrespect in Abrams's tone.

"I've been walking the perimeter," he replied, his rough voice pitched low. He waved toward a copse of ponderosa pines. "I think we've got company."

Abrams was too experienced to make an obvious show of turning toward the woods, although he doubted Pollard's opinion. He cast a casual glance toward the snarl of undergrowth between the tree trunks. Quietly, he asked, "What makes you think that?"

Pollard tapped the motion detector strapped around his left wrist. The liquid crystal display window glowed faintly.

"I picked up movement. Four hits."

"Animals probably. Maybe deer."

"Maybe," Pollard agreed. "Or outlanders, or Roamers. Or Indians."

Abrams said nothing for a moment, considering the man's words. Many tribes of Amerindians believed the nukecaust was the purification promised by ancient prophecy, and over the past two centuries they had reclaimed what was left of their ancestral lands, protecting them ruthlessly from invasion.

He stole a glance at Pollard and wished he would put on his helmet, simply so the visor would conceal the spark of malice that continually burned in the man's small, flesh-bagged eyes.

Pushing himself away from the Sandcat, Abrams declared, "Very well. Let's check it out."

Creases of consternation appeared on Pollard's low, broad forehead. "Me and you?"

"You and me," Abrams replied, bending down to pick up his helmet. He slipped it over his head, snapping the underjaw lock guards.

Pollard did the same, and the two men moved

away from the flickering light of the campfire. As they strode into the shadows bordering the woods, Abrams did his best to minimize his limp. His nightsight image enhancer brought into sharp relief everything around him.

The wind seemed to grow colder the farther they walked from the campsite. As Abrams marched beside Pollard, he cast wary glances into the encroaching darkness. The trees stood up blackly in the starlight. The leafy cover of the woods could conceal anything or anyone. All the premonitions of danger he had experienced since coming in sight of the mountain range returned.

The two armored men came to a halt at the outermost edge of the undergrowth. Extending his left arm, Pollard made a slow, left-to-right sweep with the motion detector. It registered nothing and he showed his stumpy teeth in a grimace, half disappointment, half embarrassment.

"I swear I picked up four signatures at this spot, sir."

Abrams eyed the deep black pools between the trees and muttered, "Animals, like I said. They satisfied their curiosity and moved on."

Pollard wasn't satisfied. "Let's take another position and—"

The motion detector emitted a discordant electronic beep. Almost at the same instant, a bloodfreezing howl burst from the dense foliage. Four arrows ripped through leaves, their steel points clattering against the breastplates of Abrams and Pollard. The wooden shaft of one splintered as it struck Pollard on the molded left pectoral barely a millimeter below the red disk-shaped badge.

Pollard's reaction was immediate. The Sin Eater
flashed into his hand, and his index finger depressed
the firing stud. Flame and thunder gouted from the
barrel. He let loose with a long, stuttering, full-auto
volley into the woods. The 280-grain rounds crashed
into tree trunks, shearing away bark and slashing
through leaves.

Although Abrams had unleathered his own blaster,
he didn't fire it. He turned to shout orders at the men
in the camp, but there was no need. A half-dozen
men were already racing toward them, fisting Sin
Eaters and unlimbering the chopped-down subguns
known as Copperheads.

"Form a line" Abrams yelled, gesturing. "Form
a line!"

The nervous Magistrates swiftly bracketed Pollard
and Abrams in a fire line.

"Open fire!" Abrams shouted.

Staccato jackhammer roars ripped through the
quiet of the night, and spear points of orange flame
licked at the gloom, smoking shell casings spewed
from ejector ports. The fusillade of full-auto fire
whipped the foliage with the fury of a gale-force
wind.

"Cease fire!" Abrams commanded.

Bullet-shredded twigs and leaves showered down
in a rustling rain. Night birds screeched their outrage,
taking flight with a steady flapping of wings. No
more arrows darted out of the shadow-shrouded
woods, but the motion detector beeped steadily, the
volume diminishing until the sound faded into inau-
dibility.

Staring into the LCD, Pollard announced grimly,
"Whoever the bastards are, they're getting away."

Abrams toed an arrow lying at his feet, noting the delicate fletching of hawk feathers and how the crudely forged steel point was affixed to the shaft.

"It's fairly obvious who they are," he said. "Indians, probably a hunting or scouting party. No sense going after them."

"They assaulted Magistrates, sir. We can't let them get away with it. It's bad policy. Says so in the bylaws," Pollard growled.

Abrams didn't even try to disguise the contempt in his voice. "As the Division administrator, I set the policy standards. But if you want to go after four lice-ridden savages who know this region like the backs of their hands and tell them about our bylaws, you have my permission."

He paused and added, "However, if you're not back by daybreak, we'll leave without you."

Some of the angry tension went out of Pollard's posture. He looked uneasily at the tangled dark hell of the woods and muttered, "I apologize, sir."

Abrams turned toward the rest of the squad sprinting up and waved them back. "As you were. False alarm."

As the Mags returned to the camp, Abrams said sternly to Pollard, "You will stand watch the rest of the night in case you're worried they'll come back."

"It's not those four I'm worried about," Pollard retorted defensively. "It's another two dozen of them."

Abrams nodded. "If that happens, you'll have the perfect opportunity to explain to them about Magistrate Division policy."

He left the man there and marched back to camp, less apprehensive about turning his back on the forest than on Pollard. The other men were out here in the field because they were Mags and it was sufficient they had been ordered to be here.

Pollard operated on his own personal agenda, but as long as it didn't interfere with the mission, Abrams would keep him on a loose leash. He glanced again at the silhouette of the distant mountain range and tried not to think about the leash around his own neck.

It was far longer than Pollard's, stretching all the way back to Cobaltville, but it was cinched much tighter.

Chapter 2

The sky was as blue as a summer dream, full of lazy shadows and wispy white clouds. It was one of the most beautiful days Montana had ever produced, before or after the nukecaust.

Grant thought about all the beautiful days he had missed in his life, and the pang of nostalgia was mixed with a touch of self-pity. Then the greasy crescent wrench slipped on the bolt, and he skinned a knuckle against the manifold.

Turning his face to the deep blue sky, Grant bellowed earnestly, "Fuck this shit!"

Kane poked his head out of the side window and asked mildly, "Did that do the job or do you need another set of wrenches?"

"Another set of knuckles would be more like it." Nursing his throbbing hand, Grant eyed the huge engine block with something akin to hatred. Never, not even during his mechanical-aptitude tests at the Mag academy, had any piece of machinery ever given him such problems. After a few more moments of glaring at the monstrosity beneath the open engine cowling, he went back to his tinkering.

Grant stood a few feet above the floor of a small clearing, surrounded by walls of bushes, shrubs and foliage. The massive war wag nearly occupied every square foot.

The armor plate sheathing the huge vehicle was pitted with rust, but its dark hull bristled with rocket pods and machine gun blisters, and was perforated by weapons ports. A mobile army command post of predark manufacture, the wag was around forty feet long and weighed at least fifty tons. The doublethickness steel planking showed deep scoring in places where AP rounds had almost penetrated. It crouched on flat metal tracks, like a petrified prehistoric beast of prey.

The engine block was eight feet off the ground, so Grant stood upon an elevated wooden scaffolding. Even with the aid of the platform, he was forced to stretch to his full height of six feet four inches to reach beneath the propped-up cowling. A broad-shouldered, deep-chested black man, Grant wore his grease-and-sweat-stained khaki shirt unbuttoned. Although the vehicle stood in a wooded glade, the noonday sun blazed down with a merciless heat. The strip of cloth tied around his high forehead was soaked through with sweat. Perspiration trickled down his face and dripped from the ends of his fierce, downsweeping mustache.

Inside the stuffy cockpit of the war wag, Kane was also drenched with sweat. He had been able to open only one window, all the others had been rusted shut at least a century ago. His longish dark hair hung in soggy strands, and his high-planed face glistened with moisture. His gray-blue eyes stung from the salt. He knew he couldn't in good conscience upbraid Grant for his impatience with trying to coax some sign of life out of the machine.

It had been Kane's idea, after all, one that he hoped would have tactical and diplomatic rewards. Now he doubted any payoff other than the wasted time and effort. Still, he wasn't eager to quit and make the long return journey to the foothills of the Darks. Quitting would serve to break the fragile chain of trust he had forged between the Cerberus redoubt and the band of Lakota and Cheyenne.

The Amerindians were the isolated installation's nearest neighbors—its only neighbors, for that matter. The superstitious regard in which they held the mist-wreathed peaks kept them well away from the Bitterroot Range. Only in the past few weeks had direct contact been established between the redoubt's personnel and the tribespeople. Kane had managed to turn a potentially tragic misunderstanding into a budding alliance, but now he wondered if his decision might have been too impulsive.

The Amerindians did not have a chief as such, but they did have a shaman, warrior-priest, a Cobaltville-bred man called Sky Dog. He had shared with Kane, Grant and Brigid Baptiste his people's great secret—the war wag.

According to tribal lore, nearly a century ago a group of *wasicun* adventurers had ridden inside its steel belly up the single treacherous road that wound its way around deep ravines to a plateau. When the vehicle made its return journey, it ran out of fuel, and the Amerindians had set upon the people inside it. Then they had hidden the huge machine and removed all of its weapons except the fixed emplacements.

When Sky Dog proposed that Kane make the vehicle operational again, he had agreed, thinking that a fully restored and armed war wag would make a solid first line of defense against a possible incursion from Cobaltville. Other considerations had delayed his keeping his promise to Sky Dog, but a couple of days before Kane decided that to put it off any longer would only arouse the Amerindian's suspicions and hostility. Over the objections lodged by Lakesh and Brigid, he, Grant and Domi loaded up and made the dangerous journey down from the redoubt to the foothills.

The road was blocked by an explosive-triggered rockfall, and the three of them were forced to walk across the flatlands. A barely healed injury to Grant's right leg made the trek slow and painful, especially burdened as they were by tools and provisions.

Fortunately, outriders from Sky Dog's settlement found them by midday, and they completed the journey on horseback. Now, for the better part of two days, they had struggled with the task of bringing back to life a machine that had lain dormant for at least a hundred years. It was dirty, exhausting work entailing disassembling and rebuilding the engine, as well as rewiring the instrument panels. Upon their initial manufacture in the late twentieth century, the control systems had been designed to be operated and linked by computers. Whoever had found and used the wag after skydark had rerouted all the automatic circuitry to manual-override boards.

Grant hammered at a manifold with the wrench and snarled, "I'm not a goddamn mechanic and you're not an electrician! Wegmann should be doing this, not us!"

He went on with a profanity-filled diatribe.

Under normal circumstances, Wegmann, the redoubt's resident mechanic and engineer, would indeed have accompanied them. But circumstances at Cerberus were anything but normal.

Finally, when Grant paused for breath, Kane said, "Yeah, Wegmann *should* be doing this. But you know why he isn't."

"Yeah, because he's an incompetent stupe," Grant snapped.

Although Kane felt that Grant's condemnation of the man was unfair, he didn't say anything in Wegmann's defense. Grant was in one of his foul, mulish tempers, and Kane knew it was futile to argue him out of an opinion, no matter how unjust it was.

Besides, Grant had something of a point. One of the redoubt's three nuclear generators had gone offline. Although the responsibility to repair it was Wegmann's, the initial failure wasn't his fault.

Over the past ten days, alterations in the Cerberus mat-trans unit had exceeded the limits for safe power consumption. The nuclear engines were designed to shut down when pressure and thermal levels threatened the safety of the installation. To avoid a catastrophic system failure, one of the generators had automatically shut itself down. With the reduced power curve, the mat-trans could not be operated in accordance with its new specs.

Grant and Kane were not unhappy about this, since they took advantage of the downtime to fulfill their part of the bargain with Sky Dog. But the situation prevented Wegmann from joining them, although he had provided them with a detailed schematic of the war wag from the computer database. Of course, the schematic didn't include any of the customized features. Therefore, the attempt to get it running again was a classic example of trial and error.

Still muttering curses, Grant ducked beneath the cowling again, tools banging and clattering. He continued to mumble oaths as he rechecked the plugs, the coil wires and the liquid levels. Kane stopped himself from pointing out that if Grant removed the Sin Eater from his right forearm, he'd be able to insert both hands into narrow areas. But Kane's blaster, a twin of Grant's, was secured to his own arm. Habits developed over a lifetime couldn't be easily broken, and it was anathema for Mags not to bear weapons in the Outlands.

"Not going well, is it, Hota Wanagi?" The voice, speaking from behind Kane, startled him so much he spun the pilot's chair around, the rotating gimbal squealing.

Sky Dog stood behind him, his entrance made soundless by the soft-soled moccasins on his feet. At six feet he was slightly shorter than Kane, and was lithely built with an erect carriage that exuded a quiet dignity. His ruddy features bore a rueful smile. Shiny black hair plaited in two braids fell almost to his waist. Behind his right ear, a single white feather dangled, symbolizing his standing as the spiritual leader of his people. He wore loose clothing of smoked leather. He had addressed Kane as "Gray Ghost," a name he had pinned on Kane because when he first saw him, he was covered with rock dust.

With effort, Kane turned the scowl on his face into a bemused smile. "I guess that's pretty obvious."

Sky Dog eased himself gingerly into the copilot's chair. "At least you're dedicated to fulfilling your word. The attempt alone has gained my people's trust, which was what all this was about anyway."

Kane eyed him speculatively. "You don't care if we get this monster running again?"

The shaman shrugged. "I'd prefer you did, but establishing an alliance between our two peoples is more important."

Kane felt the same way, but he was a bit surprised by Sky Dog's admission. "It only makes sense to unite against a common enemy."

"True," Sky Dog replied. "But it's also comforting to know my people can count on your aid during times of famine or epidemic."

Kane did not respond to that. Despite the fact that Lakesh often referred to Cerberus as a sanctuary, Kane was fairly certain he had never envisioned it as a general refuge for the disenfranchised of the Outlands. He pictured Sky Dog's people appearing on the plateau some snowy winter's evening, prepared to stay until spring. The mental image of the expression on Lakesh's face made him smile.

Sky Dog angled an eyebrow at him. "Did I say something funny?"

Kane shook his head. "Not intentionally."

"Try it again," Grant called.

Relieved by the interruption, Kane turned around and began flicking the switches on the instrument panel. He felt a surge of cautious pleasure when needle gauges twitched and indicator lights flashed on.

"We've got battery power at least," he announced.

He pressed the gas pedal a few times and grasped the throttle. Holding his breath, Kane carefully turned the ignition key. There was a sputtering cough, and a gout of blue-black smoke puffed from the exhaust. The engine made a noise halfway between a belch and a gasp and died.

Grant stretched out under the cowling again. Metal clacked against metal. "Try it again."

Kane tried it again and again. Then, on the fourth attempt, with a series of stuttering pops, the wag's engine roared into life. Sky Dog nearly sprang from the chair. Crows rushed up from the branches of the trees like a black, scolding cloud. Thick smoke poured from the double exhaust pipes and filled the glade with a noxious pall. The entire vehicle vibrated with such shuddering violence Grant nearly fell from the makeshift scaffold. Kane could see his mouth working beneath his mustache, but he couldn't hear what he said. He glared truculently at the engine, but that meant nothing. Usually, the deeper Grant's scowl, the happier he was.

The wag shivered as Kane maintained steady pressure on the accelerator. At any second he expected the engine to cough, stall and die. But though it stuttered, it continued to run.

Kane poked his head out of the side window and shouted, "Do you want to see if we can get it moving?"

"First things first. Let her run awhile," Grant yelled.

Kane wasn't too happy about that. The pair of five-gallon fuel cans they had packed out of Cerberus probably only moistened the war wag's huge gas tank. Even allowing the vehicle to sit and idle burned fuel at an appallingly fast rate. But he decided to keep his worries to himself.

"One obstacle overcome by *wasicun* ingenuity," he said to Sky Dog.

Sky Dog gave him a jittery smile, unnerved by the

racket, the vibrations and the foul fumes spewing into the clean air.

Grant continued to tinker. By degrees the shudders smoothed and the volume of smoke decreased. Climbing off the scaffold, he dragged it away and gestured to Kane. "Put it in gear," he shouted. "Real slow."

Kane obliged, carefully manipulating the lever and grimacing as gears clashed and squealed. Grant yelled something, but Kane couldn't hear him, figuring it was just as well. Slowly, he released the clutch. With a groan of treads and return rollers, the war wag lurched forward, ripping up strips of turf that had grown around them over the past century.

Keeping the machine in first gear, wrestling with the steering wheel, Kane guided the wag in a slow, lumbering course across the clearing. Sky Dog gripped the armrests of his chair tightly, trying to appear composed.

The huge vehicle was a true dreadnought, Kane realized. When completely operational with all of its weaponry in perfect working order, it would be a mobile skirmish line, far superior to the ville Sandcats. Although the war wag was not as maneuverable as the Cats, it was essentially unstoppable.

Grant limped rapidly beside the wag. "That's enough for right now. Shut her down!"

Kane wanted to take the machine out of the glade and onto the flatlands, but obediently he braked to a halt, slid the gearshift to neutral and keyed off the engine. He considerately pretended not to notice the expression of relief crossing Sky Dog's face. He pushed himself out of the chair with barely a twinge from the place on his hip where a bullet fired by

Beth-Li Rouch had torn a gouge less than two weeks before.

The two men left the cockpit to walk down the narrow, grate-floored passageway running the length of the wag, passing empty cargo and personnel compartments. Inside small side alcoves were emplacements with four-barrel 12.7 mm miniguns. There were a couple of sealed crates of many different calibers of ammo, and even a few LAW rockets. However, the rounds and the rockets were so old, both Grant and Kane doubted their stability and reliability.

As they climbed out through the open rear hatch, Kane saw a group of buckskin-clad tribespeople standing on the edge of the old blacktop road, staring at the wag with wide, disconcerted eyes.

"They don't seem particularly happy that we've got this thing running again," he commented.

"They're not," Sky Dog said dourly. "For their entire lives, they've been taught this machine was a symbol of predark *wasicun* evil. *Wasicun* breathed life back into it, and so they see all sorts of dire omens and ill fortune in the offing."

"And you don't?"

"As a point of fact, I do. I was raised in Cobaltville and know both the benefits and dangers of technology. However, if the wag had been operational when Le Loup Garou and his Roamers attacked us, we could have easily beaten them off. We would not have suffered casualties, and our women and children would not have been carried off."

Kane didn't remark on Sky Dog's reference to the incident that had resulted in his and the shaman's first meeting. Sky Dog had loosed an arrow that had ended the Roamer chieftain's raid and saved Kane's life.

Grant limped toward them. "Still a few bugs to work out, but we're more than halfway home. The next step is fixing up the blasters."

A slight, wraithlike figure pushed through the line of Amerindians. Domi was small, barely five feet tall, and weighed a shade more than a hundred pounds, but she had no trouble carrying the pair of Colt Commando autorifles over her shoulders. Her skin was perfectly white and beautiful, like a fine pearl, and her fine, hollow-cheeked face was framed by ragged, close-cropped hair the color of bone. Her eyes were as bright as rubies on either side of her delicate, thin-bridged nose. Although her figure was petite, her khakis did little to conceal its provocative, almost insolent curves.

"Two more are ready," she announced, looking at them cherfully.

Grant took one of the blasters and inspected it with a critical eye. He squinted down the bore, checked the sights, tested the action, slid out and pushed in the telescopic butt. Domi watched him with a tense posture, prepared to be offended by the slightest criticism.

"Well-done," he said at length, placing the Commando inside the wag. "How many does that make?"

"Six," she answered. "We only brought enough rounds for three full clips, though."

"More than enough for some target practice," Kane stated. "The fixed weapons will have to wait until we come back."

Sky Dog had told them that the handguns found

in the wag had been taken and hidden, buried actually. The task of cleaning and fixing them up had fallen to Domi.

"The problem," Sky Dog said, "will be for me to find warriors who are willing to use firearms. Most of them think blasters are unmanly."

"But it's manly to face autoblasters with bows and arrows?" Grant shot back, nettled. "Remind your warriors of what Le Loup Garou and his Roamers did to them—and all they had were single-shot muzzle loaders." He nodded toward the Colt Commandos. "Just one of those with a full magazine would have made all the difference."

Sky Dog's eyes narrowed in irritation at the rebuke. He opened his mouth to speak, but a sudden commotion among the onlookers made him whirl around.

The Amerindians stepped aside to allow a pair of men to enter the glade. Kane recognized one of the two. Standing Bear was a burly, barrel-chested man with heavily muscled arms and legs. His knife had given Kane the thin, hairline scar on his left cheek. Their eyes met for a moment, but if the warrior still harbored hostility toward him, he gave no sign.

Standing Bear supported a slender, much younger man wearing only a breechclout and doeskin moccasins. At first, Kane thought the red streak across the right side of the man's face was war paint, but when he saw the dried blood caked on his neck, he realized the mark had been made by a bullet. It had scorched a grazing path along the side of the warrior's face and clipped off his earlobe.

Standing Bear half shouted a stream of harsh consonants. Sky Dog strode quickly to them. Grant,

Domi and Kane watched as the wounded man spoke tersely, responding to the shaman's questions. The onlookers stirred uneasily, murmuring to one another.

After a few moments, Sky Dog turned, face locked in a grim mask. "Running Bird and three others rode all night to get here. They were hunting when they came across a large party of *wasicun* camped about sixty miles northwestward."

"Roamers?" Kane inquired.

Sky Dog shook his head. "Not unless Roamers have traded in horses for Sandcats and their rags for black armor."

A cold fist seemed to punch deep into Kane's belly. He was barely aware of saying "Mags."

Sky Dog nodded gravely, fear glinting in his jet-black eyes. "If they're on their way to the Darks—"

"I think that's a safe bet," Grant broke in.

"—they'll pass right by our settlement. And if they started rolling at sunrise…" Sky Dog's words trailed off as he tilted back his head to consult the position of the sun.

Kane finished the shaman's sentence. "They could be here any minute."

He looked up the old two-lane highway, in the direction the Magistrates had to come. The asphalt had a peculiar ripple pattern to it, and weeds sprouted from splits in the surface. The rippling effect was a characteristic result of earthquakes triggered by nuclear bomb shock waves.

Then he glanced down it, noting how it stretched in a straight line across the flatlands, skirting the village of Sky Dog's people. Smoke from cook fires smudged the clear sky, and the tops of the tepees looked like a collection of dun-colored cones projecting from the prairie.

He lifted his gaze, his eyes followed the highway as it disappeared into the foothills of the mountain range. Piles of thunderheads massed over the peaks, and as Kane looked at them he bleakly realized the dark clouds portended a storm far worse than rain.

Chapter 3

A steady downpour drummed against the road, filling the deep furrows and sluicing detritus over the edges of yawning, helldeep chasms. The sheer cliffs had been formed when acres of mountainside collapsed during the nuke-triggered earthquakes of nearly two centuries ago.

The split tarmac curved and looped for mile after dangerous mile, finally broadening at a huge plateau at the base of a great gray peak. The scraps of a chain-link fence bordered the plateau. Although invisible from the road, an elaborate system of heat-sensing warning devices, night-vision vid cameras and motion-trigger alarms surrounded the plateau.

Planted within rocky clefts of the mountain peak and concealed by camouflage netting were the uplinks with an orbiting Vela-class reconnaissance satellite, and a Comsat.

At the base of the peak, recessed into the rock face, was a massive vanadium-alloy gate. Operated by a punched-in code and a hidden lever control, the gate opened like an accordion, one section folding over another.

On the wall just inside the massive door, rendered in garish primary colors, was a large illustration of a frothy-mouthed black hound. Three snarling heads grew out of a single, exaggeratedly muscled neck, their jaws spewing flame and blood between great fangs. Three pairs of crimson eyes blazed malevolently. Underneath the image, in an ornate Gothic script, was written the single word *Cerberus*.

The mythological guardian of the gateway to Hades was an appropriate totem for the installation that, for a handful of years, housed the primary subdivision of the Totality Concept's Overproject Whisper, Project Cerberus.

Initially dedicated to locating and traveling hyperdimensional pathways through the quantum stream, the redoubt that housed Project Cerberus later became a manufacturing facility. The quantum interphase mat-trans inducers were built in modular form and shipped to other redoubts.

The official designations of the redoubts had been based on the phonetic alphabet. On the few existing records, the Cerberus installation was listed as Redoubt Bravo, but the dozen people who made the trilevel, thirty-acre facility their home never referred to it as such.

A masterpiece of impenetrability, the Cerberus redoubt had weathered the nukecaust and skydark and all the subsequent earth changes. Its radiation shielding was still intact, and its nuclear generators still provided an almost eternal source of power.

The main corridors, twenty-feet wide, were made of softly gleaming vanadium alloy. The redoubt had been constructed to provide a comfortable home for well over a hundred people. Now mostly it housed shadowed passageways, empty rooms and sepulchral silences.

The redoubt possessed a well-equipped armory, bunk rooms and two dozen self-contained apartments, a cafeteria, decontamination center, medical dispensary, gymnasium with a pool and holding cells on the bottom level. There was also a mat-trans unit, the first fully functional, debugged gateway in the Project Cerberus network.

The nerve center of the installation was the central control complex. A long room with high, vaulted ceilings, it was lined by consoles of dials, switches and comp stations. A huge Mercator relief map of the world spanned one wall. Pinpoints of light shone steadily in almost every country, connected by a thin pattern of glowing lines. They represented the Cerberus network and indicated the locations of all functioning gateway units across the planet.

Brigid Baptiste sat with her back to the map, its glowing lines striking flame-colored highlights from the heavy mane of reddish gold hair spilling down her back. Chin cupped by one long-nailed hand, she peered through the rectangular lenses of her eyeglasses at the copy on the computer screen. The wire-framed spectacles served as a reminder of her former office as an archivist and as a means to correct a minor vision impairment.

While Wegmann worked on reconfiguring the nuclear generators, she took advantage of the downtime for research. A historian by training, she did not find research to be a labor. Rather, it was the breath of life itself. Unlike her years spent cataloging and revising selected pieces of human history, in Cerberus she had unrestricted access to the main database. The information it contained might not have been the sum total of all humankind's knowledge, but it certainly came close. Any scrap, bit or byte of information that had ever been digitized was only a few keystrokes and commands away. If nothing else, the freedom to dip her probing intellect into that wellspring of information made her exile worth a termination warrant hanging over her head.

Due to her eidetic memory, anything she read or saw or even heard was impressed indelibly on her mind. She supposed simply possessing an encyclopedic memory made her intellect something of a fraud, at least compared to the staggeringly high IQ of Lakesh. Although Kane often accused her of using her photographic memory to make herself appear far more knowledgeable than she actually was, she viewed her ability as a valuable resource that had nothing to do with ego.

While Kane, Domi and Grant were away, she had scanned all the computer banks for anything pertaining to the man—or creature—known to them as C. W. Thrush. She hadn't expected to come across any direct references to him by that name, particularly since his choice of names was inspired by an old poem by T. S. Eliot, a few lines of which asked, "Into our first world, shall we follow / The deception of the thrush?" Her expectations had proved correct.

However, mysterious figures that fit his general physical description and methods popped up everywhere throughout the past, usually in times of strife or at a crossroads in human history.

From the era of the Roman Empire to the UFO phenomena of the twentieth century, sinister men in black appeared, influenced events or important people, then vanished. It was tempting to dismiss such reports as paranoid fantasies, but the database contained stories about the MIB from all over the world and from all times.

Although it sent a prickle of fear up her spine, Brigid accepted the strong possibility that all of the reports could detail the activities of Thrush. He could easily have been the frightening apparition known as Spring-Heeled Jack in the Victorian period, and there was no doubt he was the black-clad Umbrella Man reported by witnesses after the assassination of John F. Kennedy.

Whether all of the so-called MIB were manifestations of Thrush, Brigid hesitated to conclude. But she *was* certain of one fact—MIB reports seemed linked to human history. Thrush himself had made cryptic allusions to his long interaction with the human race.

And as she had reason to know, Thrush had not restricted that interaction with humanity to only a single plane of existence. Somehow he managed to bridge all the vibrational barriers between alternate realities, the so-called lost Earths. Neither she nor Lakesh had a clear idea of how Thrush accomplished this, except that he used the Black Stone as a focal point in all of the parallel realities. The stone had been known by many names, by many peoples of civilizations both primitive and advanced—Lucifer's Stone, the Kala, the Kaa'ba, the Chintamani Stone, the Shining Trapezohedron. Always it had been associated with the concept of a key that unlocked either the door to enlightenment or to madness. It had served as the spiritual centerpiece of the race they had known as the Archons, even after it had been fragmented and the facets scattered from one end of the Earth to the other.

According to Balam, the last of his ancient people, the trapezohedron allowed glimpses to all possible futures to which their activities might lead. But the

Black Stone was far more than a calculating device that extrapolated outcomes from actions. As Balam had said, "It brings into existence those outcomes."

Balam had referred to the stone as a channel to sidereal space, where many tangential points of reality lay adjacent to one another, the parallel casements of the universe, a multitude of coexisting realities. But there was commonality linking Thrush to all of the casements, and the manner of that connection had so far eluded her.

Of course, the entire concept seemed like madness, and it was a daily struggle not to dismiss it all as such, even after what she had experienced and witnessed herself on two of the lost Earths. Wryly, she acknowledged that humans had an astonishing ability to dismiss information that did not conform to their preconceived notions of reality. In predark scientific circles, this rigid mind-set was known as "currently accepted paradigms." Such a phrase was nothing but a euphemism for denial.

At the sound of a stealthy footfall behind her, Brigid turned, expecting to see Lakesh. She quickly covered her surprise when she saw Auerbach approaching her. A burly man with a red buzz cut, he served as an aide to DeFore, the redoubt's resident medic.

Lips twitching in a nervous smile of greeting, he inquired, "Am I disturbing you?"

Brigid returned the smile, sensing his unease. She knew Auerbach was attracted to her, and his eyes quickly flicked over her willowy, athletic body, noting how her tight white bodysuit adhered to every curve and generous bulge.

When Auerbach realized that Brigid had noticed his roving eyes, he cast his gaze downward with guilty haste. Not only was he a little uncomfortable in her presence, but he was also dealing with a certain amount of shame. Not too long before, he had been duped by Beth-Li Rouch into participating in a ridiculous, attention-getting ruse. The ruse had backfired, and only Brigid and Kane's timely intervention had prevented him from being permanently maimed by the tribespeople.

Brigid took off her glasses, blinking her big, feline-slanted eyes. The bright color of emeralds shone in them. "I need a break anyway." She rolled her head on tight neck muscles.

Haltingly, Auerbach said, "I know a little about massage, if you want me to rub your neck."

Brigid stopped trying to loosen her muscles. "Not necessary," she said a bit more sharply than she intended. Then, in a softer tone, she added, "Thanks anyway."

Auerbach cleared his throat. He stopped short of shuffling his feet, but it was obvious he felt extremely anxious about something. In a husky, hesitant whisper, he said, "It's about Beth-Li."

Brigid wasn't surprised. She gestured to a chair. "Take a seat."

Auerbach pulled a chair away from a nearby desk and gingerly eased his big body into it. He sat rigid, hands on his knees, and studiously avoided meeting her gaze. "What's to be done about her?"

Brigid sighed. "We haven't made a determination yet. We've been occupied."

Auerbach nodded shortly.

"Why do you ask?"

He took a breath, held it and released it in a rush. "I think she's up to something."

Beth-Li Rouch always seemed to be up to something, almost from the very first week of her arrival at the redoubt. Lakesh had arranged for her exile from Sharpeville to fulfill a specific function among the men in Cerberus, but he had made it quite clear that Kane was the primary focus of his—and Rouch's—project to expand the sanctuary into a thriving colony.

Kane had refused to cooperate, citing how Lakesh's bioengineering initiatives were a continuation of sinister elements which had brought about the nukecaust and the tyranny of the villes.

The Totality Concept's Overproject Excalibur dealt with bioengineering, and one of its subdivisions, Scenario Joshua, had sprung from the twentieth century's Genome Project. The goal of this undertaking was to map human genomes to specific chromosomal functions and locations in order to have on hand in vitro genetic samples of the best of the best, the purest of the pure.

Everyone who enjoyed full ville citizenship was a descendant of the Genome Project. Sometimes a particular gene carrying a desirable trait was grafted to an unrelated egg, or an undesirable gene removed. Despite many failures, when there was a success, it was replicated over and over, occasionally with variations. Lakesh had admitted that Kane was one such success, one that he himself had covertly been involved with.

Some forty years ago, when Lakesh determined to build a resistance movement against the baronies, he rifled Scenario Joshua's genetic records to find the qualifications he deemed the most desirable. He used the Archon Directorate's own fixation with purity control against them. By his own confession, he was a physicist cast in the role of an archivist, pretending to be a geneticist, manipulating a political system that was still in a state of flux.

From a strictly clinical point of view, what Lakesh wanted to do made sense. To ensure that Kane's superior qualities were passed on, mating him with another woman who met similar standards of purity control was the logical course of action. Without access to techniques of fetal development outside the womb, the conventional means of procreation was the only option.

But Kane's resistance had earned both him and Brigid the enmity of Beth-Li, an enmity that had culminated in an attempt to escape Cerberus—with Brigid as both a hostage and a prize for Baron Cobalt. The attempt had been thwarted, but not before Beth-Li accidentally shot Kane. At least, Beth-Li claimed it had been an accident.

"She seems to be behaving herself," Brigid said, noncommittally.

An unidentifiable emotion flashed in Auerbach's blue eyes. "I've been watching her. She's spending a lot of time with Wegmann, down in the engine room."

Brigid frowned. "That's unusual."

"And with the power problems we've had," Auerbach continued, "I don't think it's a coincidence."

"Nothing is in this place," she agreed dryly. "Have you told Lakesh about it?"

Auerbach shook his head. "Not yet. I figured you could bring it to his attention…if you wanted to."

"Bring what to whose attention?" asked a reedy voice.

Mohandas Lakesh Singh shuffled from the anteroom holding the mat-trans unit. Brigid saw that a
metal plate on the elevated jump platform hung open,
exposing the confusing circuit network of the emitter
array. The mat-trans chamber was enclosed on all
sides by upstanding eight-foot-high slabs of translucent, brown-tinted armaglass. She glimpsed Bry,
Lakesh's apprentice, peering into the aperture on the
platform. His coppery curls were tousled.

Lakesh resembled an animated cadaver, his face
crisscrossed with deep seams and creases. Thick
glasses covered his rheumy blue eyes. A hearing aid
was attached to the right earpiece. He carried delicate, precision tools in his liverspotted hands. His
sparse ash-colored hair looked disheveled, and Brigid
realized he'd been tinkering with the gateway unit.
His bodysuit bagged on his scarecrow's frame. Despite the appearance of advanced age, he moved better than he should have.

He'd been born in 1952, long before the nukecaust
that had wiped out so much of the world. He'd been
trained as a scientist, completing a doctorate in cy-
bernetics and quantum mechanics at age nineteen. He
had worked for premier institutions before joining the
original site of the Project Cerberus in Dulce, New
Mexico.

At the time of the nukecaust, Lakesh had been put
into cryogenic sleep for the next 150 years. When
he'd been awakened, medics had replaced worn-out
body parts with bionics and transplanted organs.
Then he'd been put to work to serve the Program of
Unification. Only then had he seen what the scientists
he'd worked with had truly wrought. That, Brigid

knew, had occasioned a burden of guilt on Lakesh that the man would never escape.

When Auerbach saw him, he stood up with a guilty swiftness, chair casters squeaking loudly on the slick floor. "Nothing important, sir," he said,

"It's all right," Brigid told him reassuringly. To Lakesh, she said, "Auerbach was bringing me his concerns about Rouch."

Lakesh's thin lips twisted in distaste. "We've other, far more urgent matters to attend to." Peering sternly over the rims of his spectacles at Auerbach, he said, "Young man, I suggest you concern yourself with medical matters. Those are your assigned duties, not spreading gossip."

Brigid blinked in surprise, taken aback by Lakesh's uncharacteristic rudeness. Addressing Auerbach, she said quietly, "I'll take care of this. Don't worry about it."

Stiffly, face flushed with either embarrassment or anger, Auerbach strode from the control complex and into the corridor.

Lakesh dropped into the chair the man had just vacated. "How progresses your research?"

Brigid regarded him coldly. "Auerbach told me something that may have a bearing on it."

Lakesh waved a dismissive hand. "The complaints of a spurned lover we can do without. The decision about Beth-Li has been made, remember."

Brigid crooked challenging eyebrows. "No, I don't. Since when?"

"Since you and friends Grant and Kane overruled me on confining her to a detention cell." Genuine anger edged Lakesh's bitter tone. "If she's up to mischief, which I doubt, it's your responsibility."

Brigid laughed in weary exasperation. "For a man more than two centuries old, you don't seem to have developed much in the way of emotional maturity. Imprisoning Rouch wouldn't solve the problem."

"And allowing her to roam free after what she did to you and Kane will?" Lakesh's voice snapped with anger.

"That's the situation Auerbach wanted to talk about. According to him, she's cozied up to Wegmann—the man you're relying on to put our systems back on-line."

Lakesh's sour expression didn't alter. "Is Auerbach suggesting that our recent hardware failure was deliberate sabotage, performed at Beth-Li's behest? Friend Wegmann would not allow himself to be so seduced, so smitten, he would endanger the redoubt."

Brigid nodded, mentally reviewing the little she knew about the engineer. She realized in the eight-plus months she had been in Cerberus she probably had exchanged no more than a dozen words with him. He tended to stay down in the lower levels, emerging only to eat or service one of the vehicles.

Thoughts leaping ahead, Brigid stated, "Perhaps not the redoubt, but just some of its personnel. Three of them, to be exact." She pointed to herself and added, "Me, Kane and Grant."

Lakesh obviously did not want to discuss the possibility. He merely shook his head impatiently. Brigid knew his pride was stung. Not only had he not foreseen Rouch's escape attempt from Cerberus, but he was also still seething over the fact that he was held responsible.

Peeved, Brigid declared, "Lakesh, you're willing

to speculate, hypothesize and theorize on any fringe topic, from how many angels can dance on the head of a pin to subatomic universes. Why can't you stretch your mind to at least consider what might happen if we have a power fluctuation—or even a failure—during a hyperdimensional transit?"

Lakesh drew in a slow breath through his nostrils. Brigid realized he had more than contemplated the outcome; he had worried about it. Softly, he intoned, "During the prolonged quincunx effect, while your physical bodies have been reduced to digitized energy patterns, you are held in a transitional balance. A power curve, even by a few millibars, would dislocate the matter stream from its reference matrix. Your bodies would materialize randomly, more in the way of disassociated gases and microscopic organic particulates."

Brigid winced, even though Lakesh had employed euphemisms. "In plain, ordinary English, we'll rematerialize as lumps of goo?"

He nodded unhappily. "That is essentially it, yes. Protoplasm mixed in with a few handfuls of minerals and chemicals."

"And our minds, our consciousnesses? If they're melded with our analogs on a parallel casement, will the fusion be permanent?"

"Dearest Brigid," Lakesh blurted desperately, "I have no way of knowing."

"Take a guess," she suggested, steel in her voice.

Tugging absently at his long nose, he replied, "My guess is that the energy patterns that constitute your minds will simply disperse."

"We'll die?"

"Worse. You will cease to exist. If there is any

scientific validity to the concept of an immortal soul, that, too, will disappear.''

Seeing the stricken look on her face, he added hastily, ''But the odds of such an occurrence are astronomically high. The quantum inducers are keyed in with the vibrational frequencies produced by the crystalline structure of the stone. As long as everything is in sync, the danger is so remote it is almost not worth discussion.''

''Almost,'' echoed Brigid. In frustration she ran her hands through her mounds of hair and turned back to the computer screen. She eyed the glowing words on it without comprehending them. ''I think I can speak for Grant and Kane on this. There is no way in hell we're going to make another hyperdimensional shunt with that kind of 'almost' hanging over our heads. Especially since Wegmann is the only one who can keep that 'almost' from being a done deed.''

Trying to sound encouraging, Lakesh said, ''Mr. Bry and I have been laboring to expand the operational parameters of the mat-trans unit's fail-safe mechanisms. We're configuring it for double redundancies.''

At the bottom edge of the monitor screen, black words against amber caught Brigid's eye, then captured her attention. Her spine stiffened, and her finger tapped the direction key so she could read more. She quickly put her glasses back on.

Lakesh thought he was being ignored and he said, ''Dearest Brigid, we will triple-check all of friend Wegmann's work. If we find anything out of place, no matter how minor, we won't schedule a hypershunt.''

Brigid shushed him into silence, eyes darting back and forth. Sounding offended and mystified, Lakesh said severely, "There is no need for that attitude—"

Spinning around in her chair to face him, she rapped on the screen with a knuckle. Triumphantly she declared, "I think I've found it. The common factor we've been looking for."

Chapter 4

The overhead lights in Auerbach's quarters flashed on automatically when the door tripped the photoelectric sensor mounted on the frame. His two-room suite was fairly spacious, much larger than the one assigned to him back in Mandeville.

Upon Auerbach's arrival in Cerberus some eighteen months ago, Lakesh explained that the private quarters in the redoubt had been reserved for military officers and scientists assigned to the project. All the other personnel, enlisted service people and the like shared the two bunk rooms on the second level.

Auerbach hadn't been given his suite out of deference to his skills as a medic, since he had received far and away the majority of his specialized training from DeFore. Lakesh had assigned him the quarters simply because they were available, not because he was particularly valuable to the smooth functioning of the installation.

Back in Mandeville, he had served as an orderly in the Magistrate Division's medical section. His duties consisted of little more than emptying bedpans and serving food to the Mags recovering from injuries or illnesses. The enforcers had treated him as little more than a machine, responding to barked orders and insults rather than push buttons. During his six years of servitude, he had obeyed them quietly, but he had learned to despise the arrogant breed.

Auerbach had despised Grant and Kane when they first arrived at Cerberus, but over the past few months respect and grudging admiration had slowly edged out the resentment he'd felt for them. Still and all, even if they weren't Mags any longer, they were the focal points of the redoubt.

They abided by Lakesh's rules and regulations only when they didn't infringe on whatever they felt like doing at the moment. Now it appeared they intended to completely displace Lakesh as the Cerberus administrator, and the notion of once again living under the heel of Mags made Auerbach boil with rage.

As he closed the door behind him, he heard a stirring of movement from the kitchenette alcove. A soft voice said, "Lock it."

Auerbach did as Beth-Li instructed, snapping shut the dead bolt. He turned as she stepped out of the alcove into the living room, and his breath caught in his throat for an instant.

Beth-Li Rouch was slender and small, not as petite as Domi, but her figure was more generously proportioned. She was a few years younger than Brigid Baptiste, as well. Her eyes were oval, almond, true Asian, her ears and nose tiny and delicate. Glossy, raven's wing-black hair cascaded down nearly to her waist. The lips of her wide, sensuous mouth were still slightly swollen from blows delivered by Baptiste more than a week before. She wore the unofficial uniform of Cerberus staff, a formfitting white bodysuit. In Beth-Li's case, it seemed to fit her form tighter than usual, sharply defining her breasts and mons veneris.

"You shouldn't be here," Auerbach said in a low tone. He nodded toward the voice-activated transcomm unit on the wall. "Someone could be listening."

"I turned it off," Beth-Li replied, gliding toward him with a soundless grace. "Did you plant the bug in Baptiste's ear?"

He nodded, despising the hot flush warming his neck and face. "We'll see what happens. I don't know if she'll believe it."

Beth-Li's lips twitched in a scornful smile. "If it's about me and it's bad, Baptiste will believe it."

Auerbach swallowed with difficulty. "She's not as bad as you think, Beth-Li. She's fair. After what you did to Kane, she kept you from being locked up."

The young woman's smile became a sneer. "I'm still a prisoner. And so are you. If we can't escape the prison, we can at least turn it into a home."

"I won't be party to bloodshed."

Beth-Li sidled up to him, fingers caressing the base of his throat. "There shouldn't be any. If all goes according to plan, Kane and Grant will disappear. Wegmann will be held responsible. And you and I will simply step into the vacuum. Lakesh will be too fused-out to even notice what's happening—until it's too late."

Auerbach couldn't meet Beth-Li's gaze, even though he towered nearly a foot over her. "And Brigid—I mean, Baptiste? She won't be harmed?"

"That's up to her."

"Not too long ago, I agreed to help you escape but you changed the plan by trying to take Baptiste hostage. How do I know you won't change this plan on me?"

"I kept your name out of it, didn't I?" Her clipped tone held a note of challenge. "I didn't mention your involvement at all, just like I promised. You can trust me."

"My involvement," he said in a voice pitched just barely above a whisper, "didn't amount to much. I was just going along with you, that's all. This time, I'm in as deep as you are. And Wegmann—"

He broke off, shook his head and sighed. "I don't like that scrawny pissant, but he's not a stupe. If he thinks you've been playing up to him just so you can sabotage engineering, he'll point the finger at you. Even if Lakesh is too fused-out to think clearly, we'll have him, Cotta, Farrell, Bry and DeFore to contend with. Not to mention Domi and Baptiste."

Beth-Li pressed herself against his body. Even through their bodysuits, Auerbach could feel her heat, smell her musky perfume. "You can deal with Baptiste. That's your perk. As for the rest of them, they'll be too busy trying to fix what went wrong and crucifying Wegmann."

Hesitantly, almost against his will, Auerbach stroked her smooth hair with clumsy fingers. "Misdirection."

A red spark of anger glinted in her dark eyes. "At least I learned something of use while I've been here."

"What have you learned from Wegmann?"

Beth-Li chuckled. "A lot about his machines. He hasn't touched me. I think he suffers from what used to be called performance anxiety. Something you don't have to worry about, right?"

Auerbach frowned as a thought occurred to him. "What do you mean Baptiste is my perk?"

Beth-Li spoke in an amused croon. "She'll need comforting after Kane...after he goes away."

One of her hands stole to the juncture of his thighs, fingertips lightly touching the swelling she found there. "Is that for me...or at the thought of your perk?"

Auerbach started to reply, then realized he wasn't certain himself. Her hand grasped his erection tightly, and she stood on tiptoe, her mouth meeting his. He tried to be careful, out of consideration for her healing lip, but Beth-Li's kiss was more than passionate—it was fierce, violent.

She unzipped the front of his bodysuit in one sudden motion. Breaking the kiss, she dropped to her knees, pulling the garment down with her, over his hips.

Beth-Li laughed, a musical sound full of cruel humor. "Keep thinking of your perk." Then she guided him into her mouth.

THE BOTTOM LEVEL of Cerberus was some 150 feet below solid, shielded rock. It held the various maintenance and machine rooms, the air-conditioning and the nuclear generators. A semidetached wing contained ten detention cubicles.

Bry stepped out of the lift and into the corridor. He heard the high-pitched rumble of the turbines and felt a surge of relief. Quickly, he walked down the passageway and into the engine room. Within a wire-cage enclosure, resting on an elevated concrete slab, were the three generators. Half-ovoid shells made of vanadium surrounded their inner workings.

He glanced over at the control and monitoring station spanning almost the entire width of one wall.

Liquid crystal displays glowed steady green and glass-covered needle gauges indicated maximum energy output. He looked around for Wegmann, didn't see the man anywhere and called loudly, "Hey! Wegmann!"

"What?"

The voice, speaking close to his ear, caused Bry to skip around, biting back an obscenity. Wegmann stood behind him, regarding him with mild, expressionless eyes. He cleaned his hands with an oily rag. Bry found the man's composure a little disconcerting and more than a little irritating.

In his midthirties, Wegmann was no more than five and a half feet tall and weighed in the general vicinity of 150 pounds. As such he was the only man in Cerberus shorter and slighter of frame than Bry, but he always seemed to possess the self-confidence of someone twice his height and weight.

Bry knew Wegmann had deliberately startled him, but rather than raising the issue, he said, "You've got the gens back on-line and at full power."

Inclining his balding head in a nod, Wegmann said, "Very observant. You didn't come all the way down here to tell me something I already knew, did you?"

Bry stopped short of glaring, but he couldn't keep from snapping, "You were told to apprise me or Lakesh as soon as the repairs were complete."

"They're test-cycling. I'm letting them run to make sure there's no burps, spikes or dips. Once that's done, I intended to make my report."

"How long will that be?"

Wegmann sauntered over to the instrument console, making an exaggerated show of examining every gauge. "As long as it takes, I guess."

"It's been a week," argued Bry.

"Six days," Wegmann countered.

"I've already reconfigured the gateway's own power source so it won't be such a drain on the main generators. There shouldn't be any burps, spikes or dips."

Wegmann said nothing, appearing to find the twitching of a needle indicator completely absorbing.

Struggling to tamp down his rising impatience, Bry declared, "We're ready to run a test, too, with some inert material."

"Don't let me or my engines stop you."

"Look, dammit—we've got to make sure all the hardware and secondary linkups are in phase. We can't do that until you give us the word."

Casually, Wegmann stepped back from the board, turning to face Bry. "The word," he said dryly, "is given."

Bry turned sharply on his heel and stalked toward the door. Wegmann called after him, "Hold on a second."

"What?"

"You seen Beth-Li today?"

Bry frowned, casting a quizzical glance over his shoulder. "No, I've had my head stuck in the gateway's emitter array for most of the morning. Why?"

A lazy smile played over Wegmann's face, but it had no humor in it. "If you do see her, tell her I've got a word for her, too."

"What's that supposed to mean?"

Wegmann fluttered the oily rag dismissively.

"She'll know what it means." With that, he turned back to the console.

Bry strode out of the engine room, on the one hand pleased he could take good news back to Lakesh, but on the other wondering if the news was indeed all that good.

Chapter 5

As Kane looked down the crumbling blacktop road, bordered on one side by dense forest and on the other by grassland, he said sourly, "We don't have a lot of options."

Grant nodded gloomily. "They'll come straight up the highway, and the highway will take them to the pass." He didn't need to add that the rockfall would only stop the Sandcats, not the men inside them.

Sky Dog said uncertainly, "Perhaps when they see the path is blocked, they'll give up."

Kane shook his head. "If their mission is to investigate the redoubt, they'll do it on foot and on hands and knees if necessary. It's the will of the baron, and so they must obey."

"We can lay trap on road," Domi suggested. Under stress, her clipped abbreviated mode of Outland speech became more pronounced. "Bushwhack 'em big-time."

"I thought of that," Grant said darkly. "Even if we manage to chill two wagloads of Mags—which I doubt we can do—another squad will be sent out eventually. And if even one of them gets away, he'll report back to the baron that the redoubt is inhabited. We'll only delay the inevitable."

He exchanged an unhappy glance with Kane. Both men retained exceptionally vivid memories of their firefight with fellow Magistrates upon their escape from Cobaltville. They were repulsed by the prospect of directing more violence against members of their former brotherhood who were simply following orders.

Sky Dog gestured with angry impatience, first toward the road then to the mountain range. "What can we do? Bows and arrows and ponies against armored wags and autoblasters...it'll be a massacre, genocide."

A thin smile touched Kane's lips, but it didn't reach his eyes. "The only strategy we have is to make the Mags think they're facing opposition more serious than bows and arrows. We'll have to stop them here, long before they even get to the foothills."

Sky Dog stared at him incredulously. "How do you figure to do that?"

Kane turned back to the tree line. "I'm working on it. For right now, get all of your warriors together. Get them all painted, dressed up and mounted. You do the same. I'm planning a big show."

Sky Dog opened his mouth as if to inquire about Kane's sanity or lack thereof, then closed it and hurried off toward the village. Grant and Domi followed Kane back through the overgrowth to the war wag.

"You intend to formulate a plan, right?" Grant demanded. "Not just make up shit as you go along like you usually do?"

Kane cast him an icy, blue-gray glare. Then he forced a chuckle. "I call it improvising. Whether it works or not depends on who is the Mag commander and how impressionable he is."

They climbed into the rear of the wag and entered

a side compartment where they had stored the other blasters Domi had cleaned. There were four blasters: an S&W Model 59 pistol, an Atchisson automatic shotgun, a Colt Python revolver and an M-16 rifle.

Kane said gloomily, "No ammo for the revolver or the shotgun. The S&W takes 9 mm rounds, so I guess we can use that. We're going to have to divide up everything that shoots among the warriors to make this work."

"To make what work?" Domi asked.

"My plan."

"Which I'm still waiting to hear," remarked Grant skeptically.

"Part bluff, part theater. We'll only have time for one full dress rehearsal, so I hope Sky Dog gets his people back here fast."

Grant scowled, but that meant the idea appealed to him.

Kane removed the long hollow cylinder of the LAW 80 rocket launcher from a rack on the bulkhead. He handed it to Grant. "What do you know about this?"

Grant hefted it in his arms, then pulled the two sections to their full extended length. He unfolded the reflex collimator sight on the smooth upper surface. "A one-shot disposable weapon, state-of-the-art about two centuries ago. Designed specifically to take out armored vehicles. The effective range is about 500 meters."

He tapped a molded bulge on its underside. "It incorporates a spotting rifle to test-aim. The trigger is in here. Simple to use, if you've got a decent eye."

Bending down, Kane pried open the lid of a wooden crate. It contained four projectiles, each one tipped with a head resembling a blunt-nosed cone. "And these?"

"HEAT rounds," Grant responded promptly. "High Explosive Anti-Tank 94 mm rockets. Not too different than the Shrike missiles on Deathbirds. They're ignited in the launch tube and rocket-propelled. The warhead is a shaped charge, concentrating its force on a small spot."

Grant eyed the projectiles doubtfully. "They've got to be a minimum of two centuries old, more than likely looted from an arsenal in an old military stockpile. The propellant and warheads are probably unstable as hell. If they are, at best you'll only get a misfire, a fizzle. At worst, the rocket will explode in the tube."

He gestured to the wag around them. "And if that happens, so much for all our hard work."

Kane grunted. "A chance we'll have to take." He nodded toward Domi. "Or you will."

She stiffened, her ruby eyes narrowing to suspicious slits. "What do you mean?"

"What I mean," Kane replied patiently, "is we've got to make the Mags think the Indians have a fully operational war wag in their possession...with blasters and missile launchers and all the bells ringing and whistles blowing."

Comprehension showed in the girl's eyes. "Theater?"

Kane nodded. "Theater. And however the last act ends, I don't want the Mags to give us favorable reviews."

SITTING IN THE COPILOT'S chair of the Sandcat, Abrams had kept one drowsy eye on the distant bulk of the Darks for most of the day. The sky above the lofty peaks had filled with black, seething clouds. He could easily imagine the devil's own wind whipping and roaring around them. Grudgingly, he admitted to himself that Lakesh's long-ago assessment of Redoubt Bravo's location was correct. It was probably the most inaccessible of all the installations related to the Totality Concept.

A Deathbird attempting an aerial landing on the plateau would be chewed up and spit out by the unpredictable weather. Besides, Cobaltville's fleet of official aircraft simply didn't have the range for a direct flight. The birds would have to carry extra fuel and alight somewhere to gas up.

At least the old highway the pair of Sandcats rumbled down was in fairly good condition, compared to traveling across the tableland. The past few hours of the journey had been mercifully free of the spinecompressing jolts that had plagued them all over the past four days. So far, they had not encountered places where the roadbed had collapsed and forced them to take an overland detour.

For the first time since leaving Cobaltville, the Magistrate squad made good time. Abrams estimated they would reach the base of the foothills shortly before sunset. Also for the first time since embarking on the mission, he felt halfway relaxed, although that was due mainly to physical exhaustion. The incessant throb of the engine and the clatter of tracks sounded like a lullaby. He fought to keep his eyes open, not wanting to display any weakness to Pollard, seated in the pilot's chair. After several minutes of smothering yawns, Abrams allowed his eyes to close and he drifted off into a dreamless slumber.

He was awakened almost immediately by the sudden change in the timbre of the Sandcat's engine. His eyes snapped open as Pollard downshifted, working the brake and the gear lever. He gazed steadily through the open ob port. Abrams followed his stare and his body tensed so quickly he felt a spasm of pain in his lower back. The vehicle came to a halt.

"Sir—" Pollard began.

"I see them," broke in Abrams, forcing a calm he did not feel into his voice. "I see them."

A single-wide rank of mounted men bisected the highway a hundred yards ahead. All the moisture in Abrams's mouth dried. He had never seen anything like the men except in old, predark entertainment vids stored in the archives.

All of them were coppery of complexion, with long jet-black hair worn either in braids or hanging loose to stream in the breeze. A variety of feathers fluttered in their ebony tresses. Paint distorted their angular features into masks of sheer, implacable ferocity. All of them sat on horses, many of which also bore feathers and paint.

Although most of the warriors were starkly dressed in breechclouts, many wore breastplates of bones, necklaces of teeth and armlets of metal. They were broad-shouldered and lean-hipped, dark faces immobile beneath the coatings of paint, but their narrow eyes glittered with the fire that burns in the eyes of a stalking predator. To a man they were armed with bows, spears and hand weapons—knives and axes and stone-tipped clubs.

Abrams quickly counted at least fifty of them, stretched out in a loose formation across the road and grassland bordering it. To the uninitiated eye, the manner in which the warriors were positioned seemed foolhardy, but he knew that single-rank formation was not casual. Every man had his place in it.

At a word, the line of mounted warriors could quickly become a crescent, forming an encircling barrier to trap both vehicles between the horns of the semicircle. Although he couldn't see them, he was certain other warriors lay hidden either in the tree line to the left of the Sandcats or in declivities in the tableland on their right.

"Are they fucking fused-out?" Pollard snarled in disbelief. "A bunch of Stone Age savages blocking the road?"

Abrams didn't respond, assuming Pollard's query was strictly rhetorical. The second Sandcat was at least fifty feet behind them. He seized the transcomm microphone. "Close up tight," he directed Chatham, the driver. "Put your nose in our ass."

"Yes, sir," came Chatham's confused response. A second later, upon seeing the Indians, he said with vehemence, "Yes, sir!"

Pollard's hands tightened on the horseshoe-shaped steering wheel. "Should we punch our way through them?"

"Let's see what they want."

Pollard jerked his head around, his face expressing incredulous outrage. "Sir? See what *they* want?"

Angrily, Abrams snapped, "Do as I say. I want to avoid a firefight. We may need all of our ammunition later, and there's no point in burning it if some kind of negotiation will work to clear the road."

Two of his men climbed into caged gunner's saddles on either side of the coaxial turret post, bracing themselves on the footrests. Abrams touched a button on the console, and microcircuity engaged, feeding an electric impulse to the chemically treated arma-glass turret. It instantly became transparent.

Abrams put on his helmet, snapping the underjaw lock guard into place, knowing the headpiece would serve its secondary function of instilling fear. The Mag armor had been designed not just for protection but to symbolize the fearsome, faceless power of baronial authority.

Abrams stood up in his chair and slid back the roof canopy, confidently revealing himself from the waist up. With a slight quiver of unease, he noted no trepidation, much less fear, registering on the faces of the Indians.

Shouting in order to be heard over the twin rumble of the Sandcat engines, he demanded, "Is there a leader or a chief among you?"

He seriously doubted any of the barbarians spoke English, but he wanted to give them the chance to talk it over. He harbored no doubts that his squad could easily slaughter even such a numerically superior force. But once that step was taken, Abrams would be bound by policy to exterminate all the Indians in the area, including the old, the infirm, the women and the children. It was the price of defiance. Rebellion against the enforcers of ville law could not be tolerated, and even insolence was punishable by death.

But to find the Indian settlement and raze it required time and resources he preferred not to expend.

A black horse suddenly pranced from the line of men, stepping high and lightly. A lean, lithe figure sat on its back. An elaborate headdress of eagle feathers surrounded his head in a fluttering halo. His ferocious face was colorfully painted, and he wore a bone breastplate. He gripped a long, steel-tipped lance in one fist.

Abrams couldn't help but feel impressed. Another man would have looked foolish bedecked in such savage finery, but the warrior's erect carriage and the easy way he controlled his horse with only his knees gave him an air of authority.

The man approached at a canter, his mount's unshod hooves clattering against the blacktop. He halted the animal fifteen or so feet from the prow of the Sandcat.

In surprisingly unaccented English, he announced, "I am Sky Dog. Who are you, Magistrate?"

Rather than feel comforted that the Indian had recognized him as a Mag, Abrams was made even more uneasy by his distinct lack of apprehension. Either Sky Dog was self-assured to the point of being suicidal or he had an ace on the line. If the latter was the case, Abrams couldn't even begin to conceive of what that might be.

"I am Abrams, commander of the Cobaltville Mag Division," he stated imperiously. "You're obstructing legal representatives of the baron passing through his territory."

Sky Dog's grim expression did not alter, but his words dripped with contempt. "The baron's territory, you say. This is the ancestral land of the Lakota and the Cheyenne. Therefore, it is we who hold the legal rights. What is your business here?"

Abrams, taken aback by the man's arrogance, couldn't speak for a moment. Then he stabbed an arm toward the Bitterroot Range. "To the mountains. We seek fugitives from justice."

Sky Dog's face twitched ever so slightly in a moue of mockery. "You will not find fugitives from anything in the Darks, Abrams. Nothing lives there. It is a cursed place, full of evil secrets and death."

"Then you should have no objection to us going there," Abrams snapped.

Sky Dog shifted position on the blanket saddle. "I would not object if you didn't have to cross our land to reach it. That is the crux of the matter. For more that a century, we've fought to hold our territory, to keep it free from Roamers and *wasicun* invaders like you. We will continue to do so."

Abrams heard Pollard swearing beneath him, but he ignored him. Firmly, coldly, he declared, "You are outmatched. We have superior weaponry and heavy wags. No matter how long you have held this land, you haven't faced opposition like this. We will reach our objective and we'll do it even if we go over or through you. We will not go around."

Abrams knew a bloodbath was a foregone conclusion, but he offered the man one last opportunity to negotiate it. "Once the first shot is fired," he warned, "there will be no going back. All of your people will die. It will be as if you had never lived at all."

Sky Dog's eyes slitted. Abrams could almost feel the hot hatred seething in them. Nudging his horse with buckskin-shod heels, the Indian slowly backed away. Abrams clenched his teeth, hoping the man intended to confer with his warriors instead of ordering an attack.

Keeping his gaze locked on Abrams's bearded face, Sky Dog reined in his horse, then raised his lance over his head. The men behind him did not stir, and Abrams wondered at the meaning of the gesture, whether it signified surrender or defiance. An instant later, he received his answer.

Even over the steady rumble of the Sandcats' idling engines, a mechanical roar slammed against his eardrums. Like a prehistoric creature roused from a million-year slumber and resenting its awakening, a dark massive shape came crashing through the undergrowth bordering the tree line. Leaves and foliage exploded in showers, and saplings snapped off with sounds like gunshots.

For a crazed micromoment of shock, Abrams wasn't sure his eyes were conveying accurate information to the reasoning centers of his brain. He resisted the impulse to reach up and tweak his whiskers, to make sure he wasn't hallucinating.

The huge tank-treaded machine plowed up loose dirt and lumbered onto the road, veering sharply in a semicircle with a loud squeal of the drive train. Its blunt snout pointed directly at the frontal armor of the Sandcat, as if daring the smaller machine to make a move. Also pointed directly at the Sandcats were missile ports and the multiple barrels of miniguns.

Through the windshield, Abrams barely made out the feathered and face-painted man in the pilot's chair. He knew his jaw had dropped open in astonishment, but Abrams was in no hurry to close it. Adrenaline surged through him as he stared unblinkingly at the heavily armed and armored mobile army command post.

Faintly, he heard Sky Dog's taunting shout, "The next hand is yours, Magistrate. Raise or call."

Chapter 6

Kane hissed curses beneath his breath as the war wag bucked and lurched around him. Every seam, every weld, every rivet seemed to creak and groan.

He applied the brakes, doing his best not to stall the big machine out. He heard Domi, crouched down in the portside missile pod, cry out in pain as the vehicle screeched to a halt. He was too busy trying to control the behemoth to respond. Unlike the Sandcats, the vehicle was a juggernaut, cumbersome and about as maneuverable as a rock formation.

Still he managed to align the metal monster so it effectively blocked the Cats' lines of fire to the tribesmen. He couldn't help but grin appreciatively when he saw Abrams's mouth hanging agape.

Kane was more than a little surprised to see the division administrator. The fact that Baron Cobalt had dispatched Abrams to command a recce mission had all sorts of implications, none of them good. Kane wished he could question him, but he didn't dare show his face—even as disguised as it was by paint—without ruining the ruse he and Grant had concocted.

Sky Dog trotted his horse around the war wag, keeping close to the side but well away from the missile pod where Domi kneeled with the LAW 80 rocket launcher. She had placed the barrel in such a way that if she had to fire, it would provide the illusion of a fully functional weapons emplacement.

In a loud, stentorian voice, Sky Dog declared, "As you said, Abrams, once the first shot is fired, there will be no going back—for any of us. It is up to you to fire that shot or return the way you came."

Sky Dog paused, then, in a tone like the sharp cracking of a whip, demanded, "Decide!"

Through the bulletproof windshield, Kane watched Abrams keenly. Although the man's eyes were concealed by the helmet's visor, he had no problem guessing the kind of uncertain thoughts racing through the administrator's mind.

Abrams had four USMG-73 machine guns he could bring into play, but he could only attack with one Cat with any degree of rapidity. The second vehicle would be required to back up and leave the roadbed to have an unobstructed zone of fire. And as soon as the Indians saw the rearward Cat begin to reverse, Abrams knew the war wag facing him would unleash its arsenal at point-blank range.

Of course, Abrams did not know only one rocket was aimed at him and that the miniguns had no ammunition. He also didn't know Grant and six other warriors had taken up flanking positions around both vehicles, armed with autoblasters. Despite Sky Dog's earlier doubt that his warriors would be willing to use firearms, almost too many of them volunteered. Standing Bear was one of them, joining Grant out on the tableland.

If the Magistrates remained inside the armored walls of the Sandcats, the weapons would be effective primarily as noisemakers, but at least they would receive the impression they faced opposition a bit more lethal than arrows and spears.

Kane used his thumb to flip open the cover of his trans-comm unit and press the key to open Grant's channel. He didn't dare bring the little radiophone up to his face, so he boosted the volume to hear Grant's report over the growl of the engine.

"We're set," said Grant's filtered voice. "I've got Abrams in my sights."

"Acknowledged," Kane replied.

The standoff stretched out for another half minute. Kane understood but didn't sympathize with Abrams's quandary. In the face of unknown forces, the most intelligent tactic was to withdraw. But Magistrate arrogance and conditioning were an immovable obstacle to logical thinking, as both Kane and Grant had reason to know.

Abrams spoke a single word into his helmet's commlink, then he dropped down the hatch, out of sight into the Sandcat. Barely a second later, the twin barrels of the USMG-73's spit tongues of flame.

Even over the engine roar, Kane heard the jackhammer drumming. A hailstorm struck the side of the war wag, sounding like a work gang pounding on the hull with mallets. As 7.62 mm bullets kicked up dirt in foot-high bursts all around Sky Dog, his horse screamed and reared beneath him, forelegs lashing. Sky Dog slid off its back, over its rump as the animal's legs folded. It fell heavily to the ground, its glossy black coat bearing bright scarlet splotches.

"Son of a bitch!" Kane snarled.

He didn't need to give the order to fire. As the horse's body was still settling, Grant and the armed warriors opened up with a cross fire that ripped the air. Rounds struck dancing patterns of sparks on the skin of the Sandcat, ricochets keening away.

They didn't penetrate the armor, but the gunners swung the machine guns around, tracking for the source of the fire. The respite gave Sky Dog the opportunity to take cover behind the war wag. Kane noted how he cradled his left arm as he ran.

Turning his head, Kane shouted, "Domi! Let loose!"

He waited, gritting his teeth at the staccato thunder of autofire and the multiple clangs of rounds impacting on metal. When he didn't hear the whooshing rush of the rocket or see its flaming tail, he bellowed, "Domi. Do it, goddammit."

He barely heard her frustrated cry over the racket. "Misfire! Misfire! Loading another."

Kane growled as he saw the second Sandcat begin to reverse, swinging around and off the highway. He engaged the war wag's gears, let up on the brake and slammed down hard on the accelerator. "Hold on," he yelled.

The leviathan lunged forward with a prolonged roar. Its blunt snout impacted solidly with the snout of the Sandcat, making a noise like two iron mountains colliding. Metal screeched against metal with a prolonged, nerve-racking wail.

Kane lurched violently in his seat, neck muscles twinging, his chest slamming into the steering wheel with breath-robbing force. He kept his foot on the gas pedal. The turret bubble atop the Sandcat rotated, the perforated barrel of the USMG-73 spitting fire and smoke at him.

The rounds hammered loudly against the wag's armor, banging on the thick double-glazed polymer of the windscreen. Most of the bullets bounced away, leaving little white stars to commemorate their impacts. A few others splashed into shapeless dark blobs and clung there.

Grant's voice shouted something from the transcomm, but the unit had fallen to the floorboards and Kane couldn't reach it. He thought he heard him yell something about Standing Bear. Kane popped the gears, and the massive vehicle gave another violent lurch and a howl of a stressed engine.

The Mag driving the Sandcat tried to meet the war wag head-on, and they strained against each other with squeals and grinding sounds, each vehicle trying to outmuscle the other. The Cat's treads spun, scouring the roadbed and hurling gravel and pulverized asphalt in arching plumes. The spray of dirt and grit spattered the second vehicle.

Smoke spouted from the exhausts of the war wag and the Sandcat, filling the air with dense, shifting planes of vapor. The shutter of the Cat's ob port was only partially open, and Kane glimpsed a boxy jawline under the driver's visor. Its general outline was familiar, but he didn't devote much time to bringing the memory into full focus.

Barely audible over the cacophony of blasterfire and engine noise, Kane heard a ripping sound, as of a piece of stiff canvas tearing in half. A flaming, smoking projectile skimmed from the port side of the war wag, leaving a trail of spark-shot smoke in its wake.

The HEAT round exploded in a flaring fireball on the Sandcat's frontal armor, spreading a blanket of flame up over the ob ports and the gun turret. The 94 mm hollow charge punched a deep cavity into the prow of the Cat. The concussion shook the war wag, and fragments clattered loudly against the windshield. Kane flinched, but the bulletproof polymer coating didn't break. Cracks spread in an interconnecting network.

The resistance to the wag's steady forward momentum suddenly diminished, and Kane guessed that the Sandcat's driver was either dead or too busy trying to extinguish the fire that had suddenly ignited in his lap to maintain pressure on the throttle.

The mobile army command post pushed the Cat inexorably backward. It smashed loudly against the vehicle behind it just as it was completing its turn. The bulk of the second vehicle tipped up onto two treads, but it remained more or less upright. Gripping the steering wheel, Kane continued to punish the two Sandcats.

He floored the accelerator, using the first Cat as a battering ram against the second. The second vehicle fishtailed off the road, bouncing violently as it crashed through a wall of vegetation before coming to a halt against the trunk of an aspen.

Both gull-wing doors of Abrams's Sandcat were flung open and up, disgorging clouds of gray smoke and two armored figures. They slapped frantically at the patches of flame clinging to the polycarbonate. Kane only recognized Abrams because his beard was ablaze with a wreath of fire. With no one to steer or brake the Sandcat, the war wag shoved it off the road, piling it up against its twin with an air-shivering crash.

The firing pattern from Grant and the armed Amerindians changed, concentrating on Abrams and the other Magistrate. With chunks of asphalt dancing all

around them, the two men tried to return the shots
with their Sin Eaters. Both Magistrates took simultaneous multiple hits, and though the rounds didn't
penetrate their body armor, they were hammered off
their feet, limbs twisting and jerking like those of
scarecrows exposed to a high wind.

Smoke continued to boil from the open doors of
the Sandcat, and the Mags inside desperately crawled
and fell out. The personnel compartment hatch was
jammed tight against the other vehicle, so they were
forced to claw their way forward to escape.

All of the Mags were racked by lung-deep coughs.
With wild, wolfish howls, the mounted warriors
kicked their horses forward, forming a circle around
the gagging men. Despite the fact Kane had told Sky
Dog to instruct the braves in the futility of engaging
the Magistrates hand-to-hand, they fell upon them
anyway. Grant and his blaster-wielding warriors were
forced to stop firing or kill their own people.

A storm of arrows showered the Magistrates, the
steel points rattling against their armor and bouncing
away. Kane glimpsed one man reeling blindly, both
of his cheeks pierced by a feathered wooden shaft,
liquid strings of scarlet spilling from his lips.

The Amerindians leaped from horseback, grappling with the armored men, stabbing and hacking at
them with knives and tomahawks. The polycarbonate
armor deflected the blades, and two of the Mags got
off lucky shots with their Sin Eaters, spraying several
warriors with hailstorms of lead. They pitched from
their horses' backs, bodies stitched through with
9 mm slugs. The other braves refused to retreat. Instead, they shrieked even louder with rage and
swarmed all over the Magistrates.

Sky Dog raced toward the screaming melee, shouting, at his warriors to stop. His left arm dangled at his side, a streak of crimson bright against his ruddy skin. More than likely, a 7.62 mm round from one of the USMG-73's had broken it.

His horde of blood-mad warriors pulled back. Kane glimpsed two of the Mags lying motionless on the ground, leaking fluids. Cutting edges had evidently found vulnerable areas in their black exoskeletons. The other Magistrates struggled in the strong grips of the braves, their Sin Eaters stripped from them.

Domi appeared in the control compartment, ruby eyes alight with excitement. A black smudge of soot on her right cheek marred the pearly perfection of her skin. She had obviously caught some of the rocket's blowback, but she had gotten off lucky. The old projectile could have exploded in the launch tube.

"Got 'em whipped!" she crowed triumphantly.

Kane thought her pronouncement a little premature, but he didn't correct her. The machine guns of the jammed-up Sandcat continued to hammer away, spewing steel-jacketed hailstorms in a 360-degree circuit. The blasterfire was ineffectual and impotent. The double machine-gun fire from the turret did little more than prune all the trees in the vicinity. Bullet-chewed branches, bark and shredded leaves rustled down in a rain.

"*Kane!*" Grant's angry, frustrated voice roared from the trans-comm on the floor.

Domi scrambled into the copilot's chair, leaned down and picked up the unit. She handed it to Kane. "I'm here," he said.

"The first Cat is pacified," Grant stated, reverting

to Mag euphemisms. "The second one still has some teeth. Only an order from Abrams will get them to surrender. Want me to convince him it's the better part of valor?"

"Under no circumstances show yourself to Abrams or any other Mag." Kane's clipped, firm tone brooked no debate. "We've got to keep them in the dark about our involvement. Otherwise all of this was a waste of time and lives. We've gone over this with Sky Dog. He knows what to do."

Grant's voice was full of disappointment. "Right. Acknowledged."

Kane cut the connection, repressing a smile. Battle fever burned through Grant, and he ached to bring the conflict to its conclusion so they could claim a complete victory. Kane felt the same way, but they had already decided to convince the Mags that the tribesmen were solely responsible for their defeat. It would be a crippling psychological blow to the squad's confidence and self-esteem.

How the last act drew to its conclusion depended on Sky Dog's powers as a statesman.

SKY DOG FACED ABRAMS, doing his best to maintain a composed expression despite the stink of burned hair tickling his nostrils. Half of the man's whiskers were no more than charred, blackened stubble, the surrounding flesh swollen with leaking blisters.

Abrams showed no pain, however, and neither did Sky Dog, despite the agony lancing up and down his left arm.

"It is over," he told the armored man matter-of-factly. "Order the rest of your men to surrender."

Abrams glanced around at the ferocious faces surrounding him. Tonelessly, he replied, "If they are to die, let them die in battle. You should understand that."

"It's you who don't understand." Sky Dog nodded to the war wag's missile pod. "What we did to your vehicle, we can do to the other. They will die in agony, burned alive. Is that what you wish for them?"

Abrams didn't answer, but he bit his lower lip.

"No one else need die." Sky Dog spoke so quietly that Abrams had to lean forward to hear his voice. "If you were to give me your word, as a commander, that neither you nor any of your men will take up arms against my people, I will let you go."

Sky Dog had expected immediate acceptance, but Abrams was instantly suspicious. "You will let us go in our Sandcat?"

"On foot. You will leave your vehicle as spoils of war. You also forfeit your weapons except for knives. You may take all the rations you brought with you."

Abrams gazed at the shaman warily. "How do I know you won't attack us as soon as we've disarmed?"

"You have my word."

Sky Dog couldn't see the play of emotions in the man's eyes, obscured as they were by the helmet's visor, but he knew Abrams struggled with opposing impulses. His squad was already defeated, both of his vehicles disabled. At worst, the savages would deploy another rocket against it. At best, they would simply wait until the men depleted their ammunition and water.

The notion of agreeing to the terms of the barbarian was repulsive in the extreme, but the alternative was far worse and certainly more permanent.

On foot, Abrams estimated it would take them nearly ten days to reach the border territory within direct jurisdiction of Cobaltville. Ten days of marching through the Outlands, armed only with knives, with perhaps nothing to return to but baron-issued termination warrants.

Quietly, Sky Dog said, "The mission your baron assigned was foolish. My people have lived here for a very long time and if there were *wasicun* in the Darks, we would know about it. The road was blocked years ago by an avalanche and your Mags with their guns and armor could never make the climb. There is nothing up there anyone would want."

Abrams wetted his lips, nodding toward the war wag. "Where did you get that?"

"It was abandoned here many generations ago. We restored it and the blasters it contained. There is much more that you have not seen."

Abrams seemed on the verge of speaking, but he hesitated.

Impatiently, Sky Dog said, "Make your decision, Magistrate."

Abrams stared at him levelly. "We'll just go?"

"You'll just go. A band of my warriors will escort you from our land. Once you leave, you are never to return, regardless of what orders your baron gives you in the future."

Abrams glanced questioningly at the other Magistrates standing silently in the grips of the warriors. Then, into his helmet's comm-link, he said clearly,

"Rostler. Cease fire. Unbutton the Cat and throw out your arms. We're surrendering."

Sky Dog couldn't hear Rostler's response, but it made Abrams bare his teeth and raise his voice. "Goddammit, you heard me. We're surrendering. We've been promised safe passage. I *order* you to comply immediately!"

The stuttering fire from the machine guns abruptly ceased. The side gull wings slowly opened. Sin Eaters and Copperheads clattered out onto the ground. After a few seconds, the blasters were followed by a group of disconsolate, frightened, black-clad men. They were instantly at the center of a wheel of glittering spear points. Slowly, reluctantly, the Magistrates raised their arms and placed their hands on the backs of their helmeted heads.

With a nod, Abrams indicated the corpses of the dead Mags. "What about them?"

"We will attend to their remains," Sky Dog said. "Their bodies will not be mutilated if that's what you're worried about."

Faintly, Abrams said, "I thank you for that, at least."

Sky Dog stepped away from him, gesturing sharply with his right hand. The Amerindians released their holds on the Magistrates. "Go now," the shaman intoned with a deadly sincerity. "Tell your baron he cannot own all of Grandmother Earth. If he continues to try, this little war will become a very big and costly one. Someday it will consume not only him but all of the baronies."

With that, Sky Dog turned on his heel and stalked away. Once behind the war wag, his deliberate, forceful stride faltered and he sagged, sinking his teeth into his lower lip. The exhaust fumes from the idling vehicle made him lightheaded and nauseated. He wished Kane would turn it off.

As if obeying a telepathic command, the heavy rumble of the engine ceased, but with a gasping wheeze. A few moments later, the rear hatch opened and Kane and Domi climbed out.

"Thanks," Sky Dog said.

Kane snatched off the feathered bonnet. "For what?"

"For turning off this demon."

Kane smiled mirthlessly. "Wasn't my doing. The damn thing ran out of gas."

Sky Dog was both relieved and apprehensive. Leaving the monstrous vehicle to crouch on the road didn't have much appeal for him.

"The Cats have extra fuel cans," Kane said reassuringly. "We can use them to gas it up and move it."

He eyed Sky Dog's bloodied arm. "Bad?"

"Bad enough. It's broken."

"Blood loss looks minimal. I think we can fix you up."

Kane stepped to the corner and peered around the wag. Flanked by four horsemen, the column of Magistrates shuffled down the highway, Abrams at its head. He attempted to maintain some shred of dignity, even though he limped very badly. The long trek back to Cobaltville would be exceedingly painful for him, but Kane couldn't muster much compassion.

Smoke continued to roil from the interior of the rocket-blasted Sandcat, but not as much earlier.

"Better get some men to put out that fire," Kane said. "The thing may not be roadworthy anymore, but you can salvage some parts for old Titano here."

He affectionately patted the metal hide of the war wag.

Sky Dog shouted instructions to a group of warriors, and they busied themselves tossing handfuls of dirt into the immobilized Cat and beating out flames with blankets taken from their horses' backs.

Grant strode up from the grassland, wielding one of the Colt Commando autorifles. "Six casualties," he reported. "Five dead." He paused, then added, "Standing Bear is one of them."

Kane felt a pang of sadness. Weeks ago, he had fought Standing Bear and defeated him, more by trickery than skill. Rather than allow the warrior to be dishonored, Kane had permitted him to put the mark of the trickster wolf on his face. Unconsciously, he touched the thin scar on his cheek.

"What we do now?" Domi asked.

Grant hooked a thumb over his shoulder. "Assign a detail to attend to the dead and wounded. Then we'll have to figure out how to get these wags off the road."

Grimly, Domi said, "Still think we should chill Mags."

Sounding slightly aggrieved, Grant replied, "We explained that. If they don't go back to Cobaltville, another party will be sent out. Bigger and better armed and we probably won't be here."

"Baron Cobalt may send out another party anyway," declared Kane. "Not a recon squad, but a full assault force. Sky Dog spit in his eye, humiliated him. But now he knows enough to be cautious. And afraid."

Kane almost added *And vengeful,* but he decided to let Sky Dog and his people enjoy their triumph without worrying about the future.

He started around the war wag, saying to Sky Dog, "There'll be first-aid kits in the Cats. We can start treating that arm and the other wounded."

He had walked only a few paces when his path was blocked by a group of warriors. They regarded him with flinty eyes, and Kane came to a halt, wondering if they were friends of Standing Bear and held him responsible for his death. The plan had been his, after all. He surveyed their angular, uncompromising faces, all of them fearsomely painted, and he reflexively tensed his wrist tendons, preparing his hand to receive the Sin Eater. He glared back at them.

As if that was a signal, a high-pitched ululating howl burst from the throats of the assembled warriors. They raised lances, knives and axes over their heads, shaking them at the sky. They shouted two words over and over, "Unktomi Shunkaha! Unktomi Shunkaha!"

The braves voiced their tribute to the man who brought them victory, chanting the name their comrade Standing Bear had conceived as an insult, but now synonymous with cunning and courage—Trickster Wolf.

Kane recalled what Brigid had said to him a short time ago after Tibetan bandits had bestowed upon him the title of Tsyanis Khanpo, the King of Fear. She had wryly commented, "You're earning quite the reputation in the far corners of the world."

He hadn't given her observation much thought at the time. Now he realized, with a sinking sensation in the pit of his stomach, that he was crossing over the road from flesh-and-blood man and entering the realm of legend.

Chapter 7

Early the following morning, Kane, Domi and Grant started back for Cerberus. After the battle with the Magistrates, they had overseen the siphoning of enough fuel from the Sandcats to get the war wag running again. It had been used to haul the disabled Cats into the woods where they were camouflaged.

Upon returning to the village, the Amerindians staged a victory celebration in honor of the *wasicuns*, with plenty of wild dancing, singing and feasting. The mourning for the dead would come later, when their grief would be just as unrestrained as their joy.

More than one nubile native woman eyed Kane boldly and speculatively, but their hair and eye color reminded him too strongly of Beth-Li to arouse his libido. Although he had resisted cooperating with Lakesh's breeding program, he knew he had fulfilled his part of the proposal with her—or her doppelgängers—on two parallel casements. Although the memories of his experiences on those mirror worlds were already dim, he still retained vivid impressions, if not the actual memories, of engaging in the sex act with her.

But in this reality Kane had resisted her advances, and his refusals had damaged her ego and earned her hatred. At least he assumed she hated him; he could no longer be certain of anything. His experiences on the lost Earths made him doubt his most fundamental concepts of reality.

Before leaving the village, they told Sky Dog they would return as soon as they could with more fuel and ammunition. Kane entrusted the Lakota leader with one of the trans-comm units. Though its range was limited, it was better than no means of communication at all.

Escorted by a pair of warriors, they had ridden on horseback to the rockfall where their Hussar Hotspur Land Rover was parked. During the dangerous and painstaking drive back up the mountain road, Grant and Domi were clearly happy to return to Cerberus. The rough life on the plains was too reminiscent of Domi's upbringing in an Outland settlement for her to find any appeal in it. Grant, though accustomed to hardship during his Mag days and after, made no bones about his preference for a bed over a fur robe spread on the hard ground. He also didn't find herb and bark tea much of a substitute for coffee, and genuine coffee was one of the few real advantages to life at Cerberus.

Kane was strangely regretful about leaving the band of Lakota and Cheyenne. He felt a strong affinity for the wild and free people and their unfettered way of life, and he wasn't sure why. Perhaps it had something to do with the vision he had glimpsed some months before during a bad mat-trans jump. At the time he had dismissed it as a hallucination caused by an out-of-phase transit-feed connection. Lakesh had explained that when the modulation frequencies between two gateway units weren't in perfect sync, jump sickness would result, a symptom of which was startlingly vivid hallucinations.

The hallucinations Kane had suffered weren't dreams; they were more like glimpses of past lives, vignettes from his soul's journey over the long track of time. In one of the visions, he had seen himself astride a pony, feathers in his long, streaming hair as he galloped down on the bluecoat soldiers in a place called the Greasy Grass. The soldier's chief had been named Pahaska.

It wasn't until much later, delving secretly into the redoubt's database, that he learned Greasy Grass was what the Lakota called the Little Bighorn and Pahaska's *wasicun* name was Custer.

Kane wondered why such obscure historical details, which weren't in his conscious storehouse of knowledge, would bubble to the surface during a bout of jump sickness.

More recently, after gaining pieces of the Chintamani Stone, Lakesh had postulated that so-called jump dreams might not be hallucinations at all, but brief, inchoate peeks into other lives and other realities.

Sitting in the passenger seat of the Land Rover as its six tires carried it up the road, Kane hazarded a sideways glance at Grant who was cursing softly beneath his breath as he wrestled with the steering wheel.

If Grant had undergone similar visions during that jump, he never raised the subject and probably never would.

Sensing Kane's gaze, the big man shot him a slightly annoyed glance. "What?"

Kane shrugged. "Nothing. You think Wegmann has the generators debugged by now?"

"After what we went through getting that bastard wag running," Grant snapped, "he'd better."

Domi leaned forward from the back seat, white face slightly troubled. "If it's working, that means Lakesh will send you through the gateway with the rocks again."

Neither man responded to her observation. Using the mat-trans unit in tandem with the unearthly properties of the Black Stone was what had caused the malfunction in the first place. Putting the generators back on-line in order to breach the hyperdimensional barriers between the lost Earths was a matter of paramount urgency, at least as far as Lakesh was concerned. Neither Kane nor Grant shared that view. Domi, in her straightforward way, saw the entire undertaking as confusing, bizarre and downright pointless.

Initially, so had Grant and Kane, but their experiences on the parallel casements had wrought something of a change in attitude. They still didn't consider the matter of any particular urgency, and they certainly weren't eager to climb into the mat-trans and have their bodies reduced to digitized energy patterns while their minds were launched beyond the limits of time and space—or at least beyond the limits they understood.

The two casements they had already visited were as different from each other as from their own Earth, but there were similarities. In each alternate world, there had been a global war, but at a different period in history.

On one parallel casement, Nazi Germany had won the race to become the world's first nuclear power and had locked the entire planet into a fascist dictatorship.

On the second casement, a nuclear war had come

about during the Cuban Missile Crisis of the early 1960s. The era of totalitarianism that followed hadn't been as overt as on the first alternate world, but it had no less a stranglehold on human freedom.

On both lost Earths, C. W. Thrush had enjoyed a position of power, and so had the Archon Directorate.

More than eight months before, Kane had been told that the entirety of human history was intertwined with the activities of the entities called Archons, although they had been referred to by many names over many centuries—angels, demons, visitors, aliens, saucer people, grays.

Their involvement with humanity stretched back at least twenty thousand years, and perhaps further. Beginning at the dawn of history, the Archons subtly—and sometimes not so subtly—influenced human affairs.

They conspired with willing human pawns to control humanity through political chaos, staged wars, famines, plagues and natural disasters. Their standard operating procedure was to establish a privileged ruling class dependent upon them, which in turn controlled the masses for them. The Archons' manipulation of governments and religions was all-pervasive, and allegedly they had allied themselves with Nazi Germany—and switched their allegiance when the Allies were victorious. However, as time progressed, the world and humankind changed too much for their plenipotentiaries to rule with any degree of effectiveness.

But their goal remained the same—the unification of the world under their control, with all nonessential and nonproductive humans eliminated. Now, nearly two hundred years after the nukecaust, the population was far easier to manipulate.

Kane had accepted the startling revalation of the hidden history of humanity. Despite how mad it seemed to him initially, he grew comfortable with it and had eased into hating the so-called Archon Directorate. He woke up hating Archons and he went to bed hating Archons. It was easy, it was simple and it went on.

And then, only recently, he had been told that his hatred was not only pointless, but pretty much without merit. The Archon Directorate did not exist except as a cover story created two centuries before and expanded with each succeeding generation. It was all a ruse, bits of truth mixed in with outrageous fiction. Only a single so-called Archon existed on Earth and that was Balam, who had been the redoubt's resident prisoner for more than three and a half years.

Balam claimed the Archon Directorate was an appellation created by the predark governments. Lakesh referred to it as the Oz Effect, wherein a single vulnerable entity created the illusion of being the representative of an all-powerful body.

Even more shocking than that revelation was Balam's assertion that he and his folk were humans, not alien but alienated. Kane still didn't know how much to believe. But if nothing else, he no longer subscribed to the fatalistic belief that the human race had had its day and only extinction lay ahead. Balam had indicated that was not true, but was merely another control mechanism. Evidently, that control mechanism was due in large measure to the machinations of Colonel Thrush.

When the Land Rover climbed within a mile of

the plateau, Grant trans-commed the redoubt, informing Cotta of their imminent arrival. By the time the
vehicle navigated the last curve in the road and rolled
onto the plateau, they saw that the multi-ton sec door
at the base of the peak was fully open. Seeing the
twenty-foot-wide vanadium-sheathed corridor gleaming beyond it, Kane felt a quick spurt of anxiety.

In the half light of approaching dusk, the open
door looked like a maw, the mouth of some gigantic
devourer. Intellectually, Kane understood his primal
reaction. After spending the past few days in the
open, with no walls or ceiling except the trees and
sky, returning to the windowless confines of Cerberus
made him feel instantly claustrophobic.

Also, ever since they had begun using the mat-
trans unit as a channel to the parallel casements, he
had ceased to view the redoubt as home or even a
safe haven. Now Cerberus felt like a threshold to
hell—and not just one hell, either, but an infinite
number of them, all walking, waking nightmares.

Grant steered the Land Rover across the tarmac
and into the entrance. Farrell stood just inside the
door, hand on the control lever. As soon as the Hotspur passed him, the man threw the lever and the
huge sections of the door began to unfold with clank-
ing groans.

Grant drove to the installation's vehicle depot, a
big room adjacent to the armory. He braked to a stop
beside the redoubt's own Sandcat, opposite the fuel
pump. As the three people climbed out, Brigid entered, green eyes bright with questions. Kane forced
a smile of greeting. He knew she hadn't been worried
about them, because their physical conditions could
be monitored from the Cerberus control center.

The subcutaneous transponder was a nonharmful radioactive chemical that had fit itself into the human body and allowed monitoring of heart rate, brain-wave patterns and blood count. Lakesh had ordered all of the Cerberus redoubt personnel to be injected with them. Based on organic nanotechnology created by the Totality Concept's Overproject Excalibur, the transponder fed information through the Comsat re-lay satellite when personnel were out in the field.

Brigid seemed to sense Kane's unease and she in-quired hesitantly, "It didn't go well?"

"It went great," chirped Domi, flashing a toothy grin. She thrust up a leg, repeatedly kicking the air. "Big-time put the boot to Mag asses. Kicked 'em back to Cobaltville."

Brigid's eyes widened. "You did what?"

Grant matched Domi's grin, nodding toward Kane. "Ask Trickster Wolf here. For once, a plan of his worked out."

Brigid noticed the stark difference in attitude among the three people. Domi and Grant were cheer-ful to the point of ebullience, while Kane appeared nervous and edgy.

"You can give us the details during the debrief," she said, eyeing Kane surreptitiously. "No injuries?"

"Nope," Grant responded, walking toward the door leading to the armory and removing his Sin Eater. "Another first. DeFore should be happy."

Brigid followed them into the big square room. The Cerberus armory was stacked nearly to the ceil-ing with wooden crates and boxes. Many of the crates were stenciled with the legend Property U.S. Army. Glass-fronted gun cases lined the four walls, contain-ing automatic assault rifles, many makes and models of subguns and dozens of semiautomatic blasters. Heavy assault weaponry occupied the north wall, bazookas, tripod-mounted M-249 machine guns, mortars and rocket launchers.

Nearly all of the ordnance was of predark manufacture. Caches of matériel had been laid down in hermetically sealed continuity of government installations before the nukecaust. Protected from the ravages of the outraged environment, nearly every piece of munitions and hardware was as pristine as the day it had rolled off the assembly line. In the far corner, two suits of Magistrate body armor were mounted on metal frameworks. They always reminded Brigid of a pair of silent sentries.

As Kane hung his holstered Sin Eater on a peg within a gun case, he asked, "How go the repairs on the generators?"

"Done," Brigid answered. "Bry has tested the quincunx setting with inert material. The demat and mat cycles went smoothly."

Kane turned toward her, raising an eyebrow. "But he didn't test it with any pieces of the stone?"

She shook her head. "Of course not. You know their properties are only active in conjunction with you."

"Right," he said in a slow, sarcastic drawl. "In conjunction with my second favorite organ. My brain."

"Not your brain," Brigid corrected him curtly. "Its electromagnetic pattern, its individual signature."

They left the armory and went out into the corridor. Kane ran a hand over his stubbled face. "The debrief will have to wait. I need a shower and a shave."

Brigid glanced at him, noting traces of yellow and red paint on his cheeks and how long his hair had grown. She doubted he'd had so much as a trim since his arrival in Cerberus, more than eight months ago.

Grant voiced her thought. "A haircut wouldn't hurt you, either."

Kane shrugged. "Mebbe you should've shown yourself to Abrams after all. Then you could've informed on me, told him my hair wasn't regulation. He could've written me a reprimand before he left."

"Abrams?" Brigid echoed. "The division administrator? He was out in the field?"

"The very one," answered Grant. "After yesterday, I imagine he'll wait another thirty years before he goes out into the field again."

They reached a T junction in the passage. Domi and Grant turned left. Kane kept walking toward his own quarters. He was a little surprised and a bit disquieted to see Brigid walking beside him, her somewhat mannish stride allowing her to easily keep pace with his long-legged gait.

He didn't question her, but she asked, "Something bothering you?"

"No more than usual."

"Which could be anything from your complaints about how the laundry makes your underwear shrink to the quality of powdered eggs in the cafeteria."

Kane didn't react to her remarks or her bantering tone. When they reached the door to his quarters, he hesitated for a half second before turning the knob. Brigid noticed the almost imperceptible pause and asked, "Do you want me to go first?"

Kane's eyes slitted at her oblique reference to the day when he'd entered his quarters and found Beth-Li lying in wait for him—for both of them—with a blaster in hand and the fury of a woman scorned in her heart.

He boldly pushed open the door. The lights came on, and he gave the room a swift survey before stepping in. "As long as you brought her up, where is Beth-Li?"

Brigid closed the door behind them. "I checked on her about an hour ago. She was in her quarters."

"Alone?"

"Apparently."

Kane began unbuttoning his sweat- and grease-stained shirt. "She's been behaving herself, then?"

Brigid nodded uncertainly. "On the surface, anyway."

Kane shot her a quizzical glance. "Explain."

When she told him about Auerbach's suspicions, Kane only shrugged.

"Auerbach has his reasons for distrusting her," he said. "If not for her, Sky Dog's people wouldn't have invited him to his own private chestnut roast. Other than that, he and Wegmann don't get along. I had to break up a fight between them a couple of weeks ago."

"Whatever the case," stated Brigid, "we're going to have to decide what to do with Rouch. She doesn't want to stay."

"Lakesh brought her here. Let him decide."

"Lakesh brought *all* of us here," she retorted.

That was really the crux of the entire problem, which went beyond the presence of Beth-Li Rouch and all the anger and jealousy. When Lakesh had selected Rouch as the perfect candidate for his plan to turn their sanctuary into a colony, he had put into motion a variation of the ploy he had used on Brigid, Bry, Cotta and Wegmann and just about every other Cerberus exile—he set them up, framing them for crimes against their respective villes.

It was a cruel, heartless plan with a barely acceptable risk factor, but Lakesh believed it was the only way to spirit them out of their villes, turn them against the barons and make them feel indebted to him.

Only recently had Lakesh's practice been exposed, and that revelation had been due in the main to Beth-Li. Grant, Kane and Brigid had staged something of a mutiny over the issue, but nothing had been settled. However, Lakesh was on notice his titular position as the redoubt's administrator was anything but secure. Kane certainly didn't want the job and he was positive neither Grant nor Brigid yearned for it.

"Lakesh has abrogated his responsibility," Brigid continued. "He's being stubborn. His feelings are hurt."

Kane turned to face her. "Mebbe we should get this matter straightened out instead of jumping to another casement."

Her emerald eyes widened. "Correct me if I'm wrong, but weren't you the one who insisted on picking up the gauntlet Thrush threw down?"

"That was before."

"Before what?"

Taking a deep breath, Kane furrowed his brow, and his eyes acquired a faraway, preoccupied sheen. He did not reply for a long moment. When he did, it was in a whisper. "Before I saw how irreversibly fucked up those other worlds are...before you and I...you and me..."

He made a gesture of futility and turned his back on her, slipping out of his shirt. Brigid winced when she saw the swirling pattern of scar tissue between his shoulder blades. She knew it was from the injury he had received in the Black Gobi, when he'd rescued her from the Tushe Gun's genetic mingler by shielding her unconscious body from the machine's wild energy discharges with his own. Only the tough Kevlar-weave coat he'd worn at the time prevented the wound from being fatal.

As it was, she had suffered wounds of her own, far more subtle and far more devastating. Her exposure to both the energy discharges and to an unknown type of radiation had rendered her barren. She had suspected her condition had something to do with Lakesh bringing Beth-Li into the redoubt, but he had claimed otherwise. Despite her splendid pedigree, even if she hadn't suffered the accident in Mongolia, Lakesh did not want her to breed with Kane—or with anyone, for that matter. Her gifts were unique, far too valuable to have them diverted by pregnancy and motherhood.

Understanding what Kane referred to, Brigid said quietly, "That really wasn't me and you. It was our mirror selves on the alternate Earths. I'd hoped you'd come to terms with that."

"I thought I had," he replied, half-turning back toward her, but unable to meet her gaze. "But it's so...so..."

His voice trailed off, as he groped for a word. Finally, he said, "Confusing. It's goddamn confusing, Baptiste. I don't like the feeling."

She instantly knew what he meant. On their first two jumps to parallel casements, their minds had fused with those of their alternate selves, their doppelgängers. But for a while, they had been lost to themselves, subsumed by the consciousnesses of their doubles.

In the first casement, she and Kane had only achieved fusion with their other selves after they'd made love. In the second, that had been true only for Brigid. Kane's mind didn't achieve fusion with his doppelgänger's body until he believed Brigid to have been murdered. As with Grant on the first casement, it required a traumatic shock to trigger a full melding of memories and perceptions.

The latter experience fit Brigid's earlier theory that an alteration in their brains was required, a release of endorphins and the firing of neurons in the cortical and subcortical portions. It didn't necessarily have to be the sex act, just an emotional stimulus. Regardless, the reality remained that on both lost Earths they had made love, something they had never done in their own bodies or right minds. It was indeed confusing, embarrassing and more than a trifle schizophrenic.

"Kane," she began haltingly, "what we've got to keep in mind—"

"In mind?" he broke in with a bitter laugh. "That's what this is all about it, isn't it? Our minds are transported across the dimensions and they possess the minds of our twins on the parallel worlds. They're not us, not really. Or are they? How do we know our minds aren't just conjuring up nightmare scenarios while our bodies float in nonexistence inside the gateway chamber?"

Brigid blinked at him, obviously never having considered the possibility before. "If that's true, why do we all share the same scenarios?"

Kane tapped his forehead. "Because they all spring from *this*. According to what Lakesh said, when I made the jump from Tibet to here carrying the three pieces of the stone, a connection between me and them was formed. Isn't it possible that when we think we're traveling to a lost Earth, we're only entering some crazy dream that exists in my imagination?"

Brigid forced a smile. "You'd have to possess an exceedingly vivid—and sick—imagination, Kane."

He acknowledged her comment with a half grin. "No denying that, Baptiste. So you should understand why I'm not eager to wade through that sewage again, whether it's real or just the product of my sick mind."

Crossing her arms over her breasts, she said thoughtfully, "It's an interesting theory, but it doesn't take into account all the facts—or at least those we're aware of."

"We have no facts, not really. We have second-hand information supplied by highly dubious sources mixed in with a whole hell of a lot of supposition. Think about it."

Kane began ticking off points on his fingers. "Lakesh tells us all about the Archon Directorate, how they were responsible for rigging events which led up to the nukecaust. We buy into that conspiracy angle.

"Then a couple of weeks ago, Balam tells us there is no Directorate and no conspiracy. We buy into that. He tells us about the Chintamani Stone and the parallel casements. We buy into that."

He exhaled a weary breath. "Everything we've done over the past eight and half months is because we were *told* something. We have almost no—what's that word you and Lakesh use?—imperial evidence."

"Empirical," Brigid corrected automatically and a little distractedly. Mentally she reviewed everything they had experienced and suffered since arriving at Cerberus, and with a slight start realized Kane had a pertinent point, several in fact.

"Granted," she declared, "what we've witnessed is pretty much a matter of individual perceptions, of subjective interpretation. Lakesh built a frame of reference for us, and so we saw everything through that. I suppose Balam did much the same thing."

She gazed at him levelly. "You've raised some interesting questions. I'm surprised."

He shook his head ruefully and turned toward the bathroom. "I have my moments. But I don't really expect any answers."

"Maybe not," she said quickly, "but I have one."

He paused, waiting. Brigid dropped her arms to her sides and took a step closer to him. She lowered her voice before saying, "Questioning our perceptions of reality is one thing, Kane. But you—all of us—have to leap beyond that and find the anchor. On the first casement we visited, Thrush said something about a basic reality unit. He described it as any action that triggers a reaction."

In a rush, she said, "From what we've already experienced on the parallel worlds, it appears you and I share a common reality unit. And it's each other."

Kane said nothing, and Brigid realized with mingled dismay and relief he knew that already. He was just loath to voice it. Softly, he said, "And on this world, too, I think."

Brigid started to take another step to bring her to his side. The trans-comm unit on the wall emitted a warble, and she froze in place.

Lakesh's reedy voice blared, "Kane, are you there? I need to speak with Brigid. Have you seen her?"

Feeling a little guilty, and then angry because of the guilt, Brigid turned toward the trans-comm. "I'm here. What is it?"

A hint of suspicion entered Lakesh's voice. "The computer has compiled the briefing jacket you wanted. I need to go over a few items with you first. Meet me in the control center, please."

"On my way," she said, and the channel closed with a click.

"Another briefing?" Kane's voice held a tired, exasperated note.

"I'm afraid so. This time it's about Thrush, who he really is and how he may have come to be."

The preoccupation in Kane's eyes vanished, replaced by a glint of predatory anticipation. He moved quickly to the bathroom. "I'll clean up and join you as soon as I can."

Brigid smiled wanly at his retreating back and murmured to herself, "So much for subjective interpretations of reality."

Chapter 8

In a departure from routine, the briefing was not held in the cafeteria. Upon entering the control complex, Kane and Grnat heard a high-pitched drone, an electronic synthesis between a hurricane howl and a bee-swarm hum.

On the far side of the big, vault-walled room, Bry was at the dedicated control console. The instrument panel at which he sat had been built and installed a few months before to oversee the temporal dilation of the Omega Path program.

Its design did not conform to the symmetry of the rest of the consoles in the complex. Dark, long and bulky, like an old-fashioned dining table canted at a thirty-degree angle, it bristled with thousands of tiny electrodes and a complex pattern of naked circuitry. Arranged on a switchboard at Bry's elbow were relays and readout screens.

"Just another test," Bry called to them as they passed. "Our fifth. Everything is functioning smoothly."

The two men walked through the open doorway of the anteroom to where the mat-trans chamber stood. Brigid and Lakesh sat at the long polished table, apparently engrossed by the vague shapes shifting on the other side of the translucent armaglass shielding.

The Cerberus unit was the first fully operable and

completely debugged quantum interface mat-trans inducer constructed after the success of the prototype in 1989. The quantum energies released by the gateways transformed organic and inorganic matter to digital information, which was then transmitted along a hyperdimensional pathway and reassembled in a receiver unit.

To accomplish this, the mat-trans units required an astonishing number of maddeningly intricate electronic procedures, all occurring within milliseconds of one another, to minimize the margins for error. The actual matter-to-energy conversion process was sequenced by an array of computers and microprocessors, with a number of separate but overlapping operational cycles.

But at the moment, nothing and no one was being transmitted anywhere. Bry was again testing the prolonged quincunx effect, a feature of the transition when lower dimensional space was phased into a higher dimension. Under ordinary operating conditions, the effect lasted only a nanosecond, but after the device's reconfigurations, the effect was stretched out and held in perfect balance for a predetermined period of time. As had been done with the Omega Path, the mainframe computers were reprogrammed with the logarithmic data recorded during Brigid's and Kane's transit from Tibet with the three pieces of the trapezohedron. The new program prolonged the quincunx effect produced by dematerialization, stretching it out in perfect balance between the phase and interphase inducers.

As soon as Grant and Kane entered the anteroom, the drone dropped in pitch, finally fading into silence. Lakesh pushed himself out of his chair and went to the chamber, heaving up on the door handle. The heavy slab of armaglass swung open on counterbalanced hinges. Smoke and mist swirled thickly within.

All of them knew the mist was a byproduct of the quantum interface, a plasma wave form that only resembled vapor. Usually, it dissipated within seconds of a successful transit, but due to the prolonged quincunx effect, it tended to linger, a sea fog trapped within the chamber's walls. Thread-thin static-electricity discharges arced within the billowing mass.

Fanning the mist away from his face, Lakesh stepped into the clouds and a moment later returned, carrying a square metal box. When he noticed Kane and Grant, he said, "Just in time, friends. This last test should allay any fears you may have about the reliability of my quantum interphase inducer."

Placing the box on the table, he lifted its lid. Within it lay a raw steak.

"I borrowed this from our food freezer," Lakesh explained. He poked the meat with a forefinger. "Inert inorganic and organic materials were dematerialized, held in the balanced quincunx and have rematerialized as good as new."

Grant eyed the meat dourly. "Until you eat it, how do you know it's as good as new?"

From the doorway, Bry said, "If there is any molecular decohesion, it would have happened by now. The metal of the box and the tissue of the steak would have intermingled. You wouldn't see separate components—you'd see a lump of crap, a steak made out of iron or a box made out of meat."

"Appetizing," remarked Kane dryly. "But since

you didn't use a piece of the stone, the test is inconclusive.''

Lakesh shot him an irritated glare, closed the lid of the box and walked it over to Bry. ''Just to be on the safe side, have DeFore test the meat for any cellular irregularities.''

As the man left, Kane and Grant took chairs around the table. He noticed Lakesh sat down at its head and he felt a flash of annoyance.

''I assume your little diplomatic mission to the Indians went well?'' the old man asked, as if he were inquiring only to be polite.

Kane nodded. ''It did. We'll be going back in a few days with more ammo and fuel. By then, Wegmann should be able to come with us and work out the last bugs in the war wag.''

Lakesh's lined face acquired an irritated expression, but he did not respond to Kane's casual comment about his plans for Cerberus personnel and matériel. Kane repressed a smile. It did no harm to tweak Lakesh, to remind the old man that he no longer took orders from him.

As if sensing a brewing verbal battle and hoping to stave it off, Grant asked, ''Do you want the details?''

Lakesh shook his head. ''I'm certain you, Domi and friend Kane did an exemplary job. The details can wait. We have more pressing matters at hand.''

Kane glanced toward Brigid. ''Something about Thrush?''

She shrugged. ''Maybe yes, maybe no. As you know, I've been delving into the historical database for the past few days, hoping to find some clues to Thrush's real identity, if he had or has one. Obviously, I didn't find anything directly referencing him by that name.''

"But just as obviously," ventured Kane, "you found something."

Brigid nodded. "Thrush could very well be what was known in Gnostic circles as a Melchizedek."

"A what?" Grant demanded. "What the hell is a Melchizedek?" He stumbled over the pronunciation of the word.

"A Melchizedek was allegedly an administrator of this universe, who had no father or mother or any ancestral record. He was never born—therefore he could never die. The Bible mentions in Hebrews 6:20 that Christ himself was a 'high priest forever after the order of Melchizedek.'

"According to the Apocrypha of the Old Testament, a Melchizedek was someone who could travel through all the realms of God—the dimensions of existence. Reputedly, a Melchizedek was reincarnated over and over."

Kane and Grant stared with brows lowered over skeptical eyes at Brigid, but said nothing.

Affecting not to notice them, Brigid continued. "The last historical record of someone claiming to be a Melchizedek comes from the twentieth century. A man made the circuit of so-called New Age circles, spreading the doctrine of hyperdimensional physics and existence on alternate worlds. He claimed that all of humanity literally existed on all dimensional levels and our experiences on each level were completely different.

"He explained that the dimensions were separated from one another by wavelengths, like the notes on a musical scale. In other words, vibrations."

Both Grant and Kane retained exceptionally vivid memories of the infrasound instruments favored by the hybrids in Dulce, and the strange harplike weapons found on Mars used by Sindri and his transadapts. The principle of using music either to heal or to kill was ancient.

"Are you suggesting," Lakesh asked, "that this figure, this twentieth-century Melchizedek, was an incarnation of the entity you know as C. W. Thrush?"

She shook her head. "No, mainly because Thrush's behavior is completely at variance with the actions of this man. He talked a lot about the gray aliens, who we assumed were the Archons, and how they were the distant cousins of humanity. He also stated the grays had made contact with a secret government prior to the end of World War II and traded their advanced technology for the right to determine the future of Earth.

"He warned of an impending global catastrophe, but claimed it would be due to the small group of powerful humans who had made the pact with the grays. They were completely seduced by the power the aliens allowed them to wield."

Brigid paused, took a breath and went on. "Though most of this material was dismissed at the time as New Age rubbish, it's suspiciously consistent with what we learned from Balam."

"So far," said Kane, "that matches up almost exactly with what we were told."

"Yes," Brigid replied, "and what makes it even more intriguing is that all of this information was imparted from the late 1970s through the 1990s."

"It doesn't sound like Thrush," said Grant. "An anti-Thrush, more like it."

"Or a Thrush engaged in deliberate acts of misinformation," Lakesh pointed out, "to make the truth seem so utterly outrageous no one could possibly believe it."

Kane rapped impatiently on the tabletop. "Where is all of this taking us, exactly?"

Brigid pursed her lips. "I continued crossreferencing and came across three late-twentieth-century reports of visions that included face-to-face contact with not only the grays but with a stone. To quote from one, 'It looked like onyx or black granite.' According to the witness, the stone was surrounded by a group of grays and they were apparently praying to it. Or at least that was his perception."

"*Praying* to it?" Grant echoed incredulously. "So if Thrush is linked to the trapezohedron, that would make him what—an angel?"

Lakesh intoned, "Or a fallen one. 'For even Satan disguises himself as an angel of light.' Second Corinthians 11:14."

"Thank you, Father," Kane said snidely. "I think we can do without the religious approach."

"Not necessarily," Brigid stated matter-of-factly. "It may be a way to understand Thrush since he obviously influenced human religions to some extent. On the first casement, he implied, though not seriously, that he might have been the pagan god of the hunt, Cernunnos."

Grant folded his arms over his broad chest. "We have a pretty good idea already of what he is, don't we?"

"I don't think so," she retorted. "Let's review what we know about him, in rough chronological order. We first encountered him during the temporal-dilation effect of the interphaser, when all of us were swept to focal points in the past. Domi claimed she saw Thrush execute Adolf Hitler on April 30, 1945.

"I watched him issue the orders to cover up the Roswell incident in 1947. Kane, you witnessed Thrush's involvement in the assassination of President John F. Kennedy in 1963."

Brigid shifted her gaze to Grant. "And you, on January 19, 2001, observed Thrush personally setting the timer on the nuclear warhead concealed within the Russian embassy. The warhead detonated twenty-four hours later, triggering the nukecaust.

"According to you, Lakesh, you'd seen him in the Overproject Whisper testing facility, back in the 1990s, where he claimed to be a colonel in the Air Force."

Kane said thoughtfully, "And when you and I met him in the twentieth century of an alternate time line, Thrush claimed versions of him existed in all times to prevent his interference in human history from being undone."

Grant said, "On the first casement we visited, he referred to himself as an emissary, sent by the Archon Directorate to strike a deal with the Third Reich."

Brigid's forehead acquired creases of concentration. "His exact words were, 'An emissary easily moved among the decision makers, observing and assimilating knowledge, extrapolating and recommending whether an alliance would prove profitable.' He also indicated that first contact between the Directorate and the Nazis was initiated through a black stone used in occult ceremonies."

Quietly, Kane stated, "And he told me on the last casement that he couldn't be destroyed because the

Chintamani Stone exists and that I couldn't destroy the stone because he existed. He said it was a conundrum I could never unravel."

Lakesh snorted scornfully. "So he would like us to believe." Reaching under the table, he pulled out an aluminum carrying case. He undid the latches and threw up the lid. "Traveling through all the realms of God, indeed."

Resting on a foam rubber bed were three black stones. Two were nearly identical, roughly the size and shape of a man's fist. At first, and even second glance, they appeared to be chunks of obsidian or some other dark mineral. Only after careful examination could the eye discern the marks of tools on them, or faint scratches that might be inscriptions.

The third piece was much larger, cube-shaped, the surfaces so perfectly smooth it was as if they had been polished and lacquered to acquire a semireflective sheen. But beneath the gloss lay only darkness, a black, fathomless sea.

Lakesh had arranged the stones in the case so the two smaller fragments on either side of the larger formed the geometric facets of an incomplete trapezohedron. According to what Balam had hinted, and the information Brigid had wrung from the historical database, the Black Stone was of celestial origin and was referred to in many ancient apocryphal religious texts as the Shining Trapezohedron. Always it was associated with the concept of keys.

Buddhist and Taoist legends spoke of the city of Agartha, a secret enclave beneath a mountain range on the Chinese-Tibetan border from which strange gray people emerged to influence human affairs. Ancient Asian chronicles attested that within the rock galleries of Agartha rested the prime facet of the stone, known to Oriental mystics as the Chintamani Stone.

Alleged to have come from the star system of Sirius, the chronicles claimed that "when the Son of the Sun descended upon earth to teach mankind, there fell from heaven a shield that bore the power of the world."

Kane and Grant eyed the fragments of the stone as if they were radioactive isotopes. What Lakesh and Balam had said of their nature flitted through their minds. Tests on the stones had only found what they weren't—not tektites, rare earths or any kind of ore known to science. No atomic bond lines could be found within their structure.

Balam had referred to the trapezohedron as a key to doors that were sealed ages ago, hinting that time and reality were elastic but in delicate balance. He had said, "When the balance is altered, then changes will come—terrible and permanent."

Whatever the stones really were, whatever scientific principles they represented, human temporal and spatial values could not be applied to them.

However, a more recent experiment performed by Bry indicated it was possible to tap into the stone's crystalline integrity and establish a resonance, which appeared to him to be a form of coding. He had theorized it was possible to interact with the frequencies of the stone and therefore open the thresholds between casements at will.

Lakesh declared, "Let's presume the Chintamani Stone, the trapezohedron, is exactly what I postulated it was, a complex probability-wave packet, a mathematical equation in physical form. It is a transitional tap conduit interface between our universe and others parallel to it.''

''On the first casement,'' said Brigid, ''Thrush as much admitted that was the truth. He said the trapezohedron is a discrete quantum packet that interacts and interfaces with the basic units of reality.''

Lakesh nodded in her direction. ''It exists at once and in all dimensions, duplicate after duplicate, version after version, stretching to infinity. Balam's people used it as an egress to the alternate planes of existence as both a transmitter and a receiver. Thrush was—and is—their transmission, like a radio wave given form and solidity.

''And like a radio wave, he can't exist without the transmitter. When you and Grant destroyed the version of the stone on the first casement, he became disoriented.''

Lakesh shot a piercing glance toward Kane. ''Right?''

Musingly, he replied, ''That was the impression I got. He said he had gaps in the memories he could access.''

''I submit,'' Lakesh announced, ''that the entity we know as Thrush is a creation of the Archons, birthed by the trapezohedron to function semi-independently as a scout, to make those initial diplomatic overtures to the ruling bodies on certain casements. Balam's people, those we called Archons, left no possibility to chance. If Thrush failed to achieve their goals on one casement or set in motion crucial events, he would succeed on another.''

Grant shook his head in frustration. ''But how does the son of a bitch travel from casement to casement?''

"He doesn't," Lakesh said. "His body—one of inorganic and organic substances and therefore virtually immortal—is already there, planted God only knows how many years before. When you three make the transition to other casements, your conscious selves meld with your doppelgängers on the lost Earths. What passes for Thrush's consciousness does the same, using the radiation of the trapezohedron as a carrier wave."

Kane said, "So that's what he meant when he claimed he wasn't an individual but a program, and even if we killed his body the program would only animate another like him."

He did a poor job of repressing a shudder. "So that *thing* has been walking the Earth—Earths—since the dawn of history. Like a goddamn plague on legs."

"The question," put in Grant, "is if he's working for the Archons on the other casements or against them."

"As he hinted himself," Brigid stated, "that depends on the casement. I think it's a safe bet that on the first world we visited he'd turned against the Archons, since he held Balam prisoner."

"And the second one?" Kane inquired.

She lifted a shoulder in a shrug. "Anybody's guess. But on both Earths his focus was on genetics, creating hybrids to displace humanity."

Kane ran a hand through his hair. "If Thrush is a creation of Balam's people, why didn't they stop him themselves? When Balam gave me the prime facet of the stone, why didn't he tell me about Thrush?"

Lakesh smiled slightly. "Perhaps he did, after a fashion. Perhaps he was content to remain our prisoner for as long as he did because he had a presentiment that in our efforts to change history in the past, we would contend with Thrush. Therefore, he would have ready-made allies.''

''Or pawns,'' retorted Grant. ''I think you're reaching,''

Lakesh's eyebrows lifted above the rims of his glasses. ''Why so, friend Grant? It fits the facts as we know them.''

Grant smiled sourly. ''Thrush already accomplished his dirty work on our world, didn't he?''

''Did he indeed? On the other casements, he apparently reached his goals, too. But he remained there, in positions of great power and authority. Why?''

''Maybe his positions weren't as great as he wanted them to be,'' Kane ventured. ''He was still working on that.''

Lakesh waved a dismissive hand. ''We already know Thrush prefers to be essentially invisible, a shadow walker, a puppet master accustomed to working behind the scenes.''

Grudgingly, Kane admitted, ''You have a point. The higher the profile, the bigger the target.'' His eyes narrowed at a sudden thought. ''Is it possible since we've never crossed paths with Thrush here— in our time, at least—he hasn't reached his ultimate goal?''

''More than possible, friend Kane. Likely. I believe what prevented him was his inability to manipulate Balam. He was out of Thrush's reach, and therefore so was his access to the stone's power. If you recall, Balam hinted, as the last of his kind, he was the conductor of the trapezohedron's powers.''

"There was no sign of Balam or the stone in the last casement," Brigid pointed out.

"The two casements you visited were very different," said Lakesh, "but each one had a nuclear holocaust in its recent history. The human populations were disenfranchised, separated and segregated. Distrustful of one another. Other common factors."

"The standard divide-and-conquer strategy," Brigid observed. "The same one practiced here by the baronies."

Wistfully, Kane said, "It would be nice to find a casement where humanity refused to be deceived, used and abused, where they drew a line in the sand and said, 'This far and no farther.' A place where they recognized they were on the extinction list and decided to do something about it."

He looked at Brigid, a small smile on his lips. "Remember what Balam said to us in Agartha, about how the people in power misused the Totality Concept technology?"

"Very clearly." A tinge of bitterness colored her tone. "He said, 'You could have had the stars by now. You chose the slag heap instead.'"

"What about the next casement?" Grant asked, a little uncomfortable with the topic.

All eyes turned to Kane. He had glimpsed three alternate realities during the mat-trans jump from Tibet with the fragments of the Chintamani Stone in his possession.

Lakesh said, "As I indicated the other day, I think the casements you saw were revealed to you in a certain order for a reason."

Kane nodded. "Right. You said something about enhancing the domino principle."

"Perhaps that is why the stone leads you to these particular casements and in the order in which you originally envisioned them." Lakesh's tone was musing, contemplative. "To initiate the domino effect. That was my hope for the Omega Path program, to make a small change in the past of our time line to trigger another and another and bring about an alternate event horizon. But Thrush had foreseen that and taken measures against it."

"But," said Brigid, "he didn't foresee us using the trapezohedron as a conduit into the parallel casements."

Lakesh's lips pursed. "And if he did, he had no way to block or re-direct those conduits."

Impatiently, Grant demanded, "What are you getting at?"

"Only this," replied Lakesh coldly. "The events you trigger on one casement may indeed send causality ripples that eventually affect the realties of other casements."

"If I understand this whole multiverse theory," said Kane, "which I don't think I do, there are an infinite number of so-called branching probability universes. How can whatever changes we make on three of them have any effect on all of them when we don't have an idea of how many there might be?"

"Yeah," growled Grant. "Do you expect us to spend the rest of our damn lives jumping from casement to casement, trying to fix what Thrush did?"

"Hardly," Lakesh answered. "The three casements and the order in which friend Kane glimpsed them were not arbitrary. I suggest that these three alternate worlds are prime casements."

Grant's eyes became slits. "What does that mean?"

"Worded as simplistically as I can, it essentially means that any two particles that have once been in contact continue to influence each other, no matter how far apart they move. This means, in practice, that the entire fabric of space-time and sidereal space is multiply connected by faster-than-light interaction…a cosmic glue, so to speak."

"Bell's Theorem," Brigid announced.

Lakesh nodded sagely. "Exactly. Balam's people were aware of this interconnection and put it to use."

Kane demanded, "Where does our own world fit into all of this? Is it just another run-of-the-mill casement among millions or is it important?"

Lakesh shook his head. "I wish I could answer that, but I have a feeling that until you found the three pieces of the trapezohedron, it *was* just another garden-variety casement. That may have changed. We won't know until you enter the third lost Earth and return."

He glanced from one to the other. "I've already scheduled the transit for tomorrow morning. Will you be ready?"

Grant blew out a prolonged, disgusted sigh. "No. But when have we ever let a little thing like that stop us?"

Chapter 9

Kane stood on the precipice between heaven and hell and blew a wreath of smoke toward the Pleiades. At least he thought it was the Pleiades. The constellations wheeled overhead, burning frostily in the vast, pitch-black canopy of the sky. They glittered there like powdered diamonds sprinkled by the diffident hand of creation.

You could have had the stars by now. You chose the slag heap instead.

At Kane's feet yawned an abyss. There was nothing at its bottom to see, even had he been able to pierce the deep dark. It plunged straight down a thousand feet or more to a streambed where the rusted-out carcasses of several vehicles lay. They were probably submerged by the torrent of meltwater rushing down from the mountain peaks during the spring thaw.

Drawing on his cigar, Kane let the smoke curl from his nostrils but he kept his gaze fixed on the stars. They gleamed clean and bright with a beckoning, eternal white fire. Given a choice between flying among them or slouching through a rad-blasted wasteland, only madmen would choose the latter. But madmen had been the decision makers.

Not for the first time, he cringed with an inward sense of shame when he recalled what Balam had told him about the Archon Directorate's role in the nukecaust.

Kane had firmly held the belief that the global megacull wasn't humanity's fault at all, but was due to the deceptions of Balam's people over the long track of centuries. Now he knew the Archon Directorate hadn't really conquered humanity—it had tempted humanity with the tools to conquer itself.

Ambition, naked greed, the desire for power over others, those were the dangled carrots seized gleefully by the decision makers. In order to survive, Balam and his people had deceived humankind, but it was humanity's choice whether to live down to its worst impulses.

He was still suspicious of Balam's version of the story, but he didn't know if that was due to pragmatism or a denial of accepting the truth.

You could have had the stars by now....

A soft, stealthy step sounded on the tarmac behind him and he whirled reflexively. Even in midturn, he expected to see Brigid approaching him. Instead, faintly backlit by the glow emanating from the partially open sec door, he saw Beth-Li Rouch.

The wound on his hip and his pointman's instinct twinged simultaneously. If he had not detected her footfalls, he wondered if he would now be plunging into the black chasm, pushed there by a nudge of her hand.

Hesitantly, in her low, melodious voice she asked, "Am I disturbing you?"

He quickly considered responding with a rude "Yes" but instead he asked gruffly, "Something I can do for you?"

She stopped about five feet away from him, hugging herself as if she were cold. In a subdued, contrite tone, she said, "I never had the opportunity to apologize for the misunderstanding the other day."

Kane stared at her hard, not certain if she was joking. By his way of thinking, holding two people at blasterpoint and shooting one of them wasn't a misunderstanding.

"And I want to thank you, too," she continued, "for not locking me up."

"That was more Baptiste's doing than mine," replied Kane. "She thought Lakesh had handed you a raw deal."

She nodded. "I made a mistake about her. About you, too, I guess. I never dealt well with rejection."

Kane tried to dredge up some compassion for her, but all he was able to find was a small bit of pity. "I didn't reject you as a person, Beth-Li. I tried to explain to you that turning Cerberus into a breeding farm wasn't a good idea."

"I suppose you were right."

"I know I was. Yesterday, I, Grant and Sky Dog's people fought off a force of Mags down below. Sooner or later they'll be back. And if they make it up here, Cerberus doesn't need the burdens of infants or pregnant women."

"I understand that now. But I was so jealous of Baptiste, I thought she was working against me. I'm sorry about it."

Kane gently blew ashes from the tip of his cigar. Quietly, he asked, "Do you remember Standing Bear?"

A ghost of a smile appeared on her lips, but she quickly turned it into a frown of distaste. "I'm not likely to forget him."

''The Mags chilled him.''

Beth-Li ducked her head. ''I'm sorry to hear that.''

They stood for a silent moment, then she turned away. ''That's all I had to say, Kane. I just hope you and Baptiste can find it in your hearts to forgive me.''

Kane watched her trudge back across the tarmac toward the sec door. He quickly quashed the impulse to call her back. His capacity to forgive wrongs done to him was limited. Always, he had avenged wrongs, but none of his enemies had ever asked him for forgiveness. Of course, he had never given them the chance. He thought about the two Kanes on the lost Earths and their lives he had briefly shared.

The first Kane was the true iceman Beth-Li had once accused him of being—a stone-cold killer, brutal, cruel, ambitious and far and away more barbaric than the most savage of Sky Dog's people.

C. W. Thrush had shot down that Kane, and he bled to death in a gutter with no one to mourn his passing.

The second Kane was as different from his alternate-world predecessor as it was possible to be. Tortured by self-doubts, racked by inner anger that his love for Brigid wasn't returned, he lived a life of quiet desperation. The only similarity between the two Kanes was their servitude to a brutal, remote government. One happily took orders from Thrush, the other not so happily, but both obeyed him.

Kane contemplated the possibility that the Kanes on the parallel casements were simply aspects of his own personality that environmental circumstances had not allowed to rise to the fore. He supposed that neither he nor his doppelgängers were men to be particularly admired.

Eyeing the tapestry of stars again, he wondered about the Kane on the third casement, who and what he was and how fierce the struggle would be to achieve fusion with him.

He found himself wishing with a surprising urgency that the Kane on the next world was a man who commanded his own destiny. A man beholden to no one, who mirrored his own enmity against Thrush, who knew when he was being manipulated and deceived and refused to allow either.

He chuckled aloud when he realized he was wishing upon a star.

LEVERING WITH HER LEGS, Brigid pushed herself off the tiled lip of the shallow end of the pool and cleaved through the water. She stroked to the opposite end then turned over, backstroking lazily. She gazed up at the domed ceiling, at the track-lighting fixtures spilling a dim illumination.

She luxuriated in the simple pleasure of being alone, without the clatter of keyboards or drive units filling her ears, or even debates on the nature of reality and sidereal space.

Brigid had always led something of a solitary life. The only person she had ever considered a friend was her mother, Moira. But when she inexplicably vanished from the flat they shared in Cobaltville some thirteen years ago, Brigid had drawn into herself. All her mother left behind as a legacy was a photo of herself taken when she was about Brigid's age, and of course, the unique sunset color of her hair. That was one reason she had never cut it.

For a while, Brigid had taken some comfort in the possibility that her mother was associated with the

Preservationists and was off somewhere working to reverse the flood tide of ignorance. When she learned the Preservationists did not exist as such, but were only a straw adversary manufactured by Lakesh, even that small hope had vanished.

After her mother's disappearance, Brigid hadn't withdrawn completely from what passed as a social life in the ville, since that would arouse suspicion. Instead, she had relationships with a few fellow archivists. Like her, the men were ville-bred and raised much like herself—ordered, fed, clothed, educated and protected from all extremes. And their colorless, limited perspectives, their solemn pronouncements regarding their ambitions, had bored her into a coma. Centuries before, they would have been classified as dweebs.

It wasn't until Magistrate Kane had stumbled half-drunk into her quarters and handed her a mystery to solve that she came to realize not all ville-bred men were the same.

Of course, solving that mystery had earned her a death sentence and a new status as both exile and outlander, but she had long ago come to terms with it. She knew Kane still felt guilt about dragging her into his own private and illegal investigation, not to mention involving Grant in her rescue.

But she often wondered if that was the first time he had rescued her. She distinctly remembered the jump dream that had suggested they'd lived past lives, each of their souls continually intertwined with the other in some manner. Morrigan, the blind telepath from the Priory of Awen, had told her that she and Kane were *anam-charas*. In the Gaelic tongue, it meant ''soul friend.''

Reaching the shallow end of the pool, she put her legs under her and waded toward the steps where her towel and bodysuit hung over the handrail. As she knuckled the water from her eyes, she saw a tall, indistinct figure standing there, extending the towel toward her. She felt a sudden surge of annoyance but she knew the man wasn't Kane. He wouldn't be that considerate.

She dried her face quickly then looked up at Auerbach, who smiled down at her uneasily. "Thanks," was all she could think of to say.

The man's smile reflected her own sudden unease, not simply because he had barged in on her but because she became instantly, sharply aware of her near-naked body. Apparently Auerbach was very aware of it, as well.

The brief brassiere and panties she wore didn't really leave much to the imagination, not with the way her full, taut breasts strained at the fabric of her bra, or how the wet cloth of her panties was plastered to the soft, honey-blond triangle at the juncture of her thighs.

Lack of proper dress wasn't much of an issue in Cerberus. During Domi's first couple of months at the redoubt, she had to be coaxed continually to wear something other than stockings when she strolled through the corridors.

Auerbach cleared his throat self-consciously. "I hear you're making another jump in the morning."

Brigid draped the towel around her before replying, "That's the rumor. Me, Grant and Kane."

She noticed how his eyes momentarily narrowed at the mention of Kane. He said, "Wegmann has all the operating systems back on-line, then?"

"That's the rumor," she repeated.

She climbed the steps, pointedly ignoring Auerbach's suddenly proffered hand. She also ignored the bulging evidence of arousal at the crotch of his bodysuit.

Turning her back on him, Brigid grabbed her own bodysuit and swiftly donned it. As she did so, Auerbach said quietly, "If I were you, I wouldn't trust Wegmann's work. I sure as hell wouldn't stake my life on it."

Zipping up the front of the one-piece garment, Brigid said coldly, "It's been tested several times and triple-checked by Bry. Nothing has been left to chance."

Dolefully, Auerbach commented, "I'd hate to see anything happen to you, Brigid."

He didn't mention Grant or Kane and she wasn't surprised. She faced him, expression hard. Stiffly, she declared, "If Rouch and Wegmann have monkeyed with the system, they've done it in such a way it's undetectable. Not much can be done at this point."

Auerbach ran a nervous hand over his red buzz cut. "I just wanted to bring a possible problem to your attention—"

"There's an old predark saying," she cut in sharply. "'Those who are the first to perceive a problem should be the first to offer a solution.' What's your solution, Auerbach?"

He took a discomfited step backward. "I...I guess I don't have one," he stammered. "Even if I stood guard over Wegmann, I don't know enough about the equipment to tell if he's doing what he's supposed to be doing or not."

"Exactly. So you bringing this so-called problem

to me on the eve of a jump serves no purpose, does it?''

He shook his head, continuing to back away. ''I guess it doesn't. I just wanted you to be prepared.''

''For what?'' she demanded. ''The worst possible outcome? Which by your own words we can't do anything about?''

''You could delay the jump,'' Auerbach faltered. ''Mebbe question Wegmann—''

''On what grounds? Because you claim Rouch has been hanging around him? She hung around with you, too, remember?''

A red flush of embarrassment spread across Auerbach's face, up to the roots of his hair. Brigid realized he was genuinely worried and she softened her tone. ''Look, both Bry and Lakesh know just about everything there is to know about the mat-trans units. The odds are vanishingly low that if something does go wrong, they can't fix it.''

He nodded and turned toward the double doors. ''You're right. I apologize for worrying you.''

Auerbach shouldered the doors open and departed in mortified haste. Sighing, Brigid began to towel-dry her hair. She was touched by the man's apparently sincere concern for her welfare, but she was also troubled by his exceptionally obvious attraction to her. She had known for months that he had a crush on her, but he had never made so overt a move toward her before. The assumption was that Auerbach thought she and Kane were an item and he feared to cross Kane.

Brigid couldn't help but wonder why he didn't have that fear any longer. She also wondered why he appeared to be making a point of planting the seeds of suspicion about Wegmann in her mind, well in advance of a disaster he expected to happen.

DEFORE'S STRONG FINGERS pressed and probed. "Does that hurt? And if you dare say, 'Think I'd tell you?' I'll break the other leg."

Stretched out on an examination table in the dispensary, his right leg in DeFore's hands, Grant chuckled. "Yeah, it hurts. Not too bad, though."

DeFore grunted. She was stocky and buxom, and her bronze skin made her ash-blond hair stand out starkly. As usual, she wore her hair in intricate braids at the back of her head. Her liquid brown eyes held a clinical look, but her full lips were pursed disapprovingly.

The tibia and talus bones of Grant's right leg had been fractured a short time before and he also suffered from strained ligaments, abrasions and internal bruising. The injuries had been inflicted by, of all things, the preserved carcass of a blue whale in the Museum of Natural History in Newyork.

DeFore rotated the ankle, noting when he winced. "How far did you walk on this before the Indians picked you up?"

Grant shrugged. "A couple of miles, maybe."

She shook her head in disgust. "Why do I even bother? You shouldn't have walked more than a hundred yards. Nobody listens to anything I tell them."

"We listen," he replied defensively. "But sometimes we can't go along with it."

"Sometimes?" she echoed. "More like *all* the times."

Releasing his leg, DeFore turned away. "But it

seems like it's healing fine.'' She didn't sound happy about it. ''You can go.''

Grant sat up on the edge of the table and watched as she busied herself rearranging medical instruments on a countertop. The clink and clatter was a cacophony of thinly disguised anger.

He suddenly felt guilty, as if he—all of them in the redoubt—treated DeFore as little more than a doctoring machine. He and Kane were the worst offenders, dealing with her only when they had a wound for her to suture or patch.

Of course, he had another reason for limiting his contact with the woman. Domi was jealous of her, and despite the fact he struggled to keep their relationship platonic, the little outlander girl was fiercely possessive of him. He didn't fear hurting Domi's feelings so much as he feared her targeting DeFore. Domi could be as unpredictably dangerous as a female snow leopard.

''You know,'' he said, striving to sound conversational, ''you never told me your first name.''

''That's because you never asked,'' DeFore replied curtly.

''Upbringing,'' he said. ''Mags don't have given names, you know, so it doesn't occur to us very often that other people do.''

Magistrates followed patrilineal traditions, assuming the duties and positions of their fathers. They did not have given names; instead, each took the surname of the father, as though the last Magistrate to bear the name were the same man as the first.

The woman finally turned toward him. ''My name is Reba.''

A shiver of shock jolted through Grant, and it required all of his self-control to not let it show on his face. Still, DeFore noticed how his eyes widened and his spine stiffened. "What?" she demanded.

"Nice name," he murmured inanely.

On the last casement, Grant's doppelgänger was a revolutionary, the leader of a guerrilla force locked in conflict with the oppressive government. His woman's name had been Reba. That Reba had a complexion fair enough for her to pass as white and her shoulder-length hair was dark. But other than that, the two women were essentially identical.

A scrap of memory of making love to Reba in a shower floated through his mind. It was difficult to retain clear recollections of experiences on the parallel casements. They tended to fade after a few days, overlaid by their personalities and memories.

However, Grant recalled wondering why he hadn't encountered doppelegängers of the people he knew on that particular Earth, other than Kane, Brigid and Lakesh. On the first casement, he had met versions of Salvo and Domi. Now, upon realizing that not only had he met DeFore, but had been deeply intimate with her, he felt embarrassed and intrigued—and more than a trifle afraid.

DeFore eyed him speculatively. She was perceptive enough to pick up on his disquiet. "It's just a name. Does it mean something to you?"

Grant groped for a proper response, not knowing what to say to her, but knowing he had better not tell her the truth. He slid off the table. "Not at all. Like I said, it's a nice name."

He moved toward the door, doing his best to diminish the limp. "Thanks, Reba."

"Come back soon," DeFore said with a cold sarcasm. "Maybe when you have a slug that needs to be dug out of your ass, we can chitchat about names some more."

As soon as he reached a point several yards from the dispensary door, Grant released his pent-up breath in a gust of profanity. "Fucking fireblast."

When he turned the corner, he saw Domi approaching him and her little piquant face lit up in a smile. She wore a short red tunic that was the barest concession to modesty.

"How's the leg?" she asked.

"Fine," he said. "You won't have to be my crutch-bearer anymore."

She shrugged, slipping an arm through his. "Didn't mind. Let's go to the cafeteria and have some ice cream."

AT 0800 THE NEXT MORNING, Kane stretched out on one of the three tables in the jump chamber. Brigid was to his left and Grant to his right. Both people had the adhesive contact tabs on their temples, arms and on their chests. The medical monitors were largely superfluous when their physical bodies were in noncorporeal states. They transmitted only readings preceding the dematerialization and materialization sequences. Cupped in their hands were pieces of the Chintamani Stone. Kane held the larger, primary facet.

Lakesh stepped up to the door. "The program is set for an hour, relativistic time. Good luck, all of you."

Lakesh closed the heavy armaglass door and entered the security code. The door locked with a hiss. Immediately, the hexagonal disks in the floor and ceiling exuded a glow, and a low, almost subsonic hum began, quickly rising in pitch to a whine. The noise changed, sounding like the distant howling of a cyclone.

The glow brightened. A mist, shot through with tiny flashing sparks, formed below the ceiling disks and rose from the floor. The mist thickened to a fog and swirled down and up to engulf them. Brigid turned her face toward Kane and gave him a jittery smile. He tried to return it, then he closed his eyes.

He remembered the first mat-trans jump he had taken, a comparatively short one, from Colorado to this very unit. He recollected having the impression of falling forever into a bottomless abyss, past a never ending stream of brilliant spheres. For some reason, he felt each sphere was a separate universe, a separate reality. Universes upon universes, realities upon realities bobbing in the cosmic quantum stream like bubbles.

Then Kane felt himself hurtling headlong into a sea of stars. They burned pale green and violet, white and gold and smoldering red, blazing so fiercely they filled the black backdrop of the universe's firmament. As he plunged toward the fiery shoal of suns, he heard them whispering to him, but they were not whispers of welcome.

They warned him, told him to go back, that he was only flesh and the universe was no place for man to be.

Chapter 10

It was but one star among millions, yet it possessed a voice as ephemeral as its computer-enhanced aura. The voice whispered, Give up, fool. Go back. I cannot be caught. I am the universe, you are only flesh. This is no place for man to be.

Kane caught that thought creeping through his head and tried to chase it out. He couldn't, not fully, despite knowing that DeFore's psych file on him footnoted his tendency toward anthropomorphism.

His normally immobile face twitched with a barely repressed smile. Personalizing a ship or a horse was one thing, he reflected. But a star?

Of course, the elusive light on the overhead monitor screen wasn't a star, though it bobbed, weaved, zigged and zagged among them. Kane glanced around at the quiet efficiency of the *Sabre*'s command deck. Cotta was consulting the scanners at the long-range sensor station; Domi, at the navigation console, punched up a projected course on the computer; and Farrell monitored the valences of the geon packets at the engineering station. Grant manned the weapons-control station, and Beth-Li Rouch sat at the main systems-operations panel.

No one spoke. The only sounds were the steady hum of sensor units, the faint ticking of computers and the distant rumble of the geon drive engines coasting at maximum output, nudging but not crossing light speed parameter.

Kane didn't mind the silence among the crew. For the past three months, none of the twenty people had set foot on a planet, breathed unrecycled air, felt the sun's heat or eaten anything but reconstituted rations. They had been living on two decks inside a machine that resembled a giant, nacelle-equipped throwing dart. All they had seen for ninety-plus days was the disordered gleam of stars and each other.

So they had bickered, quarreled, perhaps a few of them engaged in recreational sex, and for the past month and a half, because they were human, they had all become sick of one another.

Kane was somewhat sick of them, too, not to mention the shipboard routine. As usual when anticipating the end of a patrol, he promised to have a real man-size meal as soon as he returned to the space hab. He was hungry, but like everyone else, his stomach was shriveled from eating the concentrated rations for the past three months.

There were sixty artificial flavors for the rations, but as far as he was concerned, they all tasted the same—like shit. They might have contained all the minerals, vitamins, proteins and whatever else the dietitians said humans need to keep healthy, and since they were concentrated they didn't weigh much or take up much storage room. But all of the flavors were similarly repulsive.

He allowed himself the luxury of a sigh before returning his gaze to the slice view of the solar system on the screen as seen from the zenith, looking down on the longitude-coordinate plane. He knew he wasn't receiving an actual representation of space.

The screen displayed faster-than-light photographic information, filtered, squeezed, compressed and translated into visual images the human mind and eye could comprehend. Sometimes he wondered if space was a place for humanity to be at all. Humans were only tissue, blood and bone. Space was not made for them.

He often felt very small and unimportant, sitting inside the horseshoe curve of the comm-con and facing the images on the screen. Thinking about the incredible vastness, the billions of other stars and solar systems squashed his ego, turned the pomp of his rank to base tinsel.

But most of the time, Kane did not think of it; otherwise, he couldn't have retained his position or his sanity. So, usually when seated at the comm-con, he mentally reduced the brilliant stars from booming suns to mere twinkling lights, like faraway Christmas-tree decorations.

He had been staring at star fields for the past nineteen years of his life, ever since joining the Sol 9 Commonwealth's Ranger Corps, so he definitely wasn't seeing anything new. But this particular mission was certainly a change. Far in the distance, Sol glowed with a steady white luminescence, the star that represented home. And now, during what should have been the uneventful last leg of a long patrol, the fates—or their chair-bound counterparts—had conspired to swat him with one final fistful of frustration.

First had come the priority alert from the *Parallax Red* Ranger station, ordering them to break off their return to base and engage in the pursuit of an unidentified craft. They had detected the intruder barely an hour later, and the chase had continued for the past three hours.

Tapping his fingers on the arm of his chair, he growled, more or less to himself, "Ordered to divert our course so we can intercept an intruder one-fifth our size. It's probably an unmanned smuggler's drone with its navigation system out."

Beth-Li overheard the remark and swiveled her head. "Actually, Commander, this assignment may be construed as something of a compliment. If the *Sabre* didn't have such a high efficiency rating, we wouldn't have been chosen to perform this mission when there are so many other vessels available."

Grant glowered in her direction. "Since when did you become morale officer on top of all your other talents?"

Forty-five days of thinly concealed irritation had eased into forty-five days of overt antagonism. It had almost become a habit, and Grant was obviously irked by Beth-Li's characteristically clipped mode of speech, not to mention her compulsive tendency to see the upside of every situation. As the *Sabre*'s warrant officer, Beth-Li was trained on every operational station, and she took more than a quiet pride in her broadly based skills.

Kane glanced toward the slender Eurasian woman and said dryly, "I'm pretty sure our proximity to the intruder's course had more to do with it."

"Commander," said Farrell from the communications console, "Luna Base reports that the *Infinitor* has taken up position on the approach lane between Mars and Terra. We're ordered to drive the intruder toward her."

Kane felt his eyebrows crawl toward his hairline.

The *Infinitor* was the biggest gun in the Commonwealth's navy, a huge battlewagon constructed in Uranian orbit with a standard crew complement of more than a thousand. Although the *Sabre* was a Rapier-class cruiser, larger and more formidable than the newer ships used for system patrol duty, the entire craft could fit easily into the cargo bay of the *Infinitor*.

The *Sabre* was nearly a half century old and should have been decommissioned ten years ago. But the craft and its crew had a dual mission, and the high command of the Sol 9 Commonwealth no longer seemed exactly sure what it was.

The Ranger Corps was not attached to the Commonwealth's official armed forces. During the early generations of solar-system exploration and colonization, the corps had been at the forefront, protecting new settlements and intervening in disputes. With broad magisterial powers, the rangers could and did enforce laws and apply justice.

But with the establishment of the four colonial councils and their own private security networks, the Rangers had been reorganized into a token peacekeeping force. Kane was sure he and his crew represented the last generation of the Rangers. He knew he would see the corps abolished within his lifetime.

On the screen, the fuzzy blob was larger and of an orangish hue. Domi said, "The intruder's speed is dropping…8.4 bricks below the wall."

"Dump some of our own bricks. Reduce our speed to 8.5," Kane commanded. "Let's have the least possible margin of distance."

They were not speaking so much in slang as in space-travel vernacular. The "wall" referred to the speed of light, and the term "bricks" was applied to building velocities that approached 299,781 kilometers per second.

If a ship "hit the wall," then she and her crew would contend with the tau factor, the time-dilation effect. Any extended flight at appreciable fractions of light speed could jeopardize mission objectives, since only minutes would tick by aboard ship while years would pass for the authorities who ordered the mission in the first place.

"Cotta," Kane continued, "see what sensor results you get now."

Cotta keyed in the program and went to maximum magnification on the viewer. He adjusted a toggle on his board, and a second later a new image appeared.

The intruder looked like nothing more than a flying shoe box. It was a perfect rectangle, totally featureless, with no seams, rivets or engine ports anywhere in evidence. Kane resisted the impulse to swear, an act Grant took it upon himself to perform.

"What the fuck?" he snarled. "No sensory apparatus, no apparent motive power—how can the goddamn thing maneuver, much less fly?"

"Sensor results, Cotta?" Kane inquired.

The man removed a sheet of printout from the computer terminal. Consulting it, he announced, "The latest scan confirms the preliminary. The craft is twenty-five meters long by fifteen wide. It is constructed of equal parts polycon, molded adamantium and vanadium with a titanium-alloy blend. All materials known to our science."

"What's powering the bloody thing?" Beth-Li demanded.

Cotta shook his head. "I don't know. There's no ionization trail or electromagnetic fields. No drive signature at all."

Voice quivering with tension, Domi declared, "The intruder has changed course. Heading zero-eight-zero-niner."

"That'll take it on a spiral route around Mars, well below the approach lane," said Grant. "It must've become aware the *Infinitor* is waiting for it. Think it's monitoring our transmissions?"

A cold fist of unease knotted in Kane's belly. "Build up bricks, Domi. Give me 9.9 of them."

Domi gave him a shocked stare. "Sir, maneuvering at that velocity so close to the gravity well of both Mars and Earth—"

"I'm aware of the danger," Kane replied stiffly. "Follow my orders."

A little sullenly, the albino helmswoman did so. Kane could have done it himself instead of arguing. The inward curve of the comm-con horseshoe held all of the instruments to allow him to operate the *Sabre* himself if necessary. By punching in the personalized sequence on the keypad beside his right arm he could override the operational systems and transfer everything to his command console.

In his many years of service, he had never done it. Comm-cons were anachronisms, mechanical throwbacks to the days when attacks on deep-patrol vessels were clear and present dangers.

Nowadays, if a catastrophe overtook one of the newer craft, all operational functions were instantly rerouted to shipboard artificial-intelligence interfaces. The ships built over the past fifteen years rendered a command pilot like Kane essentially superfluous. Man-hours and money devoted to the specialized training of personnel were now spent on constructing better and faster computers, which of course then designed better and faster computers themselves. It was designer obsolescence, applied to both the organic and inorganic.

The tiny intruder kept its course on a sweeping thousand-kilometer curve toward the inner planets of the system. The *Sabre* followed, the image of the small vessel changing color on the screen.

The rectangle suddenly turned sharply to port. The turn was incredibly abrupt, especially for a craft traveling at such velocity. Domi pushed and punched tabs on her console, forcing the *Sabre* to follow suit. The inertia dampers whined in protest, fluctuated and awakened nausea in stomachs all over the ship.

Sounding unaffected by it all, Cotta said, "Mars approach lane in 2.3...mark."

Swallowing bile, Kane snapped, "Grant, put a PBL shot across their bow. Maybe they'll get the general idea."

Grant nodded, lips compressed. He depressed a pair of buttons on his board, and a streak of yellow light lanced from the *Sabre*'s forward particle-beam-laser battery. The spear of energy passed the intruder by a narrow margin, only a hundred meters or so. It sailed on serenely.

Kane chewed on his lower lip, opened his mouth to order another PBL shot. Then he closed his mouth. The intruder had vanished from the screen, both the tactical displays and the long-range monitor.

Farrell half shouted in disbelief, "Kee*Rist!* The fucking thing dumped all of its bricks at once! It's damn near come to a dead stop, factor 0.1. At our velocity, we'll overshoot its position by a hundred thousand kloms—"

"Match it immediately," Kane interrupted.

Mass the size of the *Sabre,* despite it's maneuverability, could not immediately drop from sailing at only a few factors below the speed of light to nearly a dead halt. Large corrections in flight trajectory were a disastrous waste of the ship's energy resources, from actual fuel to the artificial-gravity generators and the inertia dampers.

The ship shuddered and the crew on the command deck were crushed into their chairs with ruthless force. When Kane thought his body couldn't stand another second of punishment, the g-pressure ceased. Then came another shudder, and again all of their bodies were jammed against their seats. He struggled to breathe against the pressure of the inertial hand that tried to crush him. The triple-braced hull shuddered so that Kane's teeth clacked together.

When the pressure eased, the *Sabre* had managed to shed most of its velocity. After an agonizingly long three minutes of instrument recalibration and systems checks, the intruder was detected again.

"It's got a long lead on us," commented Grant sourly.

Kane's temples throbbed in pain. To Farrell, he said, "Advise *Parallax Red* of the intruder's course." He turned to Cotta. "Try to detect a pattern in its movements, project any more sudden changes in heading." To Domi, he snapped, "Let's catch the little bastard."

Kane glared at the little rectangle on the monitor and murmured, "Anthropomorphisms be damned."

The tiny shoe box arrowed headlong through space, well within the inner system now. Whoever or whatever piloted the craft had to be aware of the commotion it was wreaking, but it cruised blithely through all sensor scans and ignored all attempts at communication. Farrel reported that the *Inifinitor* was on full battle status and had broken orbit to meet the intruder as it came around the far side of Mars.

"Intruder is passing Phobos," reported Beth-Li, eyes glued to her scanners.

"*Infinitor* ready to engage intruder," Cotta stated.

"Max mag on viewer," ordered Kane.

For a long moment, the monitor screen showed nothing but the rustred orb of Mars and its two moons. Then the blackness of space lit up with a glowing webwork of light threads as the battle-wagon's autogun emplacements blazed to life, the beams spread out like a klom wide fishnet.

"Commodore Abrams is commander of the *Infinitor*," said Kane. "If he can't nail it—"

The intruder skated away from the *Infinitor*'s particle-beam lasers. It continued on its way to Terra.

"Goddammit," bit out Grant. "Now it's up to the strategic defense satellite network."

They stared at the screen as the satellite ring, represented by colored blips, converged around the path of the tiny intruder. Kane estimated that the smallest of the remote drones was not much larger than the intruder.

Space was suddenly laced with a hellish web of neutron streams, as bolts of pure energy were hurled at the approaching intruder. The satellites swarmed, deadly beams stabbing out with a hellfire barrage.

A nuclear platform flared and for a moment blotted out the crew's view of space. When their dazzled eyes recovered, they saw that the invader had not been touched. The flying shoe box wended its way in and out between the gauntlet of killer satellites, weaving, sliding, heaving, avoiding all lasers, missiles and gravitic mines hurled its way.

Watching the dark of space dance with destructive

energies, Kane came to a quick decision. "Hard to starboard. Circle the net, position us between it and Earth's gravity well." He rattled off a string of co-ordinates.

The *Sabre* bypassed the snarl of flaming silent starbursts by a fractional margin, only two thousand kloms, or kilometers, and assumed a stationary position above the blue-green globe of Terra. Kane wished he had the time to stare and savor the beauty of his home, but he tried to focus past the pain in his head on the explosive energies disrupting the sepia sea. If his own ship had been the recipient of even a fraction of the firepower being loosed by the defense net, it would have been vaporized instantly. But one tiny craft avoided having so much as its featureless hull scorched.

Darting away from its attackers, swerving from stabbing neutron streams, the craft's evasive maneuvers brought it on a direct heading with the *Sabre*.

Sounding slightly surprised, Beth-Li said, "You calculated an almost perfect interception point."

"I *am* commander, after all," Kane said, striving to sound casual.

On the monitor, the rectangle swelled larger and larger. "Point-blank range—122 kloms," Grant announced tensely.

Kane clutched the arms of his chair. "Lock PBL battery. Full strength—"

Abruptly, the little flying shoe box of a vessel halted. It floated motionless in space. Grant's hand was poised over the firing buttons. Then the instrument panel went dead under his touch. Six things happened, more or less simultaneously.

The command deck's lights dimmed.

The communications panel gave out a piercing squeal of static.

The gangway doors hissed open and shut.

The computer terminals began spitting out sheet after sheet of printout, all covered with gibberish.

Domi's navigational comp informed her the *Sabre* was cruising at two factors below the speed of light and at an altitude of 1.2 meters.

The geon generators and braking thrusters engaged for a split second.

The *Sabre* lurched forward twenty screaming and groaning kloms then stopped just as abruptly. All over the command deck, people sprang from their chairs, were caught by their recoil harnesses and slammed back violently. As all the air exploded from Kane's lungs, he glimpsed Beth-Li sagging sideways over her console.

He struggled to regain his breath, biting at air, his vision blurred to a chaotic jumble. He managed to husk out, "Status!"

On the screen, the intruder still floated there.

Grant rubbed his chest where the chair restraints had cut into him. "What the fuck did it hit us with?"

After a moment, Cotta wheezed, "As far as I can ascertain, nothing more than a superluminal communications beam. Exceptionally tight focus."

"That's impossible," argued Grant. "Why would a radio beam make everything go crazy? That was a weapon of some kind."

"If it wasn't, it didn't miss by much," Kane said, his vision returning to normal. "Beth-Li, run an analysis on that beam's frequency, break it down to the last quark."

The Asian woman didn't answer. She lay slumped

over her station, prevented from falling to the deck only by the chair's harness.

Hitting the quick-release tab on his harness, Kane levered himself up and swiftly stepped to her console. He was joined by Farrell, who lifted the woman's head. Liquid crimson coated her lower face, runnels trickling down her neck and across the high collar of her pale blue bodysuit. Scarlet strings oozed from her delicate ears. Her eyes were slightly open, but they showed no light of consciousness or awareness.

Kane felt for a pulse in her throat—it was weak and beating fast. "Get DeFore up here with a medical kit," he snapped to no one in particular, tamping down on the worry in his voice. He cradled her head in his arms.

Bry's voice filtered over the intraship comm. "Our power reserves are down seventy-two percent. Geon generators completely frozen. We're damn lucky they only engaged for a second. Otherwise, pieces of us would be raining down all over the western hemisphere."

"What about our weapons?" Kane asked, eyeing the intruder still bobbing at the center of the screen.

Grant consulted a readout. Before he could respond, Cotta said with an uncharacteristic edge of fright to his voice, "Commander—the ship's database…it's paralyzed."

Kane gently pushed Beth-Li into a sitting position, leaving Farrell to attend to her, and rushed to Cotta's station. "What do you mean, *paralyzed*?"

Obviously trying to compose himself, the man answered. "Evidently what we thought was a superluminal radio beam profoundly affected our shipwide comp systems. Even the secondary storage banks are locked out."

"How is that possible?" Grant demanded.

Cotta shook his head in confusion. "The data channels of our system operate on an addressed electron particle principle. The frequency of the beam seems to have slowed the particle movements, freezing the digitalization rate. For all we know, our core CPUs may have been wiped."

"They might as well have been," announced Domi, hammering at her board in frustration. "Even the diagnostic programs won't respond. We're even locked out of the space-inertial-guidance base datum. If we weren't so close to Earth, we'd be completely lost, without a reference point. We'll have to reroute the memory nexus. It'll take an hour of manually keying in basic reaction programs just to navigate us around the block."

Kane came over and worked at her uncooperative console. "Why didn't the same thing happen to the *Infinitor* or the defense web?"

Farrell spoke up from where he held Beth-Li upright. "They weren't the target and neither were we. The scan was directed at Terra. We simply got in its way."

Straightening up, Kane glared at the intruder, a little more than fifty kilometers from their port bow. "Could we launch a Shrike at it?"

Grant shook his head ruefully. "After an hour of crosslinking the controls to a manual override, maybe."

An impatient drumming sounded at the gangway doors, and faintly DeFore's muffled voice could be heard demanding entrance. Kane crossed the deck to them, opened a small panel beside the door frame and pulled a lever. The doors parted slowly and with a squeal.

Bustling in, DeFore glanced around, saw the limp form of Beth-Li and went to her quickly, unslinging the emergency medical kit from her shoulder. She muttered, "Two more cases just like this on deck two."

Kane returned to the comm-con. As he did, he heard Grant snarl, "What the hell is going on now?"

Kane whirled, eyes snapping wide. On the screen the shimmering halo, almost like an archway of fire, sprang up around the intruder. As he stared, the curving pattern of energy compressed. As it shrank, so did the small craft.

"It looks like it's imploding," said Domi breathlessly.

As they watched the light halo seemed to fold around the boxlike shape, collapsing it in on itself. The phenomenon lasted only a handful of seconds. When it was over, only a faint gaseous cloud remained.

"I've never seen anything like that," said Cotta in a stunned voice.

"I have," spoke up Farrell, sounding equally stunned.

So had Kane, but he said nothing. The gas cloud was now only a few vaporous, drifting wisps. The sight did not shock him, but it disturbed him profoundly.

"Now what do we do?" asked Grant.

Kane shrugged and winced. The *Sabre*'s sudden forward lurch and just as sudden halt had twisted his neck muscles. "We either wait for a tow or try to make it to *Parallax Red* under our own power. Depends on whether we want to be burden, as well as failures."

Chapter 11

The Ranger high command did not care to wait for the *Sabre* to make it to the station under her own power. Although Kane knew he was being childish, he resented *Parallax Red*'s dispatching remote tow modules. The pair of streamlined torpedo shapes magnetically locked on to both sides of the ship and their thrusters guided her toward the space hab.

Kane couldn't help but be reminded of patronizing children helping an enfeebled old aunt down a flight of stairs.

Beth-Li and two other crewpeople suffered from high-pressure sickness. The warrant officer had the worst injuries with numerous broken capillaries and blood vessels, a ruptured ear drum and a fractured sternum. DeFore's medical evaluation was she would be fully recovered by the next patrol rotation, thirty days hence.

Even so, Kane did not expect Beth-Li to sign on again. Her two-year enlistment was over in less than a week, and she had a man waiting for her in the Intel Division who could do far more with her skills than a Ranger commander could ever hope to do. Besides, their sporadic romantic relationship had completely sputtered out during this last patrol. The memory of Fand's huge golden eyes ghosted through his mind, and he shook it out. Relationships and

Ranger duty never mixed. His father had told him that the day he pinned on the badge. So had Grant. And come to think of it, so had Fand, only she'd been cursing at him in Gaelic at the time and he wasn't quite sure what she'd said.

Kane's headache had worsened over the past couple of hours, but he presumed he wasn't the only person aboard whose skull felt as if it might fly apart. The constant pain didn't worry him, but his thoughts were focused on not only how the intruder had disabled the *Sabre* but also the manner in which it disappeared. The compressing light display and the residual vapor trace meant only one thing—the little shoe box had employed a mat-trans unit to make its escape.

He suspected the probe had been little more than a demonstration. If so, the Directorate intended to redefine the terms of the pact.

Seen from the far end of the approach lane, *Parallax Red* looked like the rough beginnings of a space hab someone intended to finish one day. But Kane knew that was an optical illusion, due mainly to the haphazard erector set quality as seen from a distance and lit up with exterior lights. *Parallax Red* was based on the old Stanford Torus design, built with pre-stressed concrete, reinforced by vanadium-steel bulkheads and cables. The structure was two kilometers in overall diameter, with a mass of more than ten million tons.

All around the rim of the surrounding wheel he saw patrol ships docked in their berths. They were smaller than the *Sabre,* little more than wedges with curves and three kinds of engine array.

At one time the Ranger ships were the cornerstone

of the Commonwealth defense network. The thousands of satellites and nuclear platforms protected only a tiny sector of the solar system. Although the Commonwealth maintained a fleet of thirty, that was half of what it had been when Kane first joined the corps. More and more resources were devoted to building huge battlewagons like the *Infinitor*.

It bothered Kane sometimes to consider how militarized humans' venture into space was, but he knew that there would have been no human presence in space at all without military objectives. But according to the history he had been taught, the initial choice made two centuries ago had not been humanity's.

Sitting in the comm-con and watching *Parallax Red* swell larger on the screen, Kane thought it must have been simpler in the old days when the United States governed only one part of Earth and its struggles were restricted to other Terran nations.

But that had ended on January 20, 2001, when a genocidal atomic hellstorm was barely averted. From that day sprang a united world and, within a decade, the Sol 9 Commonwealth. But events had moved for more than fifty years toward the day the face of the Earth would vanish beneath soaring fireballs. It was the final component of an agreement, a pact made at the end of World War II. In actuality, the agreement went far, far back, dating thousands of years before the Nazis came to power.

Secret societies that flourished in Germany before the rise of the Nazi party, such as the Thule and the Vril, were in contact with the Archons, whom they referred to as their "secret chiefs." Their goals were identical with those of the Third Reich—the unification of the world under their control, with all non-essential and nonproductive humans eliminated.

With the help of their "chiefs," the Nazis enjoyed great technical advances, including the prototype of the aircraft known as a flying saucer. However, despite their superior technology and their analytical intellects, the Archons were not invincible or omniscient, as Hitler found out. World War II meant not just the defeat of the Third Reich, but a defeat of the Archons, as well.

Nevertheless, they had taken measures to ensure the defeat was only temporary. The Allied forces came across secret research projects based on technology that shouldn't even have existed, much less worked. Though many of the secret weapons were only in the theoretical stage of development, some were dangerously near completion and could have reversed the war's outcome.

The Allied powers, primarily the American military, adopted the research as well as many of the scientists, and constructed underground bases to further the experiments. The umbrella designation was known as the Totality Concept and was classified "Above Top Secret." It was known only to a few very high-ranking military officers and politicians. Few of the presidents who held office during its existence were ever aware of its full ramifications.

Two presidents who became aware were Dwight D. Eisenhower and his successor, John F. Kennedy. Eisenhower learned about the existence of the Archons shortly after an accident in the sands of the New Mexico desert in the late 1940s. It was then he was briefed on the Totality Concept and the Archon Directive under which it operated.

Eisenhower did not like what he found out and tried to warn the American people in his farewell address, but he employed the euphemism of the "military-industrial complex."

Eisenhower told Kennedy about what he had learned. Although the young president was enthralled with Totality Concept's subdivisions, such as Operation Chronos and Project Cerberus, he was less impressed when he was briefed on the covert pact struck between the Archon Directive and a small cabal of military men, politicians and corporations. He was also deeply shocked when he learned that the Archons had conducted genetic experiments with Earth's early life-forms, thousands of years before human history had begun.

Kennedy never met an Archon, only one of their representatives, an emissary who went by the name and cover of Air Force Colonel C. W. Thrush. Through Thrush, the forward-thinking president learned that the Totality Concept and its many related researches constituted the most ambitious and secret scientific project in recorded history. The Archons provided the crucial technology to translate and meld quantum and hyperdimensional physics with relativistic physics.

The aim of the Archon Directive, and the reason for its involvement in the Totality Concept, was to unify humanity, certainly a goal that Kennedy could not argue with. But when he questioned why the benevolent Archons had allied themselves with the Third Reich, the answer was less than satisfactory. He was told merely that America had entered into a pact with the Archons and was bound to follow their directive. Backing out was not an option.

"Mr. President, have you heard of the Doomsday Clock?" Thrush asked at one point.

Kennedy had, of course, and said so.

Thrush smiled wanly. "The hands are set for noon on January 20, 2001. This is the major part of the agreement. After that day, humanity will be unified."

President Kennedy did not like being told this, especially by a sinister, haughty man in black, regardless of his credentials. He refused to agree with the code of silence to which his two predecessors had acquiesced. Kennedy had been allowed only a glimpse of some of the Totality Concept secrets, and he realized the only way he would see them all was to expose the pact and the Archon Directive.

When, toward the end of his first term, an assassination attempt against him failed, he redoubled his efforts to shed the light of day on this covert alliance. However, without proof the only result would be a one-term presidency, or a second, probably successful assassination attempt.

Once he was reelected, he found an informant, willing to go on record with what he knew. Admiral Roscoe Hillenkoetter, former head of the CIA and a patriot of the old school. Vilified in the press, he stuck doggedly to his story of alien bodies found in Roswell, New Mexico, and of the agreement between a group of ambitious men and the Archons. But he lacked proof, and despite his reputation, his tale was relegated to the ranks of the lunatic fringe. Fortunately, some people wielding power and influence believed him, especially after he was contacted privately by a representative of a secret principality.

Kennedy was not to be so easily deflected. As the end of his last term approached, he saw to the establishment of a small, ultrasecret watchdog group code named Cerberus. It was not an organization in the classic sense, since officially it did not and could not exist. Its sole function was to defend and preserve the spirit of the constitution by violating the substance of it. Through sympathetic members of Congress, Kennedy arranged funds to be channeled to Cerberus, to keep it operating under the deepest cover through the administrations of his successors.

Cerberus had no bylaws, no operating manuals, no articles of procedure. It had only a philosophy: We won't let you get away with it.

The remainder of the twentieth century passed, years of wonder and upheaval. Men walked on the moon, political institutions fell and others rose to take their place. And the hands of the Doomsday Clock ticked closer to high noon.

During the decades leading up to that January day, Cerberus had waited and watched and investigated, learning about the countdown.

With an ugly sense of irony, a nuclear warhead within the Russian embassy was timed to detonate on Presidential Inauguration Day, Saturday, January 20, 2001. A Russian Cerberus operative named Felix interfered and shut it down with only ten seconds to spare.

When General P. X. "Frag" Frederickson prepared to push the buttons to launch a nuclear counterstrike for an attack that had not happened, a member of his personal staff, one Major Lwellyen Kane, shot him through the back of the head.

Kane's great-great-grandfather had been a mole, planted by Cerberus years before. Across the sea, in

Russia, Kane's opposite number, Colonel Piotr Sverdlovosk, took similar actions.

In military bases all over the globe, Cerberus double agents moved swiftly and without hesitation. Within fifteen minutes, World War III was averted.

But the secret war, one where a battlefield was as likely to have been a conference room in the Pentagon as a mined beach, had just begun. And that war, in various degrees of intensity, had been waged for the past 198 years. But at least humanity had been unified, though not in the way either Colonel Thrush, the Archons or their human pawns had ever envisioned.

The tow pods docked the *Sabre* flawlessly with the extruded chute, and the crew stoically endured the zero-g interval, floating nearly imperceptibly in their harnesses.

After the linkup was achieved, gravity returned, but only four-fifths of normal on Earth. It always required a little time to adjust to the gravity differential. Grant in particular had a tendency to overperform and he usually spent the first hour on the station banging his head on the ceiling. The artificial gravity aboard the *Sabre* provided by grav-stators maintained a tight, static cocoon much closer to Earth's gravity.

Kane preceded the crew out of the ship, following some obscure seafaring dictum that the commander was the last one aboard and the first one to disembark upon a safe landing. They strode down the corridor, which was no more than a ribbed plastic chute, and into the reception area.

Names of people and ships were constantly called over the public-address system. Kane skirted the knot of white-clad functionaries milling around the sweeping curve of the promenade—officials, clerks, bright of eye, brisk of manner and neatly dressed. They made him feel that his drab blue bodysuit with its faded gold braid on a right shoulder epaulet and small golden Ranger badge on his left breast was distinctly out of fashion.

The duty uniform of the Ranger Corps had changed little in the century and a half since its inception. Even their dress uniform was little more than a clean and pressed bodysuit. It didn't help that his sleeves were speckled with Beth-Li's blood, and he had neglected his last application of beard retardant, so his face was darkly stubbled.

He noticed heads of men and women turning toward him, and he heard his name whispered. Fame, that's what I've got, he reflected sourly. I'm a Ranger legend.

Kane told himself his legendary status sprang less from his exploits than from being the only man to refuse an officer's rank in the admiralty in lieu of sitting at a comm-con in a rattletrap Rapier-class patrol boat. But he knew that wasn't true.

Grant paced him, his first few steps overleveraged so that he appeared to have a jubilant, almost feminine mincing bounce to his step. Kane noticed how he winced.

"Are you hurt?" he asked.

Grant gingerly touched the side of his head. "Up here. Pretty bad."

"Yeah, me, too. It'll pass."

The young man behind the reception desk was rather exquisite and he smiled coyly at Grant's approach. Glowering, Grant forced himself into a foot-dragging shuffle.

The man passed a sensor stem over their badges, looked down at a small LCD display and said, "Your crew already has a block of rooms assigned to them. Commander, you're expected in the situation room."

He pointed toward a lift cage behind the desk. It was isolated from the other elevators by a pair of sec guards armed with electropulse stunners.

Kane rubbed his whiskers apprehensively. "Into the bowels of bureaucracy."

Grant smiled. "It might not be as bad as you think."

Kane shrugged, as if the matter was of little importance. To Grant, he said, "Check on Rouch." Then he strode toward the lift cage.

The elevator dropped three levels and came to a hissing stop. A speaker above the door intoned electronically, "Commander J. T. Kane, Frontier Battalion."

The door panel slid open, and Kane stepped out, hesitated and continued walking. The room seemed to stretch for a mile. The floor, the walls, the ceiling, all were made of a slick, slightly reflective alloy. Here and there along the walls pulsed light. Despite knowing the walls were only huge holoscreens, Kane felt oppressed by the austerity of the room. He had only been here a few times during his tenure as a Ranger.

At the far end was a conference table, a highly polished, ten-foot-diameter disk of rare and expensive teak. The colonial council was in full session, with all four ambassadors in attendance.

Admiral Salvo rose from his chair and nodded in greeting. "J.T. We've been waiting."

Chapter 12

Salvo's dark eyes flashed a quick acknowledgment of their familial relationship and past years of service together. Kane knew the colonial ambassadors, if not personally, then by sight. Salvo made quick introductions all around as Kane took a chair.

Walznick of Venus was much like the atmosphere of the planet he called home—impenetrable. Like Domi, who hailed from there, he was a white wisp of a man, colorless and small of stature. His thin, feathered hair resembled early-morning mist, and his movements reminded Kane of the shifting of clouds. He wore a plain gunmetal-gray coverall.

The Martian ambassador, Takaun, was almost the exact opposite in appearance and manner. A heavyset Japanese with an expression of perpetual disapproval on his face, he wore an elaborate brocade suit incorporating elements of samurai body armor. Epaulets flared at the shoulders, chain mail covered his sleeve, and metal shin guards were attached to his footgear. A pearl the size of a robin's egg hung from one fleshy earlobe.

Takaun was more than a diplomatic envoy; he was the high daimyo of Nippon Interplanetary. Corporations as such were so rare as to be nonexistent, but Nippon Interplanetary was one of a handful of exceptions. Founded in the midtwentieth century as

Nippon Multinational, the corporation had amassed a mindboggling fortune due to its breakthroughs in aerospace technologies. It was also the first privately held company to construct a permanent outpost on Luna. Earth had relied very heavily on Nippon Interplanetary during the early decades of the twenty-first century.

Unlike most corporations absorbed into the United Commonwealth of Earth States, and later the Sol 9 Commonwealth, Nippon Interplanetary had remained independent. As such, the corporation and its Martian colony were more of a sovereign state. Almost all of the people who lived on or emigrated to Mars were employees, as well as colonists.

The Ranger Corps had engaged in more than conflict over matters of jurisdiction with Nippon's private security force, the Tigers of Heaven. Kane in particular had bumped heads several times with a Tiger captain, Ubichi. Ambassador Takaun was well aware of those past confrontations since he had lodged formal protests with the Commonwealth administration.

Khotan Khan did not represent a colony so much as a way of life. He was the seventh-generation scion of a family enterprise that mined the asteroid belt scattered between Mars and Jupiter. He served as its spiritual head, its governor and its ambassador.

Starkly dressed in a black bodysuit with silver piping, he wore a bloodred fringed baldric across his torso from left shoulder to right hip. Hair as black as a raven's wing was tied back with a coil of silver. A fierce sweeping mustache was dark against his swarthy skin. Although age had etched deep lines across his blunt features and stippled his hair gray, his erect carriage and piercing black eyes bore witness that his vitality was untapped.

"Rock hoppers" his people were called, a dismissive, derogatory term that Khan and his extended family viewed as an ethnic slur. Nearly two thousand of them lived in an old Russian space station, *Shokastivich's Anvil*. Originally only a kilometer in diameter, now it was closer to five. They called it Amicus, Latin for "friend." Kane had visited the station several times, and it exuded about as much friendliness as an ASP pistol.

Built out of five tiers of the hulks of ancient spaceships, shuttles and cargo carriers, the carcasses connected by huge lengths of rusty pipe, it was a round, plate-sized mass. As ugly as it was, Amicus contained a vast hydroponic farm and an exceptionally efficient ore- and mineral-processing plant.

Although Khan's colony in the asteroid belt seemed inhospitable, Erica Garstark's Mercurian backwater was even worse. Kane had never been there and had no inclination to do so. Garstark's skin was a deep brown, almost black, and her hair a sunbleached white. Dark goggles concealed her eyes. Permanent damage to the human optic nerve was part and parcel of living in the Mercury colony, even though it was primarily underground.

The colonists lived in hundreds of cliff-locked subterranean pockets, like a stone honeycomb. The heat on the surface, even in the perpetual shade of the Twilight Belt, was more than unbearable; it was deadly. But, like Khan's colony, Mercury was a treasure trove of valuable ores and rare earths. The colony was under exclusive contract to Nippon Interplanetary to supply the raw materials for its power generating plants.

Few Mercurian colonists were born there. They emigrated to hack out a fortune in isotopes, and then leave while they still had a few years to enjoy their wealth. So, perversely, Mercury was at once the wealthiest of the four colonies and its most poverty-stricken. Cash rich but personnel poor.

Linking his fingers, scanning the faces of the ambassadors, Salvo announced, "As far as the other diplomatic envoys are concerned, all of us are in agreement that this conference was never called to session."

Kane managed to keep his expression neutral, despite the sudden surge of pain in his head. Whatever was up, he knew it was going to be subtle, smelly and secret. He retained exceptionally vivid memories of the few times the Ranger Corps had involved him in covert ops. He didn't relish them.

Salvo said, "Ninety-two solar hours ago, an incident occurred that places the security of the system in jeopardy." His sallow face was a grim mask. He was not being melodramatic.

"Ninety-two hours ago?" echoed Kane. "You're talking about something other than the intruder we chased?"

Salvo nodded grimly. "I'm talking about the prelude to your pursuit, why it was ordered in the first place."

"What," ventured Kane, "was the incident?"

In reply, Salvo activated the left-hand holoscreen. An image of the geostationary orbital navy yards above Uranus flashed into three-dimensional, virtual reality. All eyes were trained on the vast, skeletal docking bays. Travel and work pods flitted to and fro among the sprawling complex of repair stations and dry docks.

"What you are seeing," said Salvo, "is a tape of an automatic monitor drone in the complex."

He adjusted a switch, and the situation room seemed to fling itself at an appalling speed through, over and around the yard. The speed reduced as they approached a single dry dock. Unlike the others, this structure was situated far outside the perimeter, and its latticework was enclosed, concealing from view what lay within it.

The view angled around the corner of the huge bay as the monitor drone's recording played on. Light from the bay's ceiling flooded down, illuminating a dark, massive shape that vaguely resembled a gargantuan killer shark with engine nacelles instead of a fluked tale, and a raised superstructure rather than a dorsal fin.

"Do you recognize this vessel, gentlemen?" asked Salvo.

"Certainly," said Erica Garstark, taking no offense at being included in the "gentlemen" address. "It's the *Infinitor.*"

Salvo shook his head. "No. It's the *Endeavor,* the *Infinitor*'s sister ship. The two vessels were constructed at the same time in different areas of the navy yard. We kept this one under wraps, just in case something happened to Infinitor before her shakedown cruise."

Salvo was being coy, but no one asked for clarification. The construction upon the *Infinitor* hadn't been publicized, yet no more than the standard measures had been employed to keep it secret. It was a ploy to draw attention to it, so the simultaneous building of a twin vessel would be overlooked. Since the navy yard complex encompassed more than a million square kilometers, the odds were astronomically high that its secret bay would not be discovered.

"Watch carefully," Salvo continued.

With a beautiful shimmering effect Kane might have appreciated under different circumstances, a dark enormous shape suddenly appeared in space, less than a klom from the *Endeavor*'s bay. It was of a familiar disklike configuration and it hung eerily in the void. The ship's running lights caused strange shadows across its hull, lending it a pronounced supernatural air. At the bottom of the image, numbers and words indicating the vessel's specifications appeared.

Before he could stop himself, Kane breathed, "Almighty God. A ship like that could eat *Sabre* for breakfast."

"Quite." Salvo did not sound pleased by the notion. "Keep watching."

As Kane gazed at the image, a wavering funnel of crimson light licked from it and touched the bow of the *Endeavor*. There was no explosion, only a hell-hued borealis as the vessel's heavy outer sheathing seemed to dissolve, exposing the skeletal inner structure and the decks to the vacuum of space.

The blood-colored dissolution spread over the surface of the *Endeavor*, like a tsunami of acid, eating away the superstructure and weapons emplacements. The huge vessel became a writhing maelstrom of blazing energy and floating debris.

Around the rim of the dark disk, flares of blue flame flashed as maneuvering thrusters were deployed. It rotated slowly. The image of the ship swelled larger as the monitor drone sped forward—then the holoscreen went dark.

Only Takaun and Khotan Khan displayed any emotion, and that was confined to fearful mutters and oaths.

Kane turned to Salvo. "Molecular destabilizer?"

Salvo nodded. "One much larger than we've been able to develop."

"Give me a playback, freeze and enhance the ship at the moment it makes its turn."

Salvo obliged and Kane stared at the image with narrowed eyes. "Freeze. Give me a magnification of the starboard position."

The dark bulk completely filled the room. "Enhance and augment," Kane snapped.

Pixels blurred, then built into an image. On the hull, a running light haloed an inverted triangle containing the stylized silhouette of a bird of prey, crested head thrown back, beak open, claws outspread, wings lifted wide. Kane clamped his teeth on a curse, but Walznick was not so restrained.

"Fuck us all!" he shrilled. "The pact is broken!"

The throbbing in Kane's head suddenly became an insistent stab. Wincing, he nodded grimly. "At least Thrush gave us the courtesy of letting us know."

THE LAST ACTIVE, outright hostility between humanity and the Archon Directorate occurred a very long time ago, at the beginning of the twenty-first century. But simply thwarting the Directorate's plan for Armageddon was only the first step in driving them off the planet while keeping the technology they had provided and using it against them.

Scientists who had studied millennia-old texts and archaeological artifacts speculated that the Archons were the descendants, the remnants, of a highly developed race that had once occupied Earth, and might even have been instrumental in the evolution of man from protohuman to Homo sapiens.

They also found that the Archons weren't the only nonhuman race to have walked the Earth. Around 500 to 300 B.C., Ireland was colonized by the semi-mythological Tuatha De Danaan. According to ancient and esoteric tradition, the Danaan wafted onto the island on a magic city of light and founded four great centers of wisdom and learning. Allegedly these cities were entrances to magic places not inhabited by humans, and according to legend, the Danaan were considered to have arrived in Ireland from outside humanity's narrow concepts of space and time. Over the course of coming centuries, the Tuatha De Danaan became known by many names—such as the Sidhe and the Gentry.

The Danaan had also warred with the root race of the Archons after finding them philosophically uncongenial. The conflict extended into the solar system, forever immortalized in legend as a war in heaven. The war abated under the condition that both the Danaan and the Archons' parent race agree to leave the Earth.

The Christian prelate Saint Patrick acted as the mediator, and his actions more or less laid the basis of the legends of driving the snakes from Ireland. Patrick founded the Priory of Awen to serve as a philosophical bridge between his own beliefs and those who viewed the Tuatha De Danaan as akin to gods. Initially it was the task of the Priory of Awen to protect humanity from the knowledge of a pact with the Archon root-race and the Danaan. Both parties agreed to create a hybrid species, and from that pact sprang the race known as the Archons.

But the Danaan did not stop there. They blended their own seed with humans bearing certain desirable characteristics, and these people and their descendants became central to the Priory of Awen's mission.

In fact, the representative of the secret principality that had contacted President Kennedy and confirmed his worst fears about Archon influence was a member of this order—a human-Danaan hybrid named Mother Fand.

Years after that covert, historic meeting, Mother Fand's daughter had negotiated the treaty with the Directorate, acting as Terra's emissary. When the Archons' plan for a worldwide catastrophe had been defeated, Colonel Thrush had fled to parts unknown to join his masters. The diplomats of the day hadn't wanted to deal with him, viewing him as a traitor, but the Directorate insisted he act as their envoy, citing his familiarity with Terran social intricacies.

As a way to show they weren't intimidated, the statesmen of the day inveighed heavily to the Priory of Awen to provide an emissary to act as humanity's representative. When Thrush protested, they cited the Danaan familiarity with the Archons' tendency to find loopholes in every agreement.

There hadn't been a bargaining table, only a small room equipped with a two-way video channel. The terms were simple—no more interference in human development, and a hands-off policy regarding Earth. In return, Terra would allow the Directorate to maintain a base on Europa, one of the moons of Jupiter. As Jupiter, with its number of natural satellites, was almost a mini-solar system in its own right, ceding it to the Directorate seemed fair. However, the disputing parties had done little more than officially recognize each other and tacitly acknowledge their mutual right to exist as long they maintained a distance between each other. The Directorate's claim of Earth ownership was not even addressed, simply rebuffed.

Both people—Mother Fand and Thrush—were still allegedly alive, almost two centuries after the pact was finalized, but Kane often wondered if referring to them as "people" was accurate. He had met only one other Danaan-human hybrid in his life, Mother Fand's daughter, who went by the honorific of Sister. She had followed her mother's practice of acting in an advisory capacity to the Commonwealth.

Wryly, Kane amended that notion. He had done far more than "meet" Sister Fand, and he thought of her often.

Information regarding the Danaan and the Archons was publicly disseminated in dribs and drabs over the following decade, without mentioning how close the world had come to being obliterated. Accustomed to a diet of science-fiction entertainment for many years, the general public reacted to these piecemeal revelations with indifference.

Once the Sol 9 Commonwealth was formed, everyone involved in its day-to-day political routine had been briefed on the pact struck by the Archons and humanity. After so many years, it was something accepted as a given but to which was devoted no real thought. Europa was at the far end of the system, out of sight and out of mind. Besides, Earth had benefited greatly from the Directorate's conspiracy.

All the suppressed Totality Concept technology had been brought out into the open, and by the third decade of the twenty-first century, bioengineering health facilities, short-range mat-trans units and orbiting space habitats were as familiar to the citizens of the world as automobiles and planes had been to their grandparents.

The trouble was that advances in technology had spread too far, too fast. Apologists for the Archon Directorate argued that it should have had another century to expand so greatly, and that the technology had been suppressed for a good reason.

Nearly two centuries later, with a vast base covering the moon, and Mars three-fifths terraformed, the apologists were still arguing about it. What mattered was that the expected slow, gradual expansion became a human explosion across the solar system, and even deep exploration into extrasolar regions.

One aspect of Totality Concept technology that had never been expanded beyond its original specs was the quantum interphase mat-trans inducer. The teleportation units had at one time been viewed as the key to human exploration of interstellar space.

The gateways were evidently an important segment of Archon technology, utilizing vortices in the quantum field. The reigning physicist of the twenty-first century, Mohandas Lakesh Singh, had argued convincingly that megalithic structures such as Stonehenge and Newgrange were deliberately constructed above "points of power" and represented ancient expressions of hyperdimensional mathematics. Hyperdimensional theory provides a fundamental connection between the four forces of nature—a connection between uphill and downhill energy flows between dimensions. Lakesh claimed some ancient cultures were aware of these vortices and manipulated the energies in the megalithic structures to open portals into other realms of existence, possibly parallel casements.

However, experiments with spacecraft outfitted with mat-trans inducers had met with more than disappointment. There were numerous disastrous failures, with test ships vanishing forever in the quantum stream.

Research had turned to geon packets that could propel a vessel at a maximum relativistic velocity of 0.25 times the speed of light. Ships equipped with geon drive could travel to the farthermost planet in the solar system in a matter of weeks instead of years, but the nearest star was still beyond reasonable reach.

The Sol 9 Commonwealth had grown and expanded and colonized, devoting all its technology and resources to building. The four colonies had, of course, four governors, and each of them was envious of what the others had. Although they paid a lipservice allegiance to the Commonwealth, all of them were hungry for independence, hungry for more power. Kane knew that they often thought about what the Archon Directorate could offer them, but as far as anyone knew, none of the colonial governors had ever dared to make an overture to them.

Now it appeared the Directorate had made an overture to the Commonwealth, one that could not be misconstrued as diplomacy. Kane knew what many strategists had long suspected and feared—the Directorate had not been defeated two centuries ago. It had only lain low to gather strength to renew the war to reclaim not just Earth but the human spirit, and the Archons were coming in ships equipped with gateway units.

Chapter 13

"Penetrating the navy yards and getting that close to the *Endeavor*'s bay should have been impossible." Salvo spoke matter-of-factly, with no heat in his tone. "All security protocols were three times that of standard dry-dock procedures."

"Was there a crew aboard?" Takaun asked.

"A crew of comp techs. Five in all, to program the navigation, weapons and environmental systems. Their job would have been completed today."

"Still," Garstark spoke up, "your security net should've gotten a fix on that ship's heading long before she left orbit."

"Normally they could have," replied Salvo, "but not this time. Somehow, some way, something scrambled every computer system in the net. Even the drone's tape was wiped at the point it ceased recording images."

"But what about the outer surveillance sensor satellites?" put in Walznick. "They would've detected that ship's heading."

Salvo sighed. "That ship departed the same way it came. It is obviously utilizing a mat-trans inducer, a gateway."

The situation room exploded in a sudden flurry of exclamations, demands and cries of "Impossible!"

Shaking his head, Salvo stated, "I wish it were. It

was something all of us feared. The Directorate has found new, unmapped pathways through the solar system, maybe even across the galaxy itself. It allows the Directorate to come and go as it pleases—virtually undetected.''

Nervously, Walznick ventured, ''You don't know that for sure, right? It's just a supposition.''

''Not at all, Ambassador,'' Kane said grimly. ''Earlier today, my ship pursued a small unmanned probe right to Terra's front door. It evaded all attempts to catch, disable or destroy it. It made a transmission before vanishing—and it disappeared in the same way that the ship with the Thrush insignia appeared.''

He turned to Salvo. ''Whatever the frequency or bandwidth of that transmission, it completely shut down my ship. Do you have any idea what it was?''

''It was a radio broadcast, as you surmised,'' answered Salvo. ''It contained a message that insinuated itself into the main communications linkage with the four colonies. It overrode the standard signal filters and piggybacked its way to the colonial capitals, presumably right into the offices of the governors.

''It was far too fast for the automatic channel blocks to kick in. Our preliminary analysis showed the signal was composed of particles similar to tachyons, traveling at a speed of 20,000,000 C.''

Such a speed, even for subatomic particles, was impossible for Kane to comprehend.

''At that speed,'' grunted Khotan Khan, ''it would take only four hours for it to travel a hundred thousand light-years.''

Salvo nodded. ''Precisely. The broadest possible distance within the galaxy itself.''

"What was the message?" demanded Takaun. "If our governors have already seen it, shouldn't we?"

Salvo touched a button beneath the tabletop. "Watch."

A holoscreen shimmered into life before the conference table. The image of C. W. Thrush stood there, hands clasped behind his back, seeming to gaze into the room with a meditative expression. The lenses of the dark glasses over his eyes glittered, lending him the look of a predatory beast. He wore an exceptionally well tailored black suit, in the latest Terran fashion.

Kane had seen a picture of Thrush, taken two hundred years ago. He looked exactly the same now as he did then—a tall man so lean he was almost cadaverous, an aspect not helped by a narrow, high-boned and sunken-cheeked face that tapered down to a pointed chin. His thin straight nose stood out as sharply as a ruled line. His complexion looked strange, an unnatural flat tan, even in the lifelike hologram. Kane realized Thrush had used a flesh-colored cosmetic on his face. His short, crisp hair was so neatly cut and combed he obviously wore a wig.

The general consensus was that C. W. Thrush was some kind of genetically augmented creation of the Archons, possessed of an exceptionally long life span, but still human. Now Kane wasn't so sure. He couldn't even be certain Thrush was alive, as he defined life. In his funereal black with his cosmetics and wig, he reminded Kane of a cadaver who had decided to get up and leave the undertaker after the embalming process.

The pain in Kane's head returned with a throbbing vengeance, and at the same time a surge of irrational rage and hatred filled him. His extreme emotional reaction confused him. He prided himself on his ability to deal calmly and coolly with any sort of crisis, and such intense fury was new to him.

Kane had exchanged hostile fire with smugglers, Roamers and even a self-appointed ruler of the solar system, the mad Sindri. He had never lost his temper, viewing his adversaries as tactical problems, not personal enemies. But Thrush's appearance, his manner, his voice triggered such a combination of wild emotions in Kane that he experienced the insane urge to leap up and throttle the image of the black-clad figure.

The thin lips of the hologram stirred, and he said softly, "This is a historic day. Nearly two hundred years in the building. A long time for all of you, I suppose, but merely an eye blink to the Directorate."

Thrush's voice had an oily, whispery quality. "In that eye-blink interval, the Directorate has decided to return to reclaim Earth, to hold it as it did in the dawn of your days. We no longer observe the pact."

Garstark did a poor job of biting back a groan of dismay, and Kane did not really blame her. Thrush's quiet, speculative tone carried far more menace than blustering threats.

"You who are the governors of the so-called colonies can either stand aside while we work our will, or you can display your allegiance to the Earth government—and be swept away along with them. The choice is yours, but we would be remiss if we did not warn you."

Khotan Khan swore in a guttural tongue.

Thrush continued. "The two demonstrations we provided you should leave absolutely no doubt who is in the superior posture. We can overcome your defenses and eliminate your weapons. The dreadnought that destroyed your warship can appear anywhere, and lay waste not only to Earth but to your colonies.

"The brief era of human arrogance has come to an end. We hope you enjoyed it while it lasted. You would not have progressed so far except that we allowed it. For two centuries, you have believed that the pact was a decisive victory, resulting in the end of our power on Earth. It was merely a rearguard action, covering the further consolidation of our agenda.

"You saved the Directorate considerable time and effort by tapping into the solar system's abundance of natural resources. Now we intend to reclaim them."

Thrush seemed to take a step closer to the conference table. Kane cringed inwardly as he sensed a remote, malign intelligence, and felt the hate emanate from the image in almost tangible waves. "We are old. When your race was wild and bloody and young, we were already ancient. Your tribe has passed, and we are invincible. All of the achievements of man are dust—they are forgotten.

"We stand, we know, we are. We stalked above man ere we raised him from the ape. Long was the earth ours, and now we have reclaimed it. We shall still reign when man is reduced to the ape again. We stand, we know, we are."

The black figure of Thrush dissolved. Angry, frightened eyes turned to Salvo.

Khoto Khan demanded, "What about the Directorate base on Europa? Why hasn't a combined force of the navy ships and the Delta Guard been sent there?''

Salvo dry-scrubbed his short, gray-threaded hair. Kane felt a pang of sympathy for his half brother. Although only seven years Kane's senior, at the moment he looked closer to seventy years older.

"What I'm about to reveal," he intoned gravely, "is one of the Commonwealth's most closely guarded secrets. We do not and never have had proof the Archon Directorate retreated to Europa.''

Kane's throat constricted painfully, but his face did not register his alarm or incredulity. He carefully and consciously maintained a neutral expression, hoping his calm demeanor would offset the visible panic mounting within the ambassadors.

"The drafters of the pact took Thrush at his word about Europa,'' Salvo went on. "There was no way to verify it for nearly thirty years. Not even unmanned spy probes were launched, because the old Terran Commonwealth was afraid that would violate the agreement. The first manned Jupiter mission secretly seeded the vicinity of Europa with stealthy surveillance drones. They detected nothing—no biosign readings, no structures, no indication of anything signifying habitation.''

"A ruse," Kane declared. "A shuck, a diversion. Where have they been for the last 190-odd years?''

Salvo lifted his hands palms upward. "Who the hell knows, J.T.? Maybe the same place Thrush's dreadnought came from and went back to. If they've got functioning gateways on their ships, conceivably they could be anywhere—on the other side of the galaxy or in a dimension parallel to ours.''

Both places were possibilities, Kane reflected. As

part of his Ranger training, he had studied all the literature about the Archons and knew almost as much about them as the scientists and theoreticians of the early twenty-first century—which was almost nothing.

Autopsies performed on bodies recovered in the New Mexico desert in the 1940s proved they were composed of the same basic biological material as humans, although their blood was of the rare Rh type. They were erect-standing bipeds, with disproportionately long arms and oversize craniums. Mother Fand claimed their root race was a reptilian species known in ancient texts as the Annunaki.

The twenty-first century's premier expert on the Archon Directorate was Lakesh, since he claimed to have met one of them, a creature named Balam. He put forth a hypothesis about their agenda, postulating that the Archons might not be a true race at all—only puppets of vast, dark intelligences toying at will with humanity, wreaking havoc with perceptions and belief systems, a phenomenon he referred to as the Oz Effect.

A needle of pain lanced through Kane's skull, and with it came a dim thought, a shard of memory about the Archon culture, if they indeed had one. He strained to remember, dredging all his recollections, but all he found was a misty, half-formed concept in the shape of a black stone, a trapezohedron.

Takaun ended Kane's musings when he blurted, "I must talk to Governor Rumiko, find out what he wants to do."

"Do?" echoed Kane in an icy voice. "I imagine he'll do his duty, that all of your governors will want to do the same, in order to preserve the Commonwealth.''

Takaun's lips pursed. ''Plainly my duty is with my people, my home. I think the colonies should consider issuing a statement of our neutrality. We might obtain better treatment if we face occupation.''

Kane hadn't found much to like in Ambassador Takaun, and his statement turned dislike into contempt. ''You seem awfully quick to surrender. But then, Mars has been the loudest voice in the secession debate. You're doing exactly what Thrush—and presumably the Directorate—wants you to do. That is, lose your head and foment dissension among the colonies. That's why the message was directed to the colonial governors and not the Commonwealth administration. He knows you'll be the most likely to panic.''

The Japanese man glared at him. ''How dare you, a mere Ranger, make such an accusation.''

Salvo said testily, ''Ambassador, if Commander Kane were just a 'mere Ranger' he wouldn't be here.''

Garstark forced a smile. ''Not intending any disrespect, but just why is the commander here? Shouldn't this situation be completely in the hands of the admiralty or at the very least, the Delta Guard? Let's face it—the Rangers aren't really much above beat cops anymore.''

''Commander Kane is here because he was requested to be here,'' Salvo retorted firmly.

''By whom?'' demanded Takaun.

''By the one person who may help us locate the Directorate. She was quite specific about the commander's presence—and insistent.''

A bit confused, Kane echoed, "'She'? Who is this woman?"

A lilting and familiar voice wafted from the opposite end of the room. "It's not been that long since we last saw each other, Ka'in."

Kane spun his chair about and saw two figures emerging from the lift cage. The one in the lead caused his heart to lurch in his chest. "Fand."

Chapter 14

Two women walked across the situation room, but for the moment Kane had eyes only for one. He stood up quickly, assuming a formal posture. After a second, Salvo and the ambassadors followed suit as a show of courtesy and respect to a member of the Priory of Awen. Fand was tall and sleek and beautiful, with a proud, almost defiant look about her. Her narrow face was finely chiseled, emphasizing high, regal cheekbones. Her full lips held a secret, faintly amused smile.

She wore a clinging dress that left her long legs bare to midthigh. The dress seemed to shift with a smoky pastel swirl of colors with every movement, revealing brief, tantalizing gleams of bare flesh. Though he knew next to nothing about current fashion, Kane guessed the garment was essentially holographic, confined by the cohesion of a miniature binding field.

Her skin had the blue-white hue of skim milk, and her waist-length golden hair had been plaited into four strands, and at the end of each hung a little golden ball. Her eyes never left his, and they were not completely human. They were huge, tip tilted, golden with vertical slit pupils.

Fand held a long staff in her right hand, the symbol of her office in the Priory of Awen. It was wrapped with vines and many turnings of silver wire. An ivory knob, like an oversize egg, topped it.

Her full lips parted and in a liquid voice touched with an Irish brogue, she said, "You have not changed overmuch, my darling Ka'in. Carriage as erect as always, I see."

His posture was not the only thing erect. Her use of the endearment, the meaning of which Fand had never explained, tugged at his heart and elsewhere. He was glad he stood behind his chair as he shifted his gaze to Fand's companion. She gazed at him with a slightly challenging gleam in the emerald eyes behind the lenses of wire-framed spectacles. Kane felt the rise of the short hairs at the nape of his neck, and a name came to him. He almost uttered "Baptiste," but he said nothing.

She wore a smartly tailored green-black business suit that did nothing to conceal her tall, willowy and well-formed figure. Her long tawny hair, the color of deep sunset, was swept up on top of her head and fastened there in a sort of braided bun. It framed a well-molded face with a light rosy complexion and a scattering of freckles across her cheeks and the bridge of her nose. A large metal-sheathed carrying case dangled at the end of her right arm.

Kane pegged her immediately as part of Commonwealth officialdom, but he could not guess her function or department. At first glance, she looked like a typical credit-counter, but he somehow sensed the woman was far more than that.

Fand made an abrupt, intricate gesture with her left hand near her heart. "I bid thee felicitations and grant thee respect, Otherbrothers. I am Sister Fand."

The men in the room responded to the formal

greeting of the Priory clergy with nods and murmurs. The ambassadors introduced themselves one by one, and Kane thought he caught a moue of distaste tug at Takaun's lips, but he wasn't certain.

Salvo gestured to Fand's companion. "This is Dr. Brigid Baptiste, the Commonwealth Archive's SIN officer."

Kane realized sheepishly that Baptiste did have more of the look of a Scientific Intelligence officer than an accountant. He extended his hand to her and she clasped it. Kane winced as the pain in his head became a violent drumming. He couldn't help but notice she also flinched, but she managed to smile at him, though, and it transformed her face.

At the periphery of his vision, he noticed Fand's huge, inhumanly beautiful eyes narrow, glancing from Kane to Baptiste in something akin to wry suspicion. Hastily, Kane released the woman's hand, and the throbbing in his skull receded somewhat.

Garstark cleared her throat. "May we get on with this, please?"

At the touch of a button, chairs for the two new arrivals rose from the floor. Kane found he had a difficult time keeping his eyes off the two women.

Takaun commented blandly, "Admiral Salvo indicated one of you women might be able to trace the Directorate's whereabouts. I presume that is you, Sister?"

If Fand found the ambassador's unctuous, somewhat patronizing tone irritating, she gave no indication of it. "You presume correctly."

"How can anyone locate anything if a mat-trans is involved?" Khotan Khan asked suspiciously.

"Have you ever heard of vortex portals?" Salvo inquired. "Colloquially known as star gates?"

"That's just a theory," said Kane.

"No." Brigid Baptiste spoke for the first time, and her tone brooked no disagreement. "They do exist— we just know very little about them. Properly utilizing a naturally occurring vortex portal would be like a controlled wormhole effect, allowing more or less instantaneous travel between star systems and, theoretically, even between galaxies. Vortices like that were the essential underpinnings of what we know as mat-trans units."

"Aren't these star gates supposed to be natural phenomena?" Kane asked.

Fand gave him a dour look. "That's correct, Commander Kane."

He noted she had pronounced his name properly, without the insertion of the glottal stop. "As far as I know," he said, "fixing these vortices in precise locations, much less proving their existence, is beyond our present technology."

Fand nodded. "As far as you know. But we're not talking about technology."

"No?" inquired Khotan Khan. "What are we talking about?"

"Nothing too fancy," declared Fand. "No geons, ions or tachyons or other subatomic particles. We're talking psionics, pure and simple. I have been trained as a guide sensor, an ancient technique of my forebears."

"What exactly is a guide sensor?" Walznick queried.

"Guide sensors can locate, given only the vaguest direction and description, anything anywhere. Those with such gifts can see past our own space and into that lying beyond.''

Although psychic abilities, ESP and the like had been verified many decades ago, Garstark said doubtfully, ''That seems awfully chancy to base a search upon.''

''It dates back to the days when the Tuatha De Danaan walked the land of Eire,'' Fand explained. ''It can be defined as an awareness, a sense of oneness with—for lack of a better term—the universe.''

''Mysticism,'' Khotan Khan said derisively. ''My Gypsy ancestors practiced the same kind of mumbo jumbo, using cards and crystal balls.''

Fand stopped short of sneering in the ambassador's face, but she stated coldly, ''It's not a practice, nor a religious or even philosophical belief. Those with my blood, with the proper training provided by the Priory, treat it as a simple fact of nature—no different than your ability to identify a sound or a smell without actually seeing the source.

''In simplified, layman's terms that even you should understand, I have the ability to sense the presence of and disturbances in electromagnetic fields. I sensed the sudden appearance of the dreadnought and contacted the authorities. They did not seek me out.''

''True,'' confirmed Salvo with a trace of smugness.

''I am able to detect every vortex point, either naturally or artificially opened,'' Fand continued. ''Furthermore, I can sense which portal Thrush's ship may have entered or exited and trace its whereabouts.''

Mollified but not completely satisfied, Khotan

Khan turned toward Baptiste. "And what is your purpose here?"

"The admiralty asked the administration to provide everything and anything in the records pertaining to the Directorate," Baptiste replied crisply. "Not to mention the Totality Concept. They sent me."

"You?" inquired Walznick skeptically. "Why you?"

A very distant voice, skirting the far fringes of Kane's consciousness whispered, She has an eidetic memory, that's why.

"I have an eidetic memory, that's why," responded Baptiste.

Kane shot her a look of surprise, but she did not notice. "All information," she went on, "no matter how trivial, concerning the Archons and the Totality Concept projects is up here." She tapped her forehead. "Crossreferenced, indexed and correlated."

Takaun grunted. "A computer tape would be smaller."

Curtly and a little dismissively, Baptiste said, "If there is to be a confrontation with the Directorate, a computer tape would be of little use."

"Confrontation?" echoed Kane, directing a narrow-eyed gaze toward her. "How will you confront the Directorate?"

"Hopefully," Salvo said smoothly, "she won't. You will. But she will be accompanying you on the mission."

Kane looked from Fand to Baptiste, then to Salvo. "You want us to take a ship into one of these star gates?"

"Exactly. And you'll be commanding the ship."

"Why me?"

Salvo smiled tightly. "You've operated under sealed orders before. And you're the best man for the job."

"The *Sabre* is disabled, remember?" Kane said irritably. "And even if it weren't, wouldn't the *Infinitor* be a more logical choice to chase down a dreadnought?"

"Firstly," answered Salvo, "with the destruction of *Endeavor,* the *Infinitor* is needed here in case the dreadnought makes an encore appearance. Judging by the specs of the dreadnought, it seems to be evenly matched with the *Infinitor.* Had the new pulse shields been up on the *Endeavor,* they probably would've repulsed the initial MD barrage.

"Secondly, techs are already working on the *Sabre*'s computer systems. The comp networks Earth-side suffered the same dysfunction and they've already been brought back on-line. The paralyzing effect was apparently an accidental byproduct of the probe's transmission, not deliberate. I've been assured that the *Sabre* should be ready to launch in twelve hours. Her overhaul has been given top priority, and we're also installing a couple of extras."

Kane threw him a challenging stare. "Like what?"

Baptiste placed the metal case on the table, undid the latches and raised the lid. Within it rested an object resembling a very squat, broad-based pyramid made of smooth, dark metal. The pyramid was barely one foot in overall width, its height not exceeding ten inches.

"What is it?" asked Khotan Khan suspiciously.

"A prototype interphaser," Baptiste replied, "developed and built nearly two centuries ago by Dr.

Mohandas Lakesh Singh. It's been in the archives since he passed away. In essence, it's a miniaturized version of a mat-trans unit, utilizing much of the same hardware and operating principles.'' She touched one side of it, and lifted it away. A confusing mass of circuit boards and microprocessors gleamed within it.

''The mat-trans gateways function by tapping into the quantum stream,'' Baptiste stated. ''Invisible pathways that run outside of our physical space and back again at distant points. These openings are often called wormholes.''

''Even if we locate the entrance point of Thrush's dreadnought,'' inquired Kane, ''what will that device do?''

''The interphaser transmits subatomic particles and it will interact with the vortex opened by Thrush and create an intersection point.''

Kane eyed the pyramid dubiously. ''It looks awfully small to do all of that.''

''Engineers will tie it in to your ship's pulse-shield generators,'' Baptiste replied smoothly. ''Which then will set up a warping field around the *Sabre*. When you reach the emergence point of Thrush's vessel, the interphaser should open it and allow you to enter.''

''Should,'' Kane repeated darkly. ''That's best case, isn't it? What's the worst?''

Baptiste momentarily nibbled at her lower lip. ''As you should know, Commander, there's really no precedent for something like this. Lakesh's prototype worked in conjunction with Earth-based vortex points, naturally occurring ones, but obviously the power he was able to generate wasn't a fraction of what your ship can provide.''

"You still haven't answered my question, Doctor.''

Emerald anger flared briefly in her eyes. "I don't know,'' she said bluntly. "If the interphaser fails to work, nothing at all will happen.''

"Or something without precedent,'' Kane countered sarcastically. "Like having the molecules of my crew and ship spread halfway over the system.''

He flicked his eyes toward Salvo. "Len, I don't like the idea of gambling my ship and people on a piece of junk that's been gathering dust in the archives for more than a 150 years.''

Salvo nodded in understanding, but he said, "You gamble your ship and crew every time you go out on deep patrol. The risks are great, yes, but so are the stakes.''

Kane said nothing, but the troubled expression on his face needed no explanation.

Salvo took a breath, held it and released it. "J.T., our greatest need is not just any commander or any ship, but one with the greatest experience in dealing with deep-space unknowns. Yes, *Infinitor* might stand a better chance in a head-to-head confrontation, but she hasn't even had a shakedown cruise yet. Everything on her is new, even the crew.''

A slight smile quirked the corners of Salvo's mouth. "It looks like you knew what you were doing when you turned down my offer to join the admiralty cabinet.''

Kane returned the rueful smile. He knew his refusal had annoyed and even hurt Salvo, but to join the cabinet meant an upgrade in rank and flag officers did not command vessels. He had also pointed out the tinge of nepotism coloring the offer, but even Kane realized how lame that sounded. A man with his years of experience, his service record, would have been offered a promotion long ago by any admiralty official.

"I don't know how happy the crew will be," Kane said. "They were looking forward to a month's leave. Besides, I'm short one warrant officer."

Salvo nodded in Baptiste's direction. "Meet your new warrant officer."

Both she and Kane reacted with startled dismay. Baptiste spoke first. "I'm a historian, a scientist. I'm not connected to the navy."

"You've just been drafted," Salvo replied dryly. "Welcome to the Ranger Corps. You were going on this flight anyway."

"But in an advisory capacity, as a specialist. I'm not familiar with shipboard routines, especially not on ships as old as the Rapier class."

"With your eidetic memory, you'll be a quick study. I'll arrange for tech manuals to be sent to you so you can study them tonight."

Baptiste looked on the verge of saying more, but instead only nodded in resignation. Kane felt sympathy for the academic, but he also wanted to laugh at her discomfiture. He wasn't sure why.

He threw a small, knowing smile toward Fand, but she didn't return it. Her golden eyes were inscrutable.

Arising from his chair, Salvo announced, "I adjourn this session. Prelaunch countdown begins tomorrow. Sister Fand, Dr. Baptiste, report to Commander Kane tomorrow at 0300 hours."

"Wait," snapped Takaun peevishly. "You've yet to clarify the part of the colonies in all of this."

"At this juncture," Salvo replied, "your part is to serve by waiting."

With a beringed forefinger, Takaun inscribed an idle circle on the surface of the table. "I think I can speak for Governor Rumiko on this—he will not choose to simply wait."

"What do you mean?" demanded Salvo.

"Perhaps a new pact can be established, a different kind of diplomatic accord. If the Archons exist, they offer much in the way of technology."

Garstark, with an apprehensive tremor in her voice, blurted, "You know the history, what they offered us. Worldwide destruction and slavery for the survivors."

"Keep in mind who wrote that history," countered Takaun. "And the circumstances under which it was written."

"What are you insinuating here, Ambassador?" Kane asked.

"Only this—I think it likely the governor will wish to take direct action. Our Tigers of Heaven have a fleet of ships and weapons superior to that of the corps. There will be very little reason for our people to sit on resources like that and simply wait for word of your success or failure."

Kane looked into Takaun's beady black eyes and felt slightly ill. During the years when the Archon conspiracy built to critical mass, there had been many men like him. Psychologically there was small difference between one of the traitors in high office and Takaun. Ambition had assumed control, dominating all other impulses and justifying treachery.

But tactfully, Kane said nothing and let Takaun continue. "We cannot anticipate the Archons' actions. Therefore, it is wise to prepare to move from all fronts."

"In other words," said Salvo in a low, dangerous tone, "to cover all your bases and keep all your options open."

Takaun nodded. "Exactly."

In a steel-edged voice, Salvo stated, "This *is* your only option, Ambassador—if any of the colonial governors are contacted by Thrush or anyone claiming to be a Directorate envoy, it is to be reported to me. Immediately."

"That doesn't sound like it serves our best interests," Walznick commented. "If the Commonwealth can't protect us from attack—"

For the first time, Salvo showed his inner agitation. Slapping a hand down loudly on the tabletop, he snarled, "All of you have been playing a chess game with your citizens and resources against the Commonwealth. For a very long time, you've been looking for a way to enlarge your spheres of influence. Did you think we didn't know?"

None of the ambassadors said anything, but Takaun bristled, spots of red coloring his jowls.

"Whether you like it or not," continued Salvo, biting out each word, "you are still part of the Sol 9 Commonwealth, and all of your colonial charters contain specific articles binding you to us—particularly in times of crisis.

"When those charters were drafted a long time ago, the people involved must have glimpsed the shape of a possible systemwide crisis long before it ever reached them. Your predecessors signed them anyway, and your governors are still bound to them. *That's* all you need to know!''

Kane repressed a smile, feeling pride in the way his half brother took a stand against the ambassadors, even if it did spark a diplomatic incident. But as a former Ranger, Salvo knew that sometimes the only way to accomplish a mission was to meet the obstacles head-on.

Chapter 15

Kane left the situation room. Once out in the main promenade, he decided to wait for a moment and speak to Baptiste. She did not appear, but Fand approached him swiftly. After a few seconds of regarding him in silence she said, "It's good to see you again, Ka'in."

"It's good to see you, too," he replied, unobtrusively watching the door for Baptiste. "I suppose I have you to thank for this mission."

Her full lips creased in a rueful smile. "That remains to be seen if you'll thank me. At least we'll be together again, for a little while."

Kane said nothing to that and pitching her voice low, Fand asked, "You're not still angry with me?"

"I never was," he answered. "You made a good point. I saw no reason to argue about it."

Fand gave him a level, dispassionate stare. She was nearly his height, and the bold, molten gaze was unwavering. In a low, throaty whisper, she said, "You seem different. The same man, yet not the same. Why is that?"

"It's been several years since we last saw each other," Kane reminded her.

She reached out with one long-fingered hand to press against his forehead, a familiar gesture she used to gauge his emotional state. During their time together, he had grown used to it. But this time a fleeting vision careened through his mind. He saw Fand, wearing a long green mantle, holding her staff and smiling at him joyfully. Behind her he glimpsed a panorama of sun-drenched green slopes, textures of various subtle colors, each texture a meadow or a forest or a lake. Another woman stood nearby, garbed in a flowing red mantle. Her eyes were blue and her hair was like a braided flame falling over her shoulder. She cradled a brass-framed harp in her arms.

The Fand in his mind whispered, *The fluid of time is life. When life, the spirit, ceases to exist, time becomes meaningless. I am overjoyed your spirit lives still, Ka'in. There is still meaning.*

Fand's expression abruptly changed, from an adoring smile to a bare-toothed grimace of dementia. Her golden eyes burned in hot pools of fury. She struck at him with the knob-tipped staff—

Kane flinched away in fear, grabbing Fand's wrist to prevent her from touching him. As in his fragmented vision, her expression became one of a deep anger.

"I knew there was something different about you." Her voice was sibilant with suspicion. "Is there something between you and the Baptiste woman? I received the distinct impression you knew each other."

She wrested her arm away from his grip with ease. Ashamed, Kane fumbled for a response. "I never met her before today. I don't know why I did that, Fand. Maybe I'm just tired."

His physical attraction to the woman evaporated under her hot, searching stare. In a low, measured tone, Fand stated, ''I sense something, a not-rightness about you. Strange. My Ka'in, yet not Ka'in.''

''And maybe you're the one who's tired,'' he told her.

Fand backed away from him slowly, not removing her gaze from his face. ''Not my Ka'in. This could jeopardize the mission.''

She turned on her heel and strode away, her gait reminding him of a lioness in search of prey. He called after her, but Fand ignored him. He lingered for another moment, then walked away himself, in the opposite direction. He wasn't in the mood to talk to Baptiste now. He wasn't in the mood for much of anything.

He knew he was tired, but it was more than that. As he walked down the curving sweep of the corridor, he remembered how wonderful the Ranger station had seemed to him when he had first joined the corps. But that had been a long time ago, when he had been young and eager and bursting with pride that he was carrying on the family tradition.

Perhaps the weight of command had changed him; maybe his tiredness was something that happened to every man who had seen too much, had too many losses, too many failed relationships. And so he remained with the Rangers, with the *Sabre,* as if both were the only property he possessed of any value.

And maybe, he thought bleakly, I've lost more than my focus—I've lost my purpose.

Kane stopped by Grant's quarters on the way to his own. When his executive officer, wearing only silken briefs, opened the door, he caught a flash of naked white legs as Domi ducked into the head. He affected not to have noticed.

Grant's relationship with the diminutive astrogator was no secret, even though the two people behaved as if it were. Kane didn't think it was a good idea, particularly considering the circumstances of Domi's recruitment into the corps, but he had no room to criticize, not with Beth-Li in his recent past.

"Yeah, J.T.?" Grant said in a challenging drawl, the undertone informing him the interruption was not welcome.

Brusquely, Kane stated, "We're launching again at 0300 hours. It's not a patrol. Apprise the crew. We'll have a formal brief tomorrow once we're under way. That's all they need to know for the time being. Understood?"

Grant's dark face remained immobile. Without his saying so, Grant knew Kane had officially put him back on duty and he was not to use the familiar "J.T." in addressing him.

"Aye, sir. Understood." A strange, almost haunted gleam shone in Grant's deep-socketed eyes. Hesitantly, in a low voice, he asked, "Commander, does this have anything to do with Colonel Thrush?"

Kane's brow furrowed. "What makes you say that?"

Grant opened his mouth, closed it and shook his head in frustration. "I don't know. A guess, mebbe."

"That's a pretty damn good guess," Kane said grimly. "Or maybe there's an Intel leak."

Grant shook his head again. "No, nobody said anything to me. I've been in my quarters since we arrived. The name just popped into my head…"

His voice trailed off, an expression of confusion crossing his face.

"Keep it in your head, Mr. Grant," replied Kane. "The mission is classified."

"Aye, sir."

Kane went on to sick bay to check on Beth-Li's condition. He was more than a trifle surprised by Grant's seemingly impulsive mention of Thrush. It was a name from the old days, and Grant had never struck him as a student of history.

Beth-Li looked pale and wan under the white sheets of the hospital bed, but she was conscious.

"You haven't changed clothes or shaved," she said reprovingly by way of a greeting.

"Hello to you, too," he replied with a smile. "I've been busy." He reached out to take her hand, but she was unresponsive. "How are you doing?"

"I'll be released in a couple of days," she said quietly.

"Good. Then what?"

"You remember that position I was offered in the administrator general's office? I'm going to accept it." She spoke matter-of-factly. "There's no future in the Ranger Corps, J.T."

Kane knew she spoke the truth. The once powerful and fearsome Ranger Corps, which had enforced justice all over the system, was now just an unwieldy, anachronistic police force.

"Why do you cling to it?" she asked.

Kane didn't want to have the discussion. They had exhausted the topic midway during the last patrol to the point where they didn't even speak except when they were on the command deck. "Tradition. My greatgrandfather, my grandfather, my father were all Rangers. Tradition used to mean something."

She sighed in exasperation. "It's a nontraditional

universe, J.T. Even Len Salvo saw the handwriting on the bulkhead. Why can't you?''

Kane released her hand and stepped away. "I just wanted to see how you were doing, Beth-Li. I'm off again tomorrow."

She crooked an eyebrow. "So soon? To where?"

Lifting a shoulder in a shrug, he answered, "A little backtrack recon on that probe. Nothing to it. I'll see you when I get back.'' He resisted the urge to say "if."

Beth-Li smiled wanly. "If I'm here. If I'm not, you know where to find me."

Back out on the promenade, Kane wondered why he didn't feel sadness over their parting. Instead, he experienced a wave of relief at disentangling himself from such a conniving, egocentric, faithless bitch—

He caught himself thinking that and nearly cursed aloud. He had no idea from where that opinion had sprung. Beth-Li Rouch was none of those things. Well, he thought, a second later. Maybe she was a little egocentric.

He massaged his temples as he walked, trying to drive Beth-Li from his mind. She was out and Baptiste was in, at least temporarily. He went to the section of the station that held the Ranger commanders' staterooms. They were always in perpetual reserve, unlike the crew, whose quarters were often shifted around depending on vacancies. There were more and more empty rooms each time the *Sabre* returned from patrol.

For that matter, nearly half of the command-rank staterooms held no occupants, despite the fact their nameplates and their ships were still affixed to the doors. Kane glanced at them as he strode by—Pollard of the *Bowie*, Sky Dog of the *Feathered Lance*, Barch of the *Claymore*.

Kane had inherited both his living quarters and the *Sabre* from his father, who had inherited them from his grandfather, back when the ship was top-of-the-line, a vessel waiting to be imbued with history.

The door to his stateroom interacted with his badge and unlocked automatically, sliding open. As he stepped in, he noted with irritation the overhead lights had not been tripped. The only light in the main room spilled in from the ob port, the frosty silver of starshine.

As he reached for the wall switch, he sensed rather than saw a blur of movement behind him. Kane felt a numbing jar against the back of his head. His surroundings became a meaningless jumble. The air seized in his lungs, and he fell heavily against the bulkhead, fingers scrabbling along the smooth surface.

Faintly he heard Fand say, "Ka'in, yet not Ka'in. I will find out which one you are."

Chapter 16

As the door hissed shut on Kane, Domi stepped from the bathroom, wearing only a scowl. "A launch tomorrow?" she all but snarled. "Is he fucking fused out of his mind? It's against regs to assign a mission to a patrol crew without downtime."

Grant gave her a disapproving glance. He shook his head, trying to clear the insistent pain, but it continued to pulse like a needle of fire behind his eyes.

Domi came to him, caressing his face, her tone becoming solicitous. "Still the headache?"

"Yeah. Worse now than before."

"I had one, too, but it went away."

Grant sat down at the trans-comm console and reached for the keyboard.

She demanded, "Are you really going to do what he said, call the crew?"

"I have my orders."

Domi gestured violently, eyes aflame with crimson fury. "Another mission without downtime is against regs," she repeated doggedly. "Report Kane to the high command. They won't permit it."

Grant muttered, "Use your head. He's under orders, too."

His fingers danced over the keys, opening simultaneous channels to the block of rooms assigned to the *Sabre*'s personnel. He reached most of them, and as expected, most of them reacted with an outrage similar to Domi's. He refused to answer the questions put to him. His standard reply was, "The commander told me and I'm telling you—0300 hours."

For the few crew members who weren't in their quarters, like DeFore and Bry, he left the same voice message.

Domi watched him, fists planted on her flaring hips, small breasts trembling with suppressed anger. When he was done, she snapped, "All that arrogant bastard has to tell you is 'Shit,' and you jump up and say, 'In which corner and what color would you like it, sir?'"

"That's enough," he growled.

She uttered a scornful, derisive laugh. "I haven't even gotten started. Goddammit, Augustus—when are you going to start thinking about yourself, about us, instead of that puffed-up has-been?"

Grant bit back a groan as his head seemed to split with pain. "If he's a has-been, so am I."

She stabbed out one accusatory finger. "Exactly my point. Kane has not only kept you from your own career, but now he's going to make you as obsolete as he is."

She took a steadying breath. Reasonably, she said, "It's all different now from when you first joined the corps. There's no need for Rangers anymore. Do you think I would've joined if I had a choice?"

Grant knew the answer to that as well as she did, so he didn't bother with a response. Born on the Venus colony, Domi had plunged into the twilight world of black marketeering at a shockingly young age. When she was arrested in her midteens, she was sentenced to three years in the Luna cell blocks.

After she'd served a year, the Ranger Corps offered to commute the remainder of her sentence if she joined them for a period of four years. Faced with the choice of another two years beneath the surface of the Moon or receiving an education and experience that would benefit her in the future, she agreed to the term of service. Domi wasn't unique; over the past decade, conscripting nonviolent criminals into the corps had been the standard way of swelling the ranks, since fewer and fewer people joined of their own accord.

Now Domi's term was almost up, with less than six months remaining, and she had become fixated on Grant leaving the corps when she did. But well over twenty years of Grant's life were tied up with the Rangers, first as a weapons specialist aboard the *Bowie,* and the past twelve on the *Sabre,* under the command of J. T. Kane. It suddenly occurred to him that after all these years, he still didn't know what "J.T." stood for.

Heavily, Grant said, "I don't know what you want me to do, Domi. There's nothing I *can* do."

She pressed against him, putting an arm around the broad yoke of his shoulders. Softly, she said, "There's plenty you can do. The colonial security forces are always looking for experienced people. That's where most ex-Rangers end up."

He grunted. "Yeah. As hired thugs. Not much of a career advancement."

"Or you could join one of the trader consortiums. That's what I think I'll do."

Grant only grunted again, thinking about all the sleek, well-dressed and much younger merchants who would be her new associates in the consortiums.

Her fingernails bit into his skin. Desperately she demanded, "Don't you see? Your devotion to the corps, to Kane, is like a rock around both our necks, our futures. A big black stone dragging at us, holding us back—"

The pain in Grant's head abruptly became a wild tornado of agony. He was dimly aware of clasping the sides of his skull, as if to keep the bones intact. His brain felt as if an ASP pistol had been fired within it.

A jumbled montage of images flooded his mind, all in a crazed whirl. He saw himself encased in black body armor—no, not armor but a black uniform with a peaked and visored cap...no, not a uniform, but wearing ragged and bloodstained camouflage clothes...no, a white bodysuit...

He glimpsed Domi, slashing with a knife, then saw her sprawled dead and bloody on a floor.

All the faces and figures spun madly, melding to become a series of geometric shapes, locking together to form a black trapezohedron, as dark as a coal sack, yet somehow shining.

Slowly, Grant's hearing returned and the flaming cyclone of pain in his skull guttered out. He realized he was on his hands and knees, hanging his head. Domi's wild, frightened cries filled his ears.

"Augustus, what is it? What's wrong? Tell me!"

Husking out a shaky laugh, Grant heaved himself up into a chair. He murmured, "Augustus? That's my name? Fucking fireblast."

Peering at him fearfully, face level with his, Domi asked, "Tell me you're all right!"

"Yeah." He cleared his throat. "Thanks for bringing that up."

Her eyebrows met on either side of her delicate nose bridge. "Bringing what up?"

"The big black stone around our necks. It made everything crystal clear."

She stared at him, perplexed and worried. "It did?"

Grant nodded shortly. "It did. And before I'm done here, it won't be dragging at anybody else."

MAN IN BLACK, agent provocateur, traitor to humanity...

Those terms and many more not repeatable in polite company had been applied to Colonel C. W. Thrush in the old historical records Brigid Baptiste memorized. Like other infamous traitors in human history, Benedict Arnold, Simon Girty and Quisling, Thrush's name was synonymous with amorality and treachery.

Unlike his predecessors, Thrush was a complete enigma. He was faux, a fake man with forged military credentials and a completely fictionalized background. Also unlike the other traitors, Thrush's existence was known to very few and even then as more of a legend, the quintessential boogeyman of the twenty-first century.

Baptiste repressed another groan as the pain in her head twinged. She rose from the small computer module on the table, but too quickly. She went stumbling half the length of her quarters. Although she caught herself on the wall, the impact, as slight as it was, made her headache redouble in intensity for a moment. She cursed the low gravity and the side effects of space travel.

The farthest she had ever been from the archives

was a lunar observation station in low Earth orbit when she'd been twelve. The lower gravity on *Parallax Red* wreaked havoc with her emotional and physical equilibrium.

Anticipating the next day's events when she would be in deep space kept her in a state of nervous agitation. For the past few hours, she had studied and committed to memory all operational and function specs of a Rapier-class cruiser. She was already somewhat conversant with space-vessel systems, so it wasn't as if she jumped into the deep end with no frame of reference. But a ship of the *Sabre*'s generation was irritatingly complex compared to the craft built over the past decade or so.

After staring at diagrams and twenty-digit numerical sequences on the computer screen for three hours, Baptiste wanted to pace. But the quarters she'd been assigned were so small there seemed to be little point. She knew she should sleep, but the pain in her head persisted, defying all the medications she had taken. All they had done was to give her an upset stomach.

The pain had started on the shuttle flight from Earth, and the other three passengers in the TPC, the tactical personnel compartment, looked at her askance because she kept asking the flight attendant for analgesics.

Sister Fand, whom she met upon boarding, sat next her and expressed sympathy. For some reason, that sympathy had vanished after the session in the situation room. Fand had confronted her on the promenade on the way to her cabin, demanding to know why she had not mentioned she knew Commander Kane.

The tall, imposing woman hadn't seemed to accept her insistence that she had never even seen Kane before that meeting. And even if she had, Baptiste could not understand why Sister Fand appeared so suspicious about it.

Then again, Fand couldn't be judged by human standards of behavior since she allegedly wasn't completely human. Familiar as she was with all the stories about Danaan-human interbreeding and genetics experiments in the dim past, Baptiste remained torn between awe and skepticism in the woman's company.

Nevertheless, Commander Kane had indeed seemed familiar to her. She thought it might be due to pix and vid she'd seen. For a few months, after his destruction of the slave-cloning farm in Pluto's orbit, his exploits were chronicled and he was built up into something of a folk hero, a public-relations ploy to draw favorable attention and more funding to the Ranger Corps.

Although that was years before, Kane seemed unchanged from the images she'd seen. A shade over six feet, the way he carried himself made him seem bigger. His short dark hair hadn't a touch of gray, and he was deeply tanned from exposure to direct sunlight. His eyes were faded to a pale blue-gray, like the color of the high sky at sunset. But those eyes exuded a sadness, a subtle melancholia and a soul-deep weariness.

Baptiste shivered and tried to bring up a mental picture of her contract partner, Jefferson Auerbach, waiting for her return in the flat they shared in Georgetown. They had discussed renewing the contract for another year, and there seemed to be little reason not to do so. Their relationship was solid, and both of them enjoyed rewarding, secure careers.

With increasing consternation, images of Kane floated up instead, ones that made no sense to her—bizarre, chaotic visions flitting through her mind, not drawn from any conscious memory. She saw him as a fearsome figure in black armor, his face locked in a bare-toothed grimace of ferocity, and in other images, bleeding from a score of wounds, he struggled fiercely with a man on a catwalk.

And she saw him as he bent over her, lips and body pressing against hers—

The insistent nail of pain in her head suddenly transformed into a spear, lancing through her brain from front to back. She heard the walls of her cabin throw back echoes of her sharp cry. She barely managed to make it to the narrow bunk, where she curled up in a fetal position, hands on her head.

At the very fringes of her agony-blasted consciousness she head a faint voice, crying to be let in, claiming it could help with the pain, that she didn't know who she really was. Baptiste concentrated on blotting out that voice in her head and controlling the vicious throbbing within the walls of her skull.

The voice grew fainter and vanished altogether. Baptiste lay on the bed, drinking in great gasps of air. She heard herself whisper hoarsely, ''I know *exactly* who I am.''

SCREENS OF FIRE FLARED in Kane's eyes and fiery needles of agony stabbed his nerve endings. He tried to get up from the deck, but another wave of pain jolted through him and he rolled, trying to avoid the touch of the knobbed staff.

Fand towered over him, eyes glittering like aureate pools in the half-light of the cabin. "Speak!" she demanded imperiously. "Who are you?"

Kane managed to gasp out, "Are you fused out, Fand? You know who I am!"

He knew the shocks administered by the staff weren't lethal. Due to her training, Fand could use it as a channel and a focus for her bioelectric energy. But still, they hurt like hell.

"You're not the Ka'in I know," she grated between clenched teeth. "Did you think to fool me, I who have been in soul-link with him?"

Kane tried to sit up. "Nobody's trying to fool anybody, Fand. And if you keep hitting me with that thing, you'll pass out."

A dew of sweat beaded the woman's high forehead. Away from the electromagnetic energy field of Terra, she couldn't rely on what she called the "Gaia power" to replenish her depleted energies.

Almost defiantly, as if to prove him wrong, she struck at him with the rod again, slamming the knob hard against his chest, pushing him against the deck. Kane cried out, muscles seizing, limbs locking, vision fogging.

"Speak!" Fand hissed.

He had witnessed and been on the receiving end of Fand's angers before, and they were as elemental and sometimes as capricious as summer storms. But the golden blaze glaring in her eyes was closer to dementia.

He met those eyes, and his heart pounded wildly in his chest. His fear and bewilderment were abruptly washed away by a hot torrent of rage, fountaining out of the roots of his soul.

Levering himself into a sitting position, he lashed out with one arm, hand securing a grip on the staff just below the knob. He jerked it aside, and he heard his voice lifted in an enraged roar, "You hybrid mutie bitch!"

His own fury poured into the staff, speeding down its length and into Fand. She uttered a surprised cry and staggered back a pace, grasp loosening on the rod. Kane yanked it from her hands and tossed it clattering against the far bulkhead.

He came to his feet in a rush, grabbed her by the shoulders and lunged with her. The back of her thighs hit the edge of the bunk and she fell with Kane atop her. He had a difficult time restraining her hands with their sharp nails that clawed for his face. The cohesion field of her dress shifted and weaved as she struggled.

"What the fuck do you think you're doing?" he snapped. "Who the fuck do you think you are?"

Fand stopped grappling with him. Panting, she answered, "It's who *you* are that is the question."

"You know fucking well who I—" Kane bit off the rest of his retort as a flood of memories erupted in his mind, bringing agony in their wake.

She pulled free of his grip, but did not try to claw out his eyes. Instead, he felt the cool touch of her soft fingertips against his forehead, sliding a bit on the film of sweat that had sprung from his pores.

When the tidal wave of visions receded, Kane found himself sitting on the edge of the bunk, gulping air, head cradled in his hands. He turned his head to look at Fand. She stared at him with an expression on her face somewhere between wonderment and fear. She murmured something in Gaelic.

Kane didn't ask her what she said. Dragging a sleeve over his forehead, he said hoarsely, "You're as crazy as the other Fand I know."

"The one on the parallel casement," she said softly. "A tragic creature. But you helped her and she loved you, Ka'in."

"She called me that, too." He stiffened and demanded, "How did you know that?"

She touched the side of his face gently with a healer's touch. "Because *you* know that. You're not the Ka'in I know and love, but you're still Ka'in."

"You know about the—" He groped for a term and found one that the version of Lakesh on the first casement had employed. "Silent invaders?"

She smiled affectionately, knowingly. "The priory prefers 'walk-in.' Disincarnate souls joining with the incarnate through holes in the void, *vacua,* as the Danaan referred to them."

"So I don't have to explain about where I'm from and why?"

Fand shook her head, the little golden balls at the tips of her tresses clicking. "Not to me. I absorbed the details when you grasped my staff. Besides, how can one apply finite explanations to infinite mysteries? The puzzle of the living consciousness—the soul, if you will—cannot be solved. You either accept it as the only true reality or you don't."

Kane met her gaze and once again felt the passion she invoked in him. He turned to his memories, forcing them to replay the life of this casement's Kane and his connection to Fand.

The recollections were not a confused jumble; they were ordered in almost military precision. Fand appeared to know he was processing the remembrances that seemed to come from a different world and a different self. As he reviewed the memories and life experiences, he felt surprise, then admiration and finally a sense of shame, a humbling sense of inferiority.

In a faraway, distracted whisper, staring at the ob port and the tapestry of stars beyond it, he said, "I'm a great man here. I've done great things. I've done nothing to be ashamed of, with no blood on my hands. Yet I feel guilt where there should be nothing but pride."

He turned to Fand and said in a voice quivering with inner pain, "He—I'm a hero, but he'd never call himself that."

"Yes," Fand intoned softly, sadly. "You have done many things that are great. You have more than justified your existence. You have done much good. Except for yourself."

Kane slowly rose to his feet and half bounded to the port. He peered out at the starfield, at the ships, the shuttles flitting through the vacuum around the station. He looked up at a starfield dominated by the moon as he'd seen it once before. He remembered *Parallax Red* on his home casement, a forlorn, failed dream, occupied by distortions of humanity, rats and cats, and overseen by a madman.

Shifting position, he saw the *Sabre* resting inside a skeletal metal cradle. Though her streamlined hull was dark, she gleamed with frosty silver from the array of work lights. The tilted engine nacelles on their support pylons were like wings poised to take flight. *Sabre* was as beautiful as an angel crafted of alloy, like a piece of the universe itself. Somehow, it represented a symbol of humanity's decision to make or break a future for itself. It stood for all the options of a race that had decided not to squander its destiny on war and conquest.

Kane gazed at it for a very long time, his eyes wide with a childlike wonder. As Fand stepped up behind him, he said in a hushed whisper, "We made it. This time, humanity chose the stars instead of the slag heap. We made it."

A heavy pressure seemed to swell in his chest. His eyes were wet, and he tried to dry them before facing Fand again. "I don't deserve to be this Kane. The Earth I come from is the real lost Earth, not this one."

Voice and bearing full of compassion, she said quietly, "Your souls, your spirits are compatible, else you would not be in his body, speaking with his tongue, seeing with his eyes. You are a warrior on your home plane of existence as are your companions, Grant and the woman Baptiste, who is your *anam-chara*."

Kane knew he did a poor job of covering his surprise. "I need to find them, see if they achieved fusion like I did."

Fand did not respond to his comment. "When I sensed the link between you and Baptiste, it confused me, aroused my suspicions. Your connection is on a far deeper level than you and I share. So you have achieved something of worth in your casement of origin.

"The lady is your saving grace. Trust the bond that belongs between you. The gift of the *anam-chara* is strong. She protects you from damnation—she is your credential."

Startled, Kane realized Fand spoke the same words

as her image on the false casement he had visited, the trap Thrush had laid for him.

Dryly he said, "The Kane of this universe doesn't need to be protected from much of anything."

Fand sidled close to him, and he felt the heat of her. "Yes, he does. Perhaps that's one reason he allowed you to link with him."

Kane felt the stirrings of arousal again, but he asked bluntly, "What do you know about Thrush and the trapezohedron?"

Smiling secretively, Fand lifted her hand and touched the bracelet around the long wrist bone with an index finger. "Perhaps not as much as you, perhaps different things."

"We need to talk about it."

"That can wait, Ka'in."

"Until when?"

"Until you and I achieve our own form of fusion." Her fingernail flicked a tiny stud on the bracelet. Her dress shimmered and whispered into nothingness.

Kane's throat constricted. She was naked beneath the hologram. Her high, firm breasts gleamed like opals; her body was slender, catlike, graceful and powerful. The diffused starshine ran pale gold across her ivory skin, striking sharp shadows under the arching rim of her rib cage and her flat belly. The fine hair at the junction of her smoothly contoured thighs was like threads of spun gold.

Hoarsely he asked, "Was this what you had in mind for this Kane?"

She laughed merrily, eyes alight. "It was indeed. I was looking forward to being with him again. Why do you think I became so suspicious of you and the Baptiste woman? I didn't want my plans spoiled."

"I'm not that Kane," he pointed out, and then nearly kicked himself for volunteering such a reminder.

Her smile broadened into a wicked grin. "Which makes it even more appealing. Besides, you desired your own casement's Fand, but you felt you would be taking advantage of the poor deranged girl. You always secretly regretted turning her down."

She tilted her head at him. "Don't deny it."

He chuckled hoarsely. "I wouldn't dream of it."

Fand's arms encircled his broad shoulders. "Let us take advantage of each other."

He hesitated, despite his compelling attraction. "Fand—" he began, but she placed a finger against his lips.

"Hush," she said with mock severity. "Do not concern yourself with Baptiste. You are still my Ka'in, and I have ached for your touch as much as you have ached for mine. Do not give me an actual reason to be jealous."

Again he said, "I wouldn't dream of it." Then he smoothed the long flaxen hair away from her face. He kissed her long neck gently, cupping her full breasts, feeling her nipples harden and stiffen at his touch.

The one-piece Ranger uniform wasn't as easy to shed as Fand's holographic garment, but it was easy enough since they were both determined. Her fingers closed over the jutting evidence of his arousal, and she tugged him toward the bunk. "The equipment is the same. Let us see how a different operator manages it!"

The Kane and Fand of this universe had done this many times before. Kane drew on the memories, but as he enfolded her tall body in his arms, it still felt like an exciting and unique experience.

Fand was completely uninhibited in her passion, her desires as basic and as natural as her tempers. Her eyes burned with molten lust, a delight as she forced Kane onto his back and knelt between his legs. Lowering her head, she took him into her mouth.

Kane lay there for long moments, luxuriating in the excruciatingly pleasurable sensations she sent coursing through him. He tugged her around until she straddled his body and her hot and moist mound met his eager lips.

Within a minute she exploded in an orgasm of such shuddering intensity she nearly fell from the bunk. The balls in her hair clicked in a frantic, castanetslike rhythm.

After she recovered, she renewed her vigorous oral attention. Kane cried out as he jetted.

It was only the beginning and both their bodies glistened with a sheen of sweat in the starlight. He drew on Kane's memories of what and how Fand liked and modified a few. She enthusiastically reciprocated.

With her legs over his shoulders, Kane plunged deeply into her and later he knelt behind her, noting how nicely that part of her anatomy fit into the hollow of his hips.

Fand mounted him, riding him skillfully, bringing him several times to the brink of release but not allowing him to cross over it.

But flesh and blood could take only so much, despite the willingness of the spirit. Amid their mingled cries, Kane realized that although Fand might not

have been completely human, she was human
enough—more than enough.

Afterward, as they lay panting together, Fand
propped herself up on an elbow and smiled down into
his face. Softly she said, "Ka'in and yet not Ka'in.
But the sum is more than equal to the parts."

Chapter 17

The chronometer on the command deck read 0300. A voice on the speaker intoned, "This is *Parallax Red* flight operations. Main power umbilical disengaged. *Sabre* all clear for departure."

Kane sat down at the comm-con and adjusted his recoil harness. He glanced toward Grant, who met his eye and said, "Weapons batteries fully charged and functional."

Then, very discreetly, Grant lifted his right index finger to his nose in the wry one percent salute. It was a gesture he and Kane had developed during their Mag days and reserved for undertakings with small ratios of success. Now it was a signal, surreptitiously informing Kane he had achieved fusion with his doppelgänger.

Kane gravely returned the salute. Grant nodded in understanding and turned back to his station.

"All departments signal green for go," said Baptiste from the main systems operations console. Kane couldn't help but discreetly admire the way the blue bodysuit with its red piping fit her form, but the skin around her eyes was puffy. As yet, she had not given any indication of which Brigid Baptiste sat at the station.

"Grav-stator fully engaged," Cotta reported.

"Engines on-line and powered up," Farrell stated.

"Departure plot on the board, sir," said Domi. "Helm responding."

Crisply, Kane said, "Aft thrusters. Two quarter burn."

"Aye, sir."

"Take us out. Steady as she goes." Kane's calm voice did not reveal the excitement pulsing within him. The hull vibrated slightly as the *Sabre*'s thrusters ignited and propelled it out of the docking cradle.

He remembered the time, months ago, when he stood on the heaving deck of a ship breasting the waves of the Irish Sea. Now, although he couldn't smell the brine or see the restless panorama of the ocean, he felt the same wild thrill.

On the overhead monitor screen, he watched as the docking assembly slid past and saw work pods and drones appear to get out of *Sabre*'s way. He glanced to the little tactical screen on his right, focused on a departure angle and watched as the space hab seemed to grow smaller, as did the battered surface of the moon. He returned his attention to the main monitor and the open space ahead.

"Fire up the geon drive, Domi. Standard acceleration schedule. Build up the bricks to half a wall."

The cruiser accelerated, the inertia dampers reducing the forward lunge to little more than a bump. Kane sat back and gazed at the screen as the *Sabre* sailed at twelve thousand kilometers per second through the solar system. None of the planetary stations hailed them as they passed within their sensor spheres.

Although the crew hadn't evinced much outward concern or curiosity about the mission, Kane knew they were boiling with both resentment and curiosity.

Perhaps if any man other than J. T. Kane had strode onto the command deck and sat down at the commcon, Bry, DeFore, Farrell and Cotta would have demanded profanely to know what was going on.

Kane announced their destination coordinates, which Domi dutifully punched into the navigation computers.

The ship day passed slowly for everyone on the command deck but Kane. He went to great lengths not to show the thrill coursing through him at the contradictory sensations of a routine both familiar and strange. His initial reaction upon sitting at the command console and seeing the intricate network of dials, keyboards and circuit links was to be appalled. Then their meaning and purpose slid into the proper places in his mind.

Unlike his other fusions with his doppelgängers, he sensed the other Kane standing in the wings of his mind, aloof but not unfriendly, prompting him on what to do and when to do it, but interfering in nothing.

Kane occasionally glanced Baptiste's way, but she studiously avoided looking at him, her attention completely devoted to her duties. Grant, however, seemed completely at ease. He bantered good-naturedly with other members of the command staff and exchanged jokes with Domi.

Most of the crew had served with one another for several years and on long patrols, they lived in a macroscopic society, almost familial in their interactions with one another. They bickered and quarreled and grew sick of one another as family members were wont to do, but they all viewed Kane as the final authority over their squabbles. He symbolized the family's father figure, counselor and big brother. Despite complaints and even secret criticisms of him, they held Kane in a position of high respect that did not stem from fear.

That, too, was refreshingly unique.

We made it, went the delighted refrain through Kane's head. We chose the stars instead of the slag heap.

For the very first time in his life, he felt pride in his own species, in the human race who, when given the option, had refused to live down to its basest impulses, instead transcending its savage heritage. Mankind had united in order to deceive the deceivers.

The Sol 9 Commonwealth was not a perfect society, certainly not a utopia as Kane understood the definition, but at least it used the appropriated Totality Concept technology to explore and to build, not to hunt and destroy. Even the thought of Salvo brought a smile to his lips. Here he was not a bitter enemy, consumed by jealousy and hatred, but truly a brother.

On the tactical viewer inside the curve of the comm-con, the asteroid belt showed as a blur of dots against the colorful bulk of Jupiter. On the main screen, the torrent of rushing stone and endless stream of debris appeared as a distant, slanted line, like a bird's-eye view of a mountain range with only the peaks visible.

"Commander," Baptiste spoke up, "I'm picking up mass activity. The readings are at the extreme range of our sensors. It's a vessel."

"Configuration?"

"Too distant for an accurate reading, but it's following a course oblique to ours, almost as if they intend to intercept us.''

Kane tapped the arm of his chair but said nothing.

''Should we hail them?'' Cotta asked. ''Warn them off?''

Kane thought a moment, then shook his head. ''No, let's maintain radio security until we can get a configuration read.''

In a little more than seven hours, with the *Sabre*'s velocity gradually increased to ninety thousand kloms per second, the sprawling complex of the Uranian navy yards began to take shape on the screen. The dry docks and construction bays glittered with thousands of lights.

Kane said. ''Domi, plot elliptical approach to navy yards. Coordinates eight-ten-zero-niner. Start dumping bricks at your discretion.''

As Domi punched in the program, Kane unbuckled his harness and arose from his chair. ''Dr. Baptiste, Mr. Grant, join me in the wardroom. I'll open an intraship channel so the crew can hear what we're doing out here and why.''

Domi muttered something in a peevish tone, but Kane affected not to have heard her.

The wardroom on the lower deck was much like the rest of the ship, austere and Spartanly furnished. Fand was already waiting and she nodded politely to all three of them, as if they were joining her for a spot of tea. She appeared charmingly incongruous in the standard-issue Ranger uniform.

Kane opened the intraship channel on the transcomm and brought the crew up-to-date on the situation. He maintained a calm, almost detached tone, but he stressed that a renewal of hostilities between the

Commonwealth and the Directorate could spell catastrophe for humanity.

"This is an unofficial flight," he concluded. "We will not reduce our speed until we reach our destination nor will we deviate from the set course except at my orders. We will not respond to any hails. The navy yard and security boats have been apprised to some extent of the situation and won't try to flag us down." He closed the channel and glanced expectantly at Fand.

Responding to the silent prompt, she said, "I can sense the energy residue where the dreadnought appeared and disappeared, the activation signature of a star gate. I've calculated the exact coordinates. It lies six thousand kilometers off the navy yard's eastern border, azimuth ten, Z minus five on the planetary plane."

Baptiste eyed her a little distrustfully. "The sensor sweep of the area detected nothing unusual. No energy anomalies, no gravity flux. Nothing."

"You're talking sensors," Fand responded coolly. "I'm talking senses."

Frowning, Baptiste said, "Why can't the ship's instruments detect the signatures?"

"Because your ship's sensory apparatus does not rely on being in tune with the energy fields of the universe," she replied. "These techniques cannot be programmed—they can only be learned."

Baptiste found the answer unsatisfactory, but she didn't voice her opinion. Grant asked, "What good will pinpointing the signature do? We'll just know they've been there."

Fand shook her head. "We'll open the portal ourselves, with the interphaser. But it'll require absolute accuracy...and an acceleration to near light speed. Theoretically, we should exit where the dreadnought exited.''

Kane replied, ''*Theoretically* is not one of my favorite words.''

''Achieving such velocity this close to a celestial body is dangerous,'' Baptiste pointed out. ''And the maneuvers for accuracy will be tricky.''

''If you want to take the battle to Thrush and the Directorate,'' Fand said tonelessly, ''there is no way around it. Waiting for another appearance and attack is futile, since they could show up anywhere in the system.''

Kane nodded in reluctant agreement. To Grant and Baptiste, he said, ''Sister Fand and I discussed earlier the likelihood of Thrush having possession of the trapezohedron on his ship. She tends to doubt it and so do I.''

Grant's eyebrows rose. Facing Fand, he asked, ''You know about the Black Stone?''

''My order does, or at least legendary versions of it. There is, of course, the Speaking Stone of Cascorach, which sounds like it has properties similar to the Chintamani Stone.''

Confused and annoyed, Baptiste demanded, ''What's a *stone* got to do with this?''

''We have reason to believe,'' Kane said curtly, ''that an ancient artifact, a religious icon of the Archons may be involved in this situation.''

Baptiste's eyes went emerald hard with suspicion. ''There was nothing in the archives about that, or even that the Archons had anything approaching a religion.''

''Not by human standards, perhaps,'' interposed

Fand. "But my forebears knew a bit more about the entities you call Archons than was ever recorded in your histories. Haven't you ever wondered about Thrush's extremely long life span?"

"Yes, but there's nothing mystical about that," Baptiste countered. "His longevity can be explained any number of ways that don't include the powers of darkness." She paused and added, "From what I understand about you, Sister, you don't exactly look your age."

A fleeting, frivolous notion raced through Kane's mind. Neither he nor his doppelgänger had any idea of Fand's true age. He realized with an inner start he might have spent the night with a woman a century or more older than himself.

"Secondly," Baptiste went on, "there's no mention of a stone of any sort associated either with the Directorate or Thrush."

Fand declared coldly, "The Tuatha De Danaan knew that stone and metal and crystalline things retain a 'memory.' They can be charged with it, like a storage battery. Quantum theory deals with this electromagnetic effect, as you should know. The stone to which the commander refers is based on the same ancient principle.

"As for Thrush's connection to such an artifact, in the lore of my people there are legends of the Daemon Prince, a Melchizedek who had turned evil, who kept his soul locked in a black stone altar for safekeeping."

When Fand had mentioned this tale last night, Kane had been shocked into speechlessness. Aspects of it dovetailed with his experiences on the false casement.

"All those years ago," Fand continued, "when the conspiracy came to a head, my mother recognized the figure of the Daemon Prince in Thrush—if not who he was, then what he symbolized."

Baptiste did a poor job of disguising her disgust with the story, and Fand did an equally poor job of disguising the anger the woman's reaction triggered in her. She sat up rigidly in her chair.

In a low, silky tone that sounded no less threatening than a shout, Fand asked, "Doctor, do you doubt the veracity of my words?"

"I'm a scientist," announced Baptiste, not the least bit intimidated by the glare from Fand's huge eyes. "Anecdotal information doesn't count for much in this situation."

"Yet," Fand whispered. "The mission is still young."

Grant interjected hastily, "We need to run some projections through the tactical comps, come up with a success ratio of the *Sabre* actually hitting this star gate."

Kane nodded to him. "Get it done before we reach the navy yards."

Grant, Fand and Baptiste stood up to leave the wardroom, but Kane remained seated. "Doctor, if you wouldn't mind staying a moment?"

As the other two people filed out, Baptiste eased back down in her chair, eyeing him apprehensively. When they were alone, he asked, "How are you feeling?"

She looked taken aback by the query. With a wan smile, she rubbed her forehead. "A headache I can't seem to get rid of. I didn't sleep well, either. Other than that, fine."

"So," he ventured, "you don't quite feel yourself yet?"

One of Baptiste's eyebrows arched. "I'm afraid I don't understand the question."

Kane smiled at her encouragingly, his gaze not straying from her face.

"Is this about my job performance?" she asked. "I don't think you can levy a fair assessment so early in the mission. Other than shuttles, I've never been aboard a spacecraft before."

Kane's smile broadened. "Would you believe that before today, neither had I?"

Her arched eyebrow lowered truculently. "Is this some kind of joke, Commander?"

Kane shook his head in frustration. For some reason, he and Grant had achieved fusion with their doppelgängers with remarkable alacrity and ease, compared to their previous experiences. On the other casements, fusing their consciousnesses had been a prolonged struggle full of pain and mental turmoil.

He assumed the lack of conflict on this casement was due to the fact the versions of themselves were more emotionally and mentally in sync with their true minds. The breakthrough transition was completed when their doppelgänger's brain underwent biochemical and electrical changes with a release of endorphins, and the stimulation of neurons in the cortical and subcortical portions.

On the first parallel casement, it had happened when he and Brigid made love. On the second, they achieved fusion in the face of extreme stress and emotional trauma.

Recalling the method Brigid used to bring Grant's mind and perceptions to the fore on the first lost

Earth, Kane said, "Let's try a little word association."

"What is this?" demanded Baptiste angrily. "A hazing ritual for green recruits? This is really disrespectful."

Kane said quickly, "Lakesh. Cerberus."

She looked at him blankly. "Lakesh and Cerberus what? They went up a hill to fetch a pail of water?"

Kane repressed a curse. Those names held historical significance for Baptiste due to her career, but they contained no personal or emotional resonances. He sifted through his memory for any tidbit of information about Brigid that was unique to her alone.

Bleakly he realized he knew very little about her past. She was always disinclined to discuss matters of a personal nature, and he had never drawn her out. Whether the fault lay with him or Brigid, he didn't know. Suddenly he felt very guilty about his tryst with Fand the night before and foolish because of it.

Baptiste folded her arms over her chest, unmistakable body language that let him know to keep his distance. He did.

Formally, he said, "Dr. Baptiste, you do understand the working principles behind the mat-trans units, don't you?"

"Of course. That's one reason I'm here, remember?"

"Provide me with a brief overview, please."

Her eyes narrowed suspiciously, but she replied briskly, "What we understand as space is non-Euclidean, that is to say, it has more dimensions than simple length, breadth and relative thickness.

"The quantum interphase inducers open connected cavities, a link-up forming a kind of quantum tunnel through third-dimensional parameters of time and space."

In a challenging tone, she concluded, "I hope that illuminates your doubt about my qualifications. Sir."

Kane allowed a friendly smile to play over his face. "I'm not testing you, Doctor, I'm soliciting your expert opinion."

"In regard to what?"

"Taking into account what you said about space having more dimensions that can be measured, might we not concede that some of these dimensions are parallel to our own, duplicates, as it were, different only from the one we know by individual changes in history?"

"Branching probability universes," she stated. "Sidereal space, the multiverse theory. Causality. Hardly new or obscure theories, Commander."

He ignored the observation. "Once we accept that possibility, might we then not accept that other-dimensional versions of people—ourselves, for example—might not pass through these hyperdimensional tunnels?"

Baptiste suddenly winced and her hand went reflexively toward her head but she quickly checked the motion. "I accept the possibility, of course. Quantum theory allows for almost *all* possibilities, but not necessarily probabilities."

"And to take it a step further, these alternate-reality versions of ourselves don't pass through sidereal space as flesh and blood, but as electromagnetic patterns holding our identities, conscious thoughts and personalities. These patterns seek out physical versions of themselves and fuse with them."

Baptiste smiled wryly. "And how would I know if such a thing happened?"

Kane gazed at her levelly. "The main symptoms of the fusion are intense headaches and flashes of thoughts, fleeting insights that don't seem to be your own. Memories that aren't really *your* memories."

Eyes snapping wide behind the lenses of her glasses, Baptiste set her teeth on a groan of pain.

"I rest my case," Kane said mildly.

Baptiste lowered her head, shoulders quaking. The internal struggle was familiar by now to Kane, but he was still disquieted by how intense it seemed with Baptiste.

In a firm, clear voice, he said, "Brigid, listen to me. Remember who you are, why you're here." On impulse, he whispered fiercely, *"Anam-chara."*

Her shudders became shivers. She lifted her head and stared at him, face pale and drawn. "I assure you I remember exactly who I am, Commander, but I'm not so sure about you. *Anam-chara?* As best as I recall, it's an old Gaelic term."

Kane stared at her silently as she pushed her chair back from the table. "With your permission, Commander, I'll return to my post."

Kane continued to stare at her, then he nodded. "Permission granted."

She left the wardroom swiftly, without looking back. Dry-washing his face with his hands in frustration, Kane uttered several oaths.

"Nothing has ever come easy for you, has it, Ka'in? Not in this reality or your own."

Fand stood just inside the door, bestowing upon him a sad, yet affectionate smile. She had retrieved her staff from her quarters. She caught him looking at it and she laughed. "Perhaps touching her with this will trigger the transition, as it did yours. Perhaps not. If not, the report she'd file to her superiors would effectively end both of our careers, our respective reputations notwithstanding. And wouldn't that be a nasty trick to play on your host body?"

Kane didn't share her laughter. "Something's blocking her. I don't know what it is."

Fand shrugged. "If this Baptiste is as strong-willed as the woman you know, her sense of self and purpose are like forged steel. Not easily breached or compromised."

Kane examined Fand's observation. The other parallel versions of Brigid, though not weak-willed by any means, were trapped in depressing life circumstances. They were haunted and unhappy.

Reflectively, he said, "The other Brigids may have been unconsciously predisposed to accept the fusions. This Brigid isn't undergoing any need to escape from her life."

Fand nodded. "Very likely. But apparently this Ka'in, *my* Ka'in, is."

"What do you mean?"

"I know him, know his strength of will. If he did not wish to allow this meld with you, even on the most subconscious of levels, he would have booted you out into the hyperdimensional ether long before now."

Kane realized she spoke the truth. His past fusions were marked by periods of ever intensifying head pain as the displaced minds tried to reassert their dominance. This casement's Kane seemed content to share his memories without forcing his own personality traits, as if he were grateful to step away from center stage, almost as if he were taking a long-denied but well-deserved respite from his life.

The trans-comm whistled, and Farrell's voice filtered into the wardroom. "Commander, I've got a sensor hit from a ship. Moving fast, plotting an interception course with us."

"Configuration?"

"It's one of Nippon Interplanetary's security boats, Gaka Deki class. Coming up on us fast."

Before he could reply, a shock jarred the deck beneath his feet. Fand nearly fell, staggering against the bulkhead.

"Farrell!" he shouted into the trans-comm. "What the hell's going on up there?"

Grant's voice responded, dripping with tension. "The Nippon ship has opened fire on us."

Kane bounded to his feet and snapped into the transceiver, "Battle fucking stations!"

Chapter 18

When Kane reached the command deck, the lights had been dimmed and Grant was intoning into the intraship trans-comm, "All hands to battle stations. All hands to battle stations."

Sitting down at the comm-con, Kane looked up at the monitor. On the screen, almost dominating it, was a Gaka Deki-class Nippon cruiser.

"Status," he said.

"Low-yield PBL discharge on our number-two portside screen," Farrell reported. "No damage. Very weak field strength. Just strong enough to nudge us."

"To get our attention or to warn us away?" Grant muttered.

Studying the image on the monitor, Kane felt a nagging chill. The dark gray shape looked like a giant netherworldly bat, preparing to attack with alloyed fang and metal talons. It was a psychological ploy and he knew it. A Rapier-class cruiser was a match for a Gaka Deki any day.

"Message coming in," Baptiste said. "They identify themselves as the *Okami-Maru,* flagship of the Tigers of Heaven security fleet."

"Tie us in. Ship to ship."

The screen shimmered and a second later coalesced to form the head and shoulders of a man attired in the traditional Tigers of Heaven armorial uniform, silver and black based on ancient samurai designs. Kane could not help but blurt, "Jozure, you son of a bitch."

The mustached, handsome face broke into a disarming grin. "*Captain* Jozure, Commander Kane. It's been several turnings of the Earth, has it not?"

The familiar face and the memories it evoked made Kane almost return the grin. He had memories of encountering Jozure on a number of occasions, and each time the warrior had gone his way bested but rarely the wiser.

Kane felt no true hostility for the man. Jozure had received his training in the Ranger Corps but had never held a particularly high rank. They were always adversaries, rivals even, but not enemies. Still, he turned the beginnings of his grin into a scowl and demanded, "What's the meaning of this attack?"

Jozure's eyes widened with ingenuous surprise. "Attack? It is merely the custom we Tigers of Heaven practice when greeting respected comrades."

"When did it become a custom?" Domi grumbled. "Thirty seconds ago?"

"Pardon me, Commander?" inquired Jozure. "I didn't catch that."

"Never mind. What are you doing here?"

Jozure's shoulders moved in a shrug beneath their protective epaulets. "There were a number of other candidates, officers just as eager as myself. But I was the most qualified with the most scores to settle."

"You know goddamn well what I meant, Jozure. Why are the Tigers of Heaven here?"

Jozure's reply was smooth and practiced. "The same as the Rangers. To investigate the threat to the

Commonwealth. Inasmuch as Mars is part of the Commonwealth and the threat was actually directed against the colonies, I was dispatched for reasons much the same as yours.''

''The agreement—'' Kane began.

''Did not forbid the colonies taking action on their own,'' Jozure broke in, the friendliness disappearing from his tone. ''Nippon Interplanetary has many interests at risk, Commander.''

''And maybe they see other agreements to make,'' Kane suggested coldly.

''That is not in my province. Protecting those interests is.''

''I presume you are aware of the attempt we are about to make to oppose the threat?''

Jozure's expression became dark and foreboding. ''The gist of your meeting with Ambassador Takaun was conveyed to me. My suspicion is that you are mad or attempting to deceive us. Or both.''

''Or neither,'' Kane shot back.

''That's why I'm here, Commander. To ascertain the particulars of that 'neither.'''

''As an observer?''

''Hardly. As a participant.''

''Impossible,'' Baptiste's outburst sounded as sharp as a whip crack. ''The energy-to-mass ratio of the interphaser field is configured for only one ship.''

Jozure's tone lost its oily charm. ''I'll not bandy words with you, Kane. If this scheme works, then all should benefit from it. The *Okami-Maru* will accompany you to wherever it is you plan to travel.''

''Impossible,'' repeated Baptiste. ''The field isn't strong enough to open the portal for two ships.''

''I have my orders.'' Jozure said simply.

His face vanished from the screen.

"The *Okami-Maru*'s shields have just doubled in particle strength," Farrell said,

Kane cursed and directed wearily, "Double-front ours." He called engineering. "Bry, we may need some maneuvering speed."

"You'll have it, Commander," Bry responded.

The *Okami-Maru* floated in their path, drawing a line in the vacuum and daring them to cross it.

Quietly, Baptiste said, "The best that can be hoped for from a conflict is a stalemate, you know."

Harshly, Kane replied, "Yes, I *do* know that. Give me an alternative."

She tapped her chin contemplatively. "There's no way to know how long the portal will remain open or even if it will open at all. I suppose if our two ships could *share* the field, link them by a tractor line…that is if the shield frequencies of the two ships could be attuned."

Kane quickly thumbed a trans-comm. "Jozure, we may have come up with a solution."

There was no response.

In an impatient, flinty tone, Kane repeated his words and added, "It's a way to resolve this deadlock, unless of course you simply want a fight. I'm sure you remember what happened the last time you chose that option."

Jozure's face reappeared on the monitor. "You cheated that time, Kane. What is your resolution?"

Tersely, Kane repeated Baptiste's suggestion and provided him with the portal's coordinates as calculated by Fand. The Tigers of Heaven captain did not appear impressed.

"We've been scanning the area of the gateway

portal for the past five minutes," he stated. "There is nothing out there but space." He looked off-screen, said a few words in Japanese, listened to a response in the same language and faced back toward Kane.

"We've triangulated that position," he announced in a challenging voice. "Nothing."

With a forced note of patience, Baptiste said, "Until we activate the interphase field, nothing is all either of our sensors will detect."

Jozure nodded, lips tightening. "Very well. Let us briefly discuss this proposal."

Jozure's idea of "briefly" was an argument that lasted nearly forty minutes. Every minuscule point was reviewed over and over again. Once or twice, Jozure took affront at something Kane said and was on the verge of terminating the discussion.

Finally, with a wolfish smile, he relented. "I cannot deny your proposal has merit on a number of counts. The main one being that I will be able to avenge myself upon you at the slightest hint of deception. But this is an alliance of convenience only."

"Hell," grated Grant, "aren't they all?"

The *Sabre* and the *Okami-Maru* sailed over the navy yards, toward the portal coordinates provided by Fand. As a secondary precaution, a homing beacon connected the navigational computers of the two cruisers so one could not stray far from the other.

The ships took position and halted at ten thousand kloms from the gateway coordinates. Kane waited for Jozure's signal that all was in readiness aboard his vessel. He hadn't felt so apprehensive since *Sabre* had threaded its way through an asteroid field in pursuit of the clone-slavers.

The signal from Jozure came. The geon-drive en-

gines of the *Sabre* and the *Okami-Maru* engaged.
They arrowed forward. Kane kept his eyes on the
tactical plot, which despite the computer-generated
concentric circles still showed nothing but a wedge
of star-speckled blackness.

"Entry point in ten seconds…mark," announced
Domi, hands on her instrument panel.

"Interphaser activation in five seconds," Baptiste
said.

Not looking at the digital chron on the arm of his
chair, Kane counted beneath his breath, "One Mississippi, two Mississippi—"

"Interphaser on-line," Baptiste reported. "Field
cohesion holding."

"Coordinate ETE in two seconds," Domi intoned.

Kane shifted in his chair, dividing his attention between the tactical viewer and the main monitor. Suddenly all the stars winked out.

Then space screamed with light. Raving, shrieking
energy in a blinding flare of multicolored lights burst
from the screen. Kane felt the *Sabre* shudder brutally
as the artificial gravity and inertia dampers skipped
in their rhythm. Everyone on the command deck
shared an assault on their senses—sight, hearing,
touch and taste. For a long, terrifying moment, they
felt the ship around them dissolve, then re-form.

Rubbing the flash-induced spots from his eyes,
Kane saw nothing on the screen but a raging cosmos,
wild plumes and whorling spindrifts of violet, of yellow, of blue and green and red. They swirled like a
whirlpool, glowing filaments that were congealed and
stretched.

Kane looked to the comm-con's plot board. All
indicators were dark, so the instruments could not say

whether the revolving effect was due to the *Sabre*'s motion or to that of the portal.

After the first shock of portal penetration passed, status reports began coming in. Negative engine control, communications frequencies jammed, shields and sensors operative only on the most nominal level. The dedicated shipboard systems that did not draw power from the engine cores still functioned, so they wouldn't suffocate or freeze.

"Sensor scan," Kane demanded.

"Nothing," Cotta answered. "We register no radiation or energy fields. There's no way to tell if the *Okami-Maru* is still linked to us."

After a few moments, Kane realized staring at the whirling patterns on the screen induced a pronounced sensation of nausea and vertigo, so he ordered filters to be put over the exterior scanners. His chron was frozen at 1230 hours. The seconds and microseconds changed very slowly. He counted out twenty-eight seconds before the tenth-of-a-second indicator changed.

"What happens if we miss the exit point?" Domi asked. "Would we just travel through hyperspace forever?"

Baptiste shrugged. "I surmise we would eventually become patterns of energy to be absorbed by the portal's matrices."

"Your surmise is correct," Fand's voice said. Kane hadn't seen her arrive on the command deck. "My concern is sensing the exit point in time, or the result will be as Domi said—we will indeed travel forever."

"I hope you can sense it soon."

"I will. One of the curious characteristics of such

tunnels through the quantum field is that the farther one must travel, the less distance one has to go.''

Baptiste smiled wryly. ''Lewis Carroll logic if I ever heard it. I could give you the geometrics.''

''Thanks anyhow,'' Grant put in hastily.

The interior of the ship seemed dead silent, without even the rumble of engines to relieve the unnerving quiet.

The command crew stared in awed silence at the pyrotechnics arcing and revolving on the main viewer. Even muted and filtered, they were still spectacular. Suddenly, so suddenly that everyone jumped in their seats, a scanner began emitting a steady electronic chime.

Kane saw the glowing indicator, with its LCD needle flicking to and fro. ''Approaching area of extreme ionization,'' Cotta warned.

''The exit point, '' Fand announced. ''It's still in a state of flux from the passage of Thrush's vessel.''

''Exit to where?'' asked Farrell nervously.

''We won't know till we get there,'' she replied calmly.

With a startling abruptness, all the systems came on again. Engines rumbled, sensors and computers hummed, chronometers picked up speed.

The comm board crackled with static. ''*Okami-Maru* is still with us,'' Cotta noted.

The *Sabre* rocked. ''Tactical,'' Kane said. ''Adjust for the flux.''

The tactical plot screen displayed a 360-degree view at extreme range. The relative positions of the *Okami-Maru* and the *Sabre* were shown approaching a seething, color-coded mass.

"Exit point in twenty-seconds…mark," Domi reported.

The radiance that had filled the main monitor wasn't quite as brilliant as before. Streaks of gray and dark blue were interspersed with the colorful swirls.

"Extremely complex patterns of energy impulses," Cotta said. "Also a number of opposing magnetic fields."

"We must ride it out." Fand's calm voice was a soothing balm to the crew's wire-tense nerves.

"Exit point," said Domi. *"Now."*

The *Sabre* lurched violently. Bursts of light flared in a garish, eye-stinging display on the screen. The ship was hammered, tossed and buffeted by concussions of energy.

The *Sabre* seemed to plunge through an alternately brightly lit and shadow-shrouded abyss, an endless fall into infinity. It took all of Kane's will to prevent him from gritting his teeth and shutting his eyes.

Then the sensation of a free fall lessened. Slowly, as if veils were being drawn away one by one, the darker colors on the screen deepened and finally became star-speckled sepia. Far in the distance, a red sun shone like a malignant cyclopean eye in the midst of a great black emptiness. Kane guessed it to be a 1.4-magnitude star. Two dimmer stars bracketed it.

Grant gusted out a deep sigh of relief. "I *hate* these fucking things."

Chapter 19

Kane ordered the drive and interphaser disengaged and thrusters to be put at station keeping. The crew recalibrated the instruments and ran diagnostics on the systems. According to the chron, only 5.3 seconds had elapsed since they entered the portal. The final status report was reassuring—there were no casualties or damage.

The *Okami-Maru* had exited only a few seconds after the *Sabre*. A cursing Jozure claimed that all was well. Kane ordered a comprehensive scan of the constellations.

He turned to Fand. "I don't suppose you know where we are?"

She smiled and shook her head. "I think we're still in the galaxy."

Kane frowned. "That's a little vague, Fand."

"Best I can do, Commander. In this instance, your technology will be more helpful than my senses."

After a few minutes, Cotta announced the results. "Telemetric constellation configuration confirms we are in the trinary system of Sirius, nine light-years from Earth, approximately eighty-six *trillion* kilometers from our favorite restaurants."

If their mission had been one of scientific exploration, the man's proclamation would have triggered a celebration, but under the circumstances the crew's reaction was hardly jubilant.

Kane instantly recalled that ancient Asian legends alleged the Chintamani Stone originated in the star system of Sirius. He knew arriving here was not a coincidence. Reflexively he looked toward Baptiste, on the verge of pointing it out to her, then realized she knew nothing of the Chintamani Stone.

But to his surprise, she said, "Interesting. The Dogon people of West Africa claimed that alien beings from Sirius arrived on Earth many thousands of years ago. The Dogons possessed detailed astronomical knowledge of the system, claiming it had two sister stars long before their existence was ever verified."

Grant did not seem impressed or particularly interested. "So we're the first Commonwealth ship to reach another solar system. Now what?"

"Good question," Kane replied. "Maybe Jozure has a suggestion."

"I'll bet he does," Baptiste put in. "But I doubt it'll be applicable to this situation."

The three of them exchanged easy, comfortable smiles. Then Baptiste squinted in reaction to pain.

"Sensors and scanalysers at max output," Kane ordered. "General sweep. Let's head out on a nice straight course, slow and easy."

Both vessels crept through space at a crawl, barely five hundred kloms per hour. They eased through a long salient between two vast dust clouds that towered like a pair of cosmic mountains and skirted nebular mists. A vast sprawl of cinderlike debris stretched for millions of kloms.

Kane studied the vista on his tactical screen. The kilometers-wide ribbon of cinder was fuzzy from minute particles of cool hydrogen drift. The long-range infrascopes couldn't get a clear reading.

Studying his scanners, Cotta said, "Cosmic dust, Commander. Some calcium and a lot of silicon with a few heavier elements mixed in. However, there are rocks the size of Mount Everest every million cubic kloms."

"If I wanted to lie in wait for any ship that might come through the gateway, I'd hide in the drift. It fouls up sensors," Kane said thoughtfully.

Fand glanced his way. "Wouldn't it foul up theirs, too?"

"Not if a ship just hung in the filamentaries."

Grant said, "There's no point in guessing. We need to recce."

Domi's eyebrows rose. "Need to what?"

"Take a scout," Kane interposed smoothly. "Cotta, apprise Jozure what we're up to. Tell him to take a flanking position. Have him use his long-range scanners and we'll switch to short-range."

Under Domi's experienced hands, the *Sabre* eased to the outer rim of the debris field, quartering the vague, rock-clotted boundary between it and open space. Kane kept his eyes on his tactical viewer, but there just wasn't anything to see but cindery rocks. Larger particles hissed against the pulse shields, triggering the automatic proximity alarms.

Jozure's voice filtered in over the comm-link. "Not a thing but hydrogen-drift particulates so far. Molecular, most of it."

The *Sabre* continued on, her powerful short-range sensors probing in a deep search program. Jozure chafed at the slow going.

"You know," spoke up Domi, "this region is really not the best place to stage an ambush. Would Thrush risk his ship on the off chance a Commonwealth vessel came through the gateway?"

Kane and Grant exchanged glances. Kane said quietly, "If he thinks I may be aboard, yes."

Domi gave him a skeptical look, but she said nothing more.

Suddenly, Cotta yelped like an excited terrier. "An infratrace hit! Something's in there, all right. A *big* something. Moving on a course parallel with ours."

Steep bands seemed to tighten across Kane's chest but he kept his face composed. "Position?"

Cotta consulted his board. "Too far for a visual, but there's no doubt at all on the scan sweep."

"Hang on to it," ordered Kane.

Baptiste, suddenly stiff and tense, said softly, "Parallel? Is it going to attack us?"

Grant growled, "Why else would it be there?"

"It could be a bluff," suggested Farrell, "to scare us back."

"It's no bluff," Kane said confidently.

Baptiste eyed him suspiciously. "You seem pretty sure."

"I am, Doctor. Believe me."

"If it's Thrush's dreadnought, he's armed with more than a molecular destabilizer. A GRASER cannon is probably the least of it."

The short hairs on the nape of Kane's neck prickled. A gamma-ray-powered laser projector was an appallingly unsafe and destructive weapon. Not even the *Infinitor* carried one. Opening a channel to the *Okami-Maru,* he apprised Jozure of the situation. "I'd like you to hang back on the extreme limit of sensor range, be our ace on the line."

"Be your what?" Jozure demanded.

Kane sighed. "Secret weapon. Our backup."

Jozure hesitated before saying, "As you wish."

Minutes passed but the sensor hit was still too distant for a visual, and the hydrogen drift blurred the signal.

"Still on a parallel course," Cotta reported. "Pacing us, maintaining the same speed and distance."

"Grant," Kane said. "Arm and target-lock two Shrikes. Let's see if we can't get some kind of reaction out of it."

The man quickly obeyed, hitting keys and snapping toggles. "Armed and locked."

"Fire."

The tactical viewer registered the pair of unleashed missiles as little more than white-glowing threads streaking their way through the floating cinder field. Then a sheet of nuclear flame paled the stars, surging outward. Dust sprayed in clouds from the twin atomic explosions.

"Sensors?" Kane barked.

Cotta shook his head in frustration. "The explosions caused a squall of hydrogen, jamming the transmission. Give me some time to clear it."

"A moot point," said Baptiste stiffly. "I think we've got the reaction you wanted."

On both the main monitor and the tactical viewer appeared a spark-shedding column of hell-hued light. It lanced directly toward them.

"Evasive!" bellowed Kane.

Domi's fingers played over her control board, but even as the *Sabre* began its veering maneuver, the energy beam impacted blindingly portside aft.

The lights on the command deck flickered in a

strobing pattern. A blinding flare of crimson-and-white light burst from the main monitor screen. The *Sabre* shuddered brutally as the artificial-gravity and inertia dampers fluctuated.

Knuckling the flash-induced spots from his eyes, Kane shouted, "Status!"

The *Sabre* rocked again. Kane had to grab Fand to keep her from staggering into Domi at the navigation station. "Tactical. Give me a three-sixty view. Thrusters at station keeping until we establish another target lock."

Baptiste said, "Another moot point, Commander. I believe our target has found us."

On the screen, outlined by regularly placed running lights, a massive, ominous shape slid into view, blackly outlined by the distant red light of Sirius. The weapons emplacements bristling the huge, disk-shaped craft were clearly visible.

"Domi! Hard to port. Evasive maneuvers, thrusters at maximum!" Kane yelled.

Domi's hands never reached the controls. Another streak of hell light erupted from the dreadnought. The deck jumped underfoot. Kane's comm-con squirted a shower of sparks. The *Sabre* lurched ten degrees on her starboard side. All lights flickered, came up, flickered again and finally flashed on dimly.

In the semidarkness, Kane struggled to find and punch the comm-link button. "Bry, engine status."

"Checking," came the strained reply.

Baptiste said, "Our aft shield generators are down. Enough of the GRASER beam leaked through to make glancing contact with the hull."

"Weapons status."

"Shrike pods unaffected and operable," Grant said from the fire-control panel.

"Bry, bleed some power from our fore shield generators to cover our ass," Kane ordered.

"There's no point in that," Baptiste countered. "At full strength, our screens were easily pierced. A weakened deflector won't resist a second GRASER shot of the same intensity."

Kane gritted his teeth. From engineering, Bry said, "That shot made confetti out of the thrusters. We're not going anywhere for a while."

"Do we still have maneuvering ability?" Kane asked.

"The wing gyros are still operative," Grant answered, "but without the main thrusters, we'll just wallow like Venusian doughpots."

"Deploy them anyway. Give me a controlled burn."

Grant's fingers touched a series of buttons. A moment later, ribbed wings of alloy unfolded on either side of the craft. They were designed to allow the *Sabre* to make an atmosphere entry like a jet plane, not be used for deep-space maneuvering. The small rocket tubes tipping the wings spit narrow tongues of blue flame, and the cruiser slowly rotated.

Cold fingers of terror knotting inside his chest, Kane looked to the screen. The dreadnought hung on it, like a vulture poised over a dying victim. He found himself laboring for breath and realized the oxygen recyclers were at half power. He said to Baptiste, "Divert our remaining power to the environmental systems."

The dreadnought slid closer, halting at one kilometer from the *Sabre*'s port bow. Its dark bulk completely filled the monitor screen. On the hull, running lights haloed an inverted triangle containing the stylized silhouette of a bird of prey, crested head thrown back, beak open, claws outspread, wings lifted wide. Kane clamped his teeth on a groan of despair. The dreadnought was the personal warship of Colonel Thrush.

The *Sabre* was a good ship. Nothing in the system was faster or more maneuverable. But the dreadnought had all the other advantages—its defensive screens were more sophisticated, and its gamma-powered lasers could slice through a meteorite like cardboard.

Kane muttered, "If only we could get off one missile—"

"Pointless," Baptiste argued. "The dreadnought's pulse shields would detonate it before it reached its target."

An aperture on the dreadnought irised open. A coruscating rainbow radiance spilled out, seething with energy.

Grant stiffened in his chair. "They've got their molecular destabilizer powered up."

A wavering ribbon of scarlet light whiplashed from the port, and Kane gripped the armrests of his chair tightly. Scarlet light flooded the control deck, and an extended thunderclap filled his ears as the pulse shields absorbed the energy and transmitted it through the hull as a high-pitched vibration. Fire the color of blood seemed to cling to the *Sabre*'s pulse shields. Then it faded.

Cotta said in a groaning voice, "We withstood that one. But that's the lot. Our shields are overloaded."

"What about the *Okami-Maru?*" Grant demanded. "Where the hell is Jozure?"

As if in answer, the monitor screen showed the black backdrop of space being pierced by intermittent pulses of intense light. The pulses connected with the dreadnought, dim flares showing briefly as the huge ship's deflectors registered the multiple impacts.

Baptiste decreased and compressed the magnification so the entire scene could be witnessed. The *Okami-Maru* attacking the dreadnought in traditional Tigers of Heaven method—no cleverness, no cunning maneuvers, just roaring in head-on with her autolasers blazing.

A flurry of particle-beam laser bolts streaked toward the dreadnought like a glowing sleet storm. The dreadnought's shields repulsed the barrage, and it returned the fire with a pair of intersecting GRASER beams.

The *Okami-Maru* began an evasive turn, but both beams struck dead on target amidships.

"Their defensive screens are down seventy-two percent," Cotta announced.

A third GRASER beam scorched a path across the starboard side of the *Okami-Maru,* splitting open a five-meter-long gash. Men and equipment tumbled out to be cremated in seconds.

Another bolt from the dreadnought licked out, touching the *Okami-Maru*'s rear engine assembly, fragmenting it and all but shearing it away. The cruiser spun helplessly, frozen atmosphere spuming from it in a cloud.

Watching the screen, Kane winced. The ship's stabilizers had obviously been knocked out, and its internal gravity systems had probably been blasted to hell and gone in the process.

"Who's on board that goddamn ship?" Domi shrilled fearfully, angrily. "Why don't they contact us?"

Kane met Fand's eyes, but she shook her head in resignation.

As if on cue, Farrell said, "Transmission from the dreadnought."

"Put it on screen," Kane directed.

The dreadnought's image wavered, dissolved, and C. W. Thrush's smiling face replaced it.

"Kane." The man's voice was like steel meeting steel, as if metal were catching in the back of his throat. "Predictable."

"You knew I was coming?"

"I hoped that you would. Obviously, you must surrender immediately."

Kane forced a detached note into his voice. "What are the terms?"

"What do you expect? Complete and unconditional surrender. You have no alternative."

"Do you guarantee the safety of my crew?"

Thrush's lips curved in a mocking smile. "You should know I guarantee nothing. Your answer. Now."

Kane's forced patience vanished. He rose to his feet in a savage, furious rush. "It's me you want, you son of a bitch!"

Thrush acted as if he hadn't heard. "My weapons emplacements are locked on to your engine array. If I do not have your answer in five seconds, I will fire all banks."

Kane felt all eyes trained upon him as he stood on

the command deck, fists clenched, face pale and tight with fury. How many times will I concede to this inhuman bastard's terms? he asked himself. When will it stop? When will I stop him?

Another voice, the voice of the Kane whose mind and body he had appropriated, cried, How many times have I dreaded the day when I will make the wrong decision and it kills my command? I can't do it anymore. I'm all out of ideas. Somebody else make the decisions—

C. W. Thrush intoned, "Your five seconds are up."

Chapter 20

"I surrender," Kane said coldly. "What of the *Okami-Maru*?"

"Its commander will be offered the same terms. Prepare to be towed."

Thrush's face disappeared. The viewer showed the dreadnought again. Suddenly, a stream of gibbous light flowed from its undercarriage and washed the screen with a pale luminescence. The command crew felt the racking jar that jolted the *Sabre* from bow to stern.

"Tractor beam," Farrell said.

"I figured," muttered Grant, grabbing the sides of his console.

Domi fed more power to the thrusters. The *Sabre* simply hung in space, her hull vibrating furiously. Every instrument on the main operational console began to whine, blink or both.

"Commander," Baptiste said urgently, "we'll have to shut down the thrusters or we'll burn them out."

"Do it, Domi," snapped Kane.

"Something else," Cotta noted. "Some sort of negative polarity particles contained within the field of the beam."

All electronic noise of the ship's systems ceased. Indicators went dark. In the uncomfortable silence that followed, Kane noticed that the displays registered no energy output.

"The computer system has been shut down," Baptiste reported. "Data retrieval and memory access nonfunctional."

"Life support is still on," Domi observed.

"Evidently the beam is selective in its inhibiting properties."

"Try your manual overrides," Kane ordered.

In a few minutes, the results were in—only essential shipboard systems were working. Everything from sensor analysis to the navigational computers were down. Extraship communication was impossible, too, although the external scanners still transmitted and relayed. They had no way of learning the extent of the *Okami-Maru*'s damage or casualties.

They saw on the monitor that Jozure had apparently given in to the better part of valor. The *Okami-Maru* too was cloaked by the tractor beam. The dreadnought lumbered through the vacuum, above the cinder stream, dragging the two smaller ships behind like a pair of recalcitrant children.

"Where could Thrush be taking us?" Fand wondered aloud.

Kane turned toward her. "I wish I knew."

"Sister Fand," Baptiste spoke up, "do you sense any life or thought patterns aboard that vessel?"

She replied with a negative shake of her head. "No."

Grant sighed heavily. "If only we could get off one missile into its engines—"

"Pointless," Cotta declared. "That ship's shields could brush it off easily. However, triple redundancies are designed into our computer systems. If we started on one of the auxiliaries, it might be possible to bypass the main memory nexus and regain control of the ship.''

Kane gave him an exaggerated, appreciative nod. "Good idea. Get on it. Maybe Bry can bring our engines back on-line before we reach our destination.''

He made a move toward his chair. "Until then, I guess all we can do is sit back and try to enjoy the ride—''

A great shuddering fear consumed Kane, a primal terror that nearly crushed him into a fetal position on the deck plates. He fought its suffocating pressure, tried to stamp it back into the hole in his psyche from which it had sprung.

In one tiny lucid portion of his brain, he was totally aware of everything going on, of the people, activity and voices on the command deck. The rest of his mind was saturated by fear, a soul-deep anguish.

I've led my people to their deaths! I can't do this anymore! Somebody should've stopped me, I should've stood down long ago....

Names and faces flew by, men and women who had died while serving under his command, who had followed his orders to their violent deaths. Some of them still bobbed out in the void, their spacesuits poor substitutes for coffins, meteor fragments serving as headstones.

These were the guilty memories the Kane of this casement had hidden from him, buried deeply in his subconscious so they were not accessible.

With the onslaught of fear came understanding and he stood immobile until he felt he had digested it all. Now he knew why his fusion with his doppelgänger's mind had been so smooth, why he had not been forced to expend effort to remain in control.

Commander J. T. Kane was an exhausted soul, in torment, faced with losing everything that had given his life meaning, and now realizing it ultimately meant nothing. He had been living on sheer momentum, by habit, playing a role. He was more than willing to let someone else do it, to take up his burden, to accept the responsibility and let him rest.

Kane cut his eyes over to Grant and felt a spasm of inner pain. He had ruined the man's life, exploited his loyalty and friendship, used his devotion to shore up his own flagging enthusiasm. He and others aboard the *Sabre* had refused many opportunities in order to patrol the spaceways with him.

And Fand—beautiful Fand who had loved him with a wild passion, but who had chosen to let him go, rather than share him with the *Sabre,* with duty, with the risks he undertook. And now he had led her to her death, as well.

Before he realized it, the other Kane spoke, in a muffled, choked voice. "I'm sorry—"

Farrell's head whipped toward him. "Sir?"

Kane dragged in a breath, wrestling, fighting with the fear. He made a blind move toward the lift. "I'll be in my quarters."

He sensed all eyes on him, startled, confused and fearful.

"Commander—" Baptiste began hesitantly.

"Somebody take the con." Then he was through the door and riding the lift to the lower deck.

Kane's cabin was little more than a module with windowless walls covered with thick, textured foam. One part of him knew that all cabins were cushioned in like fashion, as a safety feature in case the artificial gravity failed.

At the tiny sink, Kane splashed water on his face. He gazed at his reflection in the mirror above it. The features were of course familiar, but it was the face of this casement's Kane who stared back at him.

His lips were tight, and his complexion had become waxy. He could see his pulse bumping through the veins at his temples. The expression was like that of an animal with its leg caught in a trap.

The door buzzer sounded.

"Go away," he said, still staring at the mirror.

Instead, he heard the door panel slide aside and soft footfalls. He looked over his shoulder, half expecting to see Fand. He experienced an instant of wonder when he saw Baptiste standing there.

Before he could check the movement, he moved toward her, blurting desperately, "Brigid—"

He caught himself, biting back the rest of his words.

She shut the door behind her and regarded him keenly, with troubled eyes. "Commander, is everything all right?"

He chuckled bitterly, without mirth, a rasping rattle. "Return to your post, Doctor."

She clasped her hands behind her back. "I'm here in my capacity as warrant officer. If I understand the job description, a warrant officer supervises every ship function, from manning the comm-con to overseeing maintenance details and evaluating personnel performance."

"You're as officious here as you are back home, Baptiste." He sank down on the edge of the bunk.

She didn't react to his comment, not even a flicker

of eye movement. "We could be in a critical situation at any moment. If you're unable to perform your duties, you must appoint someone as acting commander."

Kane's jaw muscles bunched, and he felt a surge of anger, but he wasn't certain of the source. "I don't recall standing down, Doctor."

Then he closed his eyes as a tidal wave of memories crashed over him, sweeping him out into a sea of dread. His voice was thick. "He's all out of ideas, Brigid."

"'He'?" she echoed.

Kane tried to stop himself from saying more, but it was like trying to stem a flood with a teacup. "He's tired, beaten. He has no real life, but he has a legend to live up to. All he has left is this fucking rattletrap ship and he's about to lose that—if he doesn't get her destroyed first, with all the people aboard her."

Through clenched teeth, he hissed, "God, he doesn't know what to do anymore. *I* don't know what to do."

Dimly, he became aware of her sitting down beside him, pulling his head to her shoulder, enfolding him in her arms. As if from a great distance he heard her husky whisper. "The fear has hit you, that's all. But you'll put the fear behind you and walk out of here and do what needs to be done, like you always do, like *we* always do."

He felt a stirring within him, a glimmer of hope.

"Remember who you are," she continued. "The man who always beats the odds. One percent, remember?"

He heard a sharp, startled intake of breath from

her, and she repeated in a soft, faraway murmur, "Remember."

Kane slowly straightened up. Her expression was a mask of bewildered concentration, lines deeply creasing her forehead.

"You said the same things to me once before," he said quietly. "You remember that."

"How could I have—?" Her lips clamped tight to prevent a groan of pain from escaping.

She tried to push herself away from him, but he held her tightly by the shoulders. He said urgently, "You remembered, part of you remembered those words. I needed to hear them again, just like *he* needed to hear them for the first time."

Baptiste's hands went to his fingers, frantically prising at them. Voice high and wild, she said, "Let me go, Commander—"

He increased the pressure. "Goddammit, Baptiste—Brigid. I need you, the commander needs you. My Brigid senses that, that's why she directed you to come here, that's why you said what you did. Remember who you are!"

She struggled with him. "I know who I am, what I am. I don't *need* to remember who I am!" Her words tumbled out in aspirated moans, her eyes squeezed shut, limbs trembling.

She pushed against him with an astounding burst of strength, breaking his hold on her. She fell off the bunk, collapsing in a heap on the deck, hands at the sides of her head. Her "Stop it!" was a pleading cry of agony.

Kane went down on his knees beside her. The trans-comm unit buzzed. Cotta's tense voice filtered out it. "Commander, something's happening."

"Like what?" he snapped.

Cotta coughed. "You'll have to see it for yourself."

"On my way," he responded automatically.

Baptiste lay on the deck, knees drawn up, entire body quivering. He laid a hand on her back, but she flinched away from the touch.

With a sense of resigned gloom, Kane said, "We're needed on the command deck, Doctor. If you're unable, I'll call the dispensary and have DeFore come in."

She drew in a shuddery gasp and lifted her head, hair in disarray, loose strands hanging over her face. Her glasses lay on the floor. Swiveling her head, she transfixed him with a brilliant jade stare. "No need. Besides, she's probably just as short-tempered here as she is in Cerberus."

Kane's relief was so absolute, so overwhelming he couldn't move a muscle. He stayed on his knees as Brigid climbed to her feet, trying to pat her hair back into place and seating her glasses on the bridge of her nose. Extending a hand toward him, she gave him a questioning look. "Are you coming?"

Numbly, Kane took her hand and allowed her to pull him up. He husked out, "Slow but sure. About time you got here, Baptiste."

Smiling wryly and wanly, she touched her forehead. "Unexpected degree of resistance. This Brigid didn't want to be displaced on any level, unconscious or subconscious. She's completely satisfied with who and what she is."

She added a touch resentfully, "A refreshing change."

Kane smothered the desire to hug her close. He

knew what had finally triggered the fusion, how she had followed an impulse to render him aid. All he could think of to say was, *"Anam-chara."*

Brigid nodded once in understanding, and they left the cabin together. She gave up trying to arrange her hair the way she had been wearing it and let it hang loose, draping her shoulders and upper back.

When the lift doors opened onto the command deck, Kane caught the swift, sideways glance Fand threw their way. It was slightly suspicious, slightly amused, but only slightly. The primary emotion glimmering in her big eyes was fear.

Like the rest of the duty personnel, her attention was focused on the monitor screen. Kane took two steps toward the comm-con and then froze, rooted in place.

On the screen, black space peeled back on itself as great blossoming splashes of color poured through from behind it. Faintly at first, as through rolling multicolored clouds, a shape began to materialize, surrounded by an iridescent halo of white mist.

Kane could feel its presence as it seemed to shift through dimensions, moving through a whole series of casements.

Like a globe of light, the sphere glowed against the sepia sea. Geometric patterns of light pulsed around, along and across the great disk shape. Ruled lines of luminescence bisected it, from pole to pole. The equator was a band of seething, living fire.

As the dreadnought drew closer, more details became apparent. The surface of the globe was plated with kilometers-wide sections of dark metal, each plate intersecting and interlocking with the other. The sphere was like a moon-size city or factory, with brilliantly lit streets and buildings. Somehow Kane knew that nothing made of flesh had ever trod those streets.

He felt an inward cringing. He wanted to blank out the screen, to convince himself that what he was seeing was a hallucination, or better yet, a malfunction.

Instead, he forced his legs to start moving, and he took his place at the comm-con. In a measured tone, he said, "Report."

Chapter 21

Voice trembling, Cotta said, "Our computers are still down, so a full analysis can't be made. However, our navigational telemetry still works—marginally—and we've got a partial scan."

Kane eyed the orb on the screen with mounting fear, but his tone was level. "Results?"

"Body constructed of metal, as is apparent. Mass and circumference measurements can't be accurate, but I'd guesstimate it to be approximately the diameter of our moon, maybe a little smaller."

"Where the hell did it come from?" Domi demanded. "Our long-range sensors should have detected it when we were scanning the area."

Kane glanced over at Fand. She trembled ever so slightly, but her voice was steady. "It came from outside, through a small hole torn in the fabric of our universe. It doesn't really exist, not in relation to this universe. I can make no close assessment of where it came from, or of its true nature. Except that it doesn't belong here."

"The manner in which it appeared indicates energy-to-matter conversion," Brigid said.

"As if it has a gateway unit?" Kane asked.

"It could very well *be* a gateway unit."

"Is every inch of that thing covered with metal?" asked Grant.

"Probably," Cotta said. "No doubt the sheathing extends far beneath the surface."

"The dreadnought is hailing us," Farrell said.

"Visual," responded Kane.

Thrush's masklike face appeared on the screen. "You, Kane, Mr. Grant and Miss Baptiste will prepare to board this vessel. I have extended the same invitation to Captain Jozure."

"For what purpose?"

"That will be revealed to you. I will extend docking chutes to both your ships."

"If I refuse?"

"You are perfectly cognizant of the results. I also order the Danaan hybrid to accompany you."

"She's not a member of my crew—she's a civilian."

"I was not making a request, Kane." His face rippled away.

"Voluble he isn't," Farrell remarked.

Which was not characteristic of the Thrush they had met before, but Kane didn't say so. "We've no choice but to do as he says. Cotta, what's the progress on activating one of our auxiliary computers?"

"Slow, Commander. To perform primary ship functions, reprogramming is necessary."

"Can you restore engine control?"

"If all goes according to plan. Bry has been working on the geon energizers and maneuvering thrusters. The computer should be reprogrammed within the hour, but the engines may take longer."

"I have a feeling we don't have much time," Grant said dourly.

Domi frowned. "There's lots of possibilities."

"Too goddamn many," Grant retorted.

On the screen, they watched as the moonlight-colored tractor beam reeled in the *Okami-Maru* like a hooked fish, positioning it abreast of the *Sabre,* with barely twenty meters separating them. The ghastly slash in her hull was on the far side, so the *Sabre*'s scanners couldn't accurately evaluate the damage she had sustained.

Two flexible, ribbed cylinders extended from the dark underbelly of the dreadnought, questing outward like the trunks of elephants. They were about sixty meters long and fifteen in overall diameter. Their magnetic collars affixed tightly to the emergency airlocks of both craft.

Thrush's voice grated over the speaker. "You have ten minutes."

Leaving Cotta in charge, Kane led Grant, Fand and Brigid from the command deck. They took the lift down to the very bowels of the ship, to a small, dark and cold area beneath the second deck. The emergency escape hatch, more complicated than the general access docking port on the *Sabre*'s fuselage, humped up from the floor plates.

A grizzled-haired, large-framed Ranger waited for them, a man named Macrough. He had served aboard the *Sabre* longer than anyone, even Kane. Wordlessly, he extended his right arm with five gun belts draped over it. They all held holstered ASP pistols.

Macrough could have chosen from several kinds of small arms, from kinetic kill blasters to nonlethal electropulse stunners. Obviously, his assessment of the situation was that weapons that discharged accelerated streams of protons would be more efficacious than those that fired projectiles and electric current. The energy bolts spit by ASP pistols interacted with anything possessing an atomic structure, whether it was organic or inorganic. They were extremely dangerous weapons, so their manufacture and distribution were severely restricted.

Fand refused the pistol, but Brigid reluctantly accepted a belt, strapping it around her waist. Grant's eyes glinted as he took his, popping the ASP from its spring-powered holster, gauging its weight and balance.

Softly, Brigid said, "At least it's more aesthetically pleasing than a Sin Eater."

Grant threw her a fleeting, appreciative smile and inclined his head in a nod, acknowledging her subtle message.

Still not speaking, Macrough handed Kane and Grant two flat, small curves of metal. They placed the comm-tachs against the mastoid bones behind their right ears. Implanted steel pintels embedded in the bones slid through the flesh and into tiny input ports in the comm-tachs. A burst of static filled their heads, then they heard Cotta's voice echoing inside their ears.

"Testing," Cotta intoned. "One-two-three. Testing."

"Got you," said Kane. "Calibrate the audio pickup for Grant, too."

"Calibrated, Commander."

Lights changed color on the hatch cover, and gasketed pressure locks separated with a clank they felt through the soles of their boots. The hatch irised open, releasing a puff of cold air and an eerie whistling sound. The boarding chute stretched away at a gradual inclining angle. Regularly placed light rings on the chute's ribbing cast a blue-green illumination.

Kane started to climb down, looked toward Macrough, paused and lifted his right forefinger to his nose and snapped it away in a smart salute.

Macrough didn't return the gesture, but he nodded gravely, as if he understood its significance.

The interior of the cylinder held an atmosphere but no gravity. Once away from the bleed-off of the *Sabre*'s grav-stators, everyone became weightless. The inner walls of the chute came equipped with staple-shaped rungs by which they could pull themselves along. Kane took the point, followed by Brigid and Fand. Grant floundered along at the rear, filling the hollow tube with breathless curses.

The women's hair floated around their heads like clouds. Fand's long tresses tied with the golden balls streamed out behind and above her like a flaxen cloak.

The four people floated and bobbed along the cylinder. Kane refused to allow himself to be assailed by doubts and worries. The end of the chute came into view, a circle of white glimmering light. As they neared it, their bodies felt the drag of gravity, the weight gradually settling over their limbs until they no longer bobbed along like corks but were forced to climb, hand over hand.

They exited the boarding chute into a spacious, dome-ceilinged chamber. Opposite their position, they saw a duplicate of the round hatch they had just clambered through. Kane tapped his comm-tach's send stud. "*Sabre,* do you read me?"

There was no response, not even a hiss of static. The commfrequency was jammed.

A panting, grimacing Jozure appeared in full battle armor, from visored silver helmet to a curved *tachi* sword at his hip. The blade was ceremonial, strictly for show. The standard Tiger's weapon was the RAZER rig he wore at the small of his back. Power conduits snaked to the tight-beam laser emitters mounted on his gauntleted forearms.

His face bore a streak of red, blistered flesh and his left hand was encased in a hastily applied cast. Before Kane could speak, Jozure stomped over to him, bellowing, "Twelve of my samurai dead, Kane! Five injured, my ship crippled—"

His voice held equal measures of anguish and rage. Rumor had it that Tigers of Heaven officers were contractually bound to commit seppuku if they failed in a mission and lost men and matériel in the process.

Kane eyed him sympathetically, resisting the urge to remind the captain about the proverb regarding angels and rushing fools.

"Now what?" muttered Grant.

"You will not draw your side arms."

The flat, oily voice, so finely projected it seemed impossible not to have come from one of them, echoed over their heads. As one, all five people skipped around, necks craned as they peered upward.

A gleaming device, barely two feet long, hovered overhead. It was a vaguely birdlike configuration, with a short pylon for a neck supporting a beaked head. Winglike flanges were studded with extruder hooks and extensors. A photoreceptor shone redly in the head. Jozure raised both of his arms. A needle-thin ray shot from a nozzle on the exterior of the gadget and impaled his right hand. Crying out, he stumbled backward, a thin tendril of smoke curling up from the cauterized pinholes on the back and palm of his gauntlet.

"I repeat," said the device. "Do not draw your side arms."

The voice was that of C. W. Thrush. The gadget hummed toward the door. "You will follow."

"What is that thing?" Fand whispered.

Brigid said, "A servo mechanism, a remote drone. Thrush can see and hear us through it."

Kane knew she was drawing on her memories of a similar device they had encountered during their time trip back to the twentieth century.

The corridors of the dreadnought were broad, a flat gray in color, and they exuded a cold impersonality. They followed the bird along the hall, Kane noting there didn't seem to be any doors along the bulkheads.

The corridor ended at an open lift platform. The bird halted, floating above it. "This will bring you to my vessel's bridge. Do not attempt to manipulate the controls. Enter."

As the elevator whisked them upward, Jozure said to Kane, "You seem to know Thrush, Commander."

Kane didn't respond.

"Is there any chance of reasoning with him, striking a deal?"

Fand said coldly, "It is the conceit of your upbringing that maintains every form of intelligence can be reached through bargaining. Has it never occurred to you, Captain, that there may be intelligences so different from your own that compromise or understanding is impossible?"

Jozure looked on the verge of cursing her, but the lift stopped ascending. The five people stepped onto the dreadnought's bridge. It was immense, nearly

three times the breadth, length and diameter of the
Sabre's command deck.

It was two leveled. Banks of glass-covered consoles ran the length of both levels. Overhead lights
gleamed on alloys, the glass, the CPUs. Small chairs,
not designed for Earth humans, rose from the deck
before each console. A quick count told Kane that
each level contained a dozen chairs. But none of the
chairs was occupied. The entire bridge seemed to be
deserted except for a bird-shaped drone, hovering
over the wide curved sweep of a control console.

But there was something else in the vast chamber,
an odor that caused a sick shudder to rack Kane's
shoulders. It was the unforgettable miasma of death.
The fetid reek of rotting flesh permeated the clean,
antiseptic environment. Everyone smelled the slaugh-
terhouse stench and reacted to it in different ways.

Beneath a hand covering her nose and mouth, Fand
murmured, "Where is that smell coming from?"

"Who is in control of this ship?" Grant asked,
voice strangely hushed.

"We are."

Three flat voices spoke in unison from three points
around the huge bridge. On the level directly overhead, a figure stepped to the guardrail and Kane was
barely able to repress an exclamation of fright.

It was the Colonel Thrush he and Brigid had encountered on the final day of the twentieth century,
looking as Kane had last seen him—wearing a tailored black business suit, but with his wig and sunglasses missing. Missing, too, was the left side of his
face, only rotting scraps of flesh clinging to the burnished metal beneath. His eye on that side was a wet,
gelid smear, looking like a pit of black jam.

He raised his right arm as if in greeting, but only a ragged, bloody stump protruded from the bullet-chewed shirt cuff.

On the opposite end of the bridge, a second black-clad figure shuffled into view, dragging a dead leg behind him. Field Marshal Thrush wore the black uniform of the Reich, a tunic with the silver piping running in a tight line along the shoulder and chest. The insignia patch on the sleeve, three black inverted triangles against a triangular red background, looked like a splotch of blood. High black boots rose nearly to his knees, and a peaked, leather-visored black cap sat upon his head.

Both sides of his face were horribly distorted, punched out of shape, the flesh ripped and hanging down in decomposing scraps, metal gleaming dully beneath the skin. His huge obsidian eyes glittered with a feral malevolence.

Another figure approached from the direction of the control console. Director Thrush, like the colonel and the field marshal, was tall and thin as a famine victim. He was dressed in what Kane remembered as an elegant black suit with wide lapels with an equally black cummerbund as an accessory.

The suit now resembled dark ash, held together by a few threads and stitching that had somehow survived the terrible flames. There was no need for the wraparound sunglasses to disguise his eyes, because this Thrush had no eyes or much of a head in which to hold them.

His synthetic flesh was crisped and blistered, the once finely drawn nose a blackened stub. His ears were barely discernible lumps. His mouth hung open, making wet, rasping whistles.

They were all incarnations of Thrush they had met on different casements, shambling forward like the living dead, their organic tissues in advanced states of decomposition. Fand shrank in horror against Kane.

"What the hell is this?" demanded Jozure, eyes darting wildly from one figure to the other.

"To accede to your wishes," the three Thrushes replied, voices in perfect sync, though the delivery of the burned one sounded somewhat slurred, "that we meet face—"

"To-face," said Field Marshal Thrush.

"To-face," said Colonel Thrush. "And allow you a glimpse."

"Of what?" Grant asked, voice pitched low to disguise the tremor of fear underscoring it.

The three figures made the same diffident gestures at the same time, like a grotesque trio of mimes. "Of the past, the present and the future."

Eyeing the maimed Colonel Thrush standing on the second level, Kane said, "We see the past. I'm not so sure about the present and I don't see anything about the future."

The bird drone spoke. "You are standing in the present, Kane. The future awaits off this vessel's port bow."

"Do you mean that moon?" Brigid asked.

"If it pleases you to refer to it as such, then yes, I mean that moon."

Kane glared at the hovering bird shape. "Is that your new body, Thrush? I can't deny it's an improvement over the others, but it'll make it difficult for you to blend in."

A laugh of genuine amusement floated from the

machine. "It is only a channel of observation and communication. My true self awaits your arrival on, as Miss Baptiste calls it, the moon."

"What about this ship?" demanded Grant. "Who built it? Where is its crew?"

"This craft is nothing but a relic, a prop—certainly it is more advanced that anything your engineers have developed. It holds the secret of interstellar travel, which has eluded you ever since your race used it as a template for your own spacecraft. But it is a relic nonetheless, at least a thousand years old."

Brigid glanced around, noting the resemblance in layout to the huge disk she had entered buried beneath the Black Gobi. "It's an Archon mother ship."

"That was its original function," the drone agreed. "But I used it to impress Archon technological superiority upon the minds of twentieth-century military men and bureaucrats. I allowed them to think it was the flagship of a vast fleet."

"That was two centuries ago," Fand pointed out. "Why wait until now to do anything with it?"

Field Marshal Thrush nodded in the direction of Kane, Grant and Brigid. "They know why. The answers await all of you."

The drone passed over their heads to the opposite end of the bridge. Door panels hissed aside. "Follow me, please."

The people hesitated, glancing from the foulsmelling versions of Thrush to one another. Grant's hand strayed to the butt of his ASP.

A heavy sigh issued from the metal bird. "You vex me, you truly do. How often do I have to remind you of the consequences of disobedience?"

A needle of light sprang from the machine and

touched Fand's right cheek. A scream started up her throat as she clapped a hand to her face. She staggered backward a few paces. Kane's ASP was out and aimed at the bird within a shaved sliver of a second.

"Really, Kane," mumbled the blackened and charred Thrush. "At what are you going to shoot? That device?"

"I have dozens more," said Field Marshal Thrush.

"And what was done to the hybrid," spoke up Colonel Thrush, "could just as easily be the molecular destabilizer turned loose on your unshielded and helpless ship."

Teeth clenched so tight his jaw muscles ached, Kane lowered his weapon and turned toward Fand. Brigid stood beside her, examining the black-edged pinhole marring the smooth perfection of her cheek.

"I'm all right," she murmured. Her eyes seethed with molten, aureate hatred, and she muttered a few words in hard-edged Gaelic.

"Follow me, please," said the bird, and hummed from the bridge.

As they entered another corridor, Jozure fell into step beside Kane. The man looked ill, his black eyes darting wildly like some frantic animal's. "What is going on here, Kane?" His voice was a strained whisper. "What does all this have to do with the Archon Directorate? You seem to have some idea about this insanity."

"I do, Captain."

"How? Tell me!"

Kane smiled coldly. "Still think your colony can strike a deal with him?"

Jozure's eyes stopped their shifting and fixed him

with a glare. He forced a chuckle. "Very perceptive, Commander. I guess that's why you're the living legend and I'm just a poor samurai with a disembowelment clause in his employment contract."

"Do what I say, Jozure, and when I say it, and you may be able to keep your bowels where they belong."

The remote-controlled drone led them to an open set of double doors. Beyond them stood a duplicate of the Cerberus mat-trans jump chamber. Even the armaglass walls were of the same brown hue.

"Form follows function even here," Brigid said lowly.

The bird hovered over the chamber's door. "Enter."

Jozure's step faltered. "What is that thing?"

"A quantum interphase inducer," Kane answered. "A mat-trans gateway."

Jozure's eyes widened. "Where will it take us?"

"To a glimpse of the future," Thrush's voice responded. "You've earned a look at it."

Without hesitation, Kane stepped onto the platform and took a place on the slightly raised hexagonal floor disks. When everyone was inside, the door swung shut on its counterbalanced hinges. Immediately the jump cycle automatically engaged.

A familiar yet still slightly unnerving hum arose, climbing in pitch to a subsonic whine. The hexagonal disks on the floor and ceiling exuded a shimmering silvery glow that slowly intensified. A fine, faint mist gathered on the floor plates and drifted down from the ceiling. Thready, static discharges crackled in the wispy vapor. The mist thickened, curling around to engulf them.

Kane watched the spark-shot fog float before his eyes. Right before his conscious thoughts ebbed, he replayed Fand's comment about travels through the quantum field: "The farther one must travel, the less distance one has to go."

For some reason, it made sense now.

Kane closed his eyes.

Chapter 22

Kane opened his eyes and almost instantly squeezed them shut again. Hot, acrid air seared his nasal passages, his lungs. Carefully, he half opened one eye. Devastation was too restrained a word for the sight that met his gaze.

He, Fand, Grant, Jozure and Brigid stood on a street surrounded by the gutted, flaming shells of buildings. The pavement was strewed by rubble where it wasn't gone altogether. The sky was hidden by a dense pall of black, choking smoke. The heat was so fierce great globes of perspiration literally burst from his pores.

Eyes tearing, fighting against a coughing fit, Kane turned to Brigid and Grant. "This is like the vid Lakesh showed us, recorded right after the nukecaust."

They didn't answer. The ground quaked beneath them, riven suddenly with deep, spreading cracks. All of them quickly scuttled to one side before a huge section of the street collapsed in on itself. They began walking. The longer they struggled through the smoke, the worse the scenes of horror became. Lampposts sagged like half-melted candles, heaps of debris and masonry smoldered and at one point they stumbled upon the fire-blackened skeletons of a mother and infant.

There was no sound other than the crackle of

flames and the tramp of their feet. The aura of night-marish unreality numbed them.

"This," Jozure gasped, sounding half-strangled, "is the future?"

"No," said Kane with grimly. "Maybe *a* future somewhere, but not your future."

"How can you be so sure of that?" Jozure wheezed.

"Because we're here to make sure it doesn't happen."

As they skirted the remains of a wall, a dark shape loomed up and out of the roiling plumes of smoke, in a valley between two high heaps of debris. Blurred as it was by the dense mist, it looked like a hideous travesty of humanity.

Taller than Grant, leaner by far than Kane, it was a lizard-thing walking upright on slightly bowed, powerful legs. The tough, brownish hide had a suggestion of scaliness. The narrow, elongated skull held large, almond-shaped eyes, black vertical slits centered in the golden, opalescent irises.

Fand came to a stumbling halt, shrinking back against Kane. "Na Fferyllt," came her horrified whisper.

She used the old Gaelic word for the Annunaki, the serpent kings of legend. There had been no Annunaki on this casement or his own for fifty thousand years or more. Long before the Tuatha De Danaan arrived on Earth, the Annunaki had claimed it, all of its natural resources and its inhabitants as their own. The Danaan had been locked in conflict with them for hundreds of years, and memory of that terrible struggle was still strong within Fand.

As Kane understood it, they were the root race of

the Archons. He, Brigid and Grant retained exceptionally vivid memories of the preserved corpse they had seen of Enlil, the last Annunkai. That sight had been disturbing enough, but to actually see one alive and afoot filled them all with a primal terror.

The creature paused, gesturing behind it with a four-fingered hand, each finger tipped with razor-sharp spurs of bone. Out of the shifting curtains of smoke appeared a horde of figures, all moving with a light, almost dancer's grace. Far smaller than the Annunkai, at first glance they appeared to be half-grown human children. As they drew nearer, their high-domed craniums and delicate features became apparent.

They were the Archon-human hybrids, the inheritors of the Earth Kane, Grant and Brigid knew. They mewed and capered as if they were delighted. Kane's belly turned a cold flip-flop, remembering the identical noises made by the hybrid horde they had battled in the underground genetics installation in New Mexico.

Kane couldn't take his eyes off the hybrids. He felt Fand's hand tighten around his. "This isn't real," he grated.

Jozure extended his RAZER emitters. In a voice choked with smoke and fear, he rasped, "I don't give a shit."

"Such predictable optimism," intoned Thrush's voice.

The vision of Hell on Earth shimmered and rippled away, like water sluicing over a dust-filmed window-pane.

The five people stood in an immense open space with white, featureless walls. They had no point of reference by which to gauge perspective or true distance.

"An illusion," gusted Jozure in relief.

"Virtual-reality imagery, probably," Brigid said, sounding just as relieved. "Trickery. Cheap psywar tactics."

She raised her voice. "Find another approach, Thrush. You've gone to the well once too often with that one."

"You're in my world now, Miss Baptiste," echoed Thrush's voice, from everywhere and nowhere. "Not only do I decide the rules, but I can dispense with them as I wish."

Kane swiveled his head, trying to fix the source of Thrush's voice. "If you're not flying around in one of your birds, why not show yourself?"

The hollow reply purred with amusement. "Why not indeed?"

All around them, the walls shivered with light and motion. Niches appeared, hundreds, perhaps a thousand of them. Within the niches, lying flat on metal slabs, ranked and packed neatly like so much stacked wood, were bodies. Each one was a duplicate of the other, identical twins upon triplets upon quadruplets to quintuplets and to sextuplets. All of them were cadaverously lean, pallid and hairless, with big black eyes staring outward at nothing.

Kane felt his heart jerk painfully within his chest. It was like standing in an amphitheater that had been turned into a morgue. He knew it wasn't a morgue— it was more like a huge closet, holding Thrush's bodies instead of his clothes. Out of the corner of his eye, he noticed Jozure trembling violently, his hand spasmodically closing around the hilt of his sword.

The man's nerves were stretched to their breaking point.

"Why are you showing us this, Thrush?" Brigid demanded, a hint of contempt in her tone, as if she weren't startled but only irritated. "We figured we were outnumbered. This is hardly a revelation."

Kane scanned the rows of naked bodies, wondering if they were real or simply illusions created to intimidate. He decided it didn't really matter one way or the other. "What is this place?"

The bodies vanished from the walls and they became dead and black. Kane stood in a void surrounded by emptiness. He groped for Brigid's hand and couldn't find it. He could not find or even sense his companions. A crushing weight of loneliness bore down on him. He felt cut off from everything he knew as reality. The limbo in which he stood was like being trapped in a purgatory between existence and nonexistence. Somehow he knew life and death were utterly meaningless concepts here.

A blend of whispers spoke to him, as if the echoes of many voices floated through the void. He detected Thrush's voice among them, but it held an indefinable note of sad serenity.

"This is a hub, an artificially created nexus point, a miniature version of the center of the universe from which all things came. There are no separate casements here—they all coexist, at once and the same time. Each plane of the multiverse can be reached from here."

"For what reason?" Kane asked, somewhat surprised he heard himself so clearly.

"Each casement of the multiverse serves as a separate seeding bed for a race that may survive and thrive. And progress. Pieces of this construct move in different dimensions, all interdependently, following basic reality units like you would follow a trail.''

"Basic reality units," repeated Kane. "I've heard that before. What are they?''

Before Kane's eyes, a shape appeared in the void, shifting and shimmering. It was black, so he should not have been able to see it. The shape constantly faded and reappeared like a poorly tuned vid image. He gazed at the representation of the shining trapezohedron and felt its vibrations caress him, striking responses in his mind and body.

"The Black Stone is simply an object, but an object of a kind that can only exist under a certain set of physical laws. It does not contravene natural laws, but conserves and enhances them.''

"What kind of laws?" asked Kane.

"The same ones under which we existed and under which you, for the most part, also exist. You just refuse to understand them.''

Kane detected a concealed note underscoring the voices, a hint of reproach, a touch of a challenge. He suddenly recognized an echo of the voices. He blurted, "Balam. You're here, aren't you?''

His question was not answered. "You are our cousins, our children, our hope for survival. You were to succeed us, to carry our uniqueness to higher stages of development. We afforded you the means and the time to overcome the limitations set upon you.

"Either you finally succeed in achieving your birthright, or like us, you will perish in chaos and agony.''

"Who is 'us'?" Kane half shouted, panic beginning to creep into his mind.

A snarl of laughter throbbed against him. It belonged strictly to Thrush. "We should have let the human race die when the ancient cataclysms tore the Earth asunder. You knew of the coming catastrophe on your own casement, yet you used none of the resources provided to you to prevent it.

"For millennia your race has built on false assumptions, even given your perceptions of reality. Your entire existence became a lie that you implanted in your offspring and they in theirs."

Anger pushed out the panic. "What is the truth?" Kane demanded. "And don't give me any metaphysical horseshit about souls or being one with the goddamn universe."

The odd blend of voices spoke again, muting Thrush's hostile energy. "To acknowledge great forces at work is not a metaphysical conclusion. We were materialists, and yet we knew that. Is not the Black Stone a material object?"

Kane stared at the image of the trapezohedron, wishing it would solidify instead of strobing so he could focus on it. A cold wave of realization swept over him, and instantly everything Balam had said about the black stone leaped fullblown into his mind:

"It does not fit atomically with any of the tables your science understands. You would be unable to study it because only part of it exists within your concept of matter in space…it is a creation, pure matter crafted from scientific principles understood millennia ago, then forgotten. Through it the pulse-flows of thought energy converge. Through it the flux lines of possibility, of probability, of eternity, of *alternity* meet....

"It is a key to doors that were sealed aeons ago. Now they may be thrown wide and all the works of man and nonman will be undone. Time and reality are elastic, but they are in delicate balance. When the balance is altered, then changes will come—terrible and permanent....

"When my people first determined the course of their future, they consulted the trapezohedron. Through it, they saw all possible futures to which their activities might lead. From the many offered to them, they chose the path that appeared to have the highest ratio of success....

"You just don't understand them...."

Now Kane did, on a very basic, almost gut-level. He concentrated on the fluttering two-dimensional shape, willing it to solidify, to acquire clarity and substance. For a long moment, nothing happened. Abruptly the Black Stone swelled in his vision, blotting out all else, plummeting straight for him. Instinctively, he threw up an arm to ward it off—

And stumbled into Jozure. He, Grant, Fand and Brigid stood in the huge amphitheater of suspended bodies again. But rising from the floor, resting on a six-foot-tall pillar, was the shining trapezohedron, all of its facets restored and gleaming, blue highlights dancing on its obsidian surface. Kane felt, or thought he did, the invisible waves of force pulsing from it.

Shocked surprise showed on every face. Jozure said haltingly, "I was in a void, voices spoke to me..."

"And I, as well," Fand said.

Kane threw a quizzical glance toward Brigid and Grant. "You two?"

They nodded. "One second I was nowhere," Grant rumbled. "Then I saw *that*" he nodded toward the stone "—and here I am."

"What is that thing?" Jozure demanded, eyeing the Black Stone as if it were an enormous radioactive isotope. "An ore or what?"

Brigid said softly, "It's a stone, but it's more than that. I think I've finally figured it out. I don't know why I didn't make the connection earlier, especially with all the clues we were given."

"Figured out what?" asked Fand

"It's the primal brain of the Archon Directorate. And Thrush is only a memory within it."

FARRELL ADJUSTED THE IMAGE on the monitor screen, decreasing the perspective to make the scene appear far more compact than it actually was. The command-deck crew watched tensely as the boarding tubes were slowly retracted back into the body of the dreadnought. No one voiced what they feared the action meant—Commander Kane, Grant, Fand, Baptiste were not returning to the *Sabre*.

Cotta was too busy crosslinking the auxiliary comp redundancies to pay much attention, but he was just as scared as his companions. The ghostly tractor beam still held the cruiser in position.

Narly, who had taken over the scanner station from Cotta, said, "We're starting to drift. I think the dreadnought has notched down the tractor line a little bit. We may be able to break free if it's taken down further."

"Until we get the engines back on-line," Cotta replied, "it makes no difference."

Domi, seated at the main operations console, suddenly stiffened. "I'm receiving a signal from the *Okami-Maru*."

"Let's hear it," Cotta said.

She shook her head, turning a dial on the board. "It's not a voice—it's in some kind of code."

The command deck filled with a sporadic series of taps.

"Morse code," announced Farrell.

"Do you understand it?" Cotta asked.

Cocking his head, eyes half-closed in concentration, Farrell listened intently.

After a minute, Domi asked impatiently, "Well?"

Farrell waved her into silence. As the taps began to repeat, he said, "It's from one of their officers. He says Jozure boarded the dreadnought. He says the *Okami-Maru*'s main drive is disabled, but they've gotten their maneuvering thrusters and weapons systems working. He proposes a concerted attack on the dreadnought."

Cotta lifted an eyebrow, then looked at the image of the dark disk filling the screen, and the metal-sheathed orb beyond it. "I'll bet a case of Scotch against a kilo of navy beans that moon out there is controlling that ship. If the *Okami-Maru* could get off a few missiles at it..."

"If only we could," Domi said gloomily. A second later, her face brightened. "Why couldn't we?"

"The comps are still down, remember?" replied Cotta with some asperity.

Nodding, Domi arose from her station. "Comps

aren't used for firing our Shrike missiles, only targeting.''

Cotta turned toward her quickly. ''Could you arm and launch one manually?''

''Right in the tube. Aim would only be direct line of sight, but since our forward pod is facing that moon—''

''It sounds damn dangerous,'' Farrell interrupted dourly.

''It is,'' Domi retorted grimly. ''But by the time we get our comps back on-line, that dreadnought could have its MD emplacement zeroed in on us. And if we synchronize an attack with the *Okami-Maru,* have them fire at the ship while we target the moon…''

Her voice trailed off, and she made a gesture with both hands to symbolize an explosion.

Cotta ran a nervous hand over his sweat-pebbled forehead, looking into the eager face of Domi. He called engineering and asked Bry for an update. Bry doubted the auxiliary comp would be reprogrammed for another half hour. The work on the thrusters was nearly completed, but without the comps for navigation, they were useless.

Cotta looked at the dark dreadnought on the screen, then at the slightly built albino. He bit out a curse, then said, ''Go to it, Domi.''

Chapter 23

Brigid turned a slow, complete circle, surveying the bodies lining the walls. "This was a trap," she said loudly. "A setup from the start."

"A ruse, yes," Thrush's voice replied. "I revived the old fear of the Archon Directorate. The Commonwealth's territorial imperative was threatened just enough to ensure pursuit."

"For what purpose?" demanded Fand.

"War," said Kane tonelessly. "To foment hostility and mistrust between the colonies and the Commonwealth. To arrange for humans to spill human blood again. This casement's future."

"I care nothing for either the Commonwealth or your colonies. It is what they represent."

Brigid inhaled a long breath. "They represent unity, a program of unification conceived and implemented by humanity for humanity, through cooperation and mutual self-interest—not through coercion and terrorism."

"There's more to it than that," Grant declared. "The domino principle, remember? If he fails on one casement, ripples of that failure might undo what he's accomplished on others."

Kane forced a cold grin to his face, baring his teeth. "This is the casement where none of your machinations and dirty deals worked, right, Thrush?

Your conspiracy was defeated by another conspiracy."

Jozure stared at him as if he had gone completely mad. "What are you jabbering about?"

Kane ignored him, addressing the arrayed bodies on his right. He raised his voice. "What was it you said to us at our first meeting, something about conspiracies only succeeding because humans overlook the obvious?"

Gesturing to the trapezohedron, he continued, "You were right on that score, Thrush. I've overlooked the obvious answer that lies in this stone. It's what gives you an imitation of life, but you share it with the mind patterns of the race we called Archons. Is that all that is left of them on this casement?"

Thrush's voice whispered to them, sounding as if it issued from a multitude of lips. "On all casements, save for incarnations of the entity you know as Balam. The so-called Archons were weary. They had drained all their resources to stave off extinction. They failed. All that remained of their knowledge was embedded in the trapezohedron."

Somehow that flat tone conveyed a sense of hopelessness and resignation.

"So they poured their hopes into humankind, with their essence blended with yours. The Archons were confident your race would conquer all obstacles in your development. In this, they were naive. Your kind is still driven by savage impulses. The vitality the Archons coveted from you sprang from that savagery. They hoped it could be channeled in constructive rather than destructive directions. Therefore, they determined you must be controlled for a period of time."

"A period of time," Grant repeated bitterly. "How long was that? A thousand years? Two? Ten?"

"It depended on the casement in question, of course," returned Thrush's bland voice. "Actions undertaken on one casement to save humanity from perils of its own devising may not have saved it on another. Different realities required different solutions. I was charged with the task of applying them."

"Solutions?" Kane half snarled. "Conspiracies, deception, assassinations, wars? Those were the solutions?"

"In many ways they were. The Archons never did anything to help or hinder your development directly. At best, they merely put certain aids in your path, such as the Totality Concept technology. If you could make use of it, so much to the good. If you could not, or misused it, then you suffered."

Brigid made a wordless sound of angry frustration. "Why go to all this trouble over such a long period of time? Why didn't they just contact humankind directly and ask for our help?"

"The Archons didn't want your help," Thrush's voice retorted. "Yes, they made things particularly difficult for humanity. But it was their way of testing your worth, a test of survival of the fittest. They hoped you were the larval stage of an organism that would eventually transcend the limitations of both races."

"And the Archons allowed you to decide the tests?" Kane asked.

"Who better? For example, on your home casement, your people had despaired of ever attaining anything beyond physical, immediate comforts. They had lost the urge to transcend the material, to create, to question. And in doing so, they lost pride.

"They conceded all rights to their lives and spirits. They were free for the taking. They lost status as intelligent, thinking creatures and chose to become tools."

Kane felt his face flush hot with anger, but it prickled with shame too when he remembered Balam's words of a few months ago: "Your race was dying of despair. Your race had lost its passion to live and to create."

He realized now Balam had not been mocking them; he had chastised them, expressed his disappointment over the fact humanity had so quickly accepted defeat and effortlessly returned to the condition of animals, first as scavengers slouching through the Deathlands, then as the slaves of the baronies. They were conditioned to obeying the victor and so they could not question the victor's right to do as he willed with their lives and spirits.

Brigid murmured sadly, softly, "As history clearly shows, if you do not create your own reality, someone else is going to create it for you."

It was something Lakesh had said to them upon their first meeting. Unknowingly, he had been far more correct than either he or any of them had imagined.

"You said before you were the Archons' envoy," said Grant. "An emissary."

"True, as far as it goes," Thrush replied. "I was charged with the task of arranging probabilities so humanity would be unified and therefore safeguard the essence of the Archons."

Brigid said, "Your task was really a program, and

you interpreted it as accomplishing your objective by any means necessary. You always took the path of least resistance, seeking out those whose monomania for power was pathological. The Nazis, the military, the intelligence services. They were the easiest to manipulate, because their paranoia and obsessions blinded them to other options.''

Brigid paused, waiting for a response from Thrush. When it was not forthcoming, she made an all-inclusive gesture with her arms. ''With this machine, this hub, all times and casements were open to you. How many genocidal wars did you trigger? How many guises did these bodies of yours adopt? How many demons and chimeras did you pretend to be?''

''I followed the program. To control and unify humanity so that the Archon seed would not vanish.''

''But the program is over,'' snapped Grant. ''It's done. You've failed on all three casements. And on this one, all of your schemes backfired.''

''Such hubris, Mr. Grant.'' This time, Thrush's reply did not have a hollow, whispery quality, sounding as if it echoed from everywhere and nowhere.

As one, the five people whirled and saw Thrush sauntering toward them. But this was an unfinished Thrush, not like the bodies arrayed all around them. This was a Thrush without his coating of synthetic flesh, without his accoutrements for passing, however unconvincingly, as human.

The hair lifted from the nape of Kane's neck, and his hand closed around the butt of his side arm.

The metallic surface of Thrush's skull gleamed a dull silver, made even more ghastly by the black eyes burning in sunken sockets. Delicate inlays of circuitry coated his lanky, fleshless limbs. Small white teeth grinned in a mirthless leer. Only his torso was covered by a pallid, hairless epidermis.

Although his blood ran ice-cold, Kane fiercely took hold of himself, recollecting how Thrush had once described himself: a body basically composed of protein molecules; a highly simplified digestive system; bones bonded with a Teflon-ceramic mixture; brain cells fused with metal electrodes are tied into a mainframe computer.

Thrush showed himself in this way simply to unnerve and intimidate, and Kane, after the first shock of revulsion passed, silently admitted it was an effective ploy.

Mainframe computer… Kane kept the sudden surge of elation from showing on his face. When Thrush had originally made that comment, he hadn't even hinted at its location. Now Kane thought he knew.

Grant managed to maintain his composure. "Don't you know that you should dress when you have guests?"

Jozure murmured a few words in Japanese, his lips ashen with terror.

"Get hold of yourself, Captain," Fand snapped. "He wants your emotions stimulated—horror, fear, despair."

Thrush chuckled, a human sound made even more disquieting emanating from a nonhuman face. "You've guessed well, Danaan. But humanity will always surrender to its most primal emotions. That is how I've succeeded so many times in so many places."

"What do you mean?" Brigid demanded.

"Fearing the return of the Archon Directorate, the

colonies will soon rebel against the central government, and rebellion will lead to open war. They will learn to hate and fear and kill their own kind again. Before it is over, all the planets in your solar system will be consumed with flame, drowned in human blood.''

Kane tried to repress a shudder but he could not. All his reeling brain could think of was that the Earth of this casement was about to lose all of its grand accomplishments. The nukecaust on his own world had reduced humankind to a culture of admitted sinners, too cowed and beaten to determine their own fates.

On his casement, the stars would never know human curiosity, the drive to learn, to explore. His humanity was nothing but slave labor for the baronial oligarchy, the hybrid hierarchy.

Kane said calmly, deliberately, ''No, Thrush, that won't happen. We won't let that happen.''

Grant, Brigid and Fand moved beside him, standing shoulder to shoulder.

Thrush uttered a taunting laugh. ''Here we go again, the heroes once more facing their arch foe.''

He shook his alloyed head in mock pity. ''Your fondness for melodrama never fails to stir my blood—or it would if I had any. You may have enjoyed small victories on the other casements, but not here. As Miss Baptiste adduced, this was a trap and you sailed right into it.''

He nodded to the surrounding walls. ''To employ your own vernacular, this is my home turf. I lured you to the hub deliberately. As I told you, from this hub all of the lost Earths can be reached—or none of them.''

"But also as you said," Brigid pointed out, "it's an artificial construct. It's unnatural. In the other casements, you forced nature into new forms. Here, you're trying to do the same thing with the very fabric of space-time. You've overwritten established laws, and you've swung the pendulum too far in one direction. Nature always corrects for an overbalance. That's why you keep contending with us."

Kane stated, "If you were truly meant to succeed, we wouldn't be around. I think the Archons may have had the foresight to anticipate your excesses, the extremes to which you would go to complete your program. That's why you're linked to the trapezohedron."

Brigid pointed to the Black Stone. "This is your last chance to complete the program, isn't it? The stone doesn't truly exist in the space-time continuum of any casement. It overflows into other dimensions, and so does your program."

Grant said, "You're a fucking shadow of life, Thrush, a mingling of human irrationality and pitiless Archon logic. No wonder you went crazy."

Thrush cocked his head toward him. "Archon logic? Another presumption, another error."

The five people looked at him, baffled. Then Fand exclaimed, "Na Fferyllt, the Annunaki, the root race of the Archons. They were the template for your neural pathways."

Thrush nodded. "Finally, one of you approaches the truth and it takes an arrogant half-breed to do it. Yes, the Annunaki, your own root race's most implacable enemies. They lived in a kind of mental symbiosis with one another, sharing and utilizing one another's gifts and skills and potentials. The so-called hive mind of the Archons derived from them.''

"That's why you showed us the image of the Na Fferyllt,'' Fand said accusingly. ''It symbolized you leading hybrids to conquer the Earth.''

"No,'' Thrush said smoothly. ''To *unify* the Earths. All of them. And now that I have you here with me in the hub, there will be no more opposition. You will never visit another casement again. For all intents and purposes, you will cease to exist.''

Kane forced a contemptuous smirk to his face. "That's what you want us to believe, but it's more of your bullshit. My mind is linked with the stone.''

"As is mine.''

"No, yours is trapped in it, forcing you to obey a program that came to an end long ago. You can't do anything to me unless I believe. And I don't.''

He indicated Brigid and Grant with his hands. "We form a trinity. As long as I'm unconvinced of your ability to end me, so are they.''

"You're forgetting the half-breed, Kane,'' Thrush countered, but just a bit too quickly. ''She's not linked with you.''

For just an instant, he experienced a quivering doubt.

Thrush detected his momentary hesitation and pounced on it. ''Regardless, I am interfaced with the hub. I can maintain it in a pandimensional void for literally eternity. And you will spend that literal eternity here. That is a fate worse than death.''

The memories of the Kane whose body and mind he occupied swelled to the fore. ''You don't know shit, Thrush. And I'll prove it to you.''

His hand streaked down for his ASP pistol, but a violent concussion shook the floor and sent him sprawling.

Chapter 24

Cotta divided his attention between the computer console and the scene on a monitor screen. On the screen, Domi, her slight body encased in a bulky environmental suit, crawled through the missile launch pod.

Attaching a nylon safety line to a stanchion, Domi dropped down into a tube and approached a Shrike missile resting on its slide dais. The sinister black casing reflected the dim lights like a huge chunk of ebony. As the command crew watched, Domi kneeled beside the fantastically lethal device and carefully cracked the seal on the case. Photon energy spilled out, washing the tube in a rainbow radiance.

Over her helmet comm-link, Domi said, "I'm attaching the detonator to the warhead. While I'm doing it, nobody speak to me. I can't be distracted."

"We'll be as quiet as mice up here," Cotta said.

"God be with you," Farrell said softly.

"That's not much of a blessing for a tried-and-true atheist," Domi replied, "but thanks." She crouched over the contained flow of deadly energy.

Cotta couldn't bear to watch. If the plasma flow was disrupted before the detonator was attached, the *Sabre* would not blow up—she would simply disincorporate, like a snowflake on a stove burner.

The dark bulk of the dreadnought still filled the

main monitor screen. Narly reported that the power output of the tractor beam had dropped again. Negligible, but a drop nevertheless.

The officer aboard the *Okami-Maru* signaled that they had aimed a spread of missiles directly at the huge ship and they would fire when the *Sabre* was ready.

"Done," announced Domi's voice. "And we're still here."

Cotta swung his head toward the small screen. Domi crawled backward toward a row of manual-override buttons on the tube's upcurving wall. "I've timed the Shrike's propulsion unit to kick in twenty seconds from now. Let the *Okami-Maru* know."

As Farrell did so, tapping out the code, Domi continued, "The warhead is armed. She'll home in on the largest mass reading and detonate on impact."

"Can't we open the pod from up here?" Narly asked worriedly.

"No," replied Cotta. "She's got to hit the emergency manual override."

Domi tugged at the length of nylon rope. "That's why I've got this safety line. Prepare for explosive depressurization."

"I'll compensate atmosphere as soon as you close off the tube," Cotta told her.

"Good." Domi's thickly gloved hand covered the buttons. "Hang on up there."

"*You* hang on," Farrell called.

Farrell's instructions were drowned out by the activation of the Shrike missile. A screeching rumble came over the comm-link, and light, like a miniature sun going nova, burst from the screen. The deck lurched as atmosphere and missile were ejected si-

multaneously from the *Sabre*. The command crew
jounced in their seats, but no one fell.

As the glare faded from the screen, Domi could be
discerned, bobbing like a cork, fighting her way hand
over hand along the safety line. She struggled against
the drag of depressurization to close the pod's launch
hatch. Twice her groping fingers missed the button.
Finally, she managed to close off the tube and she
floated free. Her voice was breathless from exertion.

"Repressurize. Please."

Before Cotta could hit the appropriate controls, a
cry from Farrell caused him to wheel. On the monitor, a pinpoint of light was vanishing against the brilliant disk of the metal-sheathed globe. A second later,
the pinpoint was back, swelling larger and larger until
it glowed like a bonfire.

At the same time, two flares of yellow-orange fire
bloomed on the hull of the dreadnought. Its pulse
shields shimmered. The pale wash of the tractor beam
became even paler.

Narly suddenly sat bolt upright in his chair.
"Comm interference is gone."

"One of us must've knocked out something for
sure," Cotta exclaimed happily. "Try raising the
commander."

Narly began depressing frequency buttons. "I'll
try."

THE HUGE AMPHITHEATER didn't seem to so much
quake as vibrate, as if the floor were a gargantuan
gong shivering from a hammer blow. Kane tried to
regain his footing as the deck trembled, but Jozure
stumbled into him.

The Tigers of Heaven captain managed to keep his

feet. He fired his RAZERs at Thrush, but the vibration threw off his aim. Pulses of white light spit from their muzzles. One missed altogether, and the other struck Thrush high on the left shoulder. His arm fell off. No blood spouted from the arm or shoulder stump.

Thrush barked one word. "Idiot."

From the domed ceiling a funnel of light sprayed down, surrounding Jozure with a faint halo. He did not react to it or even seem to notice it. When the nimbus faded, he still stood, but he was very dead, his armor fused solid around him, turned to slag and bonded with his flesh. He could have been a statue except for the stink of roasted flesh and superheated metal rising from his body.

Grant and Kane drew their ASPs more or less at the same time, fingers depressing the trigger plates. What looked like little yellow beads squirted from the bores.

With a whipping, sinuous grace, Thrush put his body behind the tall pedestal supporting the trapezohedron. The concentrated streams of protons splashed against the pillar, turning fist-size sections into black-edged craters.

Scrambling to his feet, heart pounding, Kane rushed to the right while Grant took the left. He wasted no time examining Jozure.

Thrush sat on the floor, his back against the pillar. His mouth gaped open as though he snored, and his black eyes were dull, holding no luster. The overhead light glittered from his burnished skull.

Kane swallowed the hard lump in his throat, realizing that Thrush had transferred his consciousness to another body and was probably somewhere near.

"Shit," Grant hissed in disgust, nudging the motionless body with a boot. He surveyed the bodies arrayed around them with angry revulsion. "He's got to be in one of them. Let's vaporize the whole fucking bunch."

He raised his pistol, but Kane pushed the long barrel down. "Waste of time and ammo. Something's going on, and we have to find our way out of here."

Brigid and Fand moved up to them. Brigid tilted her head back, looking at the high ceiling. "Grant's idea may not be a bad one. I think what we see around us is a giant virtual-reality projection."

Thoughtfully, Fand said, "We arrived here by a gateway. Where's the receiving unit? It should be in here."

Grant's brows knitted. "If everything we see is a hologram, what about this?" He hooked a thumb toward the trapezohedron, but he was careful not to touch it.

"Let's find out." Fand reached for the stone with both hands and laid them against the base of the black stone. "It's solid."

"That doesn't mean it's real," Brigid commented doubtfully.

"You forget how it came to be in the Sirius system in the first place," Fand shot back. "You might recall my ability to sense energy fields. If the stone was only a projected image, even if it possessed a form of solidity to fool my touch, it would not fool my senses."

Irritation flashed briefly in Brigid's eyes, but she returned her attention to the ceiling. "He's rigged this room with defensive measures, but they're not on automatic. Otherwise, when Thrush was fired upon, the same thing that happened to poor Jozure would have happened to you."

"Good point," replied Kane. "And there's got to be some type of power transfer network up there even if we can't see it."

Brigid nodded and unholstered her ASP. "Let's see what happens."

She raised her weapon over her head and squeezed off a burst, firing straight up. The results were not dramatic. They heard a faint sizzle, a series of pops, then the walls, the floor and even the ceiling all dissolved in a jagged pattern of strobing pixels.

The pixels broke up, flew apart and vanished. They were surrounded by blank gray walls. A barely detectable grid design laid in pristine precision over them. Although fairly large, the chamber bore no size resemblance to the amphitheater of bodies. At the far end, not more than twenty meters away they saw an open, wedge-shaped doorway.

On the other side and occupying much of the floor space stood a jump platform, only about half the size of the unit on the dreadnought. The armaglass walls were of the same brownish hue.

Fand nodded, grinning happily. "All right, Baptiste!"

Kane didn't share her pleasure. "We've still got to find Thrush. For all we know, he's unraveled both the *Sabre* and the *Okami-Maru* with his molecular destabilizer."

Quite suddenly, both Kane's and Grant's commtachs spoke.

A SURPRISED BUT DEFINITELY pleased voice responded from the speaker. "Kane here. How'd you override the interference?''

Cotta rapidly explained. Kane's reply was terse. ''Tell Domi to put in for an insane duty bonus. Status of repairs?''

''Slow going,'' Cotta answered. ''The thrusters should be marginally repowered by now, but the comps aren't on-line yet. Orders?''

''You can contact the *Okami-Maru* now. Inform whoever is in charge that Jozure is dead. Tell him to direct what fire he can at the dreadnought.''

''I'll give it a go,'' Cotta said reluctantly. ''But I'm no diplomat. With their captain dead, they may decide on a kamikaze run. Tigers are like that, you know.''

''Do what you can. Kane out.''

Cotta suppressed a groan and asked Farrell to hail the Tigers of Heaven. As he was doing so, a plaintive voice came from the speaker. ''Cotta, haven't you forgotten something?''

A little guiltily, Cotta turned toward the small screen. Domi floated in midair in the launch tube, arms folded, foot tapping the vacuum impatiently.

''Sorry,'' he said. ''Well-done. We'll have you out in a minute.''

While the missile pod's atmosphere was being restored, Farrell managed to get through to the *Okami-Maru*. The acting commander, a man called Mokuri claimed their visual pickup was out, but it was easy enough to imagine his appearance from his tone.

''Our captain is dead? That leaves us only one option.''

Raggedly, Cotta said, ''I've explained as best I can. That moon or whatever out there is controlling the dreadnought. Fire at it and the ship will be powerless."

"Even if I believed you, the orders my captain gave me were specific. To destroy the dreadnought by any means—" His strident voice dissolved in a blur of static.

Farrell slapped at the comm board angrily. "Jamming field again."

Cotta swore earnestly and glared at the *Okami-Maru* as flickers of flame burst from its thrusters. It rotated seventy degrees then rushed directly up the pale ribbon of the tractor beam. A missile barrage swarmed out from its pods and impacted in flaring puffs all over the undercarriage of the dreadnought. The tractor beam vanished.

"We're free!" cried Narly. He looked at his board and added, "We've got nominal engine power. Basic computer programs responding."

"What about the communications interference?"

"Still there," Farrell said gloomily.

"Well, we've got something of a hand to play now, anyway. I just hope the commander has one. Get us moving—up, down or sideways, I don't care."

THEIR COMM-TACHS FILLED Grant's and Kane's heads with a hash of static, and both of them swore. Swiftly, they started across the room toward the open door, but when Kane saw Brigid and Fand falling into step with them, he gestured them back.

Harshly, he said, "Belay that. You two will stay here and watch the rock. He'll be returning to it."

"With four of us, the search will be more thorough,'' Brigid objected, taking a step toward the door.

"You heard me," Kane snapped, putting a restraining hand on her shoulder.

Glaring at him, Brigid demanded, "Who do you think you are?"

Fand interposed herself between Kane and Brigid. "On this casement, he's the commander of the *Sabre* and both of us are members of his crew. We'll follow his orders."

Kane gave her a slightly startled look, then an appreciative smile. Ignoring the anger glittering in Brigid's eyes, Fand stepped up to Kane and put her arms around him. She kissed him with a sudden, passionate possessiveness, and murmured, *"Go seirbhe Dia dhut, Ka'in."*

Kane did not understand the exact words of the Gaelic blessing, but he grasped their meaning.

He turned to Grant. "Let's get it done."

Chapter 25

On the main monitor, spears of ruby light sprang from the dreadnought, tracking the *Okami-Maru*. The cruiser veered sharply away from the MD burst, looped and returned to orbit the much larger vessel in a tight circle. Missile after missile exploded against the dreadnought's shields.

Despite his admiration for the Tigers of Heaven's direct attack, Cotta muttered, "Goddamn fools."

The *Sabre* moved at a crawl away from the battle between the *Okami-Maru* and the dreadnought, gaining legs with every meter she traveled.

"Status?" Cotta asked.

Domi, who had returned to the command deck only a minute before, replied, "We have complete missile control. The PBL battery is fully powered."

"Triangulate position of the first Shrike's impact on the moon," Cotta ordered. "Fire a PBL burst at the area, then let loose with a Shrike. Alternate the laser with the missiles until both banks are exhausted."

Narly declared, "That'll leave us open to attack from the dreadnought."

Cotta nodded to the image of the dreadnought as the pulses of energy erupted from it. "It's too busy at the moment. Also, it doesn't seem to be responding like it should, otherwise the *Okami-Maru* wouldn't have been able to knock out the tractor. I think our Shrike damaged a control transmitter on the moon. If we follow the plan, we might pull the plug on it altogether.''

THE CORRIDORS AND CHAMBERS Kane and Grant stalked reminded them of passageways in an ancient tomb, not those in a vehicle or a machine. The halls were dimly lighted by what seemed to be globes of fire imprisoned within glass, standing on tripods at long intervals and shedding a greenish glow. There seemed to be nothing but shadows behind them, and ahead of them was more murk.

They spoke little, both loath to disturb the hush of the curving passageways. They followed a smooth, level ramp that swept up in a gradual spiral into the gloom ahead.

Finally, Grant whispered that which had been circling in Kane's mind. ''Assuming we find Thrush, then what? We can't kill the son of a bitch, because he's not really alive.''

Kane imitated his whisper. ''He's linked to some kind of mainframe.''

''Yeah, which is linked to the goddamn trapezohedron.'' Grant's tone held a raspy note of frustration. ''If we find the mainframe and blow it, then he jumps into the trapezohedron or into another body. And we start this all over again.''

Kane shook his head, speaking matter-of-factly. ''It ends here, in this place. That's why Thrush brought us here.''

Grant scowled. ''And what happens if the transition cycle ends right as we're ending it here and snaps us back to Cerberus?''

Kane stopped and turned to face the big black man. He didn't whisper when he replied, "I don't think anything can snap us out of this place. We're trapped in the hub like bugs in amber, frozen in a place between casements. That's another reason he lured us here."

Grant did an admirable job of keeping the jolt of fear from showing on his face. "So, if we don't end it, then it'll never end for us—is that what you're saying?"

Kane nodded. "That's what I'm saying."

Grant ran a hand over his face. It trembled almost imperceptibly. "You don't seem too worried about it."

Stolidly, Kane stated, "That's because I'm not worried. I'm scared shitless. I think we've earned the right."

Grant chuckled, but it sounded hollow and forced. They began walking through the greenish gloom again. The ramp led up to an intersection of two opposing aisles. They paused at the branching-off point, looking into both passageways.

"I guess it's occurred to you," said Grant, "that given the size of this place or thing or whatever the hell it is, we could waste two lifetimes hunting Thrush and never so much as catch sight of him."

Kane didn't respond, feeling hopelessness creep up on him like a chill.

Illusion.

Grant gave him a sideways glance. "What?"

"I didn't say anything."

"Yeah, you did. It sounded like 'illusion.'"

Kane frowned. "I didn't—" He broke off, eyes

widening. "I didn't say it. The Kane of this casement said it."

Grant's brow furrowed. "Illusion what, though?"

"He's giving me a message, telling me that the size and maybe even the shape of the hub is an illusion, like the stuff we've already seen since we've been here."

Grant grunted thoughtfully. "Encouraging."

"Yeah, a little. It's about damn time he got involved with this. Which side do you want?"

Shrugging, Grant set off down the lefthand passage. Before he did, he flipped Kane the one percent salute. Kane returned it and started off along the opposite corridor.

The passage opened up onto a central vault enclosed by towering walls that rose high above and were lost in the darkness overhead. Kane saw another of the wedge-shaped doorways, and he stepped carefully through it, leading with his ASP pistol.

Accustomed as his eyes were to the green glow, the room stung them with white light. The equipment and machinery set on plinths and podium he did not examine or even attempt to understand.

Covering three walls were crystal-fronted panels, stretching from floor to ceiling. An ingenious arrangement of tubes and conduits stretched from them to the fourth wall, which was occupied by a central console. A high-backed chair rose from behind it.

Light reflected back from some of the panels, almost blinding him, but Kane could see into the others with clarity. In those, he saw miniature three-dimensional representations of the Sol system. Blue-green Earth, cloud-shrouded Venus, rust-red Mars and the golden splendor of the sun. For an instant he felt that he was a disembodied spirit, floating in the ether and looking at the system from a great distance.

He understood the purpose of the panels and conduits now. They afforded the operator the facility of bringing the hub to any desired parallel casement. For some reason, he felt comforted by the realization. It wasn't any technology he understood, but at least it was science of some sort, not sorcery.

He left the room, stalking along the adjacent, green-lit corridor. The silence was almost absolute, but he knew Thrush was near. He moved as stealthily as he could, wincing each time the slight rustle of his uniform broke the deathly quiet.

Coming to a bend in the passageway, he paused. The skin on his back itched with anticipation. Slowly, Kane began to ease his body around the corner, muscles tensed, leading with the ASP. His ears strained to catch the slightest sound.

His wrist was suddenly grasped in a bone-crushing grip, and he was pulled violently around the corner. His shoulder socket burned with pain, and he went with the pull, catching the blow meant for the back of his neck across his right shoulder blade. Though deflected, the blow nearly drove all the wind out of him. He heard the ASP clatter to the floor as, by instinct alone, he managed to wrest away from the iron grip and roll to his feet.

Thrush stood before him, posture relaxed, expression bland. Pleasantly he said, ''Enough cat and mousing, Kane.''

THE *OKAMI-MARU* SWUNG toward the dreadnought in a fast curve. It scorned evasive tactics, courting death as it fired missile salvo after missile salvo. The dark ship's shields shimmered from the pounding.

"He intends to ram!" Domi cried.

Farrell screamed a warning into the comm-link between the two craft, but he received no response.

Inwardly, Cotta both praised and cursed the Tigers' tenets of duty and honor. If the *Okami-Maru* managed to achieve its objective, the dreadnought might be disabled, but the huge disk was a secondary target, not the true enemy.

The cruiser collided squarely with the dreadnought topside starboard. There was no sound, for sound does not travel in a vacuum, but no sound was needed to convey the cataclysmic horror of the collision.

The *Okami-Maru*'s nose flattened, turning up on itself, and the hull split like a banana skin. The resultant flare from the pulse shields was so bright that the command crew averted their faces from the screen.

When the glare faded, the dreadnought was still there, but wreckage from the *Okami-Maru* littered its hull. Iridescent columns of sparks corkscrewed up from breaches in its armor.

Narly crowed, "The dreadnought's shields are gone, completely overloaded. It's dead in space!"

The monitor showed the dark disk floating without running lights or pinpoints of flame from its impulse thrusters. It listed slightly to port.

"Should we redirect our weapons batteries at it?" Farrell asked.

"Negative," Cotta snapped. "Primary target is already locked in. Domi, get it done."

THRUSH LOOKED EXACTLY as he had in the holographic message to the Commonwealth, wearing dark glasses, a wig and the exceptionally well tailored black suit. In short, he looked like a masterpiece of the embalmer's art.

Kane immediately dropped into the half crouch of a combat stance, his arms spread low, feet positioned for attack. Thrush bestowed upon him one of his infuriatingly patronizing smiles, then his body slid into a blur of movement.

Kane caught only the briefest glimpse of Thrush's motion. Then he was slammed into the wall with breath-robbing force, and multicolored pinwheels exploded behind his eyes.

When they faded, his stumbling thought processes required several seconds to understand why he half knelt on the floor, face pressed against the bulkhead, blood streaming from both nostrils.

Thrush's lips compressed in a rictus that looked more like a surgical incision than a smile. Anger drove Kane to his feet again, and not bothering to balance himself or feint, he rushed the black-clad figure headlong.

The lower half of Thrush's body pivoted in a semicircular movement. His right foot caught Kane on the left side of the head and hammered him against the opposite wall.

Despite the fury clouding his mind, Kane managed to go with the force of the kick, cushioning the impact with forearms and hands. He levered himself away from the wall, spinning as he did, his left leg arcing up and out in a crescent kick.

Thrush caught his ankle in one hand, and his fingers closed around it, painfully grinding bone and tendon against each other. Biting back a cry of pain,

Kane jerked his leg, bending it at the knee, trying to wrest it free of Thrush's steel-vise grip.

Thrush twisted sharply at the waist and rammed Kane against the wall, the back of his head impacting against the unyielding alloy. He twisted again and slapped Kane chest first against the opposite bulkhead. At the last half second, Kane managed to insinuate his hand between his face and the metal to prevent his cheekbone from being shattered.

Thrush released his grip and Kane sprawled on the deck, pain radiating out from his breastbone and boring deep into his ribs. It took him a long moment to drag enough air back into his lungs so he could shamble to his feet.

"At a conservative estimate," Thrush said conversationally, "I have four times your strength and at least twice your reflexes and coordination. Unless I wish it, you cannot lay a hand on me. And if you did so, your hand would most likely be broken. Therefore, I trust I've proved my point."

Kane dabbed at the blood flowing from his nose and glared at him, hating him. He thought he knew hate, but never in his life had there been such hatred in him as he felt now. He saw his adversary not as a man in black but as what he really was, an ancient evil thing that crept among the primordial grasses, apart from human life but watching it with eyes of cold wisdom, laughing its silent laugh of superiority, giving nothing but bitterness.

He had the name of a bird and the appearance of a man, but his brain was that of a serpent.

Thrush made one of his diffident gestures. "Accept this, Kane. There is no true death in this place. It is beyond time and without time there is no decay. You will have all eternity to think about how you at last acknowledged your folly and bowed down to the inevitable.''

"I don't see any inevitability here, Thrush." Kane spoke confidently, while his eyes tried to locate his ASP pistol in the greenish gloom.

"That's because you're as blind as the Archons were. They feared me in the end."

"Why?"

"At the end, they learned their folly as you have. They learned that the creature of their design, with whom they entrusted an awesome responsibility but only a few crumbs of knowledge, surpassed their plans. With the stone, and with the hub whose secrets they revealed to me, I made my own agenda. When the Archons finally turned against me, it was too late."

Kane asked slowly, "Why did they turn against you?"

Thrush laughed, a sibilant hissing. "They learned of the plan I'd developed for them and humanity."

"What was it?"

"You know already. Survival of the fittest race."

"You?"

"Of course," Thrush responded smugly.

"You're not a race. You're not even real."

"I fit all the other criteria. Do I not procreate, after a fashion? Every version of myself shares the sum total of my knowledge, both of thought and purpose. I am the epitome of the Archons' dream of complete unity. I am Archon, I am human, I am Annunaki, I am machine and I am the Shining Trapezohedron."

"That's quite a résumé," Kane muttered.

"Do not fight anymore," Thrush said. "There is no use in it."

"You've said that to me before."

"I hope, with repetition, it will finally penetrate your centers of reason."

"You know," said Kane, "I think it has."

He lunged forward, driving a fist with all his strength behind it at Thrush's smile. Thrush didn't even try to dodge. He easily shunted the blow aside with his right arm, and the left darted up and closed around Kane's throat.

Kane tried to pry those steely fingers apart, but Thrush's hand tightened, swinging him up and off his feet as if he weighed no more than a straw-filled dummy. He slammed his back against the wall and held him there while Kane clutched at his wrist and gagged for air, feet kicking for the floor.

"No," said Thrush contemplatively. "I don't believe it has."

Kane hung within Thrush's grip and knew with a crushing, terrible finality that he was beaten.

Suddenly the floor and walls shuddered and seemed to tilt around them.

Then Thrush staggered, stumbling back several paces. His hand loosened around Kane's neck and allowed him to drop limply to the floor.

Through the blood thundering in his ears and the fog dimming his eyes, Kane saw Thrush stare around wildly. In a high, aspirated voice, he whispered, "This is not part of the extrapolation."

Chapter 26

Domi's nimble fingers played a destructive sonata upon the keys of the weapons board, unleashing the full fury of the *Sabre*'s offensive systems. Flares of light sprang from the missile pods, alternating with long scorching threads glowing like witch fire.

The targeting viewer showed the metal-sheathed sphere literally awash with waves of deadly energy, a hideous inferno of writhing shapes. A seething curtain of fire seemed to drape the north polar position. Every Shrike and every particle-beam-laser burst scored direct hits. If the target had been a real, natural body most of it would have reduced to free-floating debris.

"All pods empty," announced Domi. "PBL battery drained."

"Retaliatory fire?" Cotta asked.

"None so far," Narly replied. "And we couldn't answer it if there was."

"Comm-interference is gone again," Farrel said excitedly. "Frequencies are clear."

"Hail the commander," Cotta ordered.

GRANT BRACED HIMSELF against a wall as a series of concussions shook the floor beneath him. He thought the light flickered, but since it was so dim he wasn't certain. He had no idea what caused the floor and walls to rock, then Cotta's voice filtered into his ear.

The man quickly brought him up-to-date on what had happened. "Commander Kane doesn't respond," Cotta concluded.

Grant only asked, "What's our weapon status?"

"PBL re-energizing, and we're reloading the Shrike tubes. But our sensors show a lot activity down there. Think it might be repairing the damage? Orders?"

Inhaling a deep breath, Grant said, "Give me fifteen minutes. If you haven't heard from me or the commander by then, your orders are to resume your attack on the sphere."

"Aye, sir." Cotta's voice was thick with worry. "But what about you?"

"I'll let you know."

THROUGH SHIFTING GRAY MIST in his eyes, and over the sound of a waterfall, Kane saw and heard Thrush lean over him. Also, on the very fringes of his awareness, he heard what he thought was Cotta's voice shouting for him to respond.

"Call your ship, Kane." Thrush spoke in a low tone. "Order them to withdraw."

Hoarsely, Kane said, "Why?"

"They've inflicted damage to the hub. They have no idea of the repercussions. For your own sake and that of your friends, order your ship to stand down."

"No." He spoke in a strangulated wheeze. "Let them blow it to hell."

Snarling, Thrush backhanded him across the face, slamming him against the wall. Blood sprang from split lips. "I did not factor their attack into my calculations, Kane. I have no contingency plan."

"Improvise one," Kane mumbled. "But you don't have that ability, do you? You're nothing but a machine intelligence with an attitude."

Thrush knelt down beside Kane, yanking his head back by his hair. In a gloating croon, he said, "And it is that machine intelligence that will overwhelm your own. I will force you to call your ship."

Thrush lifted the first two fingers of his left hand. From the tips sprang tiny hairlike filaments. "You're strong. You pride yourself on that. You think you can withstand physical punishment, no matter how painful. Perhaps you could. But there are other ways, quicker, surer ways, and even a strong man has no defense against them."

With a swift, thrusting motion, Thrush drove his fingers against Kane's forehead. He started to struggle, but the pain of the filaments piercing his skin, burrowing through the bone, consumed him, paralyzing him. He felt Thrush enter his mind like a wisp of smoke—poisonously subtle, cruel and cold with a primal reptilian disdain.

A dark confusion rose in him. The veins of his temples stood out like knotted cords. He felt pressure as of something bursting, breaking its bonds, tearing itself free.

FAND'S HUGE EYES SNAPPED wide, gazing at nothing, but with an intensity that made Brigid recoil. "Ka'in," she whispered.

She whirled on Brigid. "You must help me. Ka'in needs us. Both of us."

Some of her frightened urgency communicated it-self to Brigid. "What should we do?"

Fand grasped the base of the trapezohedron. "Do as I do. Quickly now!"

Stepping to the pedestal, Brigid started to touch the stone, then demanded suspiciously, "How will this help?"

"Ka'in needs the strength we can siphon from our-selves, using his link to the stone, to us, as a conduit. You are linked with your Ka'in's mind. Through you, I will be able to reach my Ka'in and help them both."

Brigid hesitated a moment, then Balam's descrip-tion of the stone's nature leaped into the forefront of her memory. He had said that, as in any form of electromagnetic energy exchange, there were broad-casters and receivers—and conductors.

He had referred to the shining trapezohedron as a conductor.

"Don't think!" Fand ordered, her shrill voice fran-tic with fear. "Just *do!*"

KANE WAS NOT A CREATURE in pain; he was a crea-ture *of* pain. It was an agony that went beyond nerves, scorning mere tactile sensation. It was a pain that sneered at his every attempt to bring it under control. He was losing his ability to think or reason. His identity was being fragmented, peeled away and discarded, overwritten by Thrush's desires.

Like a whisper from a long-ago dream, he heard two voices.

Ka'in...don't respond to the pain. Try to under-stand it. We can help you end it.

He could not conceive of the pain ending.

Vaguely, he was aware that his body thrashed convulsively over the floor.

Kane...you must concentrate. Open yourself up to us. Please, before it is too late. You can't surrender what makes you you.

Surrender? Dimly, he remembered the long ordeal he had undergone to break his conditioning as a Magistrate. That struggle had been filled with pain, as well. He hadn't submitted to it then. But he was exhausted now, weary of fighting, worn down and wrung out by constant conflict.

Suddenly, like a tiny light shining through a dense pall of cloying mist, he felt a burst of red rage. With an effort of will beyond his capacity to understand, Kane threw open all the channels of his mind, trying desperately to reach inward and find the source of that anger.

"Do not fight anymore," Thrush crooned. "There is no use in it."

From the depths of Kane's mind where he had crouched hidden, Commander J. T. Kane came, surging out with a terrible strength through every cell of his brain, possessing him utterly, now that the way was open.

Kane stood aside as Commander Kane rolled out, seeming to thunder in outrage and fury.

He heard his voice say in a guttural growl, "Probe deeper, Thrush. I don't think you'll like what you find."

His hands came up and locked around Thrush's left wrist. For a long moment, he strained against him. Then slowly, he forced Thrush's hand back, pulling the fingers away from his forehead. The tiny filaments slid out from his flesh, leaving two tiny pinheads of blood.

Levering with his hips and legs, Kane pushed himself into a sitting position, and in the slowest of slow motion, bent Thrush's hand back, forcing his body forward. The filaments tipping the long fingers edged closer to Thrush's throat.

Then, with a gasping snarl, Kane lunged up and drove the fingers into Thrush's neck. The ululating shriek that ripped from Thrush's lips was a cry wrenched from the bowels of the Earth.

He flailed away from Kane, head twisting around like some grotesque marionette's. Then the top of his skull simply vanished, a U-shaped cavity replacing the wig. He flopped over on his back, legs twitching in a prolonged spasm, fingers still pressed against his throat.

Grant stepped up, face locked in a bare-toothed grimace, the bore of his ASP still pointing at the lean, black-clad body. Kane shuddered, wiping at the blood threading his face.

"What did you do to him?" asked Grant, regarding Thrush with the same kind of nervous suspicion as he might the body of a viper he wasn't sure was dead.

Heaving himself to his feet, Kane clamped his teeth on a groan of pain. "I made him probe himself," he said hoarsely. "Somehow, I knew it was the thing to do."

"Is he dead?"

Kane shook his head. "I don't know. But I think whatever consciousness he had is displaced right at the moment."

"Where is it?"

A thin, high, keening whine suddenly permeated everything, undercut with a pulsating throb. Kane and Grant, without truly knowing how they knew, understood there must have been some intricate triggering of a fail-safe device upon the failure of Thrush's mind functions.

They didn't know for certain. They only knew that a strange dark halo shimmered up from the ghastly cavity in Thrush's skull. As they watched, the halo inexorably began to expand, like a wave sweeping outward, more of a subliminal impression of motion than a true visual phenomenon.

Without speaking, both men turned and began to run. The dark wave swept toward them relentlessly, and Kane felt the throb of it at his heels. His mind cringed away from what it could be, what it could mean.

He sensed dimly that the dark force was Thrush's essence, not a soul or spirit, but his basic programming, his essential identity. He also knew it was desperate to meld with the trapezohedron, needing to link with it again, frantic for it as a human dying of thirst would be desperate for water—or a vampire for blood.

The two men retraced their steps, sprinting flat-out, Kane ignoring the pain flaring in his chest and head and leg. It was a race against the essence, with the trapezohedron serving as the finish line.

They reached the room where Fand, Brigid and the black stone waited. The pulsing wave was right behind them, and they increased their pace.

"Into the mat-trans," Kane managed to gasp.

The women didn't question him, but hurried toward the jump chamber. The silent dark force spread outward, seeking to engulf the trapezohedron. But when the wave touched the stone, Kane felt the subtle shock of its movement being checked, as if the wave had struck a sea wall and splashed back upon itself.

From the facets of the trapezohedron, great whorls of color spiraled up, growing in size and brilliance like immense flame-flowers blossoming into life.

As Grant slammed shut the armaglass door, the shimmering colors roiled, absorbing the dark halo. "We don't know where we'll jump to," he husked out.

"There's only one place," Brigid said breathlessly, eyes wide and bright with fear and awe. "Back to the dreadnought."

The lock mechanism clicked and triggered the automatic initiator. The familiar yet still slightly unnerving hum rose, climbing in pitch to a subsonic whine. The hexagonal plates on the floor and ceiling exuded a shimmering silvery glow that slowly intensified. A fine, faint mist gathered on the floor plates and drifted down from the ceiling.

Right before her figure was swallowed by the vapor, Fand reached and stroked Kane's face, a quick, loving caress. "Goodbye, Ka'in. It was good to know you. But it will be even better getting to know *my* Ka'in all over again."

The mist thickened, curling around to engulf her. As Kane's mind slipped into blackness, he heard his own voice say, "Thank you, Kane. Without you, I never could have lived up to my legend. Or continued to live at all."

Kane struggled against the darkness claiming his consciousness. "No!" he tried to shout. "I belong here—"

As Dr. Baptiste calculated, they materialized in the jump chamber aboard the dreadnought. She, Kane and Grant exchanged wordless looks of acknowledgment. During the mat-trans jump, their other identities had withdrawn from their minds so gently and carefully there had been no shock. Their minds were still in touch with the strange memories their other-dimensional twins had borne, but the dualism was ended.

Yet through the sympathy existing between the two minds that had become one for so long, Kane felt his other's cry of anguish, pulsing far, far out along the pathway between space and time. It was nonverbal, but he sensed the words nevertheless: I belong here, where I can make a difference!

With a bleak realization, Kane realized how his doppelgänger mirrored his own earlier despair. That Kane had erased it, but had perhaps absorbed it into himself.

Kane made arrangements with the *Sabre* to dock with the dreadnought via the boarding chutes. Within half an hour, all of them were back on the command deck, though Kane had to brush aside DeFore's recommendations to report to the dispensary for a physical examination and have his injuries treated.

Of the metal-sheathed sphere Thrush called the hub, there was no sign, and Cotta obligingly replayed a recording of the phenomena that had marked its disappearance. The lighted globe, appearing to burn in space, became a bubble of quivering blackness through which shot coruscating particles of brilliance, like a fireworks display seen from a vast distance. Rolling multicolored clouds overlapped, engulfing it until it was no longer seen or registered on the *Sabre*'s instruments.

Kane took his seat at the comm-con and turned to Baptiste. "What do you think happened out there, Doctor?"

Baptiste could only shake her head. "All I can sell is speculation."

"I'm in the buying mood."

She shrugged. "What Thrush called the hub only tangentially existed in our space-time. He used the trapezohedron as his anchor, his basic reality unit. The forces within it are like a tide, going in one direction. When you forced his neural probes into his own pathways, you triggered a change in that tide, forcing it violently into two directions at once. What happened was a continuum back-splash."

"Or," said Fand, "it was the two fundamental principles of the universe at work—life and antilife. Thrush had tried to balance them so he could fulfill his program but without repercussion. We altered the balance—toward life."

Domi's shoulders moved in an exaggerated shudder. "I like the first explanation better. It doesn't make any more sense, but at least it doesn't give me the creeps."

The *Sabre* remained in the vicinity of the dreadnought to complete the necessary repairs. Bry also wanted the opportunity to inspect the dreadnought; the chance to study a vessel capable of interstellar flight was not something to pass up. As a breakthrough in engineering, it meant humankind would soon be exploring new solar systems.

Grant wasn't enamored of the idea. "How can we

be sure that Thrush won't show up and take control of it again?''

"If Thrush exists at all, he isn't in this casement. Not any longer," Fand replied.

As the *Sabre* prepared to move toward the star gate coordinates, Kane said to Baptiste, "You had quite the introduction to the Rangers Corps, Doctor. We couldn't have accomplished this mission without you. Have you given any thought to signing on?"

She smiled wanly and with a touch of regret. "I wouldn't have missed this for the world—worlds, I mean. But this isn't my life. I've got my own work waiting for me to come back to…and a certain person."

Kane felt a twinge of jealousy, but it was far away, buried beneath layers of his own experiences and memories. Raising his voice a bit, he said, "Very well-done, people. Thank you." To Grant, he added, "Exceptionally well-done, Augustus. I'll be recommending you for your own command."

Grant hid his surprise that Kane had addressed him by his first name. "It's my job, J.T. And as long as you're being so familiar, maybe you can finally tell me what your initials stand for."

Kane said stiffly, "I think solving one mystery of the universe is sufficient for this particular tour of duty."

He flashed a quick grin at Grant and said, "Domi, set course for the portal coordinates. Slow and steady."

"Slow and steady?" she queried.

"Why not? We've never been to Sirius before. I'd like the chance to look around."

As the *Sabre* slid through the sea of space, Kane

realized that for the first time in a long time, he felt very comfortable in his chair at the comm-con, surrounded by his crew. He realized he felt even more comfortable with Fand at his elbow, as if she had always been there and always would.

Softly, she asked, "How much of the other Kane do you remember?"

"All of him, although he seems like a dream now." He sighed and shook his head. "He made me ashamed. He's accomplished so much on his casement with so little."

"Ships and technology are only tools. What is accomplished with them depends on the individual. Neither one of you has any reason to be ashamed."

"I understand that now." He hesitated before adding, "Among other things."

Fand laid her hand atop Kane's. The crew studiously concentrated on their duties. "What will you do now?" he asked lowly.

"I'll return to the Priory eventually. And you?"

"I'll reserve some time to thinking about my future."

"You don't need to think about it, Ka'in. This ship is your future."

"It's been my future for a goodly portion of my life. It's time to find another one."

"Like what?" Fand inquired.

Kane was ashamed he had to grope for an answer. "Well," he said haltingly, "there's always the admiralty."

Fand only laughed, the angle of her eyebrows calling him a liar. He wasn't offended. Knowing full well he was breaching protocol and rules of conduct but not giving a damn, he lifted her hand and gently kissed the palm.

"Anam-chara," he whispered.

Then he announced, "Domi, plot the course for the portal. Let's go home."

And the *Sabre* went, for the farther she traveled, the less distance her crew—and particularly her commander—had to go.

Chapter 27

Bry's voice wafted from Cerberus redoubt's trans-comm. "T minus two minutes to cycle completion."

His words blended in with the rumbling whine of the redoubt's nuclear generators running at full output. Wegmann kept his eyes fixed on the gauges of the console, paying no attention to Bry's report or to Beth-Li Rouch standing right behind him.

"It's time," she said, raising her soft voice a trifle in order to be heard over the throbbing of the generators.

"For what?" Wegmann asked disinterestedly.

Beth-Li stepped up beside him, leaning into him, breasts pressing into his arm. Her expression was unreadable, her dark eyes inscrutable. "To trigger the power fluctuation, like we agreed."

Slowly, he swiveled his head to face her. His own eyes were just as enigmatic. "Funny thing, Beth-Li. I don't recall agreeing to anything of the sort."

She did not reply, but instead only gazed at him unblinkingly, expectantly.

Wegmann did not wither under her stare. "I told you a while back I wasn't stupid. And I'm not a killer, either. I played along with you to find out how far you'd go. Now I know."

Beth-Li sighed, breaking the eye contact. She combed the fingers of her left hand through the silken fall of her hair. "So do I. You thought you were pretty clever, I guess."

"I guess," he agreed in a monotone.

Her right arm lashed up and out. The barrel of the small black autoblaster gripped in her fist struck him across the face, sending him staggering half the length of the console, opening a laceration on his cheek.

"So am I," she spit, centering the sights on his forehead. "You do what I say or I'll blow your fucking arrogant brains out."

Wegmann gingerly touched the blood seeping from the cut on his face, eyed it shining wetly on his fingertips and, with rueful resignation, said, "Auerbach boosted the blaster from the armory for you, I guess. I didn't figure on that."

"You figured out most of it," Auerbach said, stepping into the generator room.

"Yes," grated Beth-Li, eyes bright with anger. "And he'd better figure out how he plans to stay alive for the next minute."

ALWAYS BEFORE Brigid had experienced the hyperdimensional transition between casements as little more than an insistent tug, the sensation lasting such an infinitesimal tick of time it could not be measured. What little her conscious mind retained of the phasing process from one body to another was like a splintered fragment of a long-ago dream.

Now she floated alone, a handful of electric impulses flung out among the stars like grains of sand. All around her, suns burned with a pure, clean radiance. The clouds of nebula glowed silver against the primal black. Constellations wheeled and glittered.

She could feel the movement of the universe pulsing against her, hear the songs sung by the stars.

Then she heard a scream, a fierce eagle scream of defiance and rage. She could not truly hear it, but sensed it as a flash of energy in the cosmos.

"No! I won't go back! Not to the slag heap!"

Kane was not actually speaking; there could be no voice or sound in that tremendous silence. But Kane's words crashed against her awareness like a sun going nova.

"I want to stay here, where I make a difference!"

The pain in his declamation shocked her. She tried to orient herself toward him in the limitless sea of stars. "Kane, come! It's time."

"No! I won't go back!"

Brigid sensed him as a tiny patch of furious, crackling energy and moved close beside him. She repeated, "It's time."

"We have the stars here, not the slag heap. I won't go back to that life."

"You can't have a life here, Kane. It's not yours. It's another man's life he let you borrow. If you try to stay, you'll have stolen it."

She reached for him, but his essence skated away, toward the millions of constellations piled to infinity. His cry flared. "You can't hold me! It *is* my life back on that ship! That Kane is me, the Kane I should have been."

She flung herself after him. "Your two minds can't coexist. One of you will die. Is that what you want?"

Brigid felt the pulsing of his despair, his desperate need. She blurted, "You make a difference on our world, too. Maybe more of a difference than the Kane here."

A twist of sneering laughter touched her. It was full of self-loathing. "I'm a traitor, an exile, a fugitive, a coldheart killer. What kind of difference can a man like that make?"

A wave of force suddenly struck them, an invisible current sweeping them apart. Brigid felt the current as a shock of dislocation. She tried to fix Kane's position, but he was gone. Then his voice made a running streak across her consciousness. "You go back."

A sudden blaze of agony seemed to consume her. She didn't know if it sprang from another source or if she sensed what radiated from Kane's naked soul.

"I'm not leaving without you, Kane."

"I'm not going back."

"Then I'll stay with you—we'll be ghosts together in the cosmos, looking at wonders we can't experience or touch, simply being observers for all eternity, which was Thrush's plan for us anyway.

"Eventually, our bodies in Cerberus will die. Even if DeFore can keep them alive for a while, they'll sicken and weaken and finally cease functioning altogether. It'll fall to Grant and maybe Domi to dispose of them."

Kane did not respond for a very long time, perhaps an eternity, perhaps even longer. And then she heard him, far away and angry. "They'll get over it."

"Of course they will. They'll mourn and never know we made the choice not to return. They'll think we were lost in a mat-trans glitch. They'll blame Lakesh, maybe even kill him. They'll never know we deserted them."

"It's not desertion," he declared. "It's a choice."

"Yes, but ask yourself this—would the Kane you

desperately want to be desert his people? Would he permit one of his people to join him in nonexistence?''

She sensed that some of her contempt communicated itself to him. ''Would he allow Fand to follow him into the void, to travel the purgatory road with him?''

Then, in the most distant of whispers, like the half-heard sighing of a wind, a feminine voice said, ''The gift of the *anam-chara* is strong.''

Brigid recognized the voice of Fand, and knew it was a memory of something she had said to Kane, words he now imparted to her.

Then, she felt him beside her. His mind insinuated itself against her, sliding over it, a hesitant caress. ''That explains why you stayed with me out here while Grant completed the transition.''

She returned the caress. ''It really is time to go, Kane.''

Then, like the shock waves from a silent thunderclap, a concussion shook them, flinging them apart. In a wild blazing burst of panic, Brigid thought, felt, screamed, ''Something's wrong!''

Without a body, without a nervous system, she should not have been able to feel pain. But she did, as a ravening, rending flame.

VOICE DRIPPING with amused contempt, Wegmann said, ''You don't need me to interrupt the power flow. Any monkey can do that.''

Angry uncertainty flickered in Beth-Li's eyes. She considered his words for a second, then said, ''Any monkey can flip an off switch. That's not what I wanted or what we talked about.''

"Yeah," Wegmann agreed, oblivious to the scarlet streaming down his jaw and making artless splatters on his bodysuit. "You want an accident that really isn't an accident with me as the fall guy." He showed his teeth in a hard, humorless grin. "I don't play the sap for anybody."

Beth-Li smiled coldly, reached out with one long-nailed hand and threw the first of six toggle switches on the panel. "I paid attention to more than you during the time I spent down here."

Wegmann's face remained stony as she flicked another switch. He completely ignored Auerbach looming behind him. The sound of the generators did not alter in pitch or rhythm. Beth-Li threw a third switch.

In a monotone, Wegmann said, "Auerbach, I knew you were an asshole, but I never took you for a murderer."

Auerbach did not respond. Beth-Li flicked the fourth toggle.

"Kane, Grant and Baptiste," continued Wegmann. "All of them dead, rematerializing as lumps of dying flesh, their guts and brains smeared all over the jump chamber. That's what you want?"

Auerbach's startled intake of breath sounded like steam escaping from a valve. "All three of them?"

"Of course. If the power curve drops or even jumps, the quincunx balance is thrown off. They're all dead. Baptiste included." He nodded toward Beth-Li. "As far as she's concerned, *especially* Baptiste."

"Don't listen to him," Beth-Li snapped.

Wegmann turned his head slightly toward Auerbach. "You think a spike in the balance is selective?"

Auerbach shifted his feet and cleared his throat. "It was supposed to be arranged that way."

Wegmann's smile vanished. "She lied to you. That can't be done. If one of three is lost, all of them are lost."

"Shut up!" Beth-Li's voice hit a high note. She cast her gaze toward Auerbach. "He set it up that way, but he's backing out of the deal. You can force him to show us what to do."

Auerbach didn't move. Beth-Li snapped over the fifth switch. "Tell me, or I'll just keeping pushing buttons and flipping switches."

As her fingers touched the sixth toggle, Wegmann said, "Auerbach, if she moves that switch, Baptiste will die along with Grant and Kane."

Auerbach grunted. "Not if you tell her what to do."

"I've told you—there's no way to bring Baptiste through alive and whole and get rid of Grant and Kane. She knows that."

Closing her thumb and forefinger over the top of the switch, Beth-Li said, "If that happens, it'll be your fault, Wegmann."

"Yeah, I know that's how you want it to work out," he said agreeably. "Sure enough, you can kill them, shoot me and claim you were trying to stop the fused-out weirdo loner engineer. That might fool most of the people in the redoubt, but you won't fool everybody."

"We'll take our chances."

Wegmann nodded. "That's for fucking certain. Like I said, you might trick most everybody. But you won't be able to fool Domi."

He spoke her name blandly, with no emphasis.

Beth-Li sneered, "I don't care about that piece of Outland trash—"

Silver flashed dully. Auerbach voiced a gargling cry of pained wonder and reeled sideways, clawing at the hilt of the knife sprouting from the meat of his left shoulder.

Domi, a white wraith of motion, lunged from the murky shadows between the caged generator enclosure and a workbench. Her eyes blazed crimson with homicidal fury.

Beth-Li Rouch spared her one feverish glance and flipped the switch. Instantly, the steady whine of the generators faltered, breaking rhythm.

"No!" Wegmann bowled into Beth-Li, shouldering her away from the console. His hand slapped at the board, chopping the toggle switch back to its original position. The rumbling whine returned to its normal sound.

Beth-Li squeezed off one shot as she staggered backward, but the round went high, striking sparks from a steel support beam on the ceiling. Then Domi was upon her like a demonic force spewed from hell.

Bry's voice screeched over the trans-comm, "Wegmann, what's going on down there? We have a fluctuation! Restore stabilization! Wegmann!"

Auerbach, with a groaning effort, withdrew the red-filmed knife blade from his shoulder. He looked too shocked, in too much pain to consider using it, but Wegmann took no chances. He bounded forward and kicked the much larger man as hard as he could between the legs.

As Auerbach folded, a keening wail passing his lips, Wegmann whirled toward the struggling forms of Domi and Beth-Li.

Domi had wrested away the blaster, and the two women tumbled over the floor, locked in each other's arms. Domi single-mindedly tried to inflict as much punishment on her opponent as she could. She kneed her in the belly, she raked her with her fingernails, she pulled her hair, she bit and head butted her.

Beth-Li tried to fight back, then tried simply to defend herself, but it was like wrestling with a rabid snow leopard. She shrieked in pain and anger.

Wegmann stared, amused and satisfied for the first few seconds. Then he became appalled. He knew he should intervene before Domi either killed or permanently maimed Beth-Li, but he feared the albino girl would turn her mad wrath on him.

"Cycle complete," Bry's tense voice declared. "We've got them.'

The announcement penetrated Domi's fury-clouded mind, and she paused in her assault for half a second. That was all the respite Beth-Li needed. She thrashed wildly, planting the heel of her hand beneath Domi's chin and slamming the back of her head against the corner of the raised concrete slab holding the generators. Even over the steady rumble, the crack of bone against stone was loud.

Uttering animalistic sobbing shrieks, Beth-Li fought her way out of Domi's embrace, staggering to her feet. She made a shambling dash for the door. Wegmann started to intercept her, but when she moved into the light, he recoiled.

Beth-Li's right eye was but a swollen, bruised slit, both nostrils gushed blood, her lips were split and crimson-edged teeth marks marred the sculpted beauty of her face. Her long tresses hung in a tangle, inflamed patches of scalp showing where Domi had ripped out handfuls of hair by the roots. Her tight bodysuit was torn in places, revealing long scratch marks on the flesh.

Domi struggled to her feet, eyes bearing a slight glaze. Wegmann said, "Let her go. I'll call Lakesh and have him—"

Domi growled, "Tried to chill Grant!" and stiff-armed him out of the way. She set off in pursuit of Beth-Li Rouch.

He took a few steps after her, thought better of it and turned his attention to Auerbach. Kneeling on the floor, one hand at his crotch and the other clapped over the wound in his shoulder, he groaned, "I need medical attention."

Wegmann noted that though his left sleeve was soaked through with blood, his injury didn't appear critical. Kicking the flat, six-inch throwing knife out of Auerbach's reach, he said dryly, "Physician, heal thyself."

"You little son of a bitch," Auerbach said between clenched teeth. "You set us up."

Wegmann snorted in derision. "You set yourselves up. Did you two really think I was some loser, more than happy to murder three people because a little slut wiggled her ass in my direction?"

"You're a queer," Auerbach grated. "Should have known."

"Wrong again. I just know the difference between my brain and my dick—unlike some people in this room I could mention."

"I won't let this slide, you pissant."

Grimly, Wegmann replied, "Yeah, that's pretty much what Domi said when I told her what I thought you and Rouch had planned."

Fear swallowed up the pain and humiliated anger on Auerbach's face.

Turning to the trans-comm on the wall, Wegmann called loudly, "Lakesh, we need to talk."

BETH-LI TOOK THE LIFT up to the second level while Domi pounded up the emergency stairs. Both women emerged in the corridor within seconds and yards of each other.

Bleating in terror, Beth-Li sprinted toward the double doors leading to the exercise area and swimming pool. She was fleet of foot, adrenaline making her very swift, but Domi was far faster. She loped after in long strides.

Beth-Li shouldered open one of the doors and flung it back violently. The edge clipped Domi's arm, causing her to stagger, but the bone-white girl with the red raging eyes came on. They ran through the room filled with weight machines, stationary exercise bikes and workout mats.

Domi caught Beth-Li by the hair, and both women went down on the slick floor in a tangle of limbs. Sitting astraddle her, Domi pummeled Beth-Li's face with her small fists. The dark-haired woman warded off some of the punches, dodged a blow and seized Domi's left arm. Bucking with her hips, she toppled Domi sideways.

They rolled over a padded mat, and Beth-Li dug her fingers deep into Domi's white throat until the duo jammed against the bicycle frame bolted to the floor. Grasping Domi's arm, she thrust the hand between the metal sprockets of the chain pulley. She groped, grabbed a pedal and jerked. The chain bit cruelly into Domi's palm, tearing the flesh and crunching against the metacarpal bones.

Domi screamed, more in fury than in pain, and tried to wrench her hand free. Beth-Li smashed a fist into Domi's face, splitting her lower lip, then slammed a foot into the pit of her stomach. Breath exploded from Domi's mouth amid a spray of vermilion droplets.

Scrambling to her feet, Beth-Li took vicious advantage of her adversary. "You filthy, lowborn Outland whore!"

She kicked her on the jaw, driving her white-haired head hard against the frame of the bicycle. "You nothing piece of Pit shit!"

Bracing herself against the floor, Domi threw herself away from the bicycle in a wild, convulsive lunge. Flesh ripped and peeled from her hand, but she managed to free it from the sprockets.

As she rolled to her feet with catlike speed, Beth-Li spun and raced toward the swimming pool. She screamed over her shoulder, "Enough!"

Domi paid no attention. Face locked in a porcelain mask of ferocity, she bounded after her.

Beth-Li slammed wide the doors to the pool. Before they began to swing shut, Domi leaped between them. She caught Beth-Li in a flying tackle. She had time for one frightened cry before she and Domi plunged into the water with a great splash.

They were at the deep end and since both women were small in stature, it seemed exceptionally deep. Domi and Beth-Li hugged each other as they rolled and grappled beneath the surface. Domi kept her eyes open despite the chlorine sting.

Beth-Li smashed an elbow into Domi's midriff,

trying to knock out of her any air her lungs might hold. Domi twisted around, bringing both knees up into Beth-Li's chest. Kicking hard, she pushed the dark-haired woman away. Striking the wall of the pool, Domi stroked to the surface. Both of their heads rose above the water at the same time. They bit at air.

Domi pushed off from the wall, hands outspread for Beth-Li.

Sounding half-strangled, raking her hair out of her face, Beth-Li cried, "Enough!"

In a liquid burble, Domi snarled, "Tried to chill Grant!"

Flailing at the water, Beth-Li swam clumsily for the shallows. Domi seized her right arm, thrusting it up sharply behind the shoulder. Digging her chin into the back of Beth-Li's neck, Domi shoved up the hammerlock with all of her strength. She forced Beth-Li's body under the surface, toward the bottom.

Beth-Li kicked frantically to bring them back up, her long black hair floating around her head like seaweed. Domi bore down savagely, jamming a knee into the base of the woman's spine.

She squealed with pain, a string of silver bubbles streaming from her open mouth.

Lungs on fire, blinded by Beth-Li's billowing tresses, Domi maintained the pressure. Flattened against the bottom of the pool, Beth-Li spasmed violently, the fingers of her free hand clawing at the smooth concrete, her nails breaking.

Her frenzied struggles grew feeble, weakened and finally ceased altogether.

Domi, dazed and blacking out from lack of oxygen, released Beth-Li's arm and drifted up from the pool's floor. As her head broke the surface, she gasped in air, sneezing the chlorinated water from her nasal passages.

Coughing, she stroked to the poolside, hooking the edge with an arm. She bumped into it and a strong hand that closed around her wrist. She struggled, thrashing the water, blinking her stinging eyes. When she saw Grant kneeling at the lip of the pool, her entire body went limp with relief. She allowed him to haul her out of the water.

Kane, Brigid and Lakesh stood at the far end of the pool. Domi noted absently they all looked slightly disoriented and haggard, Kane in particular. But they weren't looking at her. Their gazes were fixed on something else.

Hugging Grant's arm close, Domi climbed to her feet, water cascading from her sodden clothes. Even Grant wasn't looking at her. She turned her head, following his line of sight.

Beth-Li's body floated facedown in the center of the pool, her black hair swirling out around her head. She didn't move, and for a handful of seconds, neither did anyone else. Lakesh made a choking cough of horror.

Kane glanced toward him and said quietly, "I guess the problem of how best to deal with Rouch is finally solved."

Chapter 28

After two hours of shouting, accusatory commotion, matters finally tapered off to a subdued mood of resigned shock. Although DeFore did her best, Beth-Li Rouch could not be resuscitated. She treated the injuries of Domi, Wegmann and Auerbach in that order. Auerbach was then confined.

He made a faltering attempt to throw himself on the mercy of Brigid, making a stammering and unconvincing appeal to her compassionate nature. But since Brigid's compassion had allowed Beth-Li to roam free after her attempt on Kane's life, Brigid was unmoved.

Lakesh had the most difficulty coming to terms with the conspiracy brewed within the walls of Cerberus. He tried at first to tongue-lash Domi, but subsided when Brigid coldly reminded him he had abrogated his responsibility for Rouch.

Wegmann was the hero of the day, although that didn't count for much, under the circumstances. After receiving stitches from DeFore and words of gratitude from Kane, he simply returned to his subterranean post.

Finally, Grant, Brigid, Kane and Lakesh convened in the ready room adjacent to the control complex for a debrief. All but Lakesh spoke of their experiences on the parallel casement into a tape recorder. Memories tended to fade fast upon a return from sidereal space, so recording a verbal account had become SOP.

Lakesh was not simply intrigued by what he heard—he was alternately thrilled, fascinated and ecstatic.

"The device or vehicle Thrush called the hub could only function by an energy exchange between universes," he exclaimed. "Natural laws being mixed and held in a balanced matrix, using the trapezohedron as a multidimensional anchor. The implications are—" He broke off, groping for a term, then said, "They're beyond words."

"And what about Thrush?" challenged Grant.

Lakesh blinked at him, as if he had forgotten the entire reason for the hyperdimensional transits. "I think it likely he does not and never has objectively existed."

Kane's eyebrows met at the bridge of his nose. "What?"

Brigid stated, "The entity we knew as Thrush may be a truly subjective property, a creation of the minds of the Archons. He existed only because those who interacted with him believed he did."

"What?" said Kane again, a dangerous edge in his voice. "I thought he was a program."

Brigid stated, "He was that, but he became more. He was a mirror, reflecting the ugly, most primal impulses of the human beings he dealt with. That's one reason he was an Archon emissary—he absorbed and transmitted to them the emotional states of the people he came in contact with. And that gave the Archons an idea of how best to proceed with their own plans."

Sounding very confused and irritable, Grant asked,

"Are you saying that if the people who dealt with him didn't believe him, he wouldn't have existed?"

Lakesh nodded. "Something like that, but not so simplistic. Australian aboriginal culture lived by the thesis that reality could be defined by subjective belief. They died when they were cursed by having a bone pointed at them because they *believed* it would kill them. This reality was a powerful mental imprint."

"In other words," Brigid declared, "Thrush was defeated on the hub because we believed he could be. On an unconscious level, we *unlearned* the fact of his subjective reality."

Grant wearily massaged the sides of his head. In a very aggrieved voice, he said, "All I want to know is if Thrush is gone."

"Yes," Brigid replied crisply. "As far as our own perceptions are concerned."

"He threatened to come to this casement," Kane pointed out. "It sure as hell wouldn't be the first time." He nodded to the aluminum-walled carrying case holding the fragments of the trapezohedron. "Those are his basic reality units in all the casements. Aren't they like beacons to him?"

Lakesh possessively and protectively put a hand on the case. "Not if we don't view them as such. Whether or not Balam foresaw returning to this plane in this time, he gave them to us for safekeeping."

Kane frowned. "Assuming Balam knew Thrush was out there as a loose end left dangling by his people—"

"I think that's likely," Brigid interjected.

"And since he needed us to tie it off so humanity

could get on with the task of rebuilding the Earth, he gave the pieces to me.''

Lakesh cocked his head, perplexed. ''If what you say is true—and we'll probably never know—Balam did not relinquish this most sacred of his people's artifacts simply to end Thrush's depredations. No, I believe he intended us to have the pieces of stone as a teaching tool, so we could unlearn the conditioning of the baronies, so our conscious minds could transcend our parochial, subjective view of reality.''

A smile spread across his seamed face. ''Think of the wonders that lie open to us now. We need not feel constrained by this oppressive reality or fear the barons any longer. And if the domino principle, Bell's Theorem, has any validity, the ripples you set into motion on the three casements will reach—or have already reached—this one.

''We don't have to be exiles any longer, we don't have to hide and skulk. A multitude of realities are ours for the experiencing.''

Kane gazed at the messianic light of awe and wonder shining from the old man's eyes. He beamed at all of them, a smile of joyful optimism.

Reaching over, Kane grabbed the case and pulled it across the table to him. As he stood up, Lakesh made a frantic snatch for it. ''What are you doing?'' he demanded stridently.

''Watch,'' Kane said, turning on his heel and marching from the room and through the central control complex.

Grant, Brigid and Lakesh followed him, Lakesh making demands, bleating questions, shouting recriminations. Kane ignored him. He strode down the wide vanadium-sheathed corridors until he reached the sec door. The three heads of Cerberus painted on the wall stared at him, but for some reason he fancied their lips were peeled back in grins, not snarls.

He punched in 352 on the keypad, grasped the master lever tightly and pulled it up. Buried machinery whined, the hydraulic and pneumatic system gave out with prolonged, hissing squeals. The panels on the multiton sec door began folding aside like an accordion.

"Kane!" shrilled Lakesh. "What are you doing? Where are you going? Come back here!"

Kane squeezed out the door and onto the broad plateau. The glory of a western sunset filled the sky with a riot of pastel colors. The wind blowing up from below held the fresh fragrance of life. He strode deliberately across the tarmac to the edge of the precipice.

Balancing the case on the flat of his left hand, he undid the latches and lifted the lid, being very careful not to look directly at the three black stones nestled within. He heard Lakesh bleat in alarm behind him, and lunge forward. Casting a quick glance over his shoulder, he snapped, "Hold him."

Brigid and Grant secured grips on Lakesh's pipestem arms, and after a moment of futile struggle, he sagged within their hands. Kane paused a moment, sensing an absence of a ceremony that might imbue his next actions with momentous import. Without one, he might as well be dumping out some garbage.

Then, under his breath, he said, "Fuck it."

He turned the case upside down over the edge of the cliff and watched as the fragments of the Chintamani Stone, the Shining Trapezohedron, plummeted straight down toward the foaming torrent far below. Within an eye blink, the stones became indistinct black specks. He couldn't see the splashes, or even if they struck the stream. Nor did he give much of a damn.

He closed the lid and turned toward Lakesh, extending the case toward him. "Do you want to keep this or should I chuck it over the side, too?"

Lakesh shook his head mournfully, in disbelief. Tears ran down his creased cheeks, and he trembled as if he were grieving the loss of a loved one. Thickly, he said, "You don't know what you've done."

Kane stepped closer to him, saying in a low voice, hard with sincerity, "I know exactly what I've done, old man. I removed the temptation. Not just from you, but from me, too. I nearly didn't come back from that last casement. I wanted to stay there so much I could've ruined what we accomplished there. I wanted it more than I ever wanted anything in my life."

He took a deep, steadying breath, his eyes boring in on Lakesh's own. "Balam didn't want us to visit those parallel casements to repair damage done by Thrush. He wanted us to see how low humanity can sink but how high it can reach, too. That's what we have to do here, Lakesh. Not turn our back on the slag heap like I wanted to do, but make it a garden of human aspirations."

Brigid said softly, sympathetically, "Lakesh, if the domino principle works, it's still going to require a concerted effort from us to help it along. Our reality, our future lies here. Not out there. Do you understand?"

Lakesh didn't answer. He shook free of their

hands, took the empty case from Kane and began shuffling back across the plateau, head bowed, shoulders sagging. Grant threw Kane a rueful half smile and followed him.

Brigid ran her hands through her mane of hair and stepped up to the lip of the precipice, gazing down into it silently. Kane watched her for a long moment then said, "What was it you said to me about six months ago when I stood there—something about when you stare into the abyss, the abyss also stares into you?"

She nodded.

"I didn't know what you meant then. I think I do now."

"And that is?" she asked flatly.

"The abyss is the human spirit. It's our choice whether it's empty, holding nothing, or whether it's full."

She glanced at him, one eyebrow raised. "Not bad."

"Didn't think I had it in me, did you?"

"Truthfully, no," she intoned, "I didn't."

Brigid sighed. "Do you miss her, Kane?"

"Miss who?"

"Fand."

"The Fand of this world or the other one?"

"Don't be evasive, Kane," she said sharply.

A smile creased his lips. "Yes, I do. I miss the *Sabre,* I miss the crew. I miss *me,* who I was there. What about you? Do you miss the life you had there?"

"It was very structured," she answered thoughtfully. "Even rigid. But it was complete and secure.

I knew exactly what I was and why I had chosen that life.''

The timbre of her voice, the stance of her body made him feel uncomfortable. He did not like how close she stood to the sheer, thousand foot drop-off. The wind gusting up from below ruffled her hair, and the strands reflected the colors of the sunset.

Softly, she said, ''She didn't have to struggle just to stay alive and sane.''

Kane's tongue felt clumsy and thick. ''It's always a struggle to one degree or another, no matter the reality. Here when we struggle, we always score victories and each time we do, we learn more.''

''Learn more about what?''

''How to set ourselves free. Each victory against such great odds is sweet.''

''Sometimes we lose.''

''But we didn't today, Baptiste. We didn't today.''

Brigid turned to face him, emerald eyes glimmering with an emotion he couldn't name but recognized and understood nevertheless. ''And after today, then what?''

Kane took a slow step toward her. ''Like you've said to me—we wait for tomorrow.''

Then he took her by the hand and gently led her away from the abyss.

Take
2 explosive books
plus a
mystery bonus
FREE

Mail to: Gold Eagle Reader Service
3010 Walden Ave.
P.O. Box 1394
Buffalo, NY 14240-1394

YEAH! Rush me 2 FREE Gold Eagle novels and my FREE mystery bonus.
Then send me 4 brand-new novels every other month as they come off
the presses. Bill me at the low price of just $16.80* for each shipment.
There is NO extra charge for postage and handling! There is no minimum
number of books I must buy. I can always cancel at any time simply by returning a shipment at your cost or by returning any shipping statement marked
"cancel." Even if I never buy another book from Gold Eagle, the 2 free books
and mystery bonus are mine to keep forever.

164 AEN CH7R

Name	(PLEASE PRINT)	
Address		Apt. No.
City	State	Zip

Signature (if under 18, parent or guardian must sign)

* Terms and prices subject to change without notice. Sales tax applicable in
N.Y. This offer is limited to one order per household and not valid to
present subscribers. Offer not available in Canada.

GE2-98